ATLANTIC FURY

DATE DUE

6-02 ✓			
4-6-04			
04-19-??			

D1416439

ATLANTIC FURY

Hammond Innes

Thorndike Press
Thorndike, Maine USA

This Large Print edition is published by Thorndike Press, USA.

Published in 1998 in the U.S. by arrangement with Curtis Brown UK.

U.S. Softcover ISBN 0–7862–1307–8 (General Series Edition)

The text of this Large Print edition is unabridged.
Other aspects of the book may vary from the original edition.

Set in 16 pt. New Times Roman.

Printed in Great Britain on acid-free paper.

For Janet and Maurice,
who have painted and fished the Hebrides

Those who are familiar with the out-islands of the Hebrides will have no difficulty in recognising Laerg, just as those who have served in the Western Isles will appreciate at once the extent to which I am in the Army's debt for their co-operation. However, in a work of fiction intended to give a picture of the conditions that face men serving in an unusual environment, certain liberties are inevitable. Because of this I should like to make it absolutely clear that, whilst I have naturally adhered to correct ranks and titles, the characters themselves, and the situation, are entirely imaginary.

CONTENTS

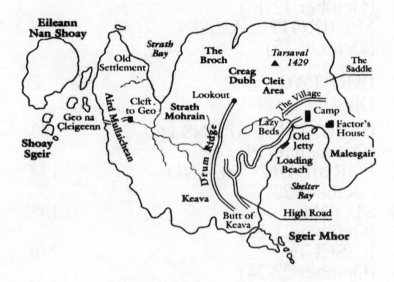

Eileann
Nan Shoay

*Strath
Bay*

Old
Settlement

**The
Broch**

▲ *Tarsaval
1429*

The
Saddle

Creag
Dubh

Cleit
Area

Cleft
to Geo

Lookout

The Village

Camp

**Strath
Mohrain**

Geo na
Cleigeenn

Camp

■ Factor's
House

**Shoay
Sgeir**

Lazy
Beds

Old
Jetty

Malesgair

Loading
Beach

*Shelter
Bay*

Keava

High Road

Butt of
Keava

Sgeir Mhor

LAERG

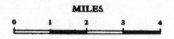

MILES

0   1   2   3   4

TO ICELAND

TO LAERG

Butt of Lewis

TO NORWAY

Cape Wrath

Loch Laxford

Stornoway

Enard
Bay

Lewis

L. Broom

Harris

The Minch

L. Ewe

Gruinard Bay

Sound of Harris

Little Minch

Gairloch

L. Torridon

North Uist

S. of Raasay

L. Carron

Benbecula

Loch
Snizort

Raasay

Inner Sound

Strome Ferry

South
Uist

Skye

Kylerhea

Glenelg

Loch Lochy

Barra

Cuillin Sound

Sound of Sleat

Canna

Rum

Fort William

Eigg

Muck

Sound of
Arisaig

Coll

Loch Linnhe

Tiree

Passage of Tiree

Mull

Iona

Firth of Lorne

Colonsay

Loch Fyne

Crinan
Canal

Jura

Islay

MILES

0   10   20   30   40   50

As to the effect of a mental or moral shock on a common mind that is a quite legitimate subject for study and description.
Joseph Conrad

PART ONE

PRELUDE TO DISASTER

DECISION TO EVACUATE
(October 12–13)

The decision to withdraw the Unit from Laerg was taken early in October. That it was a fatal decision is now obvious. It was taken too late in the year, and in the initial phases the operation was carried out with too little sense of urgency. Whether the disastrous consequences of that decision would have been avoided if the personalities involved had been different I cannot say. Certainly personality played a part in what happened. It always does. A decision that calls for action involves men, and men cannot escape their own natures; their upbringing, their training, their basic characters. Moreover, in this particular case, a series of mishaps, unimportant in isolation, but cumulatively dangerous in combination with the colossal forces unleashed against us, led inevitably to disaster . . .

*   *   *

This was the opening paragraph of a statement I found among my brother's papers. It was written in his own hand, when his mind was still lucid. Intended as a refutation of the charges brought against him, the statement was never

3

completed. Together with his notes and all his other papers, it lies before me now in the lamplight as I embark on the task of writing this account of the disaster. And the fact that I am writing of it in the solitariness of my winter isolation here on Laerg, with the same violent winds battering at the door, the same damp, salt-laden atmosphere blackening the night outside and Sgeir Mhor standing like a battlement against the Atlantic, will I hope give it a clarity not otherwise possible; that, and the fact that I was involved in it, too.

Not directly, as my brother was; and not with his burden of responsibility. Laerg was a military establishment at the time, and I am an artist, not a soldier. But for both of us it held a fatal fascination. It was in our blood, and looking back on it, our paths crossing after so many years and in such circumstances, there seems to have been something inevitable about it, as though Laerg itself were an integral part of the pattern of our lives.

There is, of course, no mention in my brother's notes of his personal reasons for wanting the Army out of Laerg, no hint of the fearful thing that drew him back to the island. And the fact that he had been so many years in the Army inhibited him in his writing. For instance, he gives no account of his interviews with Standing. He merely states the facts and leaves it at that, so that there is no indication of his relations with his Commanding Officer.

4

Fortunately I have my own notes from which to work. These last few months I have interviewed most of the men involved in the disaster. As a result I have been able to add considerably to my personal knowledge of what happened. I have also had access to the depositions taken at the Board of Inquiry and also to the transcripts covering the first two days of the abortive Court Martial. There are still gaps, of course. So many men were killed. If I could have talked with Colonel Standing, for instance . . .

However, the picture in my mind is as complete as it can ever be. And that picture is dominated, of course, by Laerg. Laerg—forbidding and mysterious, rising out of the Atlantic like the last peaks of a submerged land, its shaggy heights lost in cloud, its massive cliffs resounding to the snowflake swirl of millions of seabirds. Laerg dwarfs the men, the ships; it dominates the whole story.

Until that October I had never even seen Laerg. This may seem strange, considering my father was born there and that I'd been half in love with it since I was a kid. But Laerg isn't the sort of place you can visit at will. It lies more than eighty miles west of the Outer Hebrides, a small island group composed of Laerg itself, which with Eileann nan Shoay and Sgeir Mhor constitutes the main island; the bare rock islet of Vallay; and Fladday with its attendant stacs of Hoe and Rudha. Eighty sea miles is no great distance, but this is the North Atlantic and the seven islands of the Laerg group are a lonely cluster standing on the march of the great depressions that sweep up towards Iceland and the Barents Sea. Not only are sea conditions bad throughout the greater part of the year, but the islands, rising sheer out of the waves to a height of almost 1,400 feet, breed their own peculiar brand of weather.

Oddly enough, it wasn't my father who'd made me long to go to Laerg. He seldom talked of the island. He'd gone to sea as a young man and then married a Glasgow girl and settled as a crofter on Ardnamurchan after losing his nerve in a typhoon. It was Grandfather Ross who filled our heads with talk of our island ancestors.

This gnarled old man with a craggy face and huge hands had been a powerful influence on both our lives. He'd come to live with us following the evacuation of the islanders in 1930. He'd been the only man to vote against it when the Island Parliament made its decision, and to the day he died in 1936 he'd resented living on the mainland. It wasn't only that he talked endlessly of Laerg; in those six years he taught my brother Iain, and myself, everything he knew about the way to live in a world of rock and towering heights where sheep and birds were the raw materials of existence.

I'd tried to get there once a long time ago, hiding away on a trawler anchored in the bay below our croft. But that trip they hadn't gone within a hundred miles of Laerg, and then the war came and I joined Iain, working in a Glasgow factory making shell cases. A year in the Navy and ten years at sea, tramping, mainly in old Liberty ships, and then I had embarked on the thing I had always wanted to do—I began to study as a painter. It was during a winter spent in the Aegean Isles that I suddenly realised Laerg was the subject that most attracted me. It had never been painted, not the way my grandfather had described it. I'd packed up at once and returned to England, but by then Laerg had become a tracking station for the new rocket range on Harris. It was a closed island, forbidden to unauthorised civilians, and neither the Army nor Nature Conservancy, who leased it from the National Trust for Scotland, would give me permission to visit it.

That was the position until October of the following year when a man called Lane came to my studio and I was caught up in my brother's strange story and the events that led to the disaster. But first I must give the background to the Army's decision to evacuate Laerg, for without that decision the disaster would never have happened.

The future of the tracking station was discussed at a Conference held in the Permanent Under-Secretary's room at the War Office and the decision to close it was confirmed by the Director Royal Artillery at a meeting in his office four days later. In my reconstruction of the Conference I am indebted to the frankness with which the DRA described it to me. For the details of the subsequent meeting I have also had the benefit of talks with his Brigadier General Staff and with Brigadier Matthieson, the Brigadier Royal Artillery, Scottish Command. The latter, in addition, was able to recall for me in considerable detail his conversation with Braddock on the night train going north. These two senior officers both gave evidence at the Court Martial and my talks with them were supplementary to that evidence.

First then, the Conference. This was held on October 7 and in addition to the Permanent Under-Secretary for War, there were present the Director of Finance, the Director Royal Artillery, and, during the vital discussion on the fate of Laerg, a member of the staff of the Ordnance Board. The object of the conference was to review Royal Artillery expenditure for the current financial year. This was one of a series of War Office conferences necessitated by the Prime Minister's refusal to face the House with supplementaries to the original Estimates.

There were eleven items on the agenda for that afternoon, all affecting the Royal Artillery. Laerg was sixth on the list. It came up for discussion about half past three and I understand the Director of Finance had all the costings ready to hand, reading them out in a flat monotone that was barely audible above the roar of Whitehall traffic. It was a long list and when he'd finished he put it back in his brief-case and faced the DRA. 'I think you'll agree,' he said, 'that the cost of maintaining the detachment on Laerg is quite disproportionate to the contribution it makes to our guided weapons tests.' He then went on, I gather, to emphasise the point he wanted to make. 'Your firing season finishes when?'

'Some time in August,' the DRA replied.

'And it starts in May.'

'In May—yes. But we begin the build-up in April.'

'In other words, the station is dormant for at least seven months of the year. And during those seven months it requires a Detachment Commander, usually a Captain, a Medical Officer and two orderlies, cooks, drivers, a REME outfit, even seamen military, a total of anything from thirty to forty men. There are two LCTs Mark VIII involved in ferrying supplies and . . .'

'The tank landing craft don't function in the winter.'

'Quite so. But they are nevertheless committed to this operation and are merely withdrawn to Squadron Headquarters at Portsmouth for re-fit. They are replaced by an RASC trawler. Not so costly perhaps, but still pretty expensive. In addition, a helicopter is periodically required to deliver mail.'

Throughout this interchange the DRA explained to me that he was very much on the defensive. He knew the operation could not be justified on grounds of cost alone. 'It's the men,' he said. 'They feel cut off if they don't get regular mail. In any case, we've already decided to dispense with the trawler this winter and rely on Army helicopters for mail and relief of personnel. An experiment recommended by Colonel Standing, the Range Commandant. We've yet to find out how it will work. Conditions for helicopter flying are not all that good, particularly after the end of October.'

'That's merely a matter of detail,' the Director of Finance said. 'I have been into all this very carefully. Correct me if I'm wrong, but as I understand it the only maintenance required on the really vital equipment, the radar, is that it should be run once a day, mainly to warm it up. One man's work for a few hours each day. To keep him there you apparently require over thirty men . . .'

'I've reported on this to the Secretary for War more than once,' the DRA cut in. 'The tracking station cost a lot to establish. It isn't only the radar that has to be maintained. There's the camp, the vehicles, the boats; to abandon Laerg for seven months in the year would result in rapid deterioration through gales and the salt in the atmosphere. Moreover, trawlermen use Shelter Bay in the

10

winter—Norwegians, Belgians, French, Spanish, as well as Scots. There wouldn't be much left of our installations if there were nobody there to guard them.'

At this point the Permanent Under-Secretary intervened. 'I don't think we need query the number of men involved or the necessity for maintaining the station throughout the year in present circumstances. Presumably this was all gone into at the time and agreed as unavoidable. What we have to decide now is whether or not Laerg has become redundant in view of this new equipment we've been offered. You've had a report on it, I believe. The results of the trials were very impressive, I thought.'

The DRA didn't say anything. He was staring out of the window at the cloudless blue of the sky. From where he sat he looked across the pale stone outline the Horseguards to the trees in St James's Park. They were still in summer leaf. It had been a mild autumn and so fine were the yellow brush strokes of the early frosts that only a painter's eye would have discerned the warning breath of winter in that green canvas. The DRA was not a painter. His hobby, he explained to me, was bird-watching and he was wishing he had been able to find time to visit Laerg during the nesting season. The room was hot and airless, full of smoke, and the sun slanted golden bars of light across the table.

'Before we finally make up our minds, perhaps we should hear what Ordnance Board have to say about it.' The Permanent Under-Secretary reached for the phone and asked for the Colonel who had conducted the trials to be sent in. The discussion that followed was technical, and as the equipment concerned was secret the DRA did not discuss it with me. He did, however, say that it was American equipment and that he had pointed out that it would be costly to install. To this the Permanent Under-Secretary had replied, 'But as they are using the range themselves they are offering it to us on a long-term credit basis.' That, the DRA told me, was the decisive factor. The matter was settled and what happened later stemmed from that moment, for the Permanent Under-Secretary was under considerable pressure. 'I'd like to be able to report to the PM,' he said, 'that you'll have your men and equipment off the island and the station closed down, say by the end of the month. Would that be possible?'

'I suppose so. It depends on the weather.'

'Naturally. But we're in for a fine spell now. I heard the forecast this morning.'

'Laerg is over six hundred miles north of here and it's getting late in the season.'

'All the more reason to hurry it.'

The DRA was not disposed to argue. He had held his appointment for less than six months, and anyway he was wondering how to handle the next item on the agenda, which was of far more importance to the Artillery than Laerg. 'I've no doubt we'll manage,' he said and made a note on his pad to instruct his Brigadier General Staff.

The BGS, questioned by the President of the Court Martial about the DRA's acceptance of that time limit, made the point that some such limit was essential in an operation of this kind. If the evacuation were not completed before the winter gales set in, there would be little likelihood of getting the men and equipment off that winter. Even a partial failure to complete it would necessitate the maintenance of the station probably until the spring, with all the attendant problems of supply aggravated by the fact that essential stores would be lacking. 'Without a time limit,' he said, 'the operation would have lacked the necessary atmosphere of urgency.'

Unfortunately, all the items on the agenda could not be dealt with that afternoon and the conference was resumed again at ten the following morning. As a result, the Brigadier General Staff received his instructions about Laerg in the form of a hurriedly dictated memo that listed some half-dozen other items for his immediate attention. The BGS was a keen yachtsman, and though he had never sailed in the Hebrides, he was able to appreciate better than most people in the War Office the difficulties that could arise in an evacuation involving landing craft operating across an open beach. With the weekend imminent he decided to shelve the matter until Monday when Brigadier Matthieson was due in London. He marked it in his diary for the morning of October 11, the final decision to be taken after discussion with the DRA. Meantime, he teleprinted Matthieson at Scottish Command ordering him to have a plan of operations prepared for the immediate withdrawal of all stores, equipment and personnel.

Having established that there was a delay of four vital days between the DRA's original agreement to the principle of evacuation and the final decision to go ahead, I should perhaps add that only exceptional circumstances would have produced speedier action, and in this case the exceptional circumstances had not arisen. The pressure at this stage was from the Permanent Under-Secretary, not from the weather; a full two weeks was to elapse before that freak meteorological brew began to ferment in the sea areas Bailey, Hebrides and Faeroes. There was, in any case, a good deal of preliminary work to be done. In particular, the agreement of the RASC to the use of the landing craft had to be obtained and the plan itself worked out. This last the DRA, Scottish Command, brought with him to London so that once it was agreed it only needed an executive order to start the thing moving.

After reading the plan and discussing it with Matthieson, the BGS took him in to see the General. It was then just after midday and again the weather was fine in London, the sun shining out of a clear sky. In describing this meeting to me, Matthieson made it clear that though the DRA was under considerable pressure at the time and obviously determined to proceed with the evacuation, he had, nevertheless, been at some pains to allay any fears his subordinates might have. 'I suppose you're worrying about the weather,' was his opening remark. 'Naturally, I raised the point myself. The Permanent Under-Secretary was not impressed. The sun was shining and it was damnably hot in his room.' He glanced towards the windows. 'The sun is still shining. Did you listen to the shipping forecast this morning?' This to the BGS. And when he admitted he hadn't, the General said, 'Well, I did. Made a special point of it. I know you sailing types. There's a high pressure system covering the British Isles and the nearest depression is down in the German Bight. As to the alternative we've been offered, the responsibility rests with Ordnance Board. I made that perfectly plain. If it doesn't work . . .'

'Oh, I expect it'll work, sir,' the BGS said.

'Well, what's worrying you then?'

'Apart from the weather—Simon Standing.'

'Standing? He's one of our best instructors.'

'That's just the trouble. He's a wizard at

15

ballistics, but this is his first independent command and if anything went wrong . . .'

'Have you any reason to suppose that anything is going to go wrong?'

'Of course not. All I'm saying is that this operation doesn't call for the qualities that make a brilliant Instructor-in-Gunnery. It calls for a man of action.'

'Fine. It will give him some practical experience. Isn't that why you recommended him for the job? Practical experience is essential if he is to go on getting promotion at his present rate. How old is he?'

'Thirty-seven, thirty-eight.'

'That makes him just about the youngest IG with the rank of full Colonel. And he's ambitious. He'll make out all right. I seem to remember he's got Hartley as his second-in-command. Met him at Larkhill. Excellent at administration and a sound tactician. Just the man Simon needs.'

'Unfortunately he's in hospital—jaundice.'

'I see. Well, there's an adjutant presumably.'

'Young fellow by the name of Ferguson. He's not very experienced.'

'And you're not happy about him?'

'I can't say that. I don't know anything about him. He's only twenty-six, just promoted Captain and filling in a vacancy.'

'What's wrong with him then?'

'Well . . .' I don't think BGS wanted to go into this, but it was essential to the point he was

16

making. 'His record shows that he volunteered for paratrooping and didn't complete the course.'

'Funked his jumps?'

'Something like that. He was posted to BAOR.'

'All right then. Get on to AG6. Have them post somebody up there temporarily just to hold Simon's hand—an older man with practical experience. The AGG ought to be able to rake up somebody to fill in for a few weeks. Anything else on your mind?'

'Only the timing. The operation had been planned on the basis of completing by the end of the month, but nobody can possibly guarantee that. Fortunately we'd agreed to Standing's idea of cutting the size of the wintering unit and maintaining contact by helicopter. As a result one of the huts had already been dismantled. Nevertheless, I must emphasise that the maintenance of a planning schedule as tight as this depends entirely on the continuance of the present fine weather.'

'Of course. That's understood. Service Corps have already made it clear that they're not taking any chances with their landing craft. And rightly.' He turned to Matthieson. 'That satisfy you?'

Matthieson hesitated. He was well aware of the dangers. He told me he had tried to visit Laerg twice and each time had been turned back by bad weather. He had held his present

17

post for almost two years and he knew the difficulties that must arise if conditions deteriorated and the operation became a protracted one. But this was only the second interview he had had with the DRA since the General's appointment. Doubtless he felt it wasn't the moment to voice his misgivings. My impression is that he decided to play his luck. At any rate, all he apparently said was, 'Captain Pinney, the present Detachment Commander, is pretty experienced; so is the skipper of one of the landing craft—the other was a replacement halfway through the season. Still, I think the whole thing should go off quite smoothly.' However, to cover himself, he added, 'But Laerg can be the devil if it blows up and we're getting on towards winter in the north.'

The DFA nodded. 'Well that settles it then. We pray for fine weather and get on with the job, eh? Signal them to go ahead with the operation right away.'

And so the decision was finally agreed. Matthieson sent off the necessary signal and the BGS phoned about the temporary attachment of an officer to assist Standing.

He was immediately offered a Major George Braddock.

The reason given by the AGG for recommending this particular officer was that he wanted to be posted to the Hebrides. Not only had Braddock written twice from Cyprus, where he commanded a battery, but a few days

18

before he had sought a personal interview with the AGG to press the matter. He had then just arrived in London on leave.

To the BGS it seemed the perfect answer to the problem. Braddock was about forty, his rank was right, and so was his record. He had an MC and two Mentions in Dispatches, awarded during the last war, as well as an excellent record during the Malayan trouble. Moreover, he was in England and immediately available. Locating him took a little time. His wife, who with her two children lived at Hertford, had apparently been separated from him for a number of years and did not know where he was. All she could say was that he liked fishing and usually went to Wales for his leave. He was eventually traced to a Country Club near Brecon. By then it was late at night and Braddock didn't reach London until the following afternoon.

That was Tuesday and as far as I can gather that was the day Ed Lane arrived in Lyons. I suppose almost every disaster requires something to trigger it off—a catalyst, as it were. *A decision that calls for action involves men, and men cannot escape their own natures . . . their basic characters.* In writing that I believe my brother was thinking of this Canadian businessman from Vancouver. Lane wasn't, of course, involved in the operation. He was probing Braddock's background and to that extent he exerted a pressure on events and was, in a sense, the catalyst. He had seen Braddock in Cyprus a fortnight before and had then gone on to the Middle East on business for his firm. Now that business was finished and he was free to concentrate on his private affairs. Whilst Braddock was travelling up to the War Office, Lane was interviewing one of the few people who could help him in his inquiries.

The BGS saw Braddock just after four. In his evidence, the Brigadier simply said that the interview strengthened the favourable impression already created by his record. He was satisfied that Major Braddock was the right man for the job. He was not asked for any details, only for confirmation that he had warned Braddock about weather conditions. As a result, the Court was not aware that the Brigadier was puzzled, even a little disturbed, by the answers Braddock gave to certain rather searching questions.

In the talk I had with him later the Brigadier admitted that he had been curious to know why Braddock had applied for a posting to the Guided Weapons Establishment, particularly as his record showed that he had been one of the few survivors of the *Duart Castle*, sunk in those waters during the war. 'I should have thought your memories of that area . . .'

'That's got nothing to do with it, sir. It's just that—well, I guess it's because I spent part of my boyhood in Canada. I like cold climates.

The farther north the better. And I like something to get my teeth into. Malaya was all right for a bit. But Cyprus . . .' And then with an intensity that the Brigadier found disconcerting: 'Is there any particular reason why I'm being posted to the Hebrides now— other than to deal with the problem of this evacuation of Laerg?'

'No, of course not. Why should there be?'

Braddock had seemed to relax then. 'I just wondered. I mean, when you apply for a posting and then suddenly get it . . .' The lined, leathery-hard face had cracked in a charming smile. 'Well, it makes you wonder what's behind it.'

'Nothing's behind it,' the Brigadier told him. 'I was simply referring to what happened to you up there in 1944.' He told me he was wishing then that he knew the man better, feeling instinctively that there was more to it than he'd admitted. 'How many of you were on that raft at the outset?' He watched the tough, poker face, saw the nerve quiver at the corner of the mouth and the eyes fixed wide in a flat, blank stare. 'No, I thought not. It's something you'd rather forget. Have you ever visited the Hebrides since?'

'No.'

'Then why do you want to be posted there now?'

But Braddock either couldn't or wouldn't answer that. 'It's just that . . . well, as I said—it

21

sort of calls to me. I can't explain exactly.' And he'd smiled that engaging smile. 'It's a bit like Canada, I suppose.'

The Brigadier hesitated. But it was nothing to do with him and he'd let it go at that, staring down again at Braddock's record. The Normandy landings—anti-tank role—the MC for gallantry at Caen after holding a bridge with a single gun against repeated attacks by tanks—command of a troop two months later—promoted captain just before the dash for the Rhine—temporary rank of major at the end of the war ... 'Now about this operation. Do you sail at all?'

'I've done a little.'

'Good. Then you'll have some idea what the weather means to the LCTs, particularly in view of your previous experience ...' He had got up from his desk and turned towards the window. 'However, that isn't why I wanted to see you personally.' The sky was blue and the sun beat down on the stone ledge of the tight-shut window. 'Ever met Simon Standing?' He turned as Braddock shook his head. 'No, I didn't think your paths would have crossed. Can't imagine two people more entirely different—which may be a good thing, or again it may not. Colonel Standing is Commandant and Range Controller. He's a few years younger than you and it's his first independent command. Now this is what I want to make clear to you, and it's strictly between ourselves.

22

Standing's up there primarily because he's an expert on ballistics and all that sort of thing. In fact he's one of the best brains we've got in the field of guided weapons. But for a job like this . . .' He had hesitated then. 'Well, his world is figures. He's not strictly an action man, if you see what I mean.' And he went on quickly, 'Officially, of course, it's his show and you come under him as acting second-in-command. Unofficially, I want you to run the operation.' Faced with the blank stare of those black eyes he probably felt it was all damnably awkward, for he admitted to me later that he thought Braddock should have been a half-colonel at least. He had the experience and he had that indefinable something, that air of confidence denoting a born leader. He may even have wondered what had gone wrong, but at the time all he said was, 'Just keep Simon Standing in the picture and get on with the job. If you bear in mind that he's quite brilliant in his own field and . . . well, use a little tact.'

'I understand, sir.'

'I hope you do.' The Brigadier had hesitated then, feeling instinctively that a clash of temperament was inevitable. Ever since Braddock had come into his office he had been conscious of the strength of the man's personality, and something else—a tension, almost a sense of urgency. But there was nothing he could do about that now. Time was too short. 'There's a sleeper reserved for you

23

on the night train. You'll be travelling up with the BRA, Scottish Command. He'll give you all the details.' And with a murmured 'Good luck' he had dismissed him.

He admitted later that Braddock should have been given the opportunity to discuss the operation. But throughout the interview he'd felt uncomfortable. The large hands, the dark moustache, the lined, leathery face with the heavy brows craggy above the black stare of the eyes—somehow, he said, the man seemed to fill the office, too big for it almost. So strong was this feeling that he'd been glad when the door had shut behind him.

The train left Euston at nine thirty-five and ten minutes after it pulled out Braddock visited Brigadier Matthieson in his sleeper. I suspect that Matthieson was one of those officers who joined the Royal Artillery for the riding, back in the days when the guns were horse-drawn. I don't think he had much of a brain, but he was certainly no fool and he was as good with men as he was with horses. He never forgot a face. 'Met you somewhere before, haven't I?' he said and was surprised to find this overture rejected almost fiercely. 'A long time ago, I think. Now where was it?'

'I think you've made a mistake, sir.'

But Matthieson was quite sure he hadn't. 'During the war.' He saw Braddock's face tauten, and then he had it—a tall, hard-bitten youngster in a blood-stained battledress coming back with a single gun buckled by a direct hit. 'Normandy. Autumn of forty-four. You'd been holding a bridge.' The craggy face towering above him relaxed, broke into the same charming, rather tired-looking smile. 'I remember now, sir. You were the major bivouacked in that wood. You gave us food—the few of us that were left. A tent, too. We were just about all in.'

They'd talked about the war then, sitting on Matthieson's berth, finishing the bottle of Scotch he'd brought south with him. It was almost midnight and the bottle empty by the time they got round to discussing Laerg. Matthieson pulled out his brief-case and handed Braddock the Plan of Operations. 'The schedule's a bit tight, but that's not my fault. About ten LCT loads should do the trick. Read it through tonight. Any points we can discuss in the morning. I've a car meeting me and I'll drive you out to Renfrew Airport.'

Braddock, leafing quickly through the Plan, immediately expressed concern about the schedule. 'I have some experience of the weather up there . . .'

'On an open raft. So the BGS told me. But you're not dealing with a raft this time. These LCTs can stand quite a lot.'

'It's an open beach. If the wind's south-easterly . . .'

'You know the place, do you?'

He saw Braddock's face tighten. 'I looked it

25

up on a map,' he said quickly, and Matthieson wondered how he'd got hold of a map with the shops closed. 'If the weather goes against us . . .'

'It's the weather you're being posted up there to deal with. The weather and that fellow Standing.' He was well aware that the schedule was too tight and he wanted to get Braddock off the subject. 'Ever met Simon Standing? Do you know anything about him?' And when the other shook his head, he went on, 'Give you a word of advice then. Don't fall out with him. War Office thinks he's wonderful. But I can tell you he's a queer fish and he's got no sense of humour.' He was very frank about the words he'd used. 'Bloody little prig, if you ask me.' I imagine he smiled then, a flash of teeth that were too white and even to be his own. 'Shouldn't be talking like this about your commanding officer, should I? But we've seen a war together. These adding machine types haven't. Probably puke if they did. A real war, I mean—blood and the stink of rotting guts, the roar of a thousand guns blazing hell out of a dawn sky. They're push-button warriors; nothing but bloody electricians.'

He was staring down at his glass then, memories of a long-dead war merging with the future. 'Anyway, I'm getting out. In a few months' time I'll be running a stud farm near Melbourne. Australia, you know. Once I get out there they can push all the ruddy little

26

buttons they like.' It was the drink in him talking, and because he was aware of that he said, 'Well, I'm off to bed now.'

It was then that Braddock surprised him by asking a series of questions that seemed to have very little bearing on the operation. First, he'd wanted to know whether the men on Laerg were free to roam around the island or whether their duties kept them confined to the area of Shelter Bay. When told that off-duty they could go where they liked, and that many of them became enthusiastic bird-watchers, Braddock asked if they'd reported any interesting finds. 'I mean traces of . . . well, old dwellings, caves, things like that with traces of human habitation?'

Matthieson wondered what he was getting at. 'Are you a student of primitive men or are you thinking of the link between the Hebrides and Greenland? There was a link, I believe. The Vikings put the sheep on Eileann nan Shoay—Shoay or Soay is the old word for sheep, you know. They may well have been on their way west to the Greenland settlement.'

'Yes, I've read about that, but . . . Well, I just thought something fresh might have been reported.' And Braddock had stared at him with disconcerting directness, waiting for an answer.

'No, of course not,' the Brigadier replied. 'The boys are just amateurs.'

'What about civilians—naturalists and so

on? Are they allowed on the island?'

Matthieson admitted he was disturbed by the other's persistence. But all he said was, 'Yes. There's usually a party of bird-watchers, a few naturalists. Students, some of them. They come in summer under the aegis of Nature Conservancy. A nuisance, but quite harmless.'

'And they've reported nothing—nothing of exceptional interest?'

'If they have, we haven't been told about it.' And he'd added, 'Anyway, you won't have time to indulge your interest. Your job is to get our boys off, and it'll be a full-time job, believe you me. You'll understand when you've had time to study that Operations Plan.' And he'd wished Braddock goodnight, wondering as the train rushed on into the night what Standing would make of his new second-in-command.

Two coaches back Braddock started going through the Operations Plan, sitting propped up in bed, the pages dancing to the sway and rattle of the train. And almost a thousand miles away another man in another sleeper was checking through the notes he'd made of his first interview with a non-Canadian survivor of the *Duart Castle*. Ed Lane was on the train to Paris, bound for London with a list of five possible names.

The night train to Glasgow got in at six-thirty in the morning. A staff car was waiting for Brigadier Matthieson at Central Station and whilst driving Braddock out to Renfrew

28

Airport he discussed with him the details of the Operations Plan. In his evidence he made it clear that he'd allowed Major Braddock the widest possible interpretation of the evacuation orders. What, in fact, happened was that Braddock not only had a list of queries, but seemed prepared to argue that the whole conception of the Plan was at fault. It was the timing, of course, that chiefly worried him. 'I agree it doesn't give you much room for manoeuvre,' Matthieson had said. 'But that's not my fault. It's the Government that's pushing the operation.' And he'd added, 'I'm a great believer in sound planning and the chaps who handled this are very good at it. If they say it can be done, then you can take it from me that it can.'

But Braddock wasn't to be put off so easily. 'LCT so-and-so to sail on such-and-such a date, arrive Laerg about twelve hours later, loading time six hours, leave at dusk, return to base at dawn. All very nice and neat if you're sitting on your backside in an office. But there's no allowance for weather or any of the hundred-and-one things that can go wrong on an amphibious operation. It's an open beach. The equipment is pretty valuable, I gather—some of it secret. What happens if a gale blows up? Do I risk a landing craft and the equipment simply to keep a schedule I don't believe in?'

'Damn it, man. Use your initiative. That's why you're being posted there.' And

Matthieson had added, quoting, as no doubt he'd often done before, from the wartime leader he'd served under, 'I never interfere in the detailed running of things. That's my speciality. I leave it to the experts. In this case, Braddock, you're the expert. Understood?'

By that time they had arrived at Renfrew. Matthieson left him then and after a leisurely breakfast Braddock caught the ten o'clock plane. At Stornoway there was an Army helicopter waiting for him. He landed at Northton on the west coast of Harris shortly after one. There he was met by the adjutant, Captain Ferguson, who informed him that Colonel Standing was waiting for him in his office. There is no record of what happened between the two men at that first meeting. But it lasted little more than ten minutes and when they came into the Mess for lunch the atmosphere between them was already strained.

The clearest impression of Braddock's impact on the operation is contained in the deposition made by Lieutenant Field, the Education Officer. This deposition, made at the Board of Inquiry, could have had considerable influence on the subsequent Court Martial. Not only was Field much older than the other officers, but his background and experience gave weight to his judgment. The first two paragraphs are the vital ones and I give them in full:

Major Braddock arrived at Joint Services Guided Weapons Establishment, Northton, on October 13. I think it is right to say that his appointment came as a shock to most of the officers, not least to Colonel Standing who had only been informed of it on the phone that morning. I say 'shock' because that is how it seemed to officers accustomed to something in the nature of a winter hibernation in the Hebrides. Major Braddock was a driver. He had a very forceful personality. He was also a man of great nervous energy, great vitality. Whatever your findings, I would like to make it clear that I regard him as exactly the sort of man the operation needed at that time.

I have some knowledge of the leadership necessary in an operation that is at the mercy of the elements, and from my own observations, and from what I heard from Captain Ferguson, who was a friend of my daughter's and often visited our croft of an evening, I may say that I already had certain very definite misgivings. Not until Major Braddock's arrival was there that thrust and pressuring of officers and men, that sense of being engaged with an enemy, that is the essential prelude to exceptional human endeavour. He made them feel they were involved in a battle. Most of the youngsters got a kick out of it; the older ones, particularly some of the officers, resented it. Later, of course, they did all that any men could do in circumstances that became virtually impossible.

31

Before he left for London, Matthieson had had the foresight to arrange with RASC (Water Transport) for both LCTs to re-fuel, cancel all leave and stand by to sail at short notice. As a result, the position on Braddock's arrival was not unsatisfactory. One landing craft had completed its first trip and was on its way back to Laerg again; the other was just entering Leverburgh, a bare two hours behind schedule. And the weather was fine, cold and clear with a light northerly wind.

But as Field pointed out, the fine weather could not be expected to last indefinitely, nor could the men. The strains were already beginning to show; at Leverburgh where the quay was inadequate, on Laerg where the bolts securing huts and equipment were rusted solid and the men, after only two days, were tiring, moving in a sleepless daze from dismantling to loading and back to dismantling again. And whilst Braddock threw himself into the work of ensuring a faster rate of turn-round for the landing craft, Ed Lane flew into London and began checking for relatives of Albert George Piper, one-time Master-at-Arms on the *Duart Castle*.

Piper's name was the first on his list. The second was my brother's.

CHAPTER TWO

MY BROTHER, IAIN
(October 15)

It was two days later, just after ten on the morning of October 15, that my phone rang and a man's voice, rather soft, said, 'Mr Ross? My name's Ed Lane. Are you by any chance related to a Sergeant Iain Alasdair Ross reported lost when the *Duart Castle* was torpedoed in February, 1944?'

'He was my brother.'

'He was?' The voice had a vaguely American accent. 'Well, that's fine. Didn't expect to strike it that fast—you're only the fifth Ross I've telephoned. I'll be with you inside of an hour. Okay?' And he'd rung off, leaving me wondering what in the world it was all about.

I was working on another book jacket for Alec Robinson, but after that phone call I found it impossible to go back to it. I went into the little kitchenette and brewed myself some coffee. And after that I stood drinking it at the window, looking out across the roof-tops, an endless vista of chimney pots and TV aerials with a distant glimpse of Tower Bridge. I was thinking of my brother, of how I'd loved him and hated him, of how there had been nobody else in my life who had made up for the loss I'd felt at his going. And yet at the time I'd been almost glad. It had seemed better that he should die like that—in the sea, a casualty of war.

I turned away from the grubby window, glanced at the jacket design lying on the table amongst a litter of paints and brushes, and then fell to pacing my studio, wondering what this fellow Lane wanted digging up the past that was dead these twenty years and more. Surely to God they weren't going to rake over the whole wretched business again. I could still remember the shock when the Military Police had come to interview me at the factory. Did I realise he'd deserted? Slinging questions at me until they'd discovered my father was dead and my mother alone and ill at Ardnamurchan. 'We'll pick him up there then.' And my bursting into tears and shouting at them that whatever my brother had done it was justified and why the hell did they pick on him and not the officer. And that MP sergeant with the big ears and the broken nose—I could have drawn his face even now—snapping back at me in a grating Glaswegian voice, 'The officer was unconscious, laddie, with machine-gun bullets spraying him as he lay on the ground with a broken jaw. Aye and damn near twenty men dead who needn't have died. Justified? Christ, it was plain bluidy murrder.'

The jacket design stared at me, the lettering of the book title already pencilled in—THE PEACE THAT FOLLOWED. I had read it, thought it good, but now I dropped a rag over it, remembering the wartime passages, the sense of futility the writer had invoked. Sounds from the street drifted up to me, the bustle of London's East End. My studio was just an attic over a butcher's shop. It was all I could afford. Bed, table and easel took up most of the space, and the canvases stacked against the wall, all the work I'd done on Milos—there was hardly room to move. A cupboard in the corner held my clothes and above it was piled the camping equipment I'd bought from the proceeds of the only two pictures I'd sold—*Milos at Dawn Seen from a Caique* and *Greek Galley Under Water*. That was when I planned to paint on Laerg, before I'd been refused permission to go there.

I crossed to the window, thinking back over my life, back to the carefree days on Ardnamurchan and Iain in the glory of his youth fighting imaginary battles among the rocks below our croft, always in defence of Laerg with myself cast in the role of invader— a Viking, a pirate, a marauding trawlerman, anything that had recently captured his fancy. And in the evenings, sitting by the peat fire listening to the old man talking in that thick burr—tales of the Lovers' Stone, of cliff-crawling in search of puffins, of boat journeys to Fladday for the gannets which he called solan geese; wild tales of gales and ships being wrecked.

So long ago and yet so vivid, and Iain tall and handsome with his dark face, and his black hair

35

blowing in the wind; a wild boy with a streak of melancholy and a temper that flared at a word. He could have done something with his life. I pushed up the window, leaning out to feel the warmth of the sun, thinking of my own life, stuck here in this dirty back street doing hack work for a living. I should be painting on Laerg, getting the lost world of my grandfather down on canvas. That would be something, a justification. Eleven years at sea, followed by the years learning to paint, and it all added up to this miserable little room and a few pounds in the bank.

A taxi drew up in the street below and a man got out. All I could see of him was his wide-brimmed hat and the pale sheen of his coat as he paid the driver. It crossed my mind that it was a good angle from which to paint a picture of a London street—but in the same instant I knew I wouldn't do it; nobody would buy it. He disappeared from sight and a few moments later I heard his footsteps labouring up the bare stairboards. I opened the door and ushered him in, a tubby, round-looking man with small eyes in a smooth face. His clothes were a businessman's clothes, but not English. The small eyes took in the cluttered studio, scanning the walls as though in search of something. 'I guess you're an artist, Mr Ross. That right?'

'I kid myself sometimes.'

But there was no answering smile. The small

36

eyes stared at me, cold and humourless. 'You got a picture of your brother?'

'Just why are you here?' I asked him.

He took his hat off then and sat down on the bed, a little out of breath. 'It's a long story.' Brown-stained fingers fumbled for his cigarettes. 'Smoke?' I shook my head. He flipped one out of the pack and lit it. 'It's about the *Duart Castle*. As I told you over the phone, my name's Lane, Ed Lane. I come from Vancouver. I'm over here on business—oil and gas; my company runs pipelines. I mention that just to show you I'm a man of some standing. The reason I've come to see you is a private one. I'm investigating something that concerns my wife's family. A matter of a Will. There's a lot of money involved.' He paused for breath, reached into the pocket of his light-coloured raincoat. 'I've got some photographs here.' He had come up with an envelope. But instead of producing the pictures, he sat dragging at his cigarette and staring round the room. 'An artist,' he breathed as though he'd just thought of something. 'Do you do portraits?'

'No.'

He frowned. 'You mean you can't draw heads, faces, people's features?'

'I don't paint portraits, that's all.'

He looked at the table then, twisting his head round and reaching for the rag I'd dropped over the jacket design. Behind the lettering I had already painted in the first of a series of heads representing humanity in fear. 'There you are. That's the sort of thing.' The little button eyes stared at me as though I'd purposely misled him. 'You remember your brother, do you? You haven't forgotten what he looked like?'

'Of course not. But I don't see . . .'

'You could draw me a portrait of him, couldn't you?'

'I could.'

I think he saw I was getting annoyed, for he smiled and said, 'Sure. You want to know what it's all about first.'

'You mentioned some pictures,' I said.

He nodded. 'Later,' he said. 'Later. First, there are the press-cuttings.' He pulled some clippings from the envelope, selected one and handed it to me. 'You saw that at the time, I expect.'

It was from the *Daily Telegraph*, dated 24th February, 1944, the news of the sinking of the *Duart Castle* and the arrival at Donegal, Northern Ireland, of two boatloads of survivors, together with the list of their names, thirty-five in all. Pinned to it was a cutting dated 2nd March giving the official account of the torpedoing and the names of those who were missing, presumed dead. Iain Alasdair Ross. There it was to bring back to me after all these years the sense of loss I'd felt at the time, the feeling of being alone in the world, all my family dead. 'I read it in *The Scotsman*,' I said

38

and passed it back to him.

'Sure. It was in most of the papers.' He was riffling through the bunch of cuttings. 'That all you read about the *Duart Castle*?'

'That's all there was, as far as I know. Papers were small and a lot of ships were being sunk. They'd plenty of other news . . .'

'Then you didn't see this?' He handed me another clipping. 'It's from a Stornoway paper of March 14.'

'Stornoway's in the Outer Hebrides,' I pointed out. 'I'd hardly be likely to see a copy of that.'

'Sure, it's way up north and this is a local story. No other paper seems to have printed it. You read it. Then I'll tell you why I'm interested in your brother.'

The cutting was headed: 'ORDEAL BY RAFT— Terrible Story of Lone Survivor: On Tuesday evening Colin McTavish, seventy-two-year-old lobster fisherman of Tobson on Great Bernera, whilst rowing out in his boat to visit his pots, came upon a Carley float lodged amongst the rocks of Geodha Cool. The figures of two men lay on the raft, both apparently lifeless. The raft belonged to the *Duart Castle*, sunk by torpedoes some five hundred miles out in the North Atlantic on February 18th. They had, therefore, been adrift on the raft for twenty-two days. Colin McTavish took the bodies into his boat and rowed back to Tobson. There it was discovered that despite the long time at

39

sea, one of the men was still alive. His name is George Henry Braddock, 2nd-Lieutenant Royal Artillery, aged twenty. The terrible story of his ordeal cannot be told yet for a Merciful God has wiped it from his mind. He has been transferred to the hospital at Stornoway suffering from exposure and loss of memory. But we all know what he must have suffered out there in the open sea exposed to bitter cold and severe storms with no protection but the tattered remnants of a sail and his only companion dying before his eyes. The dead man is Pte. André Leroux, a French-Canadian from Montreal. He has been buried at the old cemetery above the bay at Bosta. Colin McTavish's rescue of 2nd-Lieutenant Braddock brings the total of survivors of the *Duart Castle* to thirty-six and this doubtless writes *finis* to the tragic story of a ship that was transporting Canadian reinforcements to aid the fight for freedom.'

'I didn't know about it,' I said. 'But I don't see what that's got to do with my brother—or with me.'

'Your brother was on that raft when the ship sank.'

'Well, he's dead,' I said. 'What difference does it make?'

He didn't say anything; simply handed me one of the photographs from the envelope. It showed a man in a light suit walking along a street—tall, black-haired, with a dark

40

moustache and what looked like a scar running down the centre of his forehead. It wasn't a very clear picture, just a snapshot taken very bright sunlight. He passed me another. The same man getting out of a car. 'And here's one taken with a telephoto lens.' Head and shoulders this time, the face heavily shadowed by sunlight. 'You don't recognise him?' He was watching me closely.

'Where were they taken?'

'Famagusta in Cyprus.'

'I've never been to Famagusta,' I said.

'I asked you whether you recognised him.'

'Well, I don't. Who is he?'

He sighed and took the photographs back, sitting there, staring down at them. 'I guess they're not clear. Not as clear as I would have liked. But . . .' He shook his head and tucked them away in the envelope together with the cuttings. 'They're pictures I took of Braddock. Major Braddock.' He looked up at me. 'You're sure they didn't strike some chord in your memory?' And when I shook my head, he said, 'They didn't remind you of your brother, for instance?'

'My brother?' I stared at him, trying to think back, remembering Iain's dark, handsome face. 'How the hell could it be my brother?' The face in those photos, lined and scarred. 'There's no resemblance at all. What are you getting at?'

'Think what he'd be like now.' The small eyes stared at me, cold and with an obstinate look.

'He's dead,' I said again, angry now, wondering what the hell this wretched little man was trying to dig up. 'And the past, that's dead, too,' I added.

'Okay, Mr Ross. If that's the way you feel. But do something for me, will you. Draw me a picture of your brother—as you think he might look now.'

'Damned if I do.' I wasn't going to help him or anyone else rake up the past. 'Why should I?'

'I'll tell you why.' His voice had a sudden bite to it. 'I don't believe the man I saw in Famagusta was Braddock.' The eyes, staring at me, still had that obstinate look. 'And if he wasn't Braddock, then who was he? That's what I want to know, and that's what I intend to find out.' He dived into his breast pocket and came out with a diary. 'I've got a list of five names.' He turned the pages quickly, spreading the diary open on his knee. 'Five men definitely identified. That's in addition to Braddock and Leroux, the two who were still on the raft when it was washed ashore in the Outer Hebrides.' He looked up at me then. 'That makes seven we know for sure were on the raft at the time the *Duart Castle* went down. No doubt there were more, but those seven have been identified by witnesses I consider absolutely reliable. Your brother was one of them, Mr Ross.'

I didn't see what he was driving at. Whether Iain was on that raft or in the water didn't seem to make much difference. It didn't alter the fact that he was dead. 'Who told you?' I asked. 'Braddock, I suppose.'

'No, it wasn't Braddock. Braddock says he doesn't remember. What you might call a mental blackout, I guess. Very convenient. No, your brother's name was given to me by a man I saw in Lyons on my way back home from the Middle East—Tom Webster, an English textile buyer. He came ashore in one of the boats.' He closed the diary. 'I've seen altogether eight of the survivors, in addition to Braddock. The first seven were Canadians, I interviewed them before I left for Europe. Only one of them remembered seeing the float. He gave me two possible names. Webster gave me a further three, and he was very positive about them because he was thrown into the water and clung to the float for a time before swimming to the boat.' He stubbed out his cigarette. 'The three men Webster was positive about were the Master-at-Arms, the second officer—and your brother. I've checked on the first two. Neither of them had any reason to change their identity. But your brother had. Did you know he was being brought back from Canada under escort to face a number of very serious charges?'

'Yes,' I said. 'I know that. But he's listed among those lost and it's over twenty years . . .'

43

'He was presumed dead.' His emphasis was on the word 'presumed', his voice flat and hard and very determined. 'There's a difference. His body was never recovered. He wasn't identified. And that brings me to the reason I'm here. The *Duart Castle* was a troopship. Most of the boys sailing in her were young Canadian conscripts. A hundred and thirty-six of them were officers, newly commissioned. Braddock was one of them.' And he went on to tell me Braddock's story.

I wanted to throw the man out. This monstrous, fantastic suggestion of his ... But he went on talking—talking in that flat Canadian monotone. It was like a river in spate and I listened to it because I couldn't help myself, because the seed of doubt had been sown and curiosity is a universal failing.

Braddock had been born in London. His father was English, his mother Canadian. When he was two the family had moved to Vancouver. That was in 1927. In 1938 they had returned to England, the father having been appointed London representative of the Canadian firm he worked for. On the outbreak of war a year later, George Braddock, then a boy of fourteen and their only child, had been evacuated to Canada. For the next four years he'd lived with his aunt, a Mrs Evelyn Gage, on a ranch in northern B.C. 'A lonely sort of place out on the old Caribou Trail,' Lane added. 'And Evie had just lost her husband. She was

44

alone there except for the stockman. She'd no children of her own and . . . well, I guess it's the old story. She came to regard young George Braddock more or less as her own son, particularly after his parents were killed. They died in the bombing—a direct hit on their flat. Now this is where I come into it. When the boy went off to join the Army she made a Will leaving everything to him "in love and affection for the boy who was like a son to me"—those are the actual words. She died last year, aged seventy-two and that Will still stands. She never made another.'

'And you're trying to break it?' Money, I thought—this smooth-faced, hard-eyed little man's whole life was money.

'Well, wouldn't you? Evie was my wife's aunt, too—by marriage; and the ranch alone is worth a hundred thousand dollars. And the boy never wrote to her, you see. All that time. It's taken lawyers six months to trace the guy. They thought at first he was dead.'

So that was it. Because the fellow hadn't written . . . 'It doesn't occur to you, I suppose, that Braddock might not be interested in a ranch in Canada.'

'There's more to it than the ranch—around a quarter of a million dollars.' He gave me a tight little smile. 'You show me the man who'll turn down that sort of money. Unless there's some very good reason. And in Braddock's case I'm convinced there is. He's scared of it.'

45

He got to his feet. 'Now then. You draw me a portrait of your brother and then I'll leave you. Draw it as you think he'd look now. Okay?'

I hesitated, my mind a confused mixture of thoughts.

'I'll pay you for it.' He pulled out his pocket book. 'How much?'

I damn near hit him then. What with his suspicions, the stupid allegations he'd made, and then offering me a bribe. 'Fifty dollars,' I heard myself say and even then I didn't realise why I'd decided to take his money.

I thought for a moment he was going to haggle over it. But he stopped himself in time. 'Okay, fifty it is.' He counted five ten-dollar bills on to the table. 'You're a professional. I guess you're entitled to your fee.' It was as though he were excusing himself for being too open-handed.

But when I came to draw it, I found it wasn't so easy. I started the first rough in black with a brush, but it was too strong a medium; you need to have your subject clear in front of your eyes. And when I switched to pen-and-ink it required too much detail. In the end I used an ordinary pencil, and all the time he stood over me, breathing down my neck. He was a chain-smoker and his quick panting breath made it difficult to concentrate. I suppose he thought he'd be more likely to get his money's worth if he watched every pencil stroke, or maybe it just fascinated him to see the picture emerge. But my mind, going back, searching for the likeness I couldn't quite capture, resented it.

It didn't take me long to realise that time had coloured my memory. Iain's features had become blurred and in that first rough I was emphasising what I wanted to remember, discarding what I didn't. I scrapped it and started again. And halfway through something happened—it began to take on a vague, shadowy likeness to the man in those photographs. I tore that sheet up, too. But when I tried again the same thing happened— something in the shape of the head, the way the hair grew down towards the forehead, the lines round mouth and eyes, the eyes themselves, particularly the eyes. A pity he'd shown me those photographs. I screwed the sheet up into a ball and threw it in the wastepaper basket. 'I'm sorry,' I said. 'I thought I could remember him. But I can't. Not clearly enough to draw you a true likeness.' And I picked up the fifty dollars and thrust the notes back into his hand. 'I can't help you, I'm afraid.'

'You mean you won't.'

'Have it your own way,' I said. I wanted to get rid of him, to be alone with time to think, and I thrust my hands in my pockets, for I knew they were shaking. *Donald my Donald*. How Iain's voice came back to me down the years— cruel and charming, gay and sombre, that queer Celtic mixture. And Laerg of our imagination that was like a Shangri-la, like a talisman—but still one thing to him, another to me. *If I go to Laerg it will be to die. Aye, Donald my Donald—death to me and life to you.* A quarter of a century and I could remember the words, still hear his voice slurred with drink in that dirty little pub. And his face, lined already, sodden that night . . . 'I'm sorry,' I said again. 'I can't do it.' And I opened the door for him, anxious to be rid of the man.

He paused, staring at me hard. 'Okay,' he said finally in that flat voice of his. I thought he was going then, but he paused in the doorway. 'If you should want to contact Braddock he's in this country.'

'I thought you said he was in Cyprus.'

'That's where I saw him on my way through to the Middle East. But he was due for leave. Now he's been posted to the Hebrides.' I didn't say anything and he added, 'You'll find him at the Guided Weapons Establishment on Harris. Just thought you'd like to know.' He was starting down the stairs when I asked him how he'd found out. 'Private inquiry agent. They've been keeping an eye on him for me.' He smiled. 'Odd, isn't it? Why should this guy Braddock get posted to the Hebrides now? And another thing, Mr Ross. I know why you wouldn't complete that drawing. I was watching your face.' He pulled his hand out of his pocket. 'I guess I'll leave these here.' He placed the dollar bills on the top step of the stairs. 'Tear them up if you like. But before you do,

48

remember they'll just about cover your fare to the Hebrides.' And with that he left me, standing there listening to his footsteps descending the bare boards, staring down at those damned dollars.

And I thought I'd covered up. How many times in the past had I covered up for Iain when he'd acted on the spur of the moment without thought of the future? Father, the police, that poor little idiot Mavis . . . I reached down and picked up the dollar bills, feeling like Judas. But I had to know. A brother is still your brother—hate and love, the old hero-worship still there, dormant, but leaving a vacuum. And I'd no one else. No one in the world I'd really cared for. I had to know.

PART TWO

DISASTER

DISASTER

I'd finished that jacket design in two hours flat and Alec Robinson had liked it sufficiently to pay me cash. Fifteen guineas. It had landed the difference, camping out, I could manage for a time, and I had my return ticket. Something else I'd got from Robinson, too—an introduction to Cliff Morgan, a meteorologist working at Northton five miles north of Rodil. I'd done the jacket for his book, Airman's Weather. He was a contact at any rate, and

GUIDED WEAPONS HQ
(October 16–19)

I left for the north the following day; the night train to Mallaig, the steamer to Rodil in the extreme south of Harris. And all the way there thinking of Iain—Iain and Braddock. The rattle of the wheels, the thump of the screws; their names pounding at my brain, till the two were one. And that Canadian . . . walking up the street to the bus stop there'd been a man in an old raincoat; he'd been on the bus with me and I'd seen him at King's Cross, just behind me waiting to get his ticket. Coincidence perhaps, but if I'd been Lane . . . I pictured him sitting by the telephone in some London hotel waiting for a report, smiling gently to himself when he was told I'd left for the north. Well, to hell with that. It was natural, wasn't it—that I should want to be sure?

I'd finished that jacket design in two hours flat and Alec Robinson had liked it sufficiently to pay me cash. Fifteen guineas. It had made all the difference. Camping out I could manage for a time and I had my return ticket. Something else I'd got from Robinson, too—an introduction to Cliff Morgan, a meteorologist working at Northton five miles north of Rodil. I'd done the jacket for his book, *Airman's Weather*. It was a contact at any rate and

53

Robinson had told me that Northton was where the Guided Weapons Establishment was.

I'd never been farther north than Ardnamurchan and all up through the islands, through the Sounds of Sleat and Raasay, I was conscious of the growing sense of familiarity, a feeling almost of contentment. The sea and the islands, and the great canopy of the sky—it called to me and my spirit sang with the smell of the salt sea air and the cold wind on my face. And then the mountains of Harris, rising abruptly from the rim of the sea, piled against a leaden sky, their tops blurred by a rainstorm. Rodil proved to be nothing but a hotel and a grass-grown quay falling into decay with an old stone church on the hill behind, built on the pattern of Iona. The boatman, ferrying us from the ship to the quay, looked at my tent and said, 'If they've nae room up yonder, I could fix ye a bed maybe.' His voice was soft as the rain that was beginning to fall and when I declined his offer, he said, 'Och weel, it's yer ain business. But it'll be a tur-rible wet night I'm thinking.'

The night was both wet and cold and I went to sleep with the sound of the waves sloshing among the seaweed that clothed the rocks, and in the morning I started to walk to Northton. Just beyond the church a girl in a small estate car stopped and offered me a lift. She wore a faded green anorak with the hood pushed back and her face had the freshness of the islands; a

54

dark, wind-browned face and bright blue eyes. 'You must have had a very uncomfortable night,' she said as we drove up the glen. Her voice was soft and that, too, belonged to the islands. 'Why didn't you come to the hotel?' Something about the way she said it, the quick, almost hostile glance she gave me—it was almost as though she resented the presence of a stranger.

But my attention was concentrated on her features, which were unusual: the dark colouring, the wide mouth below the strong, slightly beaky nose. I knew there were islands up here where Nordic blood had mixed with the Celt to produce blue eyes and dark hair and skin, and because it interested me, I said, 'You're an islander, aren't you?'

'I live here.'

'No, I meant you come from one of the islands up here.'

'My father does.' The blue eyes staring at me and again that sense of hostility. 'I'm Marjorie Field.' She said it defiantly, adding that she worked part-time at the hotel. She seemed to expect some reaction from me, and then she began asking me a lot of questions—my name, where I had come from, how long I intended to stay. At the time I put it down to the natural curiosity about strangers in an isolated community.

The fact that I was an artist seemed to surprise her. 'You mean you paint—for a living?' We were at the top of the glen then and she concentrated on her driving until the road straightened out, running down to the flat desolation of buildings scattered round marsh and loch; ugly modern dwelling houses, impermanent-looking against the misted bulk of the hills beyond. 'Artists don't come here at this time of the year,' she said quite suddenly. 'And they don't live in tents, Mr Ross—not when it's cold and wet.'

'Do you know many artists?' I asked.

'A few.' She was tight-lipped now, her manner cold, and I had a feeling she didn't believe me. We drove through Leverburgh in silence. This, according to my guide book, had been the village of Obbe until Lord Leverhulme renamed it as part of his grandiose scheme for making it the centre of the west coast trawler fleet. Beyond the village she turned to me and said, 'You're a newspaper man, aren't you?' She said it flatly, in a tone almost of resignation.

'What makes you think that?'

She hesitated, and then she said, 'My father is Charles Field.' She was watching me out of the corner of her eyes and again she seemed to expect some reaction. 'He's the Education Officer at Northton.' And then she slowed the car and turned her head. 'Please. Won't you be frank? You haven't come up here to paint. It's something else—I can feel it.'

Her reaction was disturbing, for this was

something more than ordinary curiosity. We had reached the top of the next glen and there was the sea and a cloud-capped mountain, half-obscured by rain. To distract her I asked, 'Is that Toe Head?'

She nodded. 'The hill is called Chaipaval.'

It seemed bedded on sand, for the tide was out and the bay to the north was a dull, flat gleam running out to dunes. Dunes, too, formed the neck of land that made Toe Head a peninsula. But much of the sand-bunkered area had been bulldozed flat to make a camp and a landing place for helicopters. Seaward of the camp was a wired-off enclosure with blast protection walls. The whole effect—the tarmac apron, the tight-packed ranks of the hutted camp, the flat square of the launching pad—it was raw and violent, like a razor slash on an old oil-painting. 'And that's the rocket range, I suppose?'

She nodded. 'Surprised?' She gave me a quick, rather hesitant smile. 'It always seems to surprise people. They've read about it in the papers, but when they actually see it . . .' And she added, 'Of course, being near the road, it's much more obvious than the old range down on South Uist.'

In a few minutes now we should be at the camp. 'Has a Major Braddock been posted up here?' I asked.

She nodded. 'He arrived a few days ago.' And after a moment she said, 'Is that why

57

you're going to Northton?'

'Yes,' I said. 'I'm hoping he'll be able to get me across to Laerg.'

'Laerg? Then it isn't my father . . . You really are a painter.' She gave a quick, nervous little laugh—as though laughing at her own foolishness. 'I'm sorry, but, you see, we get so few people at Rodil—only fishermen, a few tourists, the occasional bird-watcher. Why aren't you in the Mediterranean, somewhere warm and sunny? I never knew an artist come to the Hebrides, not for the winter.' Her voice ran quickly on as though by talking she could conceal from me that the presence of an unexpected visitor had scared her. 'You're Scots, aren't you? Perhaps that explains it. But an artist wanting to go to Laerg—it's so unusual. And the birds will have flown. No gannets or puffins. They've all left now. What are you going to paint?'

'The island,' I said. 'Laerg as the islanders knew it at the worst time of the year.'

She nodded. 'I've never seen it. But Mike says it can be very beautiful, even in winter.'

We were in Northton now and I could see what it had been before the Army had come, a line of small crofts clinging to an old existence in a land as old as time. It was an anachronism now, pitiful-looking against the background of the camp with its fuel dump and its MT workshops and the barrack lines of its huts. 'Where will I find Major Braddock?' I asked.

'His office is in the Admin. block. But he may not be there. He's supposed to be flying to Laerg today.' She drew up at the main gate where the model of a rocket stood and a notice board read: Joint Services Guided Weapons Establishment. 'The Admin. block is down there on the left,' she said. I thanked her and the little estate car drove off along a concrete roadway drifted with sand that led to another part of the camp.

There was no guard on the gate. I simply walked straight in. The huts stretched in two straight lines either side of a concrete road; sand everywhere and the rain driving like a thick mist. A staff car and two Land-Rovers stood parked outside the Admin. block. There was nobody about. I went in. Still nobody, and a long passage running the length of the hut with glass-panelled doors to the offices leading off it. I walked slowly down it, feeling oddly nervous, conscious of being an intruder in a completely alien world. Small wooden plaques announced the contents of each closed box of an office: RSM—WT Symes; Commanding Officer—Colonel ST Standing; 2nd-in-Command—Major G. H. Braddock (this lettered in ink on a paper stick-on); Adjutant—Captain ML Ferguson.

I stood for a moment outside Braddock's door, unwilling now to face the awkwardness of this moment. Lane and his snapshots seemed a whole world away and I felt suddenly foolish to have come so far on such an errand. How could the man possibly be my brother after all these years? But I had an excuse all worked out, the excuse that I wanted to visit Laerg. He could only refuse and at least I'd know for certain then. I knocked on the door. There was no answer. I pushed it open. There was nobody inside and I had a feeling of relief at the sight of the empty desk.

There was a sliding hatch in the partition that separated this office from the adjutant's and I could hear a voice talking. But when I went into the next office Captain Ferguson was alone at his desk. He was speaking into the telephone. He wore battledress, a ginger-haired youngster with a square freckled face and a Scots accent that took me back to my Glasgow days. '. . . I can see it is . . . Aye, well, you check with the Met. Office . . . Damned if I do. You tell him yourself. He's down at Leverburgh, but he'll be back soon. Eleven at the latest, he said, and he'll be mad as hell when he hears . . . Laddie, you haven't met the man. He'll be across to see you . . . Okay, I'll tell him.' He put the phone down and looked at me. 'Can I help you?'

'My name's Ross,' I said. 'I wanted to see Major Braddock.'

'He's out at the moment.' He glanced at his watch. 'Back in about twenty minutes. Is he expecting you?'

'No.'

60

'Well, I don't know whether he'll have time. He's very busy at the moment. Could you tell me what it's about?'

'A private matter,' I said. 'I'd like to talk to him personally.'

'Well, I don't know . . .' His voice doubtful. 'Depends whether this flight's on or not.' He reached for his pad. 'Ross, you said? Aye, I'll tell him.' He made a note of it and that was that. Nothing else I could do for the moment.

'Could you tell me where I'll find Cliff Morgan?' I said. 'He's a meteorologist at Northton.'

'Either at the Met. Office or in the bachelor quarters.' He picked up the phone. 'I'll just check for you whether he's on duty this morning. Get me the Met. Office, will you.' He cupped his hand over the mouth-piece. 'There are two of them there and they work it in shifts. Hello. That you, Cliff? Well now look, laddie, drum up a decent forecast, will you. Ronnie Adams is on his way over to see you and he doesn't like the look of the weather . . . Yes, Himself—and he'll raise hell if the flight's off. Okay. And there's a Mr Ross in my office. Wants to see you . . . Yes, Ross.'

'Donald Ross,' I said.

'Mr Donald Ross . . . Aye, I'll send him over.' He put down the phone. 'Yes, Cliff's on the morning shift. You'll find the Met. Office right opposite you as you go out of the main gate. It's below the Control Tower, facing the

61

landing apron. And I'll tell Major Braddock you're here as soon as he gets back from Leverburgh.'

I wished then that I hadn't given my name. But it couldn't be helped. I zipped up my windbreaker, buttoning it tight across my throat. It was raining harder now and I hurried out through the gate and along the road to the hangar. Pools of rain lay on the parking apron where an Army helicopter stood like some pond insect, dripping moisture. The bulk of Chaipaval was blotted out by a squall. Rain lashed at the glistening surface of the tarmac. I ran for the shelter of the tower, a raw concrete structure, ugly as a gun emplacement. Inside it had the same damp, musty smell. The Met. Office was on the ground floor. I knocked and went in.

It was a bleak dug-out of a room. Two steps led up to a sort of dais and a long, sloped desk that filled all the window space. The vertical backboard had a clock in the centre, wind speed and direction indicators; flanking these were schedules and code tables, routine information. The dust-blown windows, streaked with rain, filtered a cold, grey light. They faced south-west and the view was impressive because of the enormous expanse of sky. On the wall to my right were the instruments for measuring atmospheric pressure—a barograph and two mercury barometers. A Baby Belling cooker stood on a table in the corner and from a small room leading off came the clack of teleprinters.

The place was stuffy, the atmosphere stale with cigarette smoke. Two men were at the desk, their heads bent over a weather report. They looked round as I entered. One of them wore battledress trousers and an old leather flying jacket. He was thin-faced, sad-looking. His helmet and gloves lay on the desk, which was littered with forms and pencils, unwashed cups and old tobacco tin tops full of the stubbed-out butts of cigarettes. The other was a smaller man, short and black-haired, dressed in an open-necked shirt and an old cardigan. He stared at me short-sightedly through thick-lensed glasses. 'Mr Ross?' He had a ruler in his hand, holding it with fingers stained brown with nicotine. 'My publishers wrote me you would be coming.' He smiled. 'It was a good jacket design you did for my book.'

I thanked him, glad that Robinson had taken the trouble to write. It made it easier. The clack of the teleprinter ceased abruptly. 'No hurry,' I said. 'I'll wait till you've finished.'

'Sit down then, man, and make yourself comfortable.' He turned his back on me then, leaning on the tubular frame of his swivel seat to continue his briefing. '. . . Surface wind speed twenty to twenty-five knots. Gusting perhaps forty. Rain squalls. Seven-eighths cloud at five hundred . . .' His voice droned on, touched with the lilt of his native valleys.

I was glad of the chance to study him, to check what I knew of Cliff Morgan against the man himself. If I hadn't read his book I shouldn't have known there was anything unusual about him. At first glance he looked just an ordinary man doing an ordinary routine job. He was a Welshman and he obviously took too little exercise. It showed in his flabby body and in the unhealthy pallor of his face. The shirt he wore was frayed and none too clean, the grey flannels shapeless and without crease, his shoes worn at the heels. And yet, concentrated now on his briefing, there was something about him that made my fingers itch to draw. The man, the setting, the pilot leaning beside him—it all came together, and I knew this would have made a better jacket for his book than the one I'd done.

The background of his book was a strange one. He had written it in prison, pouring into it all his enthusiasm for the unseen world of air currents and temperatures, of cold and warm fronts and the global movements of great masses of the earth's atmosphere. It had been an outlet for his frustration, filled with the excitement he felt for each new weather pattern, the sense of discovery as the first pencilled circle—a fall in pressure of a single millibar perhaps reported by a ship out in the Atlantic—indicated the birth of a new storm centre. His quick, vivid turn of phrase had breathed life into the everyday meteorological reports and the fact that he was an amateur radio operator, a 'ham' in his spare time, had added to the fascination of the book, for his contacts were the weather ships, the wireless operators of distant steamers, other meteorologists, and as a result the scope of his observations was much wider than that of the ordinary airport weather man taking all his information from teleprinted bulletins.

How such a man came to be stationed in a Godforsaken little outpost like Northton needs some explanation. Though I didn't know it at the time, there was already a good deal of gossip about him. He had been up there over six months, which was plenty of time for the facts to seep through, even to that out-of-the-way place. The gossip I don't intend to repeat, but since the facts are common knowledge I will simply say this: there was apparently something in his metabolism that made him sexually an exhibitionist and attractive to women. He had become mixed up in a complex affair involving two Society women. One of them was married and a rather sordid divorce case had followed, as a result of which he had faced a criminal charge, had been found guilty and sentenced to nine months' imprisonment. He had been a meteorologist at London Airport at the time. On his release from prison the Air Ministry had posted him to Northton, where I suppose it was presumed he could do little or no harm. But a man's glands don't stop functioning because he's posted to a cold climate. Nor, thank God, do his wits—a whole ship's company were to owe their lives to the accuracy of his predictions, amounting almost to a sixth sense where weather was concerned.

The pilot was leaving now. 'Okay, Cliff, that settles it. No dice.' He picked up his helmet and his gloves. 'Pity they don't admit it's blowing like hell out there. No down-draughts. Shelter Bay calm as a mill-pond—that's the report I had from Laerg earlier this morning.'

'It's always the same when the boys are waiting for their mail.'

'That's true. But this time I'm under pressure from both ends. The mail could just as well go by LCT, but then this fellow Braddock . . .' A rain squall lashed the windows. 'Just listen to that. He should try his hand at landing a helicopter—that'd teach him to be so bloody enthusiastic. What's he want to do, commit suicide? When it's gusting forty it whams down off Tarsaval . . .' He stared angrily at the blurred panes. 'Thank God they're closing the place down. That idea of relying on a helicopter service through the winter months— who dreamed that one up?'

'Colonel Standing.'

'Well, it was bloody crazy. They'd have discovered the LCTs were more reliable.'

'The landing craft never operated in Scottish waters after the end of September. You know that.'

66

'Well, the trawler then. What was wrong with that?'

'A question of cost; that's what I heard, anyway. And there was still the problem of trans-shipping men and stores from ship to beach. They lost a lot of dories smashed up on the rocks or overturned.'

'Well, if it's a question of cost, dories are a damn sight cheaper than helicopters.' He turned up the collar of his flight jacket, huddling down into it with a jerk of the shoulders. 'Be seeing you, Cliff.' But as he turned towards the door, it was flung open and Major Braddock entered. In place of the light suit he wore battle-dress, but it was the same face—the face of Lane's photographs, lined and leathery, dark-tanned by the Mediterranean sun, and that scar running in a vertical line down the crease of the forehead to the nose.

'What's all this about the flight being off?' Not a glance at me, yet he knew I was there. I could feel it. And that urgent vitality, the way he leaned forward, balanced like a runner on the balls of his feet. 'Mike just told me. Is it definite?'

''Fraid so, sir,' the pilot said. 'You see . . .'

But he had turned to me. 'You the guy that's wanting to see me?' The black eyes, staring straight at me, not a flicker of recognition, only the twitch of a muscle to reveal the nervous tension.

67

'Yes,' I said. 'My name's Donald Ross.'

He smiled. And in that instant I was sure. He couldn't change that smile; he'd relied too much on its charm all his life.

'A private matter,' I said.

He nodded. 'Okay, just let me deal with this ...' He swung round on the pilot then. 'Now look here, Adams, it's all arranged. I'm staying the night there and coming back by LCT tomorrow. Just because it's a bit wet and windy ... damn it, man, what do you expect in the Hebrides?'

'It's the down-draughts,' the pilot said unhappily. 'Being slammed down on the deck—well, you ask Cliff here. It just isn't on, not in this weather.'

And Cliff Morgan agreed, nodding to the wind speed indicator. 'Blowing twenty plus now, almost forty in the gusts. And beginning to veer already. It'll be worse out there.' He shook his head. 'The forecast's bad.'

'The immediate forecast, d'you mean?'

'Well, no. That's bad enough. But I was thinking of the next forty-eight hours. I've an idea the wind's going to veer and go on veering halfway round the clock. We could have a polar air stream with a drop in temperature of perhaps ten degrees and wind speeds as high as fifty, sixty knots.'

'When?'

'How do I know? It's just a feeling I have. It may not happen that way at all.' He indicated the wall to our left, where the big weather maps hung. 'The lower one shows the position when I came on duty at six o'clock; it relates to o-o-o-one hours this morning. The upper one is my forecast of what the pattern will look like twenty-four hours later.' This map was Perspex-framed and the isobars had been drawn in with China-graph pencil on the Perspex. Here the High that had covered the British Isles for days, and which was still shown centred over Eastern Europe in the lower map, had disappeared completely, to be replaced by an intense depression behind it and a weak High over Greenland. 'A south-westerly air stream now, you see—somewhere between twenty and forty knots. But the outlook is entirely dependent upon those two depressions and what happens to that High over Greenland. My feeling is this—those depressions are going to merge, the High is going to build up. The effect would be for that depression to intensify very rapidly. By tomorrow it could be a very deep one centred over Norway and if at the same time the High builds up . . .' He shrugged. 'Wind would be north, you see, gale force at least—perhaps very strong indeed. But there's no certainty about it. Just my interpretation based on nothing more than a feeling I have.'

Braddock stared at the map. 'Well, whether you're right or wrong, the fine spell's over, eh?'

'Looks like it, Major.'

69

'Still, if you're right—northerlies; we'd still be able to use Shelter Bay.'

The phone rang and Cliff Morgan answered it. 'For you,' he said, handing it to Braddock.

I watched him as he took the call. The way the black brows came down and the lines deepened. The years had greatly changed him. His voice, too, harsher and more mature. '. . . Who? I see . . . badly hurt? . . . Okay, Mike, I'll tell Adams.' His eyes met mine for a moment as he put the receiver down. I thought he smiled, but it was so fleeting a movement of the mouth below the dark moustache that I couldn't be sure. He got up, went over to the pilot and stood facing him. 'Well now, that gives you a fine little problem. McGregor, the driver of the Scammell, has got himself badly smashed up. A piece of radar equipment toppled on him after he'd got it stuck on one of the bends of the High Road. His leg's crushed right up to the thigh, abdominal injuries, too.' And he stood over the wretched man, daring him to say that he still wouldn't go, just as he'd stood over me when we were kids. 'Doc says he must be flown out immediately.'

Adams licked his lips. 'What about the LCTs?'

'No good. Four-four-Double-o left Laerg at eleven-thirty last night. She should be in the South Ford by now. And Eight-six-one-o left shortly after two this morning . . .' He shook his head. 'It'd be almost twenty-four hours before

70

we could get him ashore by LCT, and from what I gather he wouldn't last that long. His life's in your hands. Either you fly him out . . .' He gave a little shrug and left it at that. And then he turned to me as though the matter were settled. 'If you're around when I get back tomorrow, we'll have that chat, eh?' He said it with his eyes staring straight at me, still not the slightest flicker and his voice so matter-of-fact I could easily have persuaded myself that he really was Braddock—just Braddock and nothing to do with me.

'I'll be here,' I said.

He nodded and went towards the door, opening it and marching straight out, leaving Adams standing there.

Cliff Morgan glanced again at the wind speed and direction indicators, pencilled a note or two on a piece of paper and passed it to the pilot. Adams took it, but he didn't look at it, nor did he look at the meteorologist. He didn't seem conscious that we were both of us watching him. He was facing the window, his eyes turned inwards, his whole mind given to the decision. I knew the answer, just as Braddock had known it. Adams knew it, too. I watched him bow to the inevitable, turning up the collar of his flight jacket and walking out without a word, the decision to fly made against his better judgment.

It was the moment that things began to go wrong, but none of us could know that, though

71

perhaps Cliff Morgan sensed it, or again perhaps he knew his weather better than the rest of us. 'The poor bastard!' he murmured, and I knew he was referring to the pilot, not to the injured man.

He looked at me as the door shut behind Adams. 'They vary, you know,' he said. 'In temperament.' And he added, 'If it had been Bill Harrison now, he wouldn't have hesitated. A reckless devil, Bill; but he knows his own mind. He'd never have let himself be forced into it like that.' He sucked on the end of his pencil, hollowing his cheeks, and then with a quick, abrupt movement, he went into the back room, tore off the teleprint sheets and came back reading them. 'This bloody evacuation, that's what it is, man. Thinking God Almighty would arrange the weather for them whilst they got their men and equipment off the island. I warned them.'

It was the first I'd heard about the evacuation, and realising this he began to explain as we stood by the window, watching Braddock and Adams walk out to the helicopter and climb in. But I barely took in what he was saying, for my mind had room only for one thought at that moment—the certainty that Braddock was my brother. This in itself was such a staggering revelation that it was only later that I began to consider the other factors—why, for instance, he had applied for a posting to the Hebrides, why he should have been so set on Adams making the flight?

The engine started, the rotor blades began to turn and the helicopter rose from the parking apron, drifting sideways in a gust and just clearing the hangar. Almost immediately its shape became blurred; then it vanished completely, lost in the low cloud and a squall of rain. For a moment longer the engine was faintly audible. Then that, too, was swallowed up as rain lashed at the windows.

The risk they ran in attempting that flight was something I couldn't assess; I had no experience then of the incredible malignant power of the down-draughts that come smashing down from Tarsaval and the other heights of Laerg, down into Shelter Bay. Nor was it possible for me to absorb the whole complex set-up of this military operation into the midst of which I had suddenly been pitchforked. Even when Cliff Morgan had explained to me the details of the evacuation, how Braddock had insisted on sending a detachment with towing vehicles down to the old rocket range on South Uist so that the LCTs could beach in the South Ford as an alternative to Leverburgh, the night-and-day drive to get Laerg cleared and the round-the-clock movement of landing craft, I still didn't appreciate how vulnerable the whole operation was to the weather. I had no experience of landing craft.

Nor for that matter had Cliff Morgan. But

weather to him was a living thing, the atmosphere a battle-ground. He had, as I've said, a sixth sense where weather was concerned and he was very conscious of the changed pattern. 'A polar air stream now,' he said to himself as though facing the implications for the first time. 'Jesus, man!' He lit a cigarette, staring at me over the flame. 'Know anything about weather?'

'A little,' I said, but he didn't seem to hear. 'No imagination—that's the Army for you. Look at Braddock. Up into the air and not a clue what he faces at the other end. And Standing—you'd think Standing would try to understand. He's got brains. But no imagination, you see, none at all.' He slid his bottom on to the swivel seat and drew a sheet of paper towards him. 'Look you now, I'll draw it for you. As I see it—in here.' And he tapped his forehead. 'Not the wind on my face, but a map, a chart, a picture. Imagination! But *dammo di*, they're none of them Celts. Though Braddock—' He shook his head as though he weren't quite certain about Braddock, and then he reached for a blank sheet of paper and with his pen drew a map that included North America, Greenland, Norway—the whole North Atlantic. On this he pencilled in the existing pattern: the Azores High bulging north towards Ireland and the two Lows driving that other High, that had been over England, east towards Russia.

74

'Now, the area I'm watching is down here.' His pencil stabbed the left-hand bottom edge of the map. 'That's about seven hundred miles north-east of Bermuda. It's the place where our depressions are born—the place where the cold, dry air from the north, sweeping down the east of North America, meets up with the warm, damp air of the Gulf Stream. It's the breeding place for every sort of beastliness—hurricanes bound for the States, big depressions that move across the North Atlantic at tremendous speed to give Iceland, and sometimes the Hebrides and the north of Scotland, wind speed almost as bad as the much-publicised Coras and Ethels and Janets and what-have-yous that cause such havoc in America. Now look at this.'

He picked up a red pencil and with one curving sweep drew an arrow across to the area between Iceland and Norway. 'There! That's your Low now.' He drew it in, a deep depression centred over Norway, extending west as far as Iceland, east into Siberia. And then on the other side, over towards Greenland and Canada, more isobars drawn in with long, curving sweeps of hand and pencil. A high pressure area, and between the High and the Low, in ink, he marked in arrows pointing south and south-east. 'That's a polar air stream for you. That's a real big polar air stream, with the wind roaring out of the Arctic and temperatures falling rapidly. Snow at first in the north. Then clear skies and bitter cold.'

He stared at it for a moment, an artist regarding his handiwork. 'I haven't seen that sort of weather pattern up here—not at this time of the year. But I experienced it once in Canada just after the war when I was working for the Department of Transport at Goose Bay. By Christ, man, that was something. A Low over Greenland, a High centred somewhere over the mouth of the Mackenzie River and a polar air stream pouring south across the Labrador.' He drew it for me then on another sheet of paper, adding as his red pencil circled in the pattern, 'Have you any idea what a polar air stream means up there in the Canadian North in October—to the Eskimos, the prospectors, the ships in Hudson Bay?' And when I shook my head he embarked on an explanation. I can't remember all he said; I found myself listening to the tone of his voice rather than to his actual words. It had become noticeably more Welsh, a distinct lilt that seemed to change his personality. It was his enthusiasm for the subject, I suppose, but all at once he was like a poet, painting with words on a canvas that was one quarter of the globe. I listened, fascinated; and as he talked the red pencil was constantly moving, filling in that old atmospheric battle picture until the high pressure system over north-western Canada had become a great whorl of concentric lines.

Like an artist he couldn't resist the picture as

a whole, but as his pencil flew over Greenland and down as far as the Azores, it was this big High he talked about; the effect it had had on people, animals and crops—on transportation, particularly aircraft and ships. The High represented cold, heavy air, clean, crisp, dry-frozen stuff hugging the earth's surface, weighing down on thousands of square miles of ocean, thousands of square miles of pack ice. The winds around this cold mass had been clockwise and wherever they had touched the periphery of the low pressure area to the east, the movement of the cold air stream had been accelerated to hurricane force. At first those gales had been blizzards, thick with driving snow as damp, humid masses of air were forced into the upper atmosphere and cooled to the point of precipitation. 'When that High got really established,' he said, 'there was snow in many places that didn't expect it for another month. Blizzards in the Middle West of Canada reaching south across the border into the States, and that High was like a young giant. It went on drawing strength into itself—like a boxer in training and working himself up for the big fight.'

'You make it sound very dramatic,' I said.

'Weather is dramatic, man; indeed it is, when you've got something like that building up.' He was entirely engrossed in the picture he had drawn from memory. 'It's fluid, you see; always a shifting pattern, never still. It's a battlefield of pressures and temperatures and humidity; Highs versus Lows, with the cold fronts and the warm fronts the points of engagement. A breakthrough at one point can spell disaster a thousand, two thousand miles away—a ship overwhelmed, breakwaters demolished, the flooding of lowlands, the destruction of houses, death to men and livestock.'

He was being carried away again on the tide of his imagination. But then he suddenly stopped. 'It was a long time ago. But I can remember it—by God I can.' He picked up the map he'd drawn, stared at it for a moment, then crumpled it up and threw it into the biscuit tin that acted as a wastepaper basket. 'That's just one of dozens of maps I could draw you—weather I've known ... Some of it I covered in my book. And when this High disintegrates or that Low fills in it's something different again.' He turned with a quick movement of his head to stare at the map framed on the wall, the Chinagraph bright on the Perspex. 'Those two Lows coming in ... Look at them. I'm already getting figures that complicate the whole picture. They may behave normally. They may remain separate entities. But somehow, I don't know why exactly, they worry me. That's something you learn in this game, you see—it's ninety per cent science, a matter of filling in figures, but there's the other ten per cent ... your instinct comes into it then, instinct based on experience.' He gave a little laugh and shook his head. 'Make yourself comfortable,' he said, 'whilst I catch up on my homework.' He glanced at the clock. 'Another fifteen minutes and then we'll go over to the Mess for lunch. I expect you could do with a drink. I certainly could.'

I sat and watched him checking his instruments, going through the teleprinter sheets, flying a balloon to check ceiling height, marking up his meteorological forms, phoning his report through to Pitreavie, and all the time I was thinking of Iain, trying to remember him as I had last seen him, nineteen years old and wearing battledress, the sergeant's stripes white-new on his arm. He'd been drunk that night and within the week he'd sailed with his unit out of the Clyde, bound for North Africa—Operation 'Torch'. 'Can I have a piece of paper?' I said, and when Morgan passed me a scribbling pad, I began pencilling a sketch from memory. The result was the same as when I had tried it in my studio with that bloody little Canadian businessman breathing down my neck. I wondered what Lane was doing now— would he come up here to bust Braddock's identity wide open?

I didn't like the thought of that. The wild streak in Iain had always bordered on violence. That poor devil of a lieutenant, his jaw smashed—and there had been other incidents, before that; big Neil McNeill knocked senseless with an oar after he'd shot a seal. My fault that time. I hadn't wanted the seal killed and when it was done I'd flown at Big Neil, blubbering with anger, and got a kick in the groin that sprawled me screaming in the bottom of the boat. And in Glasgow, at that factory—they'd called him Black Iain—black because of his temper and his dark features and his arrogance. They'd picked him up drunk one night and he'd knocked out three policemen and got away. That was the night he joined the Army.

'That's Braddock.' I looked up to find Morgan standing over me with a puzzled look. 'Yes, Braddock,' I said. I'd have to call him Braddock now. I'd have to think of him as Braddock. I tore the sheet from the pad, crumpled it, and tossed it into the biscuit tin.

'You made him look much younger.'

'I was just passing the time.'

He gave me a sharp, inquiring look, nodded and went back to the desk. It was a warning. I'd have to be careful. And if Lane came north . . .

Cliff Morgan was at the barograph now. He went back to his work at the desk and, watching him again, I was conscious of a tenseness. It showed in the way he paused every now and then to stare out of the window, the quick glances at the wind speed indicator. And then the phone rang. 'All right, Mike—as soon as I'm relieved.' He slammed the receiver down. 'Can I give Colonel Standing a weather briefing? No interest in this office so long as

80

the sun's shining, but now it's wet and blowing half a gale . . .' He shrugged. 'Have you met Colonel Standing?' And when I told him No, he added, 'I'll introduce you then. Alec Robinson said something about your wanting to get to Laerg and for that you need Standing's permission.'

Prompt at twelve Cliff Morgan's junior came dripping in out of the rain, a quiet, reserved man who gave me a fleeting smile as we were introduced. His name was Ted Sykes. 'I hear Ronnie took off. What's his ETA?'

'About twelve-thirty. Wind speed's twenty-five knots—almost a dead-noser.' Cliff Morgan pulled his jacket on and took a tie from the pocket.

'Rather him than me,' Sykes said, at the desk now, rifling through the teleprint sheets. 'Braddock with him?'

'Yes.'

'Well, I hope it keeps fine for them.' He said it sourly. It was obvious neither of them liked it. Cliff Morgan was standing at the desk, tying his tie, staring at the grey misery of the sky. Rain dribbled down the panes.

'There's a casualty to be lifted out.'

'So I heard.'

'Keep your fingers crossed then.' He turned abruptly and got his raincoat, and then we were out in the wind and the rain, hurrying through pools of water to the camp. 'Better not ask for a flight out to Laerg. It means a

81

bloody chit, you see, and they don't like it. Landing craft's all right. I think Standing would agree to that.' His voice came to me, staccato fragments blown on the wind. 'Perhaps tomorrow. But it'll be rough. You a good sailor?' And when I told him I'd had almost eleven years at sea, he nodded. 'That's all right then. At least you'll see Laerg as it really is. Funny thing. I've never been there. Wanted to ever since I came up here. No time, and now it's being evacuated . . .' We had reached the Admin. block. 'You might offer to do some sketches of the evacuation. Standing, you see, is not a man who's very easy with strangers, but he's artistic. Paints a bit himself and I'm told he has some interesting pictures up at his house. Nudes mostly, but not sexy— the real thing.'

Standing was waiting for us in his office, tall and slightly stooped with a thin, serious face and glasses, a tight, unsmiling mouth. He looked a cold, moody man and his long-fingered hands were seldom still, nervously shifting the papers on his desk, toying with the slide-rule or gently tapping. Cliff Morgan introduced me as an artist who wanted to visit Laerg, but all I got was a nod and a cold stare. He had Ferguson with him and he was only interested in one thing, the weather. He listened to what Morgan had to say, his eyes on the window which was tight-shut against the wind. The view was depressing—the brown creosoted back of a hut, a grey waste of sky and the rain driving.

'Can Adams get the man out? That's all I want to know.' Even then he didn't look at Cliff Morgan, but sat staring at the window, drumming with his fingers.

'Only Ronnie could tell you that,' Cliff answered, and I sensed his antagonism.

'Adams isn't here. I'm asking you, Mr Morgan.'

'I'm a meteorologist. I feed the pilot information. He makes his own decisions.'

'I know that, I'm asking your opinion.'

Cliff shrugged. 'It's dicey—but then that's to be expected when you're flying to a place like Laerg.' The native lilt was stronger now.

'The decision was made in your office, I believe. Did Major Braddock order Adams to fly?'

'How could he? It's the pilot's decision—always. You know that.'

'Very well. I will put it another way. Would Captain Adams have flown if there hadn't been an injured man to bring out?'

'No.'

Colonel Standing sighed and reached for his slide-rule, running it back and forth in his hands. 'Two men's lives and an expensive machine . . .' He was staring at the slide-rule as though calculating the risk in terms of a mathematical equation. 'Captain Fairweather has all he needs, hasn't he?' This with a quick

83

glance at his Adjutant. 'I mean the hospital is still functioning, isn't it?'

'Aye, but it's little better than a first-aid post now, sir. And Fairweather's not a surgeon.'

'He's still a member of the medical profession. If he has to operate, then he's got the means and we can link him up with Scottish Command and give him a surgeon's guidance.' He dropped the slide-rule. 'Have them contact Adams. He's to cancel the flight and return immediately. Now what's the landing craft position? Stratton is the more experienced of the two. Where's Eight-six-one-o?'

'She passed through the Sound of Harris about nine-thirty this morning. If the tide's right, she should be beaching any moment now.'

'In the South Ford.'

'Aye. They're double-banked, you see. If you remember, sir, it was to cope with just this eventuality that Major Braddock arranged for a stand-by detachment based on the old range. Four-four-Double-o cleared from Laerg on the same tide, about three hours after Stratton. She'd have been in Leverburgh by now if it hadn't been for a wee bit of trouble with one of the oil pumps. It slowed her down for a while.'

'How far out is she—an hour, two hours?'

'Two I should think. I'll check if you like.'

'No, there's no time.' Standing's fingers were drumming gently on the desk again. 'It makes no difference anyway. She's the nearest. A pity it's Kelvedon and not Stratton. But it can't be helped. Have Signals contact him: Four-four-Double-o turn round and make back to Laerg at full speed to pick up a casualty.'

'It'll be eight, maybe nine hours before she gets there. A falling tide then and it'll be dark.'

'They should be able to run their bows in, pick the man up and winch off again. There won't be much of a sea running in the Bay. He'll just have to do the best he can. See if you can speak to Kelvedon yourself, explain the urgency.'

Ferguson hesitated. 'You wouldn't have a word with Bob Fairweather first? Maybe the man's condition . . .'

'No, Ferguson. Captain Fairweather's concern is with the injured man. I have to consider what the position will be if Major Braddock and Captain Adams are injured, perhaps killed, and their machine written off. All right?'

'Yes, sir.'

'Contact Adams first. Then have a word with Kelvedon and get Four-four-Double-o turned round as soon as you can.'

'She'll still be loaded.'

'Of course she will. That can't be helped. Now get moving. Every minute counts.' He watched his Adjutant leave. Then when the door was shut he turned to me. 'You've come at an awkward time.' His voice shook slightly, so did his hands; his nerves were strung taut by the

85

decision he'd had to make.

'I didn't realise you were evacuating the island,' I said.

He was staring down at the desk. Behind him on the wall hung a six-inch-to-the-mile map of Laerg and beside it were graphs, presumably of the past season's shooting; part of the skin of a rocket, a jagged, crumpled piece of light alloy, lay on the floor beside his chair. 'There's always somebody wanting to go to Laerg—naturalists, bird-watchers, archaeologists. They're a darned nuisance.'

'My father was born in Laerg.'

I made no impression. He wasn't interested in the island as such. Later I learned that in the year he'd been in the Hebrides, he'd only visited Laerg once—a quick trip by helicopter on a fine day. 'You're an artist, you say. Professional?'

'Yes.'

He nodded to the wall behind me. 'What do you think of that?'

It was a landscape, the mountains of Harris by the look of it, in sunlight with a glimpse of the sea. The brush-work was technically quite good, but it lacked feeling. I didn't know what to say for I knew he'd done it himself, and presumably he liked it since he'd hung it in his office.

'Well?'

I hesitated; but better to be honest. I told him it was nice but that I didn't think the artist was at home with his subject. To my surprise he nodded agreement. 'I hung it there just to remind me that the sun does shine up here sometimes. It was hot when I painted that. But you're right—I'm not at home with landscapes. If you're here for a time I'll show you some others. My wife models for me.' The phone rang on his desk. 'Standing here . . . Thinks he can make it?' He glanced at the window as the rain beat against it in a gust of wind. 'Tell Adams it's an order . . . Yes. Ferguson, an order, do you hear?' He was trembling again as he put the phone down. For a moment he just sat there, drumming with his fingers at the desk. Then, as though suddenly conscious of my presence again, he said, 'All right, Ross, we'll see what we can do. Are you any good at seascapes, ships, that sort of thing?'

'Sea and mountains and rock,' I said; 'that's what I like to paint.'

'Good. A sketch or two of the evacuation— a painting perhaps; the DRA would like that, particularly if there are some birds in it.' I pointed out that the birds wouldn't be back for another three months. 'Well, there's such a thing as artists' licence. The General likes birds.' He hesitated. Finally he nodded. 'All right. Have a word with Ferguson. He'll fix it with the Movements Officer and arrange with one of the landing craft skippers to take you out. You'll have about two days there, maybe three.'

'It'll be something just to see the island,' I said.

'So long as you don't get in Captain Pinney's way. They're under considerable pressure. Where are you staying?' And when I told him I was camping at Rodil, he said, 'We can do better than that. I'll tell Ferguson to allocate you a room from the night. We've always plenty of space in the winter months.'

I thanked him and followed Cliff Morgan out of the stuffy little office into the cold, driving rain. I was feeling in a daze. First Iain, and now Laerg . . . Laerg within reach at last. 'I didn't think it would be as easy as that,' I murmured.

'Well, they're not worried about security, you see. The place is a write-off and that makes it easier than when they were lobbing missiles into the water beside it. But you wouldn't have got there if you hadn't been an artist.' And he added, 'You never know where you are with Standing. And now that Braddock's here . . .'

He left it at that. 'What about Braddock?' I asked.

'Oh, he's all right, whatever anybody else may say. By God he's woken this place up since he arrived. Yes indeed, and he'll have a drink with you, which is more than Standing will.'

The bar was deserted when we reached the Mess. But as we stood there drinking our gin-and-tonic, the officers drifted in one by one. Major Rafferty, the Quartermaster, a big beefy

88

man with a florid face and a Scots accent; the Movements Officer, Fred Flint—short and round with a button nose and the face of a pug, all bulging eyes and a way of dropping his aitches and watching with a glint of humour to see if it startled you; the Doc, also a captain, but younger, with the air of a man nothing can surprise any more; several lieutenants, much younger still; and finally Field—Lieutenant Field who was old enough to be their father. He had a strange hatchet face, grey hair and a mouth that drooped at the corners. His eyes were deep-socketed, tired—blue eyes that had a nervous blink and didn't look straight at you, but beyond, as though searching for some lost horizon. '. . . our Education Officer,' the ebullient Captain Flint added as he introduced us. 'Now what y'aving, Professor?'

'Oh, that's very thoughtful of you, Flinty. Let me see now. The usual, I think—a gin-and-tonic without the gin.' He smiled and the smile lit up his whole face so that it suddenly had a quality of great warmth. It was a striking face; moreover, it was a face that seemed vaguely familiar. But not in battledress; in some other rig. 'I take it the LCTs are all at sea since Movements can take time off for a lunchtime drink.'

'All at sea is just about right, Professor. Stratton's missed his tide and dropped his hook under the lee outside Loch Carnan. It'll be five hours at least before he can get her into the beaching position in the Ford, another three before the boys can start off-loading. Major B will like that—I don't think.'

'Braddock won't know anything about it. He's flown to Laerg.'

'Oh yes he will. I just met the Colonel. He's cancelled the flight. And he's turned Four-four-Double-o round fully loaded and sent her steaming back to Laerg to pick up a casualty. Proper box-up if you ask me.'

'Well, why not switch Stratton's ship to Leverburgh?' Major Rafferty suggested. 'Damn it, man, with Kelvedon turned back, the quay will be empty.'

'Tim, my boy, you're a genius. I never thought of that.' The quick grin faded. 'I did mention it, but Stratton told me to go to hell. His men needed sleep, and so does he. If Major B wants Eight-six-one-o at Leverburgh, then he'll have to give the order himself. I bet he gets the same answer, too. Those boys are just about out on their feet, and Stratton's his own master. He's not at the beck and call of anybody here—the Colonel or anybody else. I only hope,' he added, 'that Kelvedon gets there in time.' He looked down at his glass and then at Field. 'Did you know this bloke McGregor?' And when the other nodded, he said, 'Poor beggar. First blood to the new drive.' His voice sounded angry. 'And if you ask me it won't be the last. When they're tired they get careless. I told Command it needed more time when they were planning this flipping operation. But they wouldn't listen. I'm only the bloke that loads the ships. I wouldn't know.' Ferguson came in then, the freckles on his face showing up like spots in the electric light, a strained look about the eyes. 'You look shagged, my boy. I prescribe a night out with the fattest trollop you can find between the Butt of Lewis and Barra Head.'

'Aye, that'd do me fine.'

'What's the matter? Caught between the upper and the nether millstone again?'

'If by that you mean what I think you mean, then the answer is Yes and it'll cost you a Scotch for stating the obvious. The Colonel ordered Major B to turn back.'

'We know that. And he's bust the schedule wide open by converting Four-four-Double-o into a hospital ship.'

'This is going to put everyone in a good temper for the rest of the day.' Major Rafferty downed his drink and set his tankard on the bar top. 'That poor laddie, Doc—how is he?'

'He's still alive.' The MO ordered another Scotch.

'What are his chances?'

The dark eyebrows lifted. 'Now? Nil, I should say. If they'd got him out by air . . .' He shrugged. 'But I told the Colonel that. So did Bob Fairweather. McGregor had the whole of that crushing weight on top of him for almost an hour before they were able to release him.'

There was a hushed silence. 'Oh, well,' Flint said, 'let's have some lunch.' He stubbed out his cigarette and hitched up his trousers. 'And after lunch,' he added, 'I'm going to have a ziz. Four o'clock this morning, two the night before and stone the bloody crows it looks like four again tomorrow morning.' He glanced at me, his eyes popping with that irrepressible glint of Cockney humour. 'Four o'clock suit you—Captain Stratton driving and an iron bathtub slamming into a head sea fit to knock your block off?'

'For Laerg?' I asked.

'That's right—where the Jumblies live. The Colonel mentioned it to me just now. I'll fix it with Stratton; he'll give you the ride of your life ... that is if our weather genius 'ere doesn't frighten him so as he loses his nerve.'

'Water Transport take the shipping forecasts,' Cliff said. 'They don't trust me.'

'It isn't that, Cliff. It's just that Stratton believes in continuity—likes his forecasts all the time from the same source. But shipping forecasts—hell! What I've seen of the shipping forecasts up here, they only tell you what you've got sitting on top of you, never what you're going to get—which for my money is the only thing worth a damn.' He turned to me. 'What's your view? I gather you've put in a good deal of sea time?'

It was said of politeness to include me in the conversation, and as I stood there, sipping my drink and listening to their talk, I was conscious that this was a tight-knit, closed little world, a community not unlike a ship's company. They accepted me, as they accepted Cliff Morgan— not as one of themselves, but as an interesting specimen of the outside world, to be tolerated and treated kindly. I was even more conscious of this at lunch, which was a good meal pleasantly served by a bright little Hebridean waitress. The atmosphere was a strange mixture of democracy and paternal difference; and the youngsters calling me 'sir' to remind me how the years had flown. 'What do you think of modern art, sir?' Picasso, Moore, Annigoni—a reproduction of Annigoni's picture of the Queen hung on the Mess wall; they knew the most publicised names and seemed eager for artistic information, so that for the moment they gave me the illusion of being a visiting genius, and I hoped to God I didn't sound pompous as I tried to answer their queries.

And then Braddock came in and the table fell suddenly silent. He sat down without a word to anyone, and I could see by the way his head was tucked down into his shoulders that he was in a blazing temper.

'Too bad you didn't make it,' Major Rafferty murmured.

The black brows came down in a frown. 'Too bad, you say?' His tone was clipped and angry. 'If Adams had had any sense he'd have unplugged his radio. We'd have made it all right.'

'Have you seen the Colonel?'

'He'd gone up to his house by the time we landed. Anyway, no point. He'd made his decision.' He started in on his soup. But after a moment he glanced at the Movements Officer. 'Flint. What's the ETA for that landing craft?'

'At Laerg? Eight-thirty-nine o'clock. Maybe later. She's bucking a head sea. And that's presuming they don't have any more trouble with that oil pump.'

'Which means embarking a stretcher case from a dory in the dark.'

'Unless Kelvedon beaches her. The wind's westerly. Shelter Bay shouldn't be too—'

'He's not to beach her—do you understand? Stratton might do it. He's an old hand up here, but Kelvedon's new and if he gets his craft . . .' He gave a quick shrug. 'I'll have a word with him.' His eyes, shifting along the table, met mine for a moment. There was a hardness, an urgency about him. Maybe it was telepathy—I had always been able to sense his mood; I had the feeling that there was something he desperately wanted, something quite unconnected with the injured man. I was remembering the scene in the Met. Office, his determination to make that flight. And then from the files of my memory a sentence sprang: *It's the breath of life to you, isn't it, Donald? But I tell ye, man, it's death to me. That I know—*

deep down. Death, do ye hear, and I'll not be going there for you or anybody else. So long ago now, but I could hear his voice still. He'd been talking of Laerg—just after that trawler had brought me back. Had he forgotten? For some reason I'd never been able to fathom, he'd been afraid of the place, as though it bore him some personal animosity; and yet at the same time he'd been fascinated—a fascination that was born of his instinctive, almost primitive fear of it. And now he was desperate to get there, had had himself posted up here to the Hebrides for that purpose; why?

The table had fallen silent, an awkward stillness. One by one the officers rose, put their napkins in the pigeon-holes on the side-table and went out into the lounge for coffee. I rose with Cliff Morgan, conscious that Braddock was watching me. 'Mr Ross.' Strange that he could call me that. His dark eyes held no glimmer of a smile, his voice no trace of the old Highland accent. 'We'll have our talk—later.'

I nodded and went out. Surely to God I couldn't be mistaken. Field handed me my coffee. 'Sugar?' I shook my head. The radio was playing softly—some jazzed-up singer mouthing of love. 'You met my daughter, Marjorie, I think.' I nodded, my mind still on Braddock. 'I thought perhaps you'd care to drop in this evening. We're not far, just beyond the church at Rodil; one of the old black houses. As a painter it might interest you.

About nine o'clock. Would that suit you?'

It was kind of him, almost as though he'd known what it was like to lie alone in a small tent on the shores of a loch with a gale tearing at the nylon canopy. I felt I was very near to remembering that face then, but still the connection evaded me. In a newspaper, or a magazine, perhaps. I thanked him and added, 'But I believe I'm staying the night in the quarters here.'

He turned to Ferguson. 'Will you be along tonight, Mike? Marjorie's expecting you.'

'Yes, of course—my lords and masters permitting.'

'Then bring Mr Ross with you.'

It wasn't the sort of face you could forget, just like an axehead, keen and sharp in the features and broadening out to the head. I was still thinking about this when Cliff Morgan said he was going over to his quarters and suggested I might like to see his radio equipment.

Outside, the rain had stopped and the overcast had lifted. 'That's the warm front—it's passed over us, you see.' The wind was still as strong, west now and colder. 'Whatever Braddock says, Colonel Standing was right to recall Adams. This is no weather for a helicopter landing on Laerg.' The quarters were only a step from the Mess. He led me down a long passage and stopped at Room Number 23. As he unlocked the door, he said, 'I don't sleep here, except when I'm calling

96

Canada or some place that means staying up half the night. I've billeted myself out with a widow and her daughter in one of the crofts in Northton. Very irregular, but I like my comfort, you see.' He smiled and pushed open the door. There was a bed thrust close against one wall, a bureau and wardrobe huddled in a corner; all the rest of the room was taken up with his equipment. 'Since I published that book I've been able to buy all the things I couldn't afford before. It's been produced in the States and translated into German, Italian and Swedish. Now I have everything I need; very complete it is now.' He switched on, seated himself at the keyboard with his earphones. 'It's the weather I'm interested in. But you know that, of course. Now I want to find one or two ships who can tell me what it's like out to the west and north of here.' His hands, delicate as a pianist's, were fingering the dials, deftly tuning. The tall cabinet full of valves began to hum gently. And then his right hand thumbed the key and the soft buzz of his call sign sounded in the room. He was lost to me now, silent in a world of his own.

I sat on the bed, smoking a cigarette and watching him. Time passed. I found some paper in the bureau and began to sketch him. Periodically he spoke, but to himself rather than to me: 'The *Kincaid*. An old freighter that, six thousand tons. She's outward bound for the Saguenay to pick up a cargo of aluminium.

97

Reports wind north-easterly, force four ... *Bismuth*—that's one of the Hastings on air reconnaissance five hundred miles west of Ireland; reporting to Bracknell.' He picked up two more ships out in the Atlantic, and then he was talking to a trawler south-east of Iceland. '*Arctic Ranger*. Wind veering northerly and a swell coming down past the east coast of Iceland. Getting quite cold up there. Temperature down to thirty-eight and flurries of snow. Wind increasing, around thirty-five knots.' He took off his earphones. 'I think I'll go up to the office now and see what Ted has on the teleprints.' He switched off.

'Worried?' I asked. I had finished my sketch and was lounging back on the bed.

'No, not worried. Uneasy, though. And if it develops as I think it might ...' He pushed his chair back and stood there a moment, running his hand through his thick dark hair, biting on the pencil clenched between his teeth. 'It would be unusual—so early in the season. In January now ...' He gave that quick little shrug of his that always seemed accompanied by a sideways movement of the head, and then he was pacing up and down; half a dozen steps and then about and retrace them, back and forth with his eyes on the ground, not seeing anything but what was in his mind. He could have got the habit from his time in prison, but I thought it more likely to be the loneliness of his job. He was a solitary. Why otherwise become a meteorologist and then take to operating a 'ham' radio station as a hobby? There are countless men like Cliff Morgan—intelligent, sensitive, artists in their way. They get on all right with women, but escape from the competitive male world by burying themselves body and soul in work that is concerned with things rather than people—impersonal things. With Cliff it was the impersonal forces of the earth's atmosphere, his human contacts mostly made at one remove through the tenuous medium of the ether. I wondered what he'd do if he met opposition—direct opposition, man to man, on his own ground. I thought perhaps he could be very tricky then, perhaps behave with quite astonishing violence.

He had stopped his pacing and was standing over me, staring down at the sketch I'd drawn. 'You work pretty fast.'

'It's just a rough,' I said. 'Pencil sketch of a man who's made his work his life.'

He laughed. 'Oh, I can relax. Indeed I can—if she's pretty enough. But then there's not much difference, is there now; women and weather, they both have their moods, they can both destroy a man. That's why storms are given girls' names. Do you need that sketch? I mean, if you were just drawing to pass the time . . .'

I saw he really wanted it. 'It's your paper anyway,' I said and I handed it to him. He stood for a moment looking down at it. Then he placed it carefully on the keyboard. 'This trip to Laerg,' he said. 'Do you have to go—I mean now, tomorrow morning?'

'Of course I'm going,' I told him. 'It's what I've wanted ever since I returned to England.'

He nodded. 'Well, let's go over to the Met. Office and see what makes. But I'm telling you, man, you could have it very rough indeed.'

'No good telling me,' I said. 'Better tell the skipper of the landing craft.'

He didn't say anything, and when I glanced at him, his face was clouded, his mind concentrated on a world beyond the one in which we walked. Two big towing trucks went grinding past trundling red-painted trailers piled with stores. I don't think he even saw them, and in the Met. Office he went straight to the teleprint file and without a word to Sykes settled down at the desk to mark up a weather map.

Now that I knew something of the set-up, the Met. Office seemed somehow different—familiar ground like the bridge of a ship. The rain had stopped and it was lighter, the visibility much greater. To the left I could see the single hangar standing in the drifted sand like a stranded hulk. It was the only building in sight. Ahead, the wide windows looked out across the tarmac to a sea of dune grass rippling in the wind, humped and hollowed, as full of movement as the sea itself. And beyond the grass-grown dunes was the white blur of broken water, wind-blown waves moving in long regular lines towards the Sound of Harris.

Standing there, with the instruments of meteorology all around me, it wasn't difficult to slip into the mood of men like Cliff Morgan, to visualise the world they lived in, that great amorphous abstract world of atmosphere. I found myself thinking of Laerg, out there beyond the sea's dim horizon. I had seen photographs of it—etchings, too, by the Swedish artist, Roland Svensson. It was the etchings I was thinking of now, for I was sure Svensson had caught the mood of the wild wet world better than any photograph. Unconsciously I found my legs straddled as though to balance myself against the movement of a ship. A few hours and I should be on my way, steaming towards those sheer rock islands that for over thirty years had existed in my mind as the physical embodiment of an old man I had greatly loved.

Oddly, I felt no elation at the prospect; only a sense of awe. In my mind's eye I saw the cliffs rising sheer—black and dripping moisture. But because of my surroundings, the weather instruments and the two men working at the desk, I had also a picture of that other world comprising the moving masses of the Earth's outer skin. It was no more than the vague impression that a shipping forecast handed to the officer of the watch conjures in his mind, but it produced the same feeling of being at

101

one with the elements, so that I found myself recapturing that sense of responsibility, of being a protagonist. The phone ringing cut across my thoughts. Sykes answered it. 'Yes, he's here.' He glanced at me. 'Okay, I'll tell him.' He put the phone down. 'Major Braddock. He'll drive you down to Rodil to pick up your things.'

'Now?'

'He'll be waiting for you outside the Admin. block.'

I had known this moment would come, but I'd have been glad to postpone it. What did you say to a man who'd spent twenty years masquerading as somebody else, and that man your brother? 'All right,' I said, and went out into the wind, wishing at that moment I'd never come north to the Hebrides. Even Laerg couldn't compensate for this.

He was sitting at the wheel of a Land-Rover, waiting for me. 'Jump in.' He didn't say anything more and we drove out through the main gate and down the sand-blown road to Northton. Neither of us spoke and yet oddly enough there was nothing awkward about the silence. It helped to bridge the years, both of us accepting the situation and adjusting ourselves to it. Side-face his true identity was more obvious—a question chiefly of the shape of the head and the way it sat on the shoulders. The profile, too; he couldn't change that. And the hair and the short, straight forehead, the shape

102

of his hands gripping the wheel. 'Why didn't you contact me?' I said.

'You were away at sea.' He hunched his shoulders, an old, remembered gesture. 'Anyway, what was the point? When you take another man's identity—well, you'd better damn well stick to it.'

'Did you have to do that?'

'Do what?'

'Take Braddock's name?'

'I didn't have to, no. But I did.' A muscle was moving at the corner of his mouth and his voice was taut as he added, 'What would you have done? Given yourself up, I suppose. Well, I wasn't going to stand trial for busting the jaw of a man who hadn't the guts to lead his own men.'

'What happened?' I asked. 'What exactly happened out there in North Africa?'

'You really want to know?' He hesitated, frowning. 'Well . . . It was after we'd landed. The French had us pinned down. They'd got a machine-gun nest in one of those walled villas. We were all right. We were in a dried-up wadi. But it was murder for the lads on our right. They were caught in the open, a whole company of them lying out there on the bare rocks, and we had the shelter of that gully right up to the villa's walls. Instead of attacking, Moore ordered the platoon to stay put and keep their heads down. He was frightened to death. In the end I knocked him out and took

103

command myself. It was the only way. But by then the French had got a gun in position to cover the wadi and they opened up on us when we were halfway up it. That's when I got this.' He pointed to the scar on his forehead. 'I lost eighteen men, but we took the villa. And when it was all over, I was under arrest. If I hadn't hit the little sod I'd have been all right, but that fixed me, so I got the hell out of it and back to the beach. Wasn't difficult; everything a bit chaotic. The fact that I was wounded made it dead easy. I was taken off to a troopship that was just leaving. She'd been damaged and when we were clear of the Straits she was ordered to proceed to Montreal for repairs. That was how I landed up in Canada.' He glanced at me. 'They didn't tell you that?'

'Some of it—not all.'

'I had just over a year in Canada before they picked me up. It was conscription that fixed me. I hadn't any papers, you see. And then, when the *Duart Castle* went down . . .' He gave a quick shrug. 'Well, I took a chance and it worked out.'

But looking at the deep-etched lines of his face, I wondered. He looked as though he'd been living on his nerves for a long time. There were lines running underneath the cheek-bones and down from the sides of the mouth, others puckering the scar on the forehead, radiating from the corners of the eyes; some of them so deep they might have been scored by a knife. Those lines and the harsh, almost leathery skin could simply be the marks of a hard life, but I had an uneasy feeling they were something more than that.

Through Northton he began to talk—about the Army and the life he'd led and where he'd been. It seemed to help, for he began to relax then and become more at ease; in no time at all the years had fallen away and we were on our old, easy footing, with him talking and myself listening. It had always been like that. And then suddenly he said, 'You married Mavis, did you?'

'For my sins,' I said. 'It didn't work out.'

'And the child?'

'It died.'

I thought he didn't care, for he made no comment, driving in silence, again. But as we came down the hill into Leverburgh, he said, 'What was it—a boy?'

'Yes.' And I added, 'I had him christened Alasdair.'

He nodded as though he'd expected that. We were passing ugly blocks of Swedish pre-fabs and as we turned right past the loch, he murmured, 'I'm sorry.' But whether he was sorry for what he'd done to us or because the child had died I couldn't be sure. We were on a track now that led out to the quay. 'I just want to check that they're moving the stuff fast enough,' he said. 'Then I'll drive you on to Rodil to collect your gear.'

105

The quay looked a mess, the whole length of it littered with material brought from Laerg— piled-up sections of wooden huts, double-ended dories, trailers still loaded with stoves, radios, refrigerators, a deep-freeze, clothing, and crates full of foodstuffs, sacks of potatoes, fruit, coal; all the paraphernalia of an isolated unit being withdrawn in a hurry, and all of it soaked by the rain. One Scammell was trying to inch a trailer through the debris. Two three-ton trucks were being loaded, the men moving slowly, lethargically as though they had been doing this a long time. A single mobile crane swung its gantry lazily against the leaden dullness of the sky, and beyond the quay skerries barred the way into the Sound of Harris with here and there a light mounted on iron legs to mark the channel through the rocks.

It was a depressing sight. I wandered along the concrete edge of the quay whilst Braddock spoke to the officer in charge. 'A fine mess you'd be in,' I heard him say, 'if Four-four-Double-o had come in on schedule instead of being sent back to Laerg fully loaded.' His voice, harsh now, had a whip-lash quality.

'We're shifting it as fast as we can,' the youngster answered. 'But the men are tired. They've been at it since early this morning, and we're short of vehicles.'

'They're tired, are they? Then just think how Captain Pinney's men must be, working round the clock, crammed into only two huts, soaked to the skin. Now get moving, boy, and have this quay cleared to receive Kelvedon's ship when it comes in.'

'When will that be?'

'Dawn I should think, or a little after.' I saw him grip the young man's shoulder. 'Between now and the end of the operation this may be our one chance to catch up. See the men understand that. If Stratton's crew hadn't been dead beat you'd have had Eight-six-one-o here by now. Make the most of this opportunity, Phipps.'

'I'll do the best I can, sir.'

'Better than the best; I want miracles.' The hard face cracked in a smile. 'Okay?' He patted the lieutenant's shoulder, instilling into him some of his own urgent drive. Then he turned. 'Sergeant!' He had a word with the sergeant and then came back to the Land-Rover. 'Peacetime soldiering,' he muttered as he climbed into the driving seat. 'They don't know what it is to be beaten to their knees and still fight back. They haven't known a war. I was in Burma.' He started the engine and yanked the wheel round. 'That was after the Normandy landings. Half these guys would get shot to bits before they'd dug a slit trench. Just because they're technicians a lot of them, they think the Army's a branch of industry—a cosy factory with set hours and plenty of recreation.'

We drove out of Leverburgh and up the glen

107

with him talking about the evacuation and how he'd had his leave cut short to come up here and see the operation through. 'If I'd known what I know now I'd never have accepted the posting. It's drive, drive, drive, and they hate my guts most of them. But what can you do with the weather on top of you and time so short? And now we're at the critical stage. The run-down of accommodation and stores on Laerg has reached the point where the operation has got to be completed. Pinney's detachment haven't enough food and fuel left on the island to last a fortnight, let alone see the winter through. And the weather chooses this moment to break. Goddammit, the War Office should have had more sense.' He glanced at me quickly. 'What did you think of Standing?'

I hesitated, not knowing what he expected. 'I've only seen him for a few minutes.'

'Long enough to fix yourself a trip to Laerg.' There was a bite to his voice, a resentment almost, as though he disliked the thought of my going to the island. 'You were there when he cancelled that flight. How did he seem?'

'A little nervous,' I said. 'But in the circumstances . . .'

'Nervous! He's scared. Scared he'll make a wrong decision. In fact, he's scared of making any decision. Scared, too, of leaving it all to me. He's a bloody old woman with a mind like an adding machine. And his wife's one of the most

108

beautiful women I've ever met.'

'Are you married?' I asked.

'Yes, but it didn't work out any better than yours. Lasted longer, that's all. And I'll never get shot of her. She's a Roman Catholic.' We passed the church and a moment later drew up by the hotel. He came down to the loch-side with me and helped strike the tent and carry my stuff to the Land-Rover. It only took ten minutes or so and then we were driving back. It was as we topped the rise and sighted Northton that he said, 'D'you know a man called Lane—a Canadian?' He tried to make it casual, but the tightness in his voice betrayed him.

'I've met him,' I said. 'Once.'

'And that's why you're here.'

'Partly—yes.'

He braked so suddenly that the engine stalled and I was flung forward in my seat. 'Why do you want to go to Laerg?' The tension in his voice flared to a higher pitch. 'What's behind it? What are you expecting to find there?'

'Peace. Subjects to paint.' And I added, 'I've always wanted to go to Laerg.'

'But why now? You've managed very well for over twenty years . . . Now, suddenly, you have to go there. Why? What did Lane tell you?'

'It's nothing to do with Lane.'

'Then what the hell is it?' He had gripped hold of my arm and was almost shaking it. 'As soon as I was away on that flight you went

109

running to Standing and somehow persuaded him to ship you out on an LCT. What did you tell him?'

'Nothing about you,' I said. 'Just that my father came from Laerg and that I wanted to paint there.'

'That all?' He was staring at me, the pupils of his eyes almost black and strangely dilated. And then he let go my arm. 'You could have waited.' His voice sounded suddenly tired. 'I'd have got you to Laerg in time—if you'd asked me.'

Was he hurt that I hadn't? 'I was going to ask you,' I said. 'But you went off on that flight, and then, when I saw Colonel Standing . . .'

'Standing's not running this operation. I am. And I'm not having you or anyone else going out there and making a nuisance of themselves.' He shifted in his seat, watching me, his mouth twitching and a gleam of perspiration on his forehead. 'After all these years. Bit of a shock, isn't it?' He was smiling now, trying to recapture the old charm. But somehow the smile wasn't right. 'Be frank with me. You always were—in the old days. We never hid anything from each other.'

'I'm not hiding anything from you now.'

But he didn't seem to hear. 'What did Lane tell you? Come on now. He told you something that sent you scurrying up here with a sudden, urgent desire to get to Laerg.'

'He guessed who you were. Suspected it,

anyway. He's been interviewing survivors . . .'

'I'm talking about Laerg. What did he say about Laerg?'

'Nothing,' I said. 'He's discovered you were on that raft and he's put two and two together . . .'

'Then why are you so anxious to get out to Laerg?'

There it was again. Laerg—Laerg! Why did he keep harping on Laerg? 'He never mentioned Laerg.'

'No?'

'Just listen to me, Iain,' I said. 'I came up here with one object in mind—to find out whether you were still alive or not. Having done that, I thought it was a good opportunity to see the island. I've been wanting to go to Laerg for two years now, ever since I came back from the Aegean. I want to paint there. Just to paint, that's all. Nothing else.'

But I don't think he believed me even then. His face had a stony look as though he'd shut his mind to all reason, and I had a sudden feeling there was tragedy here, a deep, wasting wound that fed on his nerves. It was a moment of intuition, I think—blood calling to blood and the sense of his desperation very strong.

'Well, you're not going.' He said it flatly, more to himself than to me. And then, as though suddenly aware of what he'd said and the need for some explanation: 'This is a military operation. The landing craft are fully

111

committed. It's no moment for shipping tourists out to the island.'

'I'm not a tourist,' I said, resenting the implication. 'Not where Laerg is concerned.'

'You are from the Army's point of view. I'll have a word with Standing.' And he got the engine going again and we drove down into the camp, neither of us saying a word. He dropped me off at the officers' quarters. 'Room forty-two,' he said as I got my gear out of the back of the Land-Rover. 'Maybe I'll have time for a drink with you before dinner.' He was Major Braddock again and we were strangers. I watched him drive off, wishing now that I'd made more of an effort to discover what it was that was eating into his soul, for this wasn't the brother I'd known. This was quite a different man—a man driven and desperate. I had that feeling, and it scared me. Later, I said to myself. Later I'll find out.

I didn't know that there wasn't going to be a later, that time was running out and I'd missed the only chance I'd get of being alone with him before it was too late.

Room 42 was the same as Cliff Morgan's, a standard pattern and standard furniture—bed, bedside table, bureau, chair, wardrobe, all in natural oak, an armchair, wash basin and the rusted steel windows looking out on to a drab patch of coarse dune grass. I dumped my things and went for a walk, heading north from the main gate, away from the camp and the landing apron. Ten minutes and I was amongst the dunes, alone in a world that hadn't changed since the first man set foot in the Outer Hebrides. To my left Chaipaval reared heather and grass-clad slopes to the clouds. To my right the mountains of Harris stood black and sombre, their stormbound peaks shrouded in rain. I came to the last sanded bluff and ahead of me was a great stretch of sands, glistening wet, and a line of dunes standing like a breakwater between them and the sea. The island of Taransay rose misty-green beyond the dunes. There were sheep sheltering in the hollows they had worn along the edge of the bluff and below a river of water flowed towards the sea, fish marking the smooth surface with little whorls.

It was a wild wet world and I walked there until it was almost dusk, thinking of Laerg and my brother Iain, the wind on my face bringing back to me the salt taste of Ardnamurchan and my youth. The picture in my mind was of a bare, wood-lined room and the two of us, sprawled on the floor, gazing with rapt attention at the craggy, bearded face of my grandfather softened by the peat fire glow—old Alasdair Ross at the age of eighty-five or thereabouts telling two boys of the wonders of Laerg, describing the strange remote island world that had been his life and speaking all the time the Laerg brand of Gaelic he'd taught us to understand. It was a picture etched for all time in my mind. It had stood between me and the fear of death as I'd gazed down at the waxen face and the pitifully shrunken body in the big bed; it had comforted me that cold day when I stood shivering and crying bitterly beside the open grave. I could hear the rattle of the first frozen clods on the coffin lid still, but the face I remembered was the live face, vital and glowing in the firelight, the soft voice, the sea-grey eyes beneath the shaggy tufted eyebrows.

And here I stood now at the threshold of his world. In twenty-four hours I should be ashore on Laerg. Would it match my dreams, or had the old man so coloured the picture with his longing to return that he'd spoiled it for me? I wondered; wondered, too, about Iain. Was the picture the old man had painted as vivid to him as it was to me? Was that why he'd been so determined to make the flight? Or was it something else—something to do with the tension I'd sensed in him?

I had a drink with him that night in the Mess, but there were others there and I couldn't probe. In any case, his mood didn't encourage it—he had a black look on his face and was barely civil to anyone. And after dinner, Mike Ferguson drove me down to Rodil. By then the weather had closed in again, the rain slanting in the beam of the headlight. 'The forecast's not too good,' he said. 'You may be out of luck.'

I thought for a moment he was breaking it to

114

me that permission for me to sail with the LCT had been withdrawn. But then he added, 'Stratton may decide not to go.'

'But if he does . . .?'

'Then Movements will get you on board in time. Colonel Standing's orders.' And he added, 'Major Braddock wanted him to cancel your trip. Said visitors were a damned nuisance. But the Old Man dug in his toes.' He seemed preoccupied and I didn't like to ask him what had been said. In any case, it didn't matter. It wouldn't solve the mystery of my brother's extraordinary attitude. That was something deep-buried in his past, and I sat, puzzling over it, silent as the road unwound in the headlights, my interest in Laerg more urgent than ever.

The Fields' croft was just below Rodil church. It was stone built with small windows and looked like a cow byre, the thatch curving in dim silhouette and roped against the wind, each rope-end weighted with a stone. Field met us at the door, dressed now in grey flannels and an open-necked bush shirt. 'Come in, my dear fellows.' The gentleness of his voice struck me again, strangely at odds with the hard lines of his extraordinary hatchet features. 'Marjorie's seeing to the coffee,' he told Ferguson. 'You'll find her in the kitchen.' He took me through into the living-room which was spartan and furnished only with the bare essentials. A peat fire smouldered in the grate. 'We live very

115

simply, as you can see.' But they had electricity, and despite its bareness there was an intimacy, a cosiness about the room that made me feel instantly at home. 'Marjorie usually makes coffee about this time. Would that be all right?' There was a note of apology in his voice as though he thought I might have preferred whisky. 'I imagine this is the first time you've seen the inside of a black house?' And he went on quickly to explain that the word derived from the fact that the original Hebridean croft had virtually no windows and a peat fire in a central hearth that was never allowed to go out. 'The chimney was just a hole in the roof and smoke blackened the interior.' He smiled. 'I should know, I was born in one—not far from here, on the west coast of Lewis.' He was talking quickly, putting me at my ease, and all in the same soft, gentle voice.

He sat me down by the fire, gave me a cigarette, went on to talk about crofting, the subsidies, land disputes. The religion, too, and drunkenness, so that the impression left in my mind was one of a feckless, hard-drinking, lazy people. 'It's the climate,' he said. 'The remoteness of the islands. It's as insidious as a disease.' He smiled gently as though he himself were infected by it.

'It must be a pretty hard life,' I murmured.

'Aye, and they're the salt of the ear-rth.' There was a twinkle of humour in his eyes. 'Being one of them myself I understand them.

But I've been outside the islands most of my life. It makes a difference. And coming back ...' He shrugged. 'One would be more sympathetic if they made a greater effort to help themselves. Take this place; here's a dwelling ideally suited to the climate, the materials all ready to hand—but the status symbol up here is something constructed by a builder out of breeze-blocks. You try and paint the interior of any black house that's still occupied. They wouldn't let you cross the threshold.'

'Why not?' I asked.

'Because they're ashamed of them now.' He was staring into the glowing peat, his long legs stretched half across the bearskin rug. 'Islanders should never have contact with the mainland. It's destroying them here just as it's destroying the people of the out-islands. Laerg would never have been evacuated if the island had remained in isolation. It had a perfectly sound economy until the outside world brought to their doorstep the illusion of an easier life. They had their sheep—the sheep the Vikings introduced a thousand years ago—and they had the birds. In its heyday Laerg supported a population of over two hundred. They salted away huge numbers of puffins each year, splitting them open like kippers, and hanging them up to dry in the peat smoke. Puffins and guga—that's the young of the solan goose. They had the down of the birds for bedding, the

117

oil for lamps. They carded their own wool, wove their own clothes. Peat was there for the digging and the wind dried it in the loose stone cliets that litter the slopes of Tarsaval. They didn't need money.'

I knew all this—from my grandfather, from the books I'd read. What I wanted to know was how much the island had been changed by the Army. 'Not a great deal,' he said. 'There's a concrete ramp built on the storm beach in Shelter Bay for the LCTs. There's the camp, of course. That's just below the village, near to the Factor's House. And there's the High Road. That's probably changed the island more than anything else. It starts at the camp, skirts the Bay just back of the beach, climbs Keava in three hairpins, then up the ridge to Creag Dubh where the radar station is. There's a spur, too, that runs out to the Butt of Keava overlooking Sgeir Mhor. I can show it to you on the Ordnance Survey, if you're interested.'

The door opened and Marjorie Field came in; Ferguson followed with the coffee tray. 'Talking about Laerg,' her father said.

'Laerg?' She smiled. 'Everybody's always talking about Laerg, and I'm not allowed to go there.' She turned to me. 'I owe you an apology, don't I? You *are* a painter. I checked.'

'How?'

'With Cliff.' She turned to her father. 'Mr Ross did the jacket for Cliff's book.'

'Your daughter seemed under the

118

impression I was a journalist.' A shadow crossed his face and he didn't smile.

'You like it black or white?' she asked me.

'Black,' I said and she handed me my coffee and then switched the conversation by asking Ferguson if there was any more news of the Russian trawlers.

'Coastal Command had a Shackleton out yesterday. They didn't see anything.'

Field shifted in his seat and reached for his coffee. 'It's just a newspaper story, Mike.'

'Not necessarily. Visibility was bad and with the cloud base down to between four and six hundred the search was very restricted. There is no doubt whatever that they do have trawlers operating in the area.'

'So have the French, the Belgians, the Portuguese. Anyway, what information could they hope to get? It would be different if the range was operating. If they could check the accuracy of fire of the various units . . .'

'That's not half so important, sir, as the fact that we're getting out of Laerg. It means we've developed some other method of pin-pointing the fall of shot—a long-range tracking service. Moscow would be very interested to know that.'

'But, my dear fellow, they wouldn't need trawlers to tell them we're getting out. Any crofter in Harris . . .' The discussion didn't concern me and I took the opportunity to examine the room which I found much more

119

interesting. The walls were bare; no pictures, no photographs even, nothing to give a clue to Field's past. Only that bearskin rug. I wondered where that had come from. It was old, the head marked by burns. Had he shot it or was it something they'd picked up in a junk shop? The door to the kitchen had been left half open. His Service greatcoat hung there, the two pips a reminder of the incongruity of his age and rank. Below it hung a quilted jacket rather like a parka; green once, but now faded and worn and rather dirty.

My eyes turned to the daughter then; the nose, the blue eyes—I could see the likeness. But the mouth was softer, the skin darker. I wondered who her mother had been. She was perched on the arm of Mike Ferguson's chair and she looked strikingly beautiful, her face glowing in the lamplight, the skin almost nut-coloured and soft with the bloom of youth. I felt my blood stirring as it hadn't done since I'd left the Aegean. Her glance met mine and she smiled quickly, a wide-mouthed smile that had her father's warmth, lighting up her whole face. 'So you've got your wish; you're going to Laerg.'

'Yes.'

It was then that Field gave me the clue to his identity. 'Laerg,' he said, and there was a wistfulness in his voice. 'I shall miss it. One of the plums, being Education Officer here, was that I got out to Laerg once in a while. I should

120

have been going next Saturday . . .' He shrugged. 'But I can't complain. I've had three tours.' He smiled. 'I'm envious, you see. It's an experience, particularly the first time. And, of course, the cliffs—there's some of the finest rock climbing . . .'

'It's the birds he's really interested in,' his daughter said quickly.

But she was too late. That reference to climbing. I knew who he was then, for his name had been in all the papers. Pictures of him, too. Some time in the early fifties it must have been for we were still on the Far East run and the papers had come aboard with the mail at Singapore. He'd been the leader of one of the Himalayan expeditions. I couldn't remember the details, or the name of the peak, only that he'd been brought down from somewhere near the summit just before the final assault. The official statement had simply announced that he'd been taken ill, but the newspapers had reported it in a way that made it obvious there was more to it than that. As though conscious of my thoughts, he turned away from me. 'Any news of McGregor?' he asked Ferguson.

'An emergency operation. I fixed Bob up with a link through to Command on the Military Line just before I left Camp. He's doing it under instruction.'

'How horrible for him.'

He glanced up at the girl. 'Aye, an the laddie could have been in hospital hours ago.

As it is . . .' He shook his head. 'Bob's not happy about it; nobody is.'

'You think the man's going to die?' Field asked.

'Frankly, yes. I don't think he has a hope. When Bob's finished with him, the poor devil's got ten hours or more being bucketed about on a landing craft and then a flight to the mainland. If the Colonel had only left it to Ronnie Adams . . .'

'The helicopter might have crashed.'

'It might. But I doubt it. The worst the down-draughts have done to a helicopter so far is slam it on the deck so hard the rotor blades were shivered and split for about a yard from the tips. Anyway, it's for the pilot to assess the risk. That was Braddock's view, and for once I agreed with him. Not that either of them asked my views. They were too busy hammering away at each other.'

'When was this?'

'Just before dinner.'

'And you think Standing was wrong to cancel the flight?'

Mike Ferguson hesitated. 'Yes. Yes, I do; considering what was at stake—a man's life.'

Field sighed. 'Every man makes his decisions in the light of his own experience, Mike. Did you know that Colonel Standing once saw a helicopter crash? It caught fire and the chaps inside it were burned alive, right before his eyes. It makes a difference, you see.'

'And he told you about it?' Ferguson smiled. 'You've become a sort of father confessor to us all, haven't you.' There was affection as well as admiration in his voice.

'To some, yes. Not all.'

'Meaning Braddock?'

'Perhaps.' He leaned forward and poked at the fire. 'Man is a complex mechanism, each individual a solitary unit afraid of loneliness. That's something you'll discover as the years pass. Most of them seek escape from loneliness by membership of a group. The herd instinct is very strong in all of us. But there are always a few rogues—some of them men of real stature, others forced by circumstances to live solitary lives.' I thought he was speaking from experience then. The gentle voice sounded tired, weighed with weariness.

'They needn't be solitary if they're happily married,' his daughter said. And she added, 'I saw Laura this morning. She looked almost haggard.'

'Laura could never look haggard.' Her father smiled.

'Well, strained then. She knows what's going on. Ever since Major Braddock was posted up here ...'

'Braddock's only doing his job.' Field glanced at me. 'I'm afraid Mr Ross must find this very boring.' It was a signal to close the ranks in the face of the outside world, and after that the talk was general. We left just before

123

ten, and Ferguson drove fast, anxious to contact Laerg and get news of the LCT.

He was reluctant to talk about Field at first, but when he realised I'd already guessed his background, he admitted I was right. 'That business . . . it pretty well broke him up at the time. His whole life was climbing.'

'What did he do—afterwards?'

'Took to drink. That's why there's no liquor in the house.' And after a moment, he added, 'Maybe you can't understand it. But I can. I know how he must have felt—and it's not something you can control. It just takes charge . . .' We were on the hill above Leverburgh then and he slammed into lower gear. 'Damned shame. To escape it all he came up here, back to the islands where he was born. Then the Army arrived and that gave him the opportunity to do something useful again. He's all right now as long as Marjorie keeps an eye on him.'

I asked him then why she was so worried about newspaper men bothering him after all this time.

'Oh, it's his wife,' he said. 'He's quite a story—wartime hero, then all through the Karakoram and up into Mongolia. Now she's found out he's buried himself in the Army and she's threatening to put the Press on to him again if he doesn't go back to her. She's a bitch and no good to him—or to Marjorie.'

I thought he was referring to the girl's

124

mother. But he said, 'No, this is his second wife I'm talking about. The first was an islander like himself. From Pabbay, I think, though he met her out in Egypt. She was a nurse in the hospital where he was sent after getting himself shot up in a Long Range Desert Group foray. Unfortunately she was killed in a plane crash. If she'd lived it might have been different. They were very happy, I believe.' And after that he was silent and we drove down into the camp.

Back in my room I found a note waiting for me. The trip to Laerg was off. *Owing to bad weather L8610 will not be sailing on the morning tide.* It was scribbled on a sheet of paper torn from a notebook and was signed Fred Flint. I had seen a light in Cliff Morgan's quarters as we drove in and I walked across.

He was seated at the keyboard and didn't look up as I entered. He had the earphones clamped to his head and his mind was concentrated on another world. I sat down on the bed and lit a cigarette. He didn't notice me until he looked up to change the tuning. He started to speak, but then held up his hand, listening. After a moment he pushed up one earphone. 'You've heard the news, have you?'

'Captain Flint left a note in my quarters. Eight-six-one-o won't be sailing.'

'I wasn't referring to that. I thought as you were with Ferguson . . . He's calling him now.'

'Who?'

'Four-four-Double-o—Captain Kelvedon.

125

He's in trouble. I picked him up on Voice about half an hour ago asking for Major Braddock. He's got himself stuck on a falling tide. Went in to pick up McGregor ... Ah, here we are. Listen!' He switched in the loudspeaker and a metallic voice broke into the room. It was Ferguson, '... *ask him, but I'm quite sure he wouldn't agree to Adams attempting it in these conditions. I don't think Adams would go, anyway.'*

'*The Doc here says there isn't much time ...*'

'That's Kelvedon,' Cliff whispered.

'*... and I can't get out of here for another five hours at least. We're grounded hard.*'

'*What happened?*'

'*It was the wind partly. We had it westerly, bang on the nose most of the way across. Then it suddenly backed. I'd never have attempted it, but Fairweather told me the man wouldn't live if they tried to bring him off in a dory. It was dark as hell and quite a sea running, but I thought I could edge in close enough to drop the ramp with the kedge well out astern. Maybe it was badly laid. And that sandbank. I think it must have been building up without our realising it. The sea slewed us round and we touched the edge of it. Two hours after high water. When we came to winch off we found we were stuck fast.*'

'I see. And what about McGregor?'

'*He's back in his bed in the hospital hut. But Fairweather doesn't think he'll last long. The only hope is to get him out by helicopter.*'

'Okay. I'll tell the Colonel. What about you, now? Do you want me to have the Navy stand by?'

'Oh Lord, no. We're pounding a bit and it's not very comfortable. But the wind's veered now. Seems all over the bloody place. But if it stays where it is, north of west, we'll get off all right on the flood.'

'Fine. Call me again if there's anything fresh to report. Good luck.' And then he was calling Laerg. 'Are you there, Laerg? Base calling Laerg.'

'Laerg here,' a Scots voice answered. 'Go ahead Base.'

'Captain Ferguson here. Keep your set manned throughout the night. I may want to contact Captain Fairweather later.'

'Very good, sir.'

'Is Captain Pinney there?'

There was a pause and then a new voice answered, 'Pinney here.'

'How does the landing craft look from the shore, John?'

'Slewed off about twenty degrees and grounded on that ridge of sand. Nowhere near the ramp.'

'And the sea?'

'Moderate. Wind's getting round into the north-west, so the beach is sheltered, but there's still a biggish swell coming in. The old can's grinding a bit, but she'll be all right. It's this poor devil McGregor I'm worrying about. Just nothing but bad luck.' The voice sounded tired. 'Do what you can, will you? Have a talk with Major

127

Braddock.'

'He's down at Leverburgh trying to get the quay cleared.'

'Well, send a car down for him, see if he can persuade the Colonel. This boy's going to die if somebody doesn't take a chance.'

'Okay, John. Leave it with me.'

Cliff Morgan switched off and the room was suddenly dead as he reached automatically for a cigarette. He lit it, gulping a mouthful of smoke deep into his lungs, breathing it out through his nostrils. 'Not good, is it? And the wind playing tricks like that . . .' He noticed his old cigarette still burning in the ashtray at his elbow and stubbed it out. 'I don't like it when I feel like this. The number of times I've sat talking to some poor beggar riding the night sky with a load of trouble, or tapping out a message with the radio shack turning somersaults around him. I've been right too often, you see. There was that trawler, *Grampian Maid*. Nobody else could raise her and I was relaying messages until black ice turned her turtle. And a Boeing up over the Arctic—ice again and I was with him up to the moment when his message ceased abruptly. I'm not like an ordinary "ham", you see. I've got something to give them—the weather. Ships, aircraft, they live by the weather, and if you know as much about it as I do . . .' He sighed and scratched himself under the arm, his hand burrowing inside his shirt. It was an unconscious reflective gesture. 'You'd better go and get some sleep. And have your things packed ready.' He was leaning forward, tuning the dials of the radio again.

'You think the LCT will sail?' I asked.

'I don't know. Anything could happen . . .' He shifted in his seat, his body tense, his eyes fixed on the set as his fingers moved with the touch of a pianist, filling the room with the crackle of static. And behind the static a man's voice, the words indecipherable. 'There they are again. Two trawlers south-east of Iceland.' He clamped both earphones tight to his head, leaning forward, his whole being concentrated in the tips of his fingers as they hovered over the dials. He'd left the loudspeaker on and a Scots voice came faintly, a voice so broad it might have been talking in a foreign tongue: *'A' dinna ken w-what it means ony mair thin ye du yersel', mon. Twa hoors ago the wind was fra the north. Noo it's roond into the sou'east an' blowing a bluidy gale.'*

And another voice barely audible through the crackle: *'Aye, an' the glass ganging down agin.'*

'Did ye hear that noo? A bluidy great wave reecht o'er the bows, and the fish still coming in.'

'Ye're on top of a shoal, are ye, Doug?'

'Aye, blast it. But this is no' the time to be trawling whativer the bluidy fish. It's a hell of a night. You hove-to the noo, Jock?'

'Aye, hove-to and wishing to God I were in me

129

*bed with the wife and a wee dram inside o' me.
Ha' ye got the forecast?'*

'*Bluidy lot o' good the forecast was . . .*' The static overlaid the voices then and I couldn't decipher the rest.

After a moment Cliff Morgan pulled his earphones off. '*Arctic Ranger* talking to *Laird of Brora*. It's bad up there and I don't know quite what it means yet. There's no clear pattern, you see.' He was staring down at his notebook, drawing without thinking deep concentric rings. 'You go to bed,' he said. 'Get some sleep whilst you can.' He ran his hand up over his face, rubbing at his eyes. He looked tired.

'Are you going to stay up all night?' I asked.

'Probably. Maybe when they've stopped getting in the nets I'll be able to contact their radio operators—get some facts out of them. A pair of skippers blethering at each other. Doesn't tell you anything. I don't want to know how they feel with all hell let loose. I want to know what the barometer reads and how it compares with the reading three, four hours ago, what the weight of the wind is and whether the temperature is rising or falling.' He leaned back. 'Leave me to it, will you now. I want to see if I can raise some vessel further west. If not, I'll have a talk with the weather ships, see what they've got to say.'

'You get their reports anyway, don't you?'

He nodded. 'But it takes time. And talking to them is very different, you know, from reading the lists of figures they send in.' He put the earphones on again, leaning closer to the set as he began to tune, his fingers light as a caress on the dials. 'Those trawlers . . .' He was speaking to himself, not to me. 'On the fringe of the High and now that first depression's starting to come through. Still two of them, but very close. That would account for what happened to Kelvedon—the sudden changes of wind . . .' His voice died away, his expression suddenly intent. And then his thumb was on the key and the buzz of Morse, very rapid, filled the room as he made contact across miles of ocean.

I watched him for a moment longer, and then I left. Back in Room 42 I undressed, doing familiar things slowly, automatically, smoking a cigarette and mulling over the day. It had been a long one, so much packed into it, and London, my dismal attic of a studio, the years of hard work to become a painter—all seemed so far away. I was back now in a man's world of decisions and action involving ships and weather, any movements governed by the sea, and I found I was glad, as though painting had been no more than an affair with a beautiful woman and this the real love of my life. I sat on the bed and lit a cigarette from the butt of the old and thought about that. Was I painter or sailor, or was this new mood that had my blood tingling the physical reaction to the prospect of a childhood dream becoming a reality? I didn't

131

know. My mind was strangely confused. All I knew for certain was that the sea was calling.

I finished my cigarette, turned the thermostat of the central heating down to 'low' and went to bed thinking of Laerg.

CHAPTER TWO

FORBIDDEN ISLAND
(October 20)

I woke from a deep sleep with the ceiling lights blazing in my eyes and the duty driver standing over me, shaking me by the shoulder. 'There's a cuppa' tea for you, sir. Captain Flint said to tell you he's leaving at four-ten.'

'What's the time now?'

'Quarter to, I'll pick you up in twenty minutes. Okay? You are awake, aren't you, sir?'

'Yes, I'm awake, thanks.' I sat up and rubbed my eyes. Even with the thermostat turned right down the room was suffocatingly hot. I felt sweaty and drugged with sleep; the tea was black and thick and sweet. I got up, washed and shaved, and then dressed in my heaviest clothes, two sweaters and an anorak over the top. I packed my shoes and wore my gum boots; it was the easiest way to carry them. Outside, it was cold and windy; no sign of dawn yet, but the sky had cleared and there were stars. A half moon hung low over the camp, giving a frozen look to the unlighted huts. A long wheel-base Land-Rover stood parked outside the Mess, torches glimmered and the muffled shapes of men stood dark in the eerie light. 'That you, Ross?' The Movements Officer took my bag and tossed it into the back of the vehicle. 'Sorry there's no coffee laid on. No time for it anyway. Is that the lot, driver?'

'Yes, sir.'

'McGregor's replacement?'

A voice from the back of the Land-Rover said, 'Here, sir. Patridge.'

'Okay. Let's get cracking then.'

We climbed in. A big, heavy-jowled man in a beret and a sheepskin jacket squeezed in beside me. Flint introduced him as Major McDermott. 'You'll be brothers in misery for the next twelve hours—that is, if Stratton decides to go. But it's by no means certain yet. Things are in such a flipping mess this morning, nothing's certain.' He sounded tired and irritable.

We drove out by the main gate and headed towards the hangar with the moon hanging over it. The helicopter was standing on the tarmac apron. The Land-Rover drew up beside it. Adams was there waiting for us, dancing up and down on the balls of his feet to keep himself warm. The wind sifted sand in a light film across the surface of the apron. I hadn't expected to be travelling by helicopter. It seemed an odd way to be joining ship, but as we

133

settled into our seats I realised that there was no other means of getting to the landing craft. The South Ford I knew from the map was the shallow channel between Benbecula and South Uist; it was more than thirty miles away to the south with no road link because of the Sound of Harris.

The door shut and the rotors turned, gathering speed until the whole fuselage shook. And then the ground was falling away and we were slipping sideways across the hangar like a gull blown by the wind. 'Did you know we've got an LCT grounded in Shelter Bay?' Flint shouted in my ear. And when I nodded, he said, 'Stratton's standing by just in case. If the ship gets off all right, then Stratton will slip round into Carnan and land you at the quay there. If she doesn't then he'll probably have a bash at it. Even then you may land up back at Leverburgh.' He leaned across me, peering out through the window. 'Thank God I won't be with you if you do sail. My stomach doesn't like the sea.'

We were over the Sound now, the waves breaking white in the moonlight a thousand feet below us. And beyond the Sound we flew over a drowned land, all lakes, with the sea lochs reaching long, wet fingers into it. There was more water there than land. It looked wicked country in that ghostly light, and it went on and on with only a single sugarloaf hill to relieve the flat pan of its deadly monotony. At four-thirty we crossed the North Ford with the first pale glimmer of daylight showing the Isle of Skye in jagged relief on the eastern horizon. We were over Benbecula then and ten minutes later we saw the ship grounded in the South Ford with the tide creeping in over the sands; she wasn't quite afloat yet.

The helicopter dropped like a lift, turned head-to-wind and hovered just clear of her stern whilst the crew lowered the boat. Flint got up and pulled the door open. A gale of cold wind blew into the fuselage. We moved ahead then, settling gently on to the water about two hundred yards up-wind of the landing craft. As the rotors slowed and stopped a new sound invaded the cabin—the slap of waves against the floats. The buzz of an outboard motor came steadily nearer and then the dory was alongside and we were piling into it. Small waves tossed spray over the gunnel, wetting feet and baggage. A young man in a white polo-necked sweater, his fair hair blowing in the wind, jumped out on to the float. 'Flinty. You want to come aboard?'

'Not on your life. I'm going straight back to bed. Just came to see you boys were all right. What's the news?'

'Nothing yet. They're still grounded. But Captain Kelvedon was on the air about ten minutes ago to say he'd be starting to winch off any moment now.'

'Hope he makes it.'

135

'By God, so do I. It's going to be a dirty trip if we have to go out there in this. We're recording twenty-five knots, and we're under the lee here.'

'Stratton's made up his mind to go, has he?'

'If Four-four-Double-o doesn't get off, yes. We've got to.'

'Well, good luck, sonny.'

'Thanks, we'll need it.' He jumped off the float into the dory, balancing himself neatly. 'Wouldn't like a trip round the island, would you, Flinty?'

'No bloody . . .' The sound of the outboard motor drowned his voice. The dory swung away, running downwind with the steep little breaking waves. As the grey steel hull of the landing craft loomed over us I saw the helicopter lift its dripping floats from the water and go whirling away northwards in the pale light.

There was coffee waiting for us in the wardroom. It was hot in there after the raw cold outside. 'The Skipper will be along in a minute,' the fair-haired youngster told us. 'He's in the radio shack now, waiting to see what the form is. My name's Geoff Wentworth; I'm the Number One. If there's anything you want, just press the tit.' He indicated the bell-push.

I thought I had everything I wanted; hot coffee and the feel of a ship under me again— the soft, continuous hum of dynamos, the smell that is always the same, a compound of salt

136

dampness, hot oil and stale food, the slight suggestion of movement to give life to the hard steel of deck and bulkheads. 'We're afloat, aren't we?'

'Just about,' he said, and then he left us. McDermott had removed his sheepskin jacket and I saw the insignia of the Army Medical Corps, the serpent of Aesculapius, on his battledress. He was a surgeon, he told me, and he'd left Edinburgh shortly after eleven, flown to Stornoway and then been driven right across Lewis and Harris to Northton. 'I'll be honest— I hope we don't have to go. I'm a damned bad sailor and from what I hear this boy's in a mess.' He was puffing nervously at a cigarette.

Half an hour passed. Then a door slammed, a voice gave an order, somebody shouted and rubbered feet pounded aft. The dynamos changed their note as the lights dimmed momentarily. Another piece of machinery had come into action. The door opened and Captain Stratton came in, small and dark with premature streaks of grey in his black hair and a quiet air of command. Snatched hours of sleep had left his eyes red-rimmed. 'Sorry I wasn't here to greet you. As you've probably gathered by the sounds of activity, we're getting under way.'

'I take it,' McDermott said, 'this means the LCT is still stuck out there?'

'Yes. Kelvedon's made one attempt to winch himself off. Over-eager, by the sound of it.

137

Anyway, she didn't budge. And now he's going to wait for the top of the tide before he tries again.' And then he went on to explain his own plans. 'As we're afloat now, I thought I'd get started. We'll be bucking a head-wind up to the Sound of Harris; may take us three hours. If he gets off all right, then we'll put into Leverburgh. If he doesn't we'll be that much nearer Laerg.' He turned to me. 'I hear you have a lot of sea time. Master's ticket?' And when I nodded, he said, 'I hope you're a good sailor then.'

'I'm not sea-sick, if that's what you mean.'

He smiled. 'You may regret that statement. Have you ever been in a landing craft before?'

'No.'

'You'll find the movement a little different.' And he added, 'If you want to visit the bridge any time . . .' It was an invitation that accepted me as belonging to the brotherhood of the sea. He went out and a moment later the deck came alive under my feet as the main engines began to turn.

I watched our departure from the open door on the starboard side of the bridge housing. Dawn was breaking and the bulk of Mount Hecla sliding past was purple-brown against the fading stars. A seal raised its head snake-like from a rock, and then with a jerking movement reached the weed growth at the edge and glissaded without a splash into the water. A heron lifted itself from a grass-grown

138

islet, ungainly in flight as it retracted its head and trailed its feet, grey wings flapping in the wild morning air. Five cormorants stood on a ledge and watched us go, curious and undisturbed. These were the only signs of life, and though the door was on the leeward side and I was sheltered from the wind, I could see it whipping at the surface of the water.

One of the crew appeared at my side hooded in his duffel coat. 'Battening down now, sir.' He pulled the steel door to and fixed the clamps. 'In a few minutes we'll be rounding Wiay Island. We'll begin to feel it then.'

The visitors' quarters were immediately aft of the wardroom pantry, a clutter of two-tier bunks with clothing scattered around and a desk littered with papers. McDermott had already turned in fully clothed. 'Seems steady enough,' he murmured.

'We're still under the lee.'

My bag had been dumped on the bunk immediately aft of his. I stripped to my vest and pants and got into it, pulling the blankets up over my head to shut out the grey light from the portholes. The time was ten to six. I must have slept, but it wasn't a deep sleep, for I was conscious all the time of the movement of the ship, the sounds, the pulsing of the engines. I knew when we turned the bottom of Wiay Island for the bunk began to heave and every now and then there was a crash as though the bows had hit a concrete wall; at each blow the vessel staggered and a shiver ran through her. Vaguely I heard McDermott stumble out to the heads. Later he was sick in his bunk.

The steward woke me shortly after eight, a teenage youngster in a khaki pullover balancing a cup of tea. 'I don't know whether you'd care for some breakfast, sir. The Skipper said to ask you.'

I told him I would, though the battering was much worse now that I was awake. 'Where are we?'

'Off Lochmaddy, sir. Half an hour and we'll be in the Sound. It'll be quieter then.'

The cabin reeked of vomit, sickly sweet and mixed with the smell of human sweat. I dressed quickly and breakfasted in solitary state, burnt sausage and fried bread with the fiddles on the table, the blue settee cushions on the floor and the framed photograph of L8610 banging at the wall. I smoked a cigarette, thinking about Laerg and the ship stuck in Shelter Bay. Lucky for them the wind was in the north. If it had come in southerly during the night . . . I got up and went along the alleyway for'ard. A curtain was drawn across the open door to the Captain's cabin. There was the sound of gentle snoring, and behind the closed door opposite I heard the buzz of the radio operator's key. I slid back the door to the wheelhouse and went in.

The deck was almost steady now. A big, heavily built man stood at the wheel, dressed

140

like the officers in a white polo-necked sweater. There was nobody else there, but the door to the port side wing bridge stood open and almost immediately the Number One appeared framed in the gap. 'Port ten.'

'Port ten of wheel on, sir,' the helmsman repeated.

'Steady now.'

'Steady. Steering three-o-four, sir.'

Wentworth went to the chart table, checked with his parallel line against the compass rose. 'Steer three-one-o.'

'Three-one-o, sir.'

He straightened from the chart table and looked across at me. 'Skipper's got his head down. Did you manage to get some sleep?'

'A certain amount.' And I asked him if there was any news.

'He didn't get off.' And he added, 'The wind apparently—or so he says. It was round into the north-east and a gust caught him. Personally I think he dragged his kedge anchor when he tried that first time. Anyway, he's right up against the beach now, almost broadside-on to it.'

'You're going to Laerg then?'

He nodded. 'Going to have a shot at it, anyway. They've dispatched a Navy tug. But the Clyde's over two hundred miles away and she'll be butting straight into it. We're the only vessel that can reach Laerg by next high water.' He glanced through the for'ard porthole and then

141

went out on to the open wing bridge again. 'Starboard five.'

The needle of the indicator half right of the helmsman swung to five as he spun the wheel. I crossed to the port side where the chart table stood, a mahogany bank of drawers. Spread out on the top of it was Chart No. 2642; it showed the Sound littered with rocks and islands, the buoyed channel very narrow. 'That's Pabbay straight ahead,' Wentworth said, leaning his elbows on the table. 'Steer two-nine-six.'

'Steer two-nine-six.'

Through the porthole I looked the length of the ship. The tank hold was an empty shell with vertical walls and a flat bottom that ended abruptly at a steel half gate. Beyond the gate was the black hole of the beaching exit with the raised ramp acting as a bulk-head immediately behind the curved steel bow doors. Water sloshed in the open hold and sprung securing hooks banged in their racks. The vertical walls were topped by steel decking that ran like twin alleyways the length of the ship to finish at a small winch platform. This platform was swinging now against a back-cloth of sea and islands; it steadied as the helmsman reported. 'Steering two-nine-six.' Pabbay was on the starboard bow then, a smooth hump of an island, emerald-green in a drab grey world; whilst I had slept a thin film of cloud had covered the sky.

Wentworth swung himself up the ladder to

the open bridge immediately above the wheelhouse. He was back in a moment with three compass bearings which he ruled in on the chart to produce a fix. Watching him, intent, alert, entirely concentrated, I thought how young he was; a soldier in charge of a ship. That was something new to me. Later I learned that he came from a sea-faring family. Not his father, who kept a pub at Burnham Overy, but further back when every staithe along the North Norfolk coast was packed with sailing ships. He was very proud of the fact that one of his ancestors had sailed with Nelson who'd been born at the neighbouring village of Burnham Thorpe. The sea was in his blood and the fact that he was driving a ship at her maximum speed of around ten knots through a tortuous channel in a rock-infested Sound he accepted as no more than part of the day's work; accepted, too, the fact that beyond the Sound the North Atlantic waited. He ordered a slight adjustment of course and then turned to me. 'Another half hour and we'll be out of the lee of Harris. If you'd like to know what we're running into . . .' He reached across the chart table and removed a clipped sheaf of message forms from its hook. 'The synopsis makes nice reading.' His grin was friendly, unconcerned.

The top message, scribbled in pencil, read: *Weather forecast 0645. Gale warning: Warning of N gales in operation sea areas Rockall, Bailey, Faroes, South-East Iceland: NW gales areas*

Cromarty, Forties, Viking. Synopsis for 0600 GMT: a complete depression moving ENE towards Norway will affect all northern sea areas of the British Isles. This depression is likely to intensify over the next 24 hours. Another depression five hundred miles W of Ireland is almost stationary and there is a belt of high pressure over Greenland. Forecast sea area Hebrides: Winds NW or N force 7, reaching gale force 8 later. Visibility moderate to good with some rain or sleet.

'Sounds like a pleasant trip,' I said. 'What's the barometer say?'

He pushed the chart aside and pointed to the log book. 'Nine-eight-two. Falling.' In fact, the log showed that it had dropped 2 points in the last hour, 5 since we'd sailed. Wind strength was recorded as northerly. 32 knots, which is almost gale force 8 on the Beaufort scale. My eyes went involuntarily to the porthole, to the vulnerable length of that open tank deck. It wasn't difficult to imagine what it would be like with big seas breaking over the flat side of the ship, flooding the hold with water. As though he guessed what was in my mind, he said, 'We've very powerful pumps. Last summer we were hove-to for nearly six hours in force ten with a destroyer standing by. It wasn't very comfortable, but we managed.' The Army had apparently acquired the Navy's knack of embellishment by understatement.

The full force of the wind struck us as we

144

cleared the islands of Killegray and Ensay. There was a big swell coming in from the direction of Toe Head, now only a few miles away, and on top of the swell were steep, breaking waves. We were steaming north then, heading straight into it, and the movement was at times quite violent—a crash for'ard as we butted a wave, a shudder and then a lift and a twist as the comber went seething beneath us. Spray was whipped aft as far as the bridge. With Pabbay abeam, we altered course to almost due west, heading direct for Laerg. The motion was different then. We were no longer butting straight into it but steaming across the seas, rolling heavily with the wave crests breaking against the starboard bow. I could see the peak of Chaipaval clear of cloud and standing green against the darker Harris hills; even the camp was visible across a white waste of tumbled water.

* * *

It was whilst we were steaming out of the Sound of Harris that Colonel Standing was faced with the difficult choice of yielding to the views of his second-in-command or adhering to the Plan of Operations. Major Braddock saw him in his office shortly after nine and what he advised was the immediate withdrawal of all personnel from Laerg. He based his argument on the weather and he had Major Rafferty with

145

him to support his case. That he had a personal motive for wishing to hasten completion of the evacuation was not, of course, apparent to either Rafferty or Standing.

Briefly his argument was this: The weather had broken and there was a landing craft in difficulties. Even presuming that L4400 was hauled off the beach undamaged, the Squadron Commander at Portsmouth would almost certainly insist on the withdrawal of both ships from Scottish waters. The Army would then have to fall back on the RASC trawler. This vessel was anchored in the Clyde and no longer in commission. It might be a month before it was on station. The alternative would be to charter. Either way it would be expensive, and meantime the detachment on Laerg would have to be supplied by air drop.

Rafferty confirmed that the run-down of supplies on the island had reached the point where the detachment had food and fuel for less than a fortnight at full strength. He also made the point that all but one of the vital radar installations had already been shipped out. There were still four huts standing and a fair amount of equipment, clothing and stores, but the only other items of real value were the bulldozer, two towing vehicles, about a dozen trailers loaded with gear and a Land-Rover. All these could be driven straight on to the beached landing craft in a very short time.

Braddock had been up to the Met. Office

that morning and he had with him a weather map drawn for him by Cliff Morgan. It was Cliff's forecast of what the situation would be at midnight. It showed the 'complex depression' as an intense Low centred over Norway. It showed, too, the belt of high pressure over Greenland as having established itself, a massive High now extending from just west of Iceland to the Labrador coast with pressures of 1040 millibars or more at the centre. And between the High and the Low the isobars narrowed until, just east of Iceland, they were almost touching. Inked arrows indicated a strong northerly air stream.

'With northerly winds,' Braddock said, 'both landing craft could beach in safety. It may be our last chance.' And Rafferty had agreed.

If Rafferty had put the case Standing might have accepted it. At least he might have teleprinted Command for authority to act on it. Rafferty had an Irishman's gift for winning people over to his point of view. But faced with Braddock's virtual demand for immediate evacuation, Standing reacted strongly.

'I have my orders, and so have you, Major Braddock,' he said. 'Our job is to complete evacuation according to plan.'

'But the weather ... You can't just ignore the weather.' Braddock's voice was impatient, almost angry.

'All right. But there's no immediate hurry. We've got till this evening. We'll decide the matter then.'

It is always easier to postpone decisions and let events dictate the course of action. But in fairness it must be said that Cliff Morgan, alone of the men immediately concerned at Northton, had the weather constantly under review. It was being drummed into him all the time by the teleprinters—sheet after sheet of pressure figures. By eleven o'clock the picture had clarified to the extent that he was convinced beyond any doubt that his hunch had been right—the Hebrides lay full in the path of a polar air stream of considerable force. The magnitude and intensity of that low pressure area, combined with the Greenland High, would be drawing great masses of air south from the frozen wastes of the polar seas. This cold, dry air would be sliding in under the warmer, more humid air of the low pressure area, cooling and condensing it. Snow at first in the far north, up in the Barents Sea; sleet and rain further south, and in the Hebrides clear skies, or perhaps a film of cloud.

That would be the natural pattern. But before coming on duty that morning Cliff Morgan had re-established contact with *Arctic Ranger* and *Laird of Brora*. Both trawlers had reported a big swell still running from the north, but the wind backing westerly and the barometric pressure 2 to 3 millibars lower than the weather map indicated in that area. And now the Faeroes were reporting low cloud and

148

rain squalls. What worried him was the original nature of that Low; the result of two depressions merging, it had the inherent weakness of all complex systems. He thought trough lines might be developing, perhaps even some more serious weakness.

Shortly after eleven o'clock he phoned the camp. Colonel Standing was not in his office. It was Mike Ferguson who took the call. He listened to what Cliff had to say and agreed to get Colonel Standing to ring him back. Meantime he passed the information to Major Braddock and it was Braddock who raised it with the Colonel immediately on his return. It is more than likely that he used Cliff Morgan's vague fears—and they were nothing more at that time—to reinforce his own argument. Almost certainly Standing rejected them. As an Air Ministry man, Cliff had no connection with the Army. Standing was under no obligation to accept the local Met. Office's advice or even to consult him. He may well have considered that Braddock was exaggerating. At any rate, he didn't phone Cliff Morgan, deciding instead to wait for the shipping forecast which was by then due in less than two hours.

Quite a number of officers were gathered round the Mess radio at one-forty. The synopsis was much the same as before—gale warnings and the complex low pressure area intensifying to give a northerly air stream for much of the British Isles. The forecast for the

Hebrides was no worse than it had been at six forty-five—winds northerly, gale force 8 increasing to 9 later; visibility good but chance of rain squalls.

As a result, Colonel Standing took no action. There was not, in fact, much he could have done at that stage, but another commander might have thought it worth walking across to the Met. Office for a local weather briefing. There may have been something personal in the fact that Standing didn't do this; he was a man of narrow moral outlook and knowing Cliff's record he probably disliked him.

* * *

I missed the one-forty shipping forecast for I was lying in my bunk at the time. I wasn't asleep. I was just lying there because it was easier to lie down than to stand up, and even flat on my back I had to hang on. The ship was lurching very violently and every now and then there was an explosion like gunfire and the whole cabin shivered. McDermott was groaning in the bunk ahead of me. The poor devil had long since brought up everything but his guts; twice he'd been thrown on to the floor.

About four in the afternoon I got up, paid a visit to the heads and had a wash. The heads were on the starboard side and from the porthole, I had a windward view; it was an ugly-looking sea, made more ugly by the fact that we

150

were passing through a squall. Daylight was obscured by the murk so that it was almost dark. Visibility was poor, the seas very big with a rolling thrust to their broken tops and the spindrift whipped in long streamers by the wind.

I went down the alleyway to the wheelhouse. Stratton had taken over. He stood braced against the chart table staring out of the for'ard porthole. He was unshaven and the stubble of his beard looked almost black in that strange half light. A sudden lurch flung me across the wheelhouse. He turned as I fetched up beside him. 'Glad to see you haven't succumbed.' He smiled, but the smile didn't reach his eyes, and his face was beginning to show the strain. 'My DR puts us about there.' He pencilled a small circle on the chart. Measuring the distance from Laerg by eye against minutes of latitude shown on the side of the chart it looked as though we still had about eighteen miles to go. But I knew his dead reckoning couldn't be exact in these conditions.

'Will you make it before dark?' I asked.

He shrugged. 'We're down to six knots. Glass falling, wind backing and increasing. It came up like a line squall. Some sort of trough, I imagine.' He passed me the log. Barometric pressure was down to 976, wind speed 40–45 knots—force 9. 'Looks as though the weather boys have slipped up.' He gave me the one-forty shipping forecast. 'If the wind increases anymore before we get under the lee in Shelter Bay, we're going to have to turn and run before it.' He glanced at the radar. It was set to maximum range—30 miles; but the sweep lights showed only a speckle of dots all round the screen. The probing eye was obscured by the squall, confused by the breaking seas. 'We'll pick up Laerg soon.' It was less of a statement than an endeavour to convince himself and I had a feeling he was glad of my company. 'Ever sailed in these waters?' He switched the Decca to 15-mile range.

'No,' I said. 'But the Pacific can be quite as bad as the North Atlantic and the Indian Ocean isn't all that pleasant during the monsoon.'

'I've never commanded a proper ship,' he said. 'Always landing craft.' And after a moment he added, 'Considering what they're designed for, they're amazingly seaworthy. But they still have their limitations. They'll only take so much.' As though to underline his point a towering wall of water rose above the starboard bow, toppled and hit with a crash that staggered the ship. Water poured green over the sides, cascading like a waterfall into the well of the tank deck. I watched the pumps sucking it out through the gratings and wondered how long they would be able to cope with that sort of intake. The steward appeared with two mugs of tea. A cut on his forehead was oozing blood and there was blood on the mugs as he thrust them into our hands, balancing precariously to the surge and swoop as we plunged over that big sea.

'Everything all right below decks, Perkins?'

'Pretty fair, sir—considering.' I saw his eyes dart to the porthole and away again as though he were scared by what he saw out there. 'Will we be in Shelter Bay soon, sir?'

'Two or three hours.' Stratton's voice was calm, matter-of-fact. 'Bring coffee and sandwiches as soon as we get in. I'll be getting hungry by then.'

'Very good, sir.' And the boy fled, comforted, but glad to leave the bridge with its view of the wildness of the elements.

The squall turned to sleet and then to hail, but the hail sounded no louder than the spray which spattered the walls of the wheelhouse with a noise like bullets. And then suddenly the squall was gone and it was lighter. The radar screen was no longer fuzzed. It still had a speckled look caused by the break of the waves, but right at the top a solid splodge of light came and went as the sweep light recorded the first emerging outline of Laerg.

It was about half an hour later that the helmsman relayed a report from the lookout on the open bridge immediately over the wheelhouse. 'Land fine on the starb'd bow, sir.'

'Tell him to give the bearing.'

The helmsman repeated the order into the voice pipe close above his head. 'Bearing

Green o-five or it may be o-ten. He says there's too much movement for him to get it more accurate than that.'

Stratton glanced at the radar screen, then reached for his duffel coat and went out by the port door, leaving it open to fill the wheelhouse with violent blasts of cold air and a whirling haze of spray. He was back within the minute. 'Laerg all right—bearing o-three as far as I can tell. There's a lot of movement up there and it's blowing like hell.'

But at least visual contact had been established. I leaned against the chart table, watching as he entered it in the log, hoping to God that Shelter Bay would give us the protection we needed. It was now only two hours' steaming away. But even as my nerves were relaxing to the sense of imminent relief from this constant battering, the helmsman announced, 'Lookout reports something about weather coming through on the radio.'

Stratton glanced up quickly, but I didn't need the surprise on his face to tell me that there was something very odd about this. I had had a talk with one of the radio operators before I'd turned in and had discovered something of the set-up. There were two radio operators on board working round the clock in 12-hour watches. Their main contact was the Coastal Command net—either Rosyth or Londonderry. When not working the CCN, they kept their set tuned to 2182 KCS., which is

154

the International Distress frequency, and any calls on this frequency were relayed through a repeater loudspeaker to the upper bridge. 'Something about trawlers,' the helmsman reported. I think Stratton and I both had the same thought, that we were picking up a deep-sea trawler. Trawlers and some other small ships use 2182 KCS. on Voice. 'Look-out says he couldn't get all of it. There's too much noise up there.'

'Ask him whether it's a Mayday call.'

'No, sir. Definitely not Mayday. And he was calling us.'

Stratton knew better than to disturb his radio operator in the middle of receiving a message. We waited whilst the ship pounded and lurched and the outline of Laerg took clearer and more definite shape on the radar screen. At last the operator came in. 'Special weather report for you.' He steadied himself and then placed a pencilled message on the chart table. It was from Cliff Morgan. The message read: *GM3CMX to L8610. Advise weather conditions may deteriorate during night. Trawlers SE of Iceland report wind easterly now, force 9. At 0530 it was westerly their area. Suspect local disturbance. If interpretation correct could reach your area early hours tomorrow morning. This communication is unofficial. Good luck, Morgan.*

And God help you he might have added. A local disturbance on top of this lot . . .

155

Stratton was staring down at the message, cracking the knuckles of his right hand. 'How the hell can he have contacted trawlers south-east of Iceland?'

'Morgan's a "ham" operator,' Sparks said.

'Oh yes, of course. You've mentioned him before.' He straightened up. 'Get on to Coastal Command. Check it with them.' He had to shout to make himself heard above the thunder of a breaking sea. The ship lurched, sprawling us against the chart table. There was a noise like a load of bricks coming aboard and then the roar of a cataract as water poured into the tank deck. 'A local disturbance. What the hell does he think this is?' Stratton glanced at his watch and then at the radar. The nearest point of Laerg was just touching the 10-mile circle. 'Two hours to go.' And after that he didn't say anything.

*   *   *

Cliff Morgan's latest contact with the trawlers had been made at 15.37 hours. He took the information straight to Colonel Standing with the suggestion that L8610 be ordered to return to the shelter of the Hebrides until the weather pattern became clearer. This Standing refused to do. He had a landing craft in difficulties and an injured man to consider. Two factors were uppermost in his mind. The Navy tug, now in The Minch and headed for the Sound of

156

Harris, had been forced to reduce speed. A message on his desk stated that it would be another twenty-four hours at least before she reached Laerg. The other factor was the position of our own ship L8610. We were in H/F radio contact with the Movements Office at Base at two-hourly intervals and the 3 o'clock report had given our position as just over 20 miles from Laerg.

Cliff says he tried to get Standing to pass on the information. 'I warned the bloody man,' was the way he put it later. 'I warned him that if he didn't pass it on he'd be responsible if anything happened.' But Standing was undoubtedly feeling the weight of his responsibility for what had already happened. His attitude, rightly or wrongly, was that unofficial contacts such as this would only confuse Stratton. In fact, he was probably quite determined to do nothing to discourage L8610 from reaching Laerg. 'I told him,' Cliff said. 'You are taking a terrible responsibility upon yourself. You are concealing vital information from a man who has every right to it.' The fact is that Cliff lost his temper. He walked out of Standing's office and went straight to Major Braddock. My brother took the same line as Standing, though his reasons for doing so were entirely different. He wanted L8610 available in Shelter Bay to evacuate personnel. At least, that is my interpretation based on his subsequent actions. He was determined to get

157

the Army out of the island before the whole operation ground to a halt for lack of ships.

Having failed with both Standing and Braddock, Cliff decided to send the message himself. His broadcasting installation had an output of 200 watts, giving him a range of VH/F Voice of anything up to 1,000 miles according to conditions. As a result his message was picked up by another trawler, the *Viking Fisher*, then about 60 miles due south of Iceland. Her first contact with him, reporting a drop of 2 millibars in the barometric pressure in that locality, was made at 17.16.

Meantime, the Meteorological Office had begun to appreciate that the pattern developing in northern waters of the British Isles was becoming complicated by local troughs. The shipping forecast at 17.58 hours, however, did not reflect this. The gale warnings were all for northerly winds and the phrase 'polar air stream' was used for the first time.

* * *

'So much for Morgan's forecast,' Stratton said, returning the clip of forecasts to their hook above the chart table. 'Maybe there'll be something about it on the midnight forecast. But a polar air stream . . .' He shook his head. 'If I'd known that at one-forty, I'd have turned back. Still, that means northerlies—we'll be all right when we reach Laerg.' And he leaned his elbows on the chart table, his eyes fixed on the radar screen as though willing the blur of light that represented Laerg to hasten its slow, reluctant progress to the central dot.

As daylight began to fade a rim of orange colour appeared low down along the western horizon, a lurid glow that emphasised the grey darkness of the clouds scurrying low overhead. I thought I caught a glimpse of Laerg then, a fleeting impression of black piles of rock thrust up out of the sea; then it was gone, the orange light that had momentarily revealed its silhouette snuffed out like a candle flame. Dusk descended on us, a creeping gloom that gradually hid the violence of that cold, tempestuous sea. And after that we had only the radar to guide us.

At 18.57 we passed close south of Fladday, the isolated island to the east of Laerg. The two stacs of Hoe and Rudha showed up clear on the radar screen. Ahead and slightly to the starboard was the whole mass of Laerg itself. For the next quarter of an hour the sea was very bad, the waves broken and confused, the crests topping on to our starboard bow and the tank deck swilling water. The dim light from our masthead showed it cascading over the sides, torrents of water that continued to pour in almost without a break. The whole for'ard part of the ship seemed half submerged. And then, as we came under the lee of Malesgair, the eastern headland of Laerg, it became quieter, the wave crests smaller—still white beyond the steel sides, but not breaking inboard any more. The pumps sucked the tank deck dry and suddenly one could stand without clinging on to the chart table.

We had arrived. We were coming into Shelter Bay, and ahead of us were lights—the camp, the floodlights on the landing beach, and Four-four-Double-o lying there like a stranded whale. Low cloud hung like a blanket over Tarsaval and all the island heights, but below the cloud the bulk of Laerg showed dimly as a darker, more solid mass.

The home of my forebears, and to see it first at night, in a gale, coming in from the sea after a bad crossing . . . I thought that this was how it should be, and I stood there, gazing out of the porthole, fixing it in my mind, a picture that somehow I must get on to canvas—a grim, frightening, beautiful picture. In that howling night, with the wind coming down off Tarsaval and flattening the sea in sizzling, spray-torn patches, I felt strangely at peace. All my life, it seemed, had been leading up to this moment.

And then suddenly my seaman's instinct came alive and I was conscious that Stratton didn't intend to anchor. He had reduced speed, but the ship was going in, headed straight for the other landing craft. Wentworth was in the wheelhouse now. The Cox'n, too. And men were running out along the side decks, heading for the fo'c'stle platform. I caught the tail-end of Stratton's orders: '... heaving the lead and give the soundings in flashes on your torch. At two fathoms I'll go astern. Get the line across her then. Okay, Number One? Cox'n, you'll let go the kedge anchor when I give the word. And pay out on the hawser fast. I don't want to drag. Understand? We're almost at the top of the tide. We haven't much time.'

They left and Stratton swung himself up the ladder to con the ship from the square, boxed-in platform of the upper bridge. I followed him. 'Slow ahead both engines,' he ordered down the voice pipe. Their beat slowed and the ship glided, moving steadily and irrevocably nearer the beach. The stranded LCT was growing larger all the time. A spotlight had been switched on and I could see the number on her bows—L4400 painted black on grey. Wentworth and his men on the fo'c'stle were picked out in the beam's glare.

Stratton lifted a phone from its hook. 'All ready aft?' He stood, staring ahead, his eyes narrowed as he watched the approach of the shore. 'Let her go.' He replaced the phone on its hook and the ship went on with no check to show that the kedge anchor had been dropped astern. A torch stabbed five flashes from the fo'c'stle. 'Stop both engines.' The deck died under my feet. Four flashes. I could see the man heaving the lead, bracing himself against the fo'c'stle rail for the next throw. 'Slow astern together.'

Three flashes. Then two. 'Full astern both . .
. Stop both.' The ship hung motionless, heaving
to the swell, staggering like a drunkard in the
down-draughts. The howl of the wind came and
went, a thousand demons yelling murder. The
sound of the rocket was thin and insubstantial,
but I saw the line curve out and fall across the
stern of the other LCT. Men ran to grab it and
a moment later a hawser was being paid out
over our bows.

Just two minutes, and as the hawser was
made fast, Stratton was on the phone again
giving the order to winch in. For a moment
nothing seemed to be happening. Up for'ard
the lead was dropped again, the torch flashed
twice. Then I felt the tug astern as the anchor
bit to the power of the winch hauling in. Our
bows were swinging towards the shore. From
the compass platform I watched the sagging
line of the hawser come dripping out of the sea,
rise until suddenly it was bar-taut and
shivering, all the water shaken off it. Our bows
stopped swinging then. A ragged cheer came to
us on the wind. Men in oilskins lined the beach,
standing watching just clear of the surf. It was
they who had cheered.

The bows swung back towards the other
craft's stern. The hawser slackened
momentarily; then tightened again and I
sensed that the ship was straightened out now,
a direct link between stern and bow hawsers.
Stratton sensed it, too. 'Slow astern both
162

engines.' And as the screws bit, he ordered full astern. And after that we waited, tense for what would happen.

'Either she comes off now . . .' The phone buzzed and Stratton picked it up. '. . . Well, let it labour . . . All right, Cox'n. But don't let the fuses blow. Just hold her, that's all. Leave the rest to the main engines.' He put the phone down. 'The stern winch—bloody useless when you're in a jam.' His teeth were clenched tight, his face taut. 'Something's going to give soon. Breaking strain on that kedge hawser is only about forty-five tons. Not much when you're trying to hold a thousand ton vessel. And right now the Cox'n's got to control both ships, and on top of that, there's the added weight of all that sand piled up round Kelvedon's bottom.'

Time seemed to stand still with the whole ship trembling and vibrating with the effort. I left the compass platform and went aft to the port rail of the flag deck. It was dark on that side. No glimmer of light and the screws streaming a froth of water for'ard along the port side, toppling the waves so that all the surface of the water was ghostly white. I felt a sudden tremor. I thought for a moment one of the hawsers had parted, but up for'ard that single slender thread linking us to L4400 remained taut as before. A faint cheer sounded and then I saw the stern of the other ship was altering its position, swinging slowly out towards us.

Stratton joined me. 'She's coming. She's coming. Ross—do you see?' His voice was pitched high, exhilaration overlaying nervous tension. The stern swung out, the ship's profile thinning till she lay like a box end-on to us, and there she hung for a moment, still held by her bows, until suddenly we plucked her off and Stratton ordered the engine stopped for fear of over-running the stern hawser.

Ten minutes later both ships were out in the bay with their bow anchors down, manoeuvring under power to let go a second anchor. Ashore, men waded waist-deep in the surf to launch a dory. It lifted to the break of a wave and the oars flashed glistening in the floodlights. Clear of the surf, it came bobbing towards us, driven by the wind. We were at rest with both anchors down and the engines stopped by the time it came alongside. An oilskin-clad figure swung himself up the rope ladder and came dripping into the wheelhouse, a shapeless mountain of a man with tired brown eyes and a stubble growth that was almost a beard. 'Nice work,' he said. 'I was beginning to think we might be stuck here for the winter with a load of scrap iron on the beach.' He glanced around the wheelhouse. 'Where's Major McDermott? He's needed ashore.'

'I'll get him for you.' Stratton went out and the big man stood there dripping a pool of water from his oilskins, his face lifeless, dead with weariness.

'Bad trip, eh?' His voice was hoarse and very deep. The words seemed wrung out of him as though conversation were an effort.

'Pretty rough,' I said.

He nodded, briefly and without interest, his mind on something else. 'The poor bastard's been screaming for hours.' And with that he relapsed into silence until McDermott appeared, his face paper-white and walking delicately as though not sure of his legs.

'Captain Pinney? I'm ready when you are.' He looked in no shape to save a man's life.

'Can you take Mr Ross ashore this trip?' Stratton asked.

'May as well, if he's ready.' The tired eyes regarded me without enthusiasm. 'I've received instructions from Major Braddock about your visit. It's all right so long as you don't stray beyond the camp area.'

It took me only a moment to get my things. McDermott was being helped down the rope ladder as I said goodbye to Stratton. I dropped my bag to the men in the dory and climbed down the steel side of the landing craft. Hands clutched me as the boat rose to the slope of a wave and then they shoved off and we were down in a trough with the sea all round us, a wet world of broken water. The oars swung and clear of the shelter of the ship the wind hit us, driving spray in our faces.

It wasn't more than half a mile to the shore, but it took us a long time even with the

165

outboard motor. The wind coming down off the invisible heights above was so violent that it drove the breath back into one's throat. It came in gusts, flattening the surface of the sea, flinging it in our faces. And then we reached the surf line. A wave broke, lifting the stern, flooding the dory with water. We drove in to the beach in a seething mass of foam, were caught momentarily in the backwash, and then we touched and were out of the boat, knee-deep in water, dragging it up on to the concrete slope of the loading ramp.

That was how I came to Laerg that first time, in darkness, wet to the skin, with floodlights glistening on rain-soaked rock and nothing else visible—the roar of the surf in my ears and the wind screaming. It was a night I was to remember all my life; that and the following day.

We groped our way up to the road, staggering to the buffets of the wind. A Bailey bridge, rusted and gleaming with beads of water, spanned a burn, and then we were in the remains of the hutted camp. Everywhere the debris of evacuation, dismantled hut sections and piled-up heaps of stores and the mud shining slippery in the glimmer of the lights. The putter of a generator sounded in the brief intervals between the gusts and out in the darkness of the bay the landing craft were twin islands of light.

I was conscious then of a depressing sense of

isolation, the elements pressing in on every hand—the sea, the wind, the heights above, grass and rock all streaming water. A lonely, remote island cut off from the outside world. And living conditions were bad. Already more than half the huts had been dismantled. Two more had been evacuated and officers and men were crowded together in the remaining three with the cookhouse filled with stores and equipment that would deteriorate in the open. They were living little better than the original islanders and working much harder. Everywhere men in glistening oilskins toiled in the mud and the wet and the cold, grumbling and cursing, but still cheerful, still cracking the occasional joke as they manhandled hut sections down to the loading beach or loaded trailers with stores.

Pinney took us to his office, which was no more than a typewriter and a table beside his bed in the partitioned end of a hut that was crammed with other beds. The beds were mostly unmade, with clothing and odds and ends of personal effects scattered about; the whole place told a story of men too tired to care. Pinney's bed was no tidier than the rest, a heap of blankets thrown aside as he'd tumbled out of sleep to work. The two other officers' beds were the same and they shared the end of the hut with the radio operator and his equipment. 'Cigarette?' Pinney produced a sodden packet and McDermott took one. His hands were trembling as he lit it. 'If you'd like to get cleaned up . . .' Pinney nodded vaguely to the wash basin. 'Or perhaps you'd prefer a few minutes' rest . . .'

McDermott shook his head. 'Later perhaps—if I have to operate.' His face looked shrunken, the bones staring, the skin grey and sweating. He seemed a much older man than when he'd come aboard. 'I'll have a wor-rd with Captain Fairweather now and then I'd like to have a look at the laddie.'

'There's not much of him left to look at, and what's there is barely alive.' Pinney glanced at me. 'I'll be back shortly.' They went out and I got my wet things off, towelled myself down and put on some dry under-clothes. The only sound in the hut was the faint hum from the radio, the occasional scrape of the operator's chair as he shifted in his seat. He had the earphones clamped to his head, his body slouched as he read a paperback. He alone in that camp was able to pierce the storm and leap the gap that separated Laerg from the outside world.

The sound of the work parties came to me faintly through the background noise of the generator and the rattle of a loose window frame. I lit a cigarette. The hut had a musty smell, redolent of damp and stale sweat. Despite the convector heating, everything I touched was damp; a pair of shoes under Pinney's bed was furred with mould, the paper

168

peeling from his books. A draught blew cold on my neck from a broken pane stuffed with newspaper.

I was sitting on the bed then, thinking that this was a strange homecoming to the island of my ancestors, and all I'd seen of it so far was the camp litter of the Army in retreat. They were getting out and I thought perhaps old Grandfather Ross was laughing in his grave, or was his disembodied spirit roaming the heights above, scaling the crags as he'd done in life, waiting for the island to be returned to him? Those eyes sometimes blue and sometimes sea-grey, and the beard blowing in the wind—I could see him as clearly as if I was seated again at his feet by the peat fire. Only Iain was missing; somehow I couldn't get Iain back into that picture. Every time I thought of him it was Braddock I saw, with that twitch at the corner of his mouth and the dark eyes turned inwards.

Laerg and Alasdair Ross—they went together; they fitted this dark, wet, blustery night. But not Braddock. Braddock was afraid of Laerg and I found myself thinking of death and what Iain had once said. I got up from the bed then, not liking the way my thoughts were running, and went over to the radio operator. He was a sapper, a sharp-faced youth with rabbity teeth. 'Are you in touch with Base all the time?' I asked him.

He looked up from his paperback, pushed one of the earphones up. 'Aye.' He nodded. 'I

169

just sit on my backside and wait for them to call me.'

'And if you want to call them?'

'Och weel, I just flick that switch to "Send" and bawl into the mike.'

As simple as that. The radio was an old Army set, the dials tuned to the net frequency. Contact with Base was through the Movements Office. There a Signals operator sat by another set of the same pattern. The only difference was that it was linked to the camp switchboard. 'You mean you can talk direct to anybody in Northton?'

'Och, ye can do more than that, sir. Ye can talk to anybody in Scotland—or in England. Ye can get the bluidy Prime Minister if you want.' They were linked through the Military Line to the GPO and could even ring up their families. 'A've heer-rd me wife speaking to me fra a callbox in Glasgie an' her voice as clear as a bell. It's no' as gude as tha' every time. A wee bit o' static sometimes, but it's no' verra often we canna get through at all.'

A small metal box full of valves and coils and condensers, and like an Aladdin's lamp you could conjure the whole world out of the ether, summoning voices to speak to you out of the black, howling night. It was extraordinary how we took wireless for granted, how we accepted it now as part of our lives. Yet fifty, sixty years ago ... I was thinking of the islanders, how absolutely cut off they had been in my grandfather's time. There had been the Laerg Post, and that was all, the only means of getting a message through to the mainland; a sheep's inflated stomach to act as a float, two pieces of wood nailed together to contain the message, and the Gulf Stream and the wind the only way by which it could reach its destination. It had worked three or four times out of ten. At least, that's what my grandfather had said. And now this raw little Glaswegian had only to flip a switch.

The door at the end of the hut banged and Pinney came in. 'Clouds lifting. But it's still blowing like hell. Lucky for Stratton he's tucked into Shelter Bay.' He reached into his locker and passed me a plate and the necessary implements. 'Grub's up. We're calling it a day.' And as we sloshed our way through the mud to join the queue at the cookhouse, he said, 'Pity you're seeing it like this. Laerg can be very beautiful. On a still day with the sun shining and the air clean and crisp and full of birds . . . The best posting I ever had.'

The men had mess tins; it was like being back on active service. A cook ladled stew and peas and potatoes on to my plate. Another handed me a hunk of bread and a mug of tea. We hurried back to the hut, trying to get inside before the wind had cooled our food. Another officer had joined us, Lieutenant McBride. We ate quickly and in silence. A sergeant came in,

171

a small, tough-looking Irishman. 'Is it true you're wanting the generator run all through the night again, sor?'

'Not me,' Pinney answered. 'Captain Fairweather.'

'It means re-fuelling.'

'Then you'll have to re-fuel, that's all. They're going to operate.'

The sergeant sucked in his breath. 'What again? The poor devil.'

'Better see to it yourself, O'Hare. Make bloody sure no rainwater gets into the tank.'

'Very good, sor.'

He went out and Pinney, lying flat on his bed, his eyes closed, smoking a cigarette, said, 'McDermott's as white as a ghost and trembling like a leaf. He was ill coming across, I suppose.'

'Very ill,' I said.

He nodded. 'I thought so. He wouldn't have any food. Bob gave him a couple of slugs out of the medicine chest. Damned if I could operate on an empty stomach, but still . . .' His eyes flicked open, staring up at the ceiling, and he drew in a lungful of smoke. 'What the hell am I going to say to his mother? The police will locate her sooner or later and then I'll have her on the R/T and she'll be thinking it's my fault when it was his own bloody carelessness. But you can't tell her that.' He closed his eyes again and relapsed into silence, and on the instant he was asleep. I took the burning cigarette from between his fingers and pulled a blanket over him.

McBride was already in bed, stripped to his vest and pants. 'You'll have to excuse us,' he said with a sleepy, boyish grin. 'Not very sociable, but I don't seem able to remember when we had more than four hours at a stretch. We just sleep when we can.' And he pulled the blanket up over his head. A moment later he was snoring with a whistling intake of the breath and a gurgling quiver of the nostrils. 'Och, he's awa'.' The operator showed his long front teeth in a smile. 'I mind the time when a' couldna hear a worrd they were saying at Base for Mr McBride lying there snoring.'

From beyond the partition the murmur of men's voices continued for perhaps five minutes, gradually dying away to silence. And after that there wasn't a sound except for the generator and the wind blasting the four corners of the hut and McBride snoring. But not everybody was asleep. Through the uncurtained window I could see a glow of light from the next hut. The shadow of a man's figure came and went against the drawn blinds, distorted and grotesque, and I knew it was McDermott . . . McDermott, who'd retched his guts out all the way across and was now trying to put together the broken pieces of another man's body.

I must have dozed off, but it could only have been for a moment. I jerked awake in my chair to see the operator shaking Pinney by the shoulder. 'Captain Pinney, sir. Captain Pinney.' There was a movement. His head came up and his eyes ungummed themselves.

'What is it, Boyd? Somebody want me?'

'Major Braddock, sir.'

'Then it's not . . .' He glanced at his watch. 'Oh well . . .' He kicked the blanket aside and swung his legs off the bed. He was obviously relieved it wasn't the call he'd been expecting. 'What's Major Braddock want?' he asked, rubbing at his eyes.

'It's urgent, sir. We're evacuating.'

'Evacuating? Nonsense.' He stared at the operator in disbelief.

'Aye, it's true, sir. We're leaving right away, tonight. I hear-rd him give the order to Captain Stratton. Eight-six-one-o is coming in to beach noo.'

It was the moment of the fatal decision, the moment when the order was given that was to cost so many lives.

Pinney shook his head, forcing himself back to full consciousness. Then he was over at the set and had the earphones on, speaking into the mouthpiece. 'Pinney here.' He sat down in the chair the operator had vacated. 'Well, yes. The wind's off the shore, northerly. There shouldn't be any risk . . . What's that? . . . Yes, but what about the rest of the stores? According to the schedule the landing craft should be running six more trips . . . Yes. Yes, I quite agree, but . . .' He laughed. 'No, we shan't be sorry to go. Life isn't exactly a bed of roses here. It's just that my orders . . . Yes, I gathered it was a War Office appointment. But I should have thought Colonel Standing . . .' There was a long pause, and then he said, 'All right, sir. So long as it's understood that I'm quite prepared to continue here until every piece of Army equipment has been shipped out. And so are my men . . . Fine. We'll get cracking then.' He got up and handed the earphones back to the operator. 'Remain on the set, Boyd, until you're called for boarding.' He stood there a moment looking round the room as though finding it difficult to adjust himself to the fact of leaving. Then he woke McBride and in an instant all was confusion, orders being shouted and men cursing and stumbling about as they sleep-walked into the clothes they'd only just taken off. Outside, the night was clearer, no stars, but the shadowed bulk of Tarsaval just visible. The wind was still very strong, coming in raging gusts that tore at the men's clothing, bending them double against the weight of it as they stumbled towards the beach.

An engine revved and a big six-wheeled Scammell lumbered past me. Seaward the lights of the two landing craft showed intermittently through the rain. One of them had its steaming lights on and the red and green of its navigation lights stared straight at the beach, coming steadily nearer. Orders shouted above the gale were whipped away by the wind. Pinney passed me, big in the lights of a truck stuck in the mud with its wheels spinning. 'Better get straight on board.' His voice was almost lost in a down-blast.

I was standing on the beach when Stratton brought his landing craft in towards the loading ramp. There was almost no surf now, the sea knocked flat by the wind. Bows-on the landing craft was square like a box. He came in quite fast—two knots or more, and ground to a halt with an ugly sound of boulders grating on steel, the bows lifting slightly, towering over us. Lines were flung and grabbed, steel hawsers paid out and fastened to shore anchor points, and then the bow doors swung open and the ramp came down; a stranded monster opening its mouth to suck in anything it could devour.

The bulldozer came first, its caterpillar tracks churning sand and water. It found the edge of the ramp and lumbered, dripping up the slope, clattering a hollow din against the double bottom as it manoeuvred to the far end of the tank hold. The Scammell followed, towing a loaded trailer, wallowing through the shallows and up the ramp where Wentworth and the Cox'n with half the crew waited to receive it. Men straggled in from the camp and they unhitched the trailer and manhandled it into position. The Scammell reversed out and by the time it was back with the next trailer, the first had been parked and bowsed down with

176

the sprung steel securing shackles.

This went on for almost two hours; more than thirty oilskin-clad figures sweating and cursing in the loading lights and the tank deck gradually filling up. By eleven the tempo was slackening, though Pinney was still loading equipment from the camp, sending down all the small, portable, last-minute stuff.

I was working on the tank deck until about eleven-thirty. By then the Cox'n had more men than he needed. I went up to the bridge housing, took over my old bunk and cleaned myself up, and then went into the wardroom, lured by the smell of coffee. Stratton and Wentworth were there and I knew at once that something was wrong. They barely looked up as I entered, drinking their coffee in silence, their faces blank and preoccupied. 'Help yourself,' Wentworth said. Beside the coffee a plateful of bully-beef sandwiches lay untouched. 'Afraid you didn't get much of a run ashore.'

I poured myself some coffee and sat down. 'Cigarette?' I held the packet out to Stratton. He took one automatically and lit it without saying a word. Wentworth shook his head and I took one myself. A message form lay on the table close by Stratton's hand. He glanced at his watch. It was an unconscious gesture and I had the impression he knew the time already. 'Another half-hour yet before low water. If we offload—sling all this heavy stuff ashore . . .'

He left the sentence unfinished, the question hanging in the air.

'And suppose nothing happens—the wind remains in the north?' Wentworth's voice was hesitant.

'Then we'll look bloody silly. But I'd rather look a fool . . .' He shook his head angrily. 'If he'd come through just two hours earlier, before we took the ground.' He pushed his hand up wearily over his eyes and took a gulp of coffee. 'Thank God there's only one of us on the beach anyway. If Kelvedon hadn't buckled a plate . . .' He lit his cigarette. 'I'd give a lot to be anchored out there in the bay with Four-four-Double-o right now.'

'It may not come to anything,' Wentworth said. 'The midnight forecast didn't say anything about it. Troughs, that's all. And the wind northerly . . .'

'Of course it didn't. This is local. Something very local.' Stratton shook his head. 'Nothing for it, I'm afraid. We'll have to unload. Empty we'll be off—what? An hour sooner?'

'Three-quarters anyway.'

'Okay. Find Pinney. Tell him what the position is. And get them started on off-loading right away.'

Wentworth gulped down the remainder of his coffee and hurried out. Stratton lay back against the cushions and closed his eyes with a sigh. The effort of reaching a decision seemed to have drained him of all energy. I was thinking of the wasted effort, all the trailers and vehicles to be got off with the men tired and exhausted. 'You've met this fellow Morgan. How good is he?' His eyes had opened again and he was staring at me.

'I think very good,' I said. And I told him something about Cliff's background and about the book he'd written.

'Pity you didn't tell me that before. I might have taken him more seriously.' And then angrily: 'But it's all so damned unofficial. Coastal Command don't know anything about it. All they could give me was what we've got right now—wind northerly, force nine, maybe more. They're checking with Bracknell. But I bet they don't know anything about it. Read that.' He reached out with his fingers and flipped the message form across to me. 'A polar air depression. That's Morgan's interpretation. And all based on contact with a single trawler whose skipper may be blind drunk for all I know.'

The message was impersonal, almost coldly factual considering the desperate information it contained: *GM3CMX to LCTs 8610 and 4400. Urgent. Suspect polar air depression Laerg area imminent. Advise you be prepared winds hurricane force within next few hours. Probable direction between south and west. Interpretation based on contact 'Viking Fisher' 23.47. Trawler about 60 miles S of Iceland reports wind speed 80 knots plus, south-westerly, mountainous seas, visibility virtually nil in heavy rain and sleet. Barometric pressure 963, still falling—a drop of 16 millibars in 1 hour. Endeavouring re-establish contact. Interpretation unofficial, repeat unofficial, but I believe it to be correct. C. Morgan, Met. Officer, Northton.*

I didn't say anything for a moment. I had a mental picture of Cliff sitting in that room with his earphones glued to his head and his thumb resting on the key, and that big Icelandic trawler almost four hundred miles to the north of us being tossed about like a toy. I thought there wouldn't be much chance of re-establishing contact until the storm centre had passed over, supposing there was anything left to contact by then. A polar air depression. I'd heard of such things, but never having sailed in these waters before, I'd no experience of it. But I knew the theory. The theory was very simple.

Here was a big mass of air being funnelled through the gap between the big Low over Norway and the High over Greenland, a great streaming weight of wind thrusting southwards. And then suddenly a little weakness develops, a slightly lower pressure. The winds are sucked into it, curve right round it, are suddenly a vortex, forcing the pressure down and down, increasing the speed and size of this whirligig until it's like an enormous high speed drill, an aerial whirlpool of staggering intensity. And because it would be a part of the bigger pattern of the polar air stream itself, it was bound to

180

come whirling its way south, and the speed of its advance would be fast, fast as the winds themselves.

'Well?' Stratton was staring at me.

'He had other contacts,' I said. 'Those two trawlers . . .'

'But nothing on the forecast. Nothing official.' He was staring at me and I could read the strain in his eyes. No fear. That might come later. But the strain. He knew what the message meant—if Cliff's interpretation was correct; knew what it would be like if that thing caught us while we were still grounded. The wind might come from any direction then. The northerly air stream from which we were so nicely sheltered might be swung through 180. And if that happened and the wind came in from the south . . . I felt my scalp move and an icy touch on my spine. My stomach was suddenly chill and there was sweat on my forehead as I said, 'How long before you get off?'

He didn't give me an answer straight off. He worked it out for me so that I could check the timing myself. They had beached at nine-forty-eight, two and three-quarter hours after high water. Next high water was at seven-twenty. Deduct two and three-quarter hours, less say half an hour to allow for the amount the ship had ridden up the beach . . . It couldn't be an exact calculation, but as far as he could estimate it we should be off shortly after five. I glanced at my watch. It was twenty minutes to one now. We still had nearly four and a half hours to wait. Four and a half solid bloody hours just sitting here, waiting for the wind to change—praying it wouldn't before we got off, knowing the ship was a dead duck if it did. 'No way of getting out earlier, I suppose?'

He shook his head.

It was a silly question really, but I didn't know much about these craft. 'There's a double bottom, isn't there? What's in between—fuel?'

'Water, too. And there are ballast tanks.'

'How much difference would it make?'

'We'll see; I should think about eighteen inches up for'ard when we've pumped it out. Geoff's checking with the ballasting and flooding board now. About cancel out the amount we ran up the beach; give us a few extra minutes, maybe.'

Sitting there in the warmth of that comfortable little wardroom with the ship quite still and solid as a rock, it was hard to imagine that in little more than four hours' time so few minutes could possibly make the difference between getting off and being battered to pieces.

'More coffee?'

I passed my cup and lit another cigarette. The radio operator came in and handed Stratton a message. 'Coastal Command just came through with the supplementary forecast you asked for.'

182

'Stratton read it aloud. 'Winds northerly, force nine, decreasing to seven or eight. Possibly local troughs with rain squalls. Otherwise fair visibility.' He slapped the message form down on top of the others. 'Same as the midnight forecast. Nothing at all about a polar air depression; no reference to winds of hurricane force.' He turned to the radio operator. 'Anything new from Morgan?'

The operator shook his head. 'I heard him calling *Viking Fisher*, but I couldn't raise him myself.'

'Did the trawler reply?'

'No.'

'Well, see if you can get Morgan. Keep on trying, will you. I'd like to talk to him myself.' He reached for a message pad lying on the shelf below the porthole. 'And there's a message I want sent to Base. When's the next contact? One o'clock, isn't it?'

The operator nodded. 'But I can get them any time. They're standing by on our frequency.'

'Good. Give them a buzz then. Say I want to speak to Colonel Standing. And don't be fobbed off. Understand? If he's in bed, they're to get him out of it. I want to speak to him personally.' As the operator left he tossed the message pad back on to the shelf. 'Time these chaps who sit in their cosy offices issuing orders lost a little sleep on our account.'

I started in on the corned beef sandwiches

then. I had a feeling this was going to be a long night. Stratton got up. 'Think I'll go and see what the wind's doing. I'll be in the wheelhouse.' Later Perkins brought some more coffee. I had a cup and then took one through to Stratton. But he wasn't there. The door was open on the port side and the wind came crowding through it in a gusty roar. The duty watch stood sheltering there, clad in sou'wester and oilskins. 'Where's Captain Stratton?' I asked him.

'On the R/T. Radio Operator just called him.'

'And the wind's still in the north, is it?'

'Aye, just aboot. Varies a wee bit, depending which side of Tarsaval it strikes.'

I went over to the porthole and looked down on to the wet steel decks gleaming under the loading lights. They'd got about a third of the tank deck clear, but the men moved slowly now, all the life gone out of them. Stratton came in then. He didn't say anything but got his duffel coat. I handed him his coffee and he gulped it down. 'Don't know what's going on at Base. Colonel Standing says he'd no idea we were evacuating. Sounded damned angry—what little I could hear. There was a lot of static.' He pulled his coat on. 'I'd better have a word with Pinney.' He turned to the duty man. 'If anybody wants me I'll be down on the loading beach.'

After he'd gone I went over to the chart

table and had a look at the log. Barometer reading at midnight was given as 978, a fall of one millibar since the previous reading at eleven. I leaned over and peered at the glass itself—977. I tapped it and the needle flickered, and when I read it again it was 976.

Time was running out; for the ship, for the men labouring on the tank deck to undo what they had done—for me, too. I could feel it in my bones, in the dryness of my tongue—a lassitude creeping through me, a feeling of indecision, of waiting. And all because a needle in a glass instrument like a clock had moved so fractionally that the movement was barely discernible. Long years at sea, standing watch on the bridges of ships, had taught me the value of that instrument, what those small changes of barometric pressure could mean translated into physical terms of weather. Somewhere in the bowels of the ship the cook would be sweating in his galley producing food to replace the energy those men on the tank deck had consumed. Deeper still the engineers would be checking their oiled and shining diesels, preparing them for the battle to come. And out there beyond the lights, beyond the invisible peaks and sheer rock cliffs of Laerg, out across the sea's tumbled chaos, the enemy was coming relentlessly nearer, ten thousand demon horsemen riding the air in a great circle, scouring the sea, flailing it into toppling ranges of water, spilling violence as they charged

185

round that vortex pot of depressed air. Fantasy? But the mind is full of fantasy on such a night. Science is for the laboratory. Other men, who stand alone and face the elemental forces of nature, know that science as a shining, world-conquering hero is a myth. Science lives in concrete structures full of bright factory toys, insulated from the earth's great force. The priesthood of this new cult are seldom called upon to stand and face the onslaught.

The radio operator poked his head into the wheelhouse, interrupting my thoughts. 'Seen the Skipper? I've got that chap Morgan on the air.'

'He's doon to the beach to see Captain Pinney,' the duty man said.

Between the wheelhouse and the beach was the littered tank deck, and Cliff Morgan wouldn't wait. 'Can I have a word with him?' I suggested.

The operator hesitated. 'Okay, I don't see why not—as one civilian to another.' He gave me a tired smile.

I followed him into the box-like cubby-hole of the radio shack. He slipped his earphones on and reached for the mike. 'L8610 calling GM3CMX. Calling CM3CMX. Do you hear me? Okay, GM3CMX. I have Mr Ross for you.' He passed me the earphones. Faint and metallic I heard Cliff's voice calling me. And when I answered him, he said, *'Now listen, man. You're on board Eight-six-one-o, are you?'* I told

186

him I was. *'And you're beached—correct?'*

'Yes.'

'Well, you've got to get off that beach just as soon as you can. This could be very bad.'

'We're unloading now,' I said. 'To lighten the ship.'

'Tell the Captain he's got to get off—fast. If this thing hits you before you're off . . .' I lost the rest in a crackle of static.

'How long have we got?' I asked. His voice came back, but too faint for me to hear. 'How long have we got?' I repeated.

'. . . barometric pressure?' And then his voice came in again loud and clear. *'Repeat, what is your barometer pressure reading now?'*

'Nine-seven-six,' I told him. 'A drop of three millibars within the last hour.'

'Then it's not far away. You can expect an almost vertical fall in pressure, right down to around nine-six-o. Watch the wind. When it goes round . . .' His voice faded and I lost the rest. When I picked him up again he was saying something about seeking shelter.

'Have you made contact with that trawler again?' I asked.

'No. But somebody was calling Mayday a while ago—very faint. Now listen. I am going to try and raise the Faeroes or weather ship "India". It should be passing them, you see. And I'll phone Pitreavie. Tell the operator I'll call him on this frequency one hour from now. Good luck and Out.'

I passed the message on to the operator and went back into the wheelhouse. Nothing had changed. The duty man was still sheltering in the doorway. The barometer still read 976. Another trailer had been unloaded, that was all. And the wind still northerly. It was ten past one. Four hours to go.

CHAPTER THREE

STORM
(October 21–22)

A few minutes later Stratton came in, his duffel coat sodden. 'Raining again.' He went straight to the barometer, tapped it and entered the reading in the log. 'And McGregor's dead. They're bringing his body on board now.' His face was pale and haggard-looking in the wheelhouse lights.

I passed Cliff's message on to him, but all he said was, 'We're dried out for two-thirds the length of the ship and I can't change the tides.' His mind was preoccupied, wound up like a clock, waiting for zero hour. He went to his room and shortly afterwards a macabre little procession came in through the open tunnel of the loading doors—McDermott and the camp doctor, and behind them two orderlies carrying a stretcher. All work stopped and the men stood silent. A few moved to help hand the

188

stretcher up one of the vertical steel ladders on the port side. The body on the stretcher was wrapped in an oiled sheet. It glistened white in the lights. Once it slipped, sagging against the tapes that held it in place. The orderlies stopped to re-arrange it and then the procession moved aft along the side decking. I could see their faces then, the two officers' white and shaken, the orderlies' wooden. They passed out of sight, moving slowly aft. They were taking the body to the tiller flat, but I only learned that later when death was facing us too.

I went back into the wardroom and ten minutes later McDermott came in followed by Captain Fairweather. They looked old and beaten, grey-faced and their hands trembling. They didn't speak. They had a whisky each and then McDermott went to his bunk, Captain Fairweather back to the camp to get his kit.

By two-thirty the tank deck was clear, a wet steel expanse emptied of all vehicles. By three the incoming tide was spilling white surf as far as the loading ramp. The glass stood at 971, falling. No further contact with Cliff Morgan. Nothing from Coastal Command. And the wind still driving out of the north, straight over the beached bows. Pinney was arguing with Stratton in the wheelhouse. 'Christ, man, what do you think we are? The men are dead beat. And so am I.' The decks were deserted now, all the men swallowed up in the warmth of the ship, and Stratton wanted them ashore. 'My orders were to embark my men and all the equipment I could. We got the stuff on board and then you order it to be taken off again. And when we've done that . . .'

'It's for their own good.' Stratton's voice was weary, exhausted by tension.

'Like hell it is. What they want is some sleep.'

'They won't get much sleep if this depression . . .'

'This depression! What the hell's got into you? For two hours now you've been worrying about it. The forecast doesn't mention it. You've no confirmation of it from Coastal Command, from anybody. All you've got is the word of one man, and he's guessing on the basis of a single contact with some trawler.'

'I know. But the glass is falling—'

'What do you expect it to do in this sort of weather—go sailing up? All that matters is the wind direction. And the wind's north. In just over two hours now . . .'

It went on like that, the two of them arguing back and forth, Stratton's voice slow and uncertain, Pinney's no longer coming gruff out of his big frame, but high-pitched with weariness and frustration. He was a soldier and his men came first. Stratton's concern was his ship and he had a picture in his mind, a picture conjured by the falling glass and Cliff Morgan's warning and that information I had passed on about a faint voice calling Mayday on the

190

International Distress frequency. But even in these circumstances possession is nine-tenths of the law. Pinney's men were on board. They had their oilskins off and hammocks slung. They were dead beat and they'd take a lot of shifting. Stratton gave in. 'On your own head then, John.' And he gave the orders for the ramp to be raised and the bow doors shut.

Thirty-three men, who could have been safe ashore, were sealed into that coffin of a ship. The time was three-fourteen. Just over one and a half hours to go. Surely it would hold off for that short time. I watched figures in oilskins bent double as they forced their way for'ard and clambered down to the tank deck. The open gap, with its glimpse of the beach and the blurred shape of vehicles standing in the rain, gradually sealed itself. The clamps were checked. The half gate swung into place. Now nobody could leave the ship. And as if to underline the finality of those doors being closed, messages began to come through.

Coastal Command first: *Trawler 'Viking Fisher' in distress. Anticipate possibility of very severe storm imminent your locality. Winds of high velocity can be expected from almost any direction. Report each hour until further notice.*

Then Cliff crashed net frequency to announce contact with Faeroes and weather ship *India*. *Faeroes report wind southerly force 10. Barometer 968, rising. 'W/S India': wind north-westerly force 9 or 10. Barometer 969, falling rapidly. Very big seas.*

CCN again with a supplementary forecast from the Meteorological Office: *Sea areas Hebrides, Bailey, Faeroes, South-East Iceland— Probability that small, very intense depression may have formed to give wind speeds of hurricane force locally for short duration. Storm area will move southwards with the main northerly air stream, gradually losing intensity.*

The outside world stirring in its sleep and taking an interest in us. Stratton passed the messages to Pinney without comment, standing at the chart table in the wheelhouse. Pinney read them and then placed them on top of the log book. He didn't say anything. There wasn't anything to say. The moment for getting the men ashore was gone half an hour ago. Waves were breaking up by the bows and occasionally a tremor ran through the ship, the first awakening as the stern responded to the buoyancy of water deep enough to float her. And in the wheelhouse there was an air of expectancy, a man at the wheel and the engine-room telegraph at stand-by.

The time was twelve minutes after four.

The radio operator again. Base asking for Captain Pinney on the R/T. Pinney went out and an unusual quiet descended on the wheelhouse, a stillness of waiting. In moments like this, when a ship is grounded and you are waiting for her to float again, all sensitivity becomes concentrated on the soles of the feet, for they are in contact with the deck, the transmitters of movement, of any untoward shock. We didn't talk because our minds were on our feet. We were listening by touch. Perhaps that's why our ears failed to register how quiet it had become.

Through my feet, through the nerves that ran up my legs, connecting them to my brain, I could feel the tremor, the faint lifting movement, the slight bump as she grounded again. It all came from the stern. But it was a movement that was changing all the time, growing stronger, so that in a moment a slight shock preceded the lift and there was a surge running the length of the ship. It was different. Definitely a change in the pattern and it puzzled me. I glanced at Stratton. He was frowning, watching a pencil on the chart table. It had begun to roll back and forth at each surge. The bumps as we grounded were more noticeable now, a definite shock.

Wentworth came in. 'What is it? I told you to stay on the quarter-deck with the Bos'n.' Stratton's voice was irritable, his nerves betraying him. 'Well?'

'There's quite a swell building up.' The youngster's face looked white. 'You can see it breaking on the skerries of Sgeir Mhor. It's beginning to come into the bay. And the wind's gone round.'

'Gone round?'

'Backed into the west.'

193

Stratton went to the door on the port side and flung it open again. No wind came in. The air around the ship was strangely still. But we could hear it, roaring overhead. The first grey light of dawn showed broken masses of cloud pouring towards us across the high back of Keava. The moon shone through ragged gaps. It was a wild, grey-black sky, ugly and threatening. Stratton stood there for a moment, staring up at it, and then he came back into the wheelhouse, slamming the door behind him. 'When did it start backing? When did you first notice it?'

'About ten minutes ago. I wasn't certain at first. Then the swell began to—'

'Well, get back to the after-deck, Number One. If it goes round into the south . . .' He hesitated. 'If it does that, it'll come very quickly now. Another ten minutes, quarter of an hour. We'll know by then. And if it does—then you'll have to play her on the kedge like a tunny fish. That hawser mustn't break. Understand? I'll back her off on the engines. It'll be too much for the winch. Your job is to see she doesn't slew. Slack off when you have to. But for Christ's sake don't let her stern swing towards the beach. That's what happened to Kelvedon.'

'I'll do my best.'

Stratton nodded. 'This swell might just do the trick. If we can get her off before the wind goes right round . . .'

But Wentworth was already gone. He didn't

194

need to be told what would happen if the wind backed southerly—wind and waves and the breaking strain on that hawser a paltry forty-five tons. And as though to underline the point, Stratton said to me, 'One of the weaknesses of these ships, that winch gear only rates about ten horse-power.' He picked up the engine-room telephone. 'Stevens? Oh, it's you, Turner. Captain here. Give me the Chief, will you.'

He began giving instructions to the engine-room and I pushed past him, out on to the wing bridge and up the steel ladder to the open deck above. The look-out was standing on the compass platform staring aft, his face a pallid oval under his sou'wester. A ragged gap in the clouds showed stars, a diamond glitter with the outline of Tarsaval sharp and black like a cut-out; a glimpse of the moon's face, and the wind tramping overhead, driving a black curtain of cloud across it. I went aft down the flag deck where the tripod structure of the mainmast stood rooted like a pylon, and a moment later Stratton joined me. 'Any change?'

'West sou'west, I think.' I couldn't be sure, but there was a definite swell. We could see it coming in out of the half-darkness and growing in the ship's lights as it met the shallows. It slid under the stern and then broke seething along the length of the sides, lifting the stern and snapping the anchor hawser taut. Across the bay we could see spray bursting against the dim, jagged shape of the skerries. The wind was definitely south of west. I could feel it sometimes on my face, though the force of it and the true direction was masked by the bulk of Keava. Raindrops spattered on my face.

But it was the swell that held us riveted, the regular grind and bump as the ship was lifted. And then one came in higher, breaking earlier. It crashed against the stern. Spray flung a glittering curtain of water that hung an instant suspended and then fell on us, a drenching cascade. But it wasn't the water so much as the ship herself that alarmed us, the sudden shock of impact, the way she lifted, and slewed, the appalling snap of the hawser as it took the full weight, the thudding crash as she grounded again, grinding her bottom in the backwash.

'I hope to God he remembers to slip the winch out of gear,' Stratton murmured, speaking to himself rather than to me. 'All that weight on it . . . We've stripped the gears before now. I'd better remind him.' He turned to go, but then he stopped, his gaze turned seaward. 'Look!' He was pointing to the other LCT, a cluster of lights in the grey darkness of the bay. 'Lucky beggar.' She had her steaming lights on and was getting her anchor up; and I knew what Stratton was thinking that he might have been out there, safe, with room to manoeuvre and freedom to do so.

A blast of air slapped rain in my face. South—south-west. Again I couldn't be sure. But into the bay; that was definite. Stratton had felt it, too. He went at once to the compass platform. I stayed an instant longer, watching the men on the after-deck immediately below me. Wentworth was standing facing the stern, with two men by the winch on the starboard quarter, their eyes fixed on him, waiting for his signal. The sea seethed back, white foam sliding away in the lights, and out of the greyness astern came a sloping heap of water that built rapidly to a sheer, curving breaker. The winch drum turned, the cable slackened; the wave broke and thudded, roaring against the stern. The men, the winch, the whole after-deck disappeared in a welter of white water. The ship lifted under me, swung and then steadied to the snap of the hawser. The thud as we hit the bottom again jarred my whole body. I saw the mast tremble like a tree whose roots are being attacked, and when I looked over the rail again, the stern was clear of water, the men picking themselves up.

The wind was on my face now. It came in gusts, and each gust seemed stronger than the last. L4400 had got her anchor; she was turning head-to-sea, steaming out of the bay.

I went for'ard to the bridge, wondering how long it would be before the hawser snapped or the men on the afterdeck were swept overboard. The deck under my feet was alive now, the engine-room telegraph set to slow astern and the screws turning. Stratton was on the open side deck, trying to keep an eye on

197

stern and bow at the same time. If only she could shake herself free. I could feel it when she lifted, the way she was held by the bows only; for just a moment, when the wave was right under her, you could almost believe she was afloat.

Pinney came up. I don't think anyone saw him come. He just seemed to materialise. 'Would you believe it? The Old Man's countermanded Braddock's orders. Said we'd no business to be pulling out ...' There was more of it but that's all I can remember—that, and the fact that he looked tired and shaken. Nobody said anything. Nobody was listening. We had other things on our minds. Pinney must have realised this, for he caught hold of my arm and said angrily, 'What's happening? What's going on?'

'The wind,' I said. 'The wind's gone round.'

I could see it now, blowing at Stratton's hair, whipping the tops off the combers and sending the spray hurtling shorewards in flat streamers of white spindrift. We were no longer sheltered by Keava. God, how quickly that wind had shifted, blowing right into the bay now—thirty, maybe forty knots. I went down to the wheelhouse. The barometer was at 969, down another two points. *Quick fall, quick rise*—that was the old saying. But how far would it fall before it started to rise? Cliff had mentioned 960, had talked of a near vertical fall of pressure. That was what we were getting now. I hadn't seen a glass fall like that since I'd sailed into a cyclone in the Indian Ocean. I tapped it and it fell to 968.

'Full astern both engines.' Stratton's voice from the bridge above came to me over the helmsman's voice pipe. The telegraph rang and the beat of the engines increased as the stern lifted to slam down again with a deep, rending crash that jolted my body and set every moveable thing in the wheelhouse rattling. 'Stop both engines.'

I was gripping hold of the chart table, every nerve taut. Gone was the silence, that brief stillness of waiting; all was noise and confusion now. 'Full astern both.' But he was too late, the stern already lifting before the screws could bite. Stop both and the jar as she grounded, the bows still held and the hawser straining. Spray hit me as I went back to the bridge. The wind was pitched high in the gusts, higher and higher until it became a scream.

The phone that linked us to the after-deck buzzed. There was nobody to answer it so I picked it up and Wentworth's voice, sounding slight and very far away, said, 'We took in half a dozen turns on the winch that time. Either the anchor's dragging . . .' I lost the rest in the crash of a wave. And then his voice again, louder this time: 'Three more turns, but we're getting badly knocked about.' I passed the information to Stratton. 'Tell him,' he shouted back, 'to take in the slack and use the brakes.

I'm holding the engines at full astern. If we don't get off now . . .' A gust of wind blew the rest of his words away. The phone went dead as the ship heaved up. The crash as she grounded flung me against the conning platform.

I was clinging on to the phone wondering what was happening to those poor devils aft and trying to think at the same time. The wind was south or perhaps sou'west; it would be anti-clockwise, whirling round the centre of that air depression and being sucked into it at the same time. I was trying to figure out where the centre would be. If it was north of us . . . But north of us should give us a westerly wind. It depended how much the air currents were being deflected in towards the centre. I was remembering Cliff's message: the Faeroes had reported barometric pressure 968, rising, with winds southerly, force 10. Our barometer was now showing 968. If the storm centre passed to the west of us, then this might be the worst of it. I decided not to go down and fiddle with the glass again.

'We made several yards.' Wentworth's voice was shrill in the phone. 'But the winch is smoking. The brakes. They may burn out any minute now. Keep those engines running for God's sake.'

I glanced at Stratton but I didn't need to ask him. I could feel the vibrations of the screws through my whole body. 'Engines at full astern,' I said. 'Keep winching in.'

I put the phone down and dived across the bridge to yell the information in Stratton's ear. The weight of the wind was something solid now. I felt the words sucked out of my mouth and blown away into the night. 'Christ! If the winch packs up now . . . Stay on the phone, will you.' Stratton's face was white. I was lip-reading rather than hearing the words. Below him white water glistened, a seething welter of surf sucking back along the ship's side. A shaggy comber reared in the lights, curled and broke. Spray went whipping past and ectoplasmic chunks of foam suds.

The ship moved. I could feel it, a sixth sense telling me that we were momentarily afloat. And then the shuddering, jarring crash. I was back at the phone and Wentworth's voice was yelling in my ears—something about the winch gears. But his voice abruptly ceased before I could get what it was he was trying to tell me. And then Stratton grabbed the phone from my hand. 'Oil,' he said. 'There's an oil slick forming.' He pressed the buzzer, the phone to his ear. 'Hullo. Hullo there. Number One, Wentworth.' He looked at me, his face frozen. 'No answer.' There was a shudder, a soundless scraping and grating that I couldn't hear but felt through the soles of my feet. And then it was gone and I felt the bows lift for the first time. 'Winch in. Winch in.' Stratton's voice was yelling into the phone as a wave lifted the stern, running buoyant under the ship. There was no

201

grounding thud this time as we sank into the trough and glancing for'ard I saw the bows riding high, rearing to the break of the wave. 'Wentworth. Do you hear me? Winch in. Wentworth.' His hand fell slack to his side, still holding the phone. 'There's no answer,' he said. His face was crusted with salt, a drop of moisture at the end of his slightly upturned nose. His eyes looked bleak.

'You look after the ship,' I told him. 'I'll go aft and see what's happened.'

He nodded and I went out on to the flag deck. Clear of the bridge the full weight of the wind hit me. It was less than half an hour since I'd stood there and felt that first blast of the storm wind in my face. Now, what a difference! I had to fight my way aft, clinging to the deck rail, my eyes blinded by salt spray, the wind driving the breath back into my lungs. Fifty-sixty knots—you can't judge wind speeds when they reach storm force and over. It shook me to think that this perhaps was only the beginning. But we'd be round Malesgair then, sheltered under its lee—I hoped. By God, I hoped as I fought my way to the after-rail and clung there, looking down to the tiny stern platform with its spare anchor and its winch gear.

Wentworth was there. He was bending over the winch. His sou'wester had gone and his fair hair was plastered to his head. He looked drowned and so did the two men with him. They were all of them bent over the winch and the drum was stationary. A broken wave-top streaming spray like smoke from its crest reared up in the lights, a shaggy, wind-blown monster, all white teeth as it slammed rolling against the stern. It buried everything, a welter of foam that subsided to the lift of the ship, water cascading over the sides, the men still gripping the winch like rocks awash. I yelled to Wentworth, but my shout was blown back into my mouth and he didn't hear me. The winch remained motionless and the hawser, running through two steel pulleys and out over the stern, just hung there, limp.

I turned and went like a leaf blown by the wind back to the open bridge and Stratton standing there, the phone in his hand and the engines still pounding at full astern. I grabbed his arm. 'The hawser,' I yelled. 'You'll overrun the hawser.'

He nodded, calm now and in full control of himself. 'Gears jammed. I've told him to cut it.' And then he said something about taking her out on radar as he put the phone down and went quickly, like a crab, down the steel ladder to the wheelhouse. It was a relief just to be out of the wind. The radar was switched on, set to the three-mile range. The screen showed us half surrounded by the mass of Laerg, the shore still very close. And when he did try to turn—what then? Broadside to that sea with the weight of the wind heeling her over, anything might happen.

But that was something else. What worried me was the thought of that hawser. I could see it clear in my mind, a great loop of wire running from the stern down through the heaving waters and under the whole length of the ship to the anchor dug into the sea bed somewhere beyond our bows now. It had only to touch one of the propeller blades—it would strip the propeller then or else it would warp. And that wasn't the only hazard. Driving astern like this, backing into sea and wind, it might come taut at any moment. Then if it were fractionally off-centre our stern would swing. Or was that what Stratton was trying to do? I glanced quickly at his face. It was quite blank, his whole mind given to the ship as he stood just behind the helmsman, watching the compass and at the same time keeping an eye on the radar.

I thought I felt a jerk, a sort of shudder. 'Stop port. Half ahead port.'

'Port engine stopped. Port engine half ahead, sir.'

Slowly the bulk of Laerg shifted its position on the radar screen. The bows were moving to starboard, swung by the screws and the pull of the anchor against the stern. The movement slowed. A wave crashed breaking against the starboard side. The ship rolled. 'Helm hard a'starboard. Stop starboard engine. Half ahead together.'

The beat changed. The ship shuddered as she rolled. The outline on the radar screen resumed its circling anti-clockwise movement. The bows were coming round again. A big sea crashed inboard, the tank deck awash. The ship reeled, heeling over so steeply that Pinney was flung across the wheelhouse. Slowly she righted, to be knocked down again and yet again, the weight of the wind holding her pinned at an angle, driving her shorewards. But the bows kept on swinging, kept on coming round. The helmsman's voice pipe whistled.

'Number One reporting anchor hawser cut,' he said.

Stratton nodded.

'He's asking permission to come for'ard.'

'Yes. Report to me in the wheelhouse.' Stratton's whole mind was fixed on the radar. Now the bulk of Laerg was on the left-hand side of the screen, at about eight o'clock. 'Full ahead both engines.' The telegraph rang. The shuddering was replaced by a steadier beat.

And the helmsman confirmed—'Both at full ahead, sir.'

'Helm amidships.'

'Midships.'

We were round with Laerg at the bottom of the radar screen, the two sheltering arms running up each side, and the top all blank— the open sea for which we were headed. Steaming into it, we felt the full force of the wind now. It came in great battering gusts that shook the wheelhouse. Spray beat against the steel plates, solid as shot, and the bows reared crazily, twisting as though in agony, the steel creaking and groaning. And when they plunged the lights showed water pouring green over the sides, the tank deck filled like a swimming pool.

'Half ahead together. Ten-fifty revolutions.'

God knows what it was blowing. And it had come up so fast. I'd never known anything like this—so sudden, so violent. The seas were shaggy hills, their tops beaten flat, yet still they contrived to curve and break as they found the shallower water of the bay. They showed us a blur beyond the bows in moments when the wind whipped the porthole glass clean as polished crystal. The barometer at 965 was still falling. Hundreds of tons of water sloshed around in the tank deck and the ship was sluggish like an overladen barge.

Wentworth staggered in. He had a jagged cut above his right eye; blood on his face and on his hands, bright crimson in the lights. Beads of water stood on his oilskins, giving them a mottled effect. 'The tiller flat,' he said.

Stratton glanced at him. 'That cut—you all right?'

Wentworth dabbed it with his hand, staring at the blood as though he hadn't realised he was bleeding. 'Nothing much. Fenwick has hurt his arm.' And he added, 'They didn't secure the latch. There's a lot of water . . .'

'What hatch?'

'The tiller flat.'

But Stratton had other things to worry

about. The helmsman had been caught off balance, the wheel spinning. A figure moved and caught the spokes. 'All right, sir. I've got her.' It was the Quartermaster. A sea broke slamming on the starboard bow, but she was coming back again, swinging her bows back into the waves. God, what a sea! And I heard Stratton say, 'What's that on your oilskins—oil? It looks like oil.'

'There was a lot of it in the sea,' Wentworth answered. 'Every time a wave broke . . .'

But Stratton had pushed past me and was staring alternately at the radar screen and out through the porthole.

It was just on five-thirty then and dawn had come; a cold, grey glimmer in the murk.

Darkness would have been preferable. I would rather not have seen that storm. It was enough to hear it, to feel it in the tortured motion of the ship. The picture then was imaginary, and imagination, lacking a basis of experience, fell short of actuality. But dawn added sight to the other senses and the full majesty of the appalling chaos that surrounded us was revealed.

I had seen pictures of storms where sea and rock seemed so exaggerated that not even artistic licence could justify such violent, fantastic use of paint. But no picture I had ever seen measured up to the reality of that morning. Fortunately, the full realisation of what we faced came gradually—a slow exposure taking shape, the creeping dawn imprinting it on the retina of our eyes like a developing agent working on a black and white print. There was no colour; just black through all shadows of grey to white, the white predominating, all the surface of the sea streaked with it. The waves, like heaped-up ranges, were beaten down at the top and streaming spray—not smoking as in an ordinary gale, but the water whipped from their shaggy crests in flat, horizontal sheets, thin layers like razor blades cutting down-wind with indescribable force. Above these layers foam flew thick as snow, lifted from the seething tops of the broken waves and flung pell-mell through the air, flakes as big as gulls, dirty white against the uniform grey of the overcast.

Close on the starboard bow the skerry rocks of Sgeir Mhor lifted grey molars streaming water, the waves exploding against them in plumes of white like an endless succession of depth charges. And beyond Sgeir Mhor, running away to our right, the sheer cliffs of Keava were a black wall disappearing into a tearing wrack of cloud, the whole base of this rampart cascading white as wave after wave attacked and then receded to meet the next and smash it to pieces, heaping masses of water hundreds of feet into the air. Not Milton even, describing Hell, has matched in words the frightful, chaotic spectacle my eyes recorded in the dawn; the Atlantic in the full fury of a storm that had lifted the wind right to the top of the Beaufort scale.

That the landing craft wasn't immediately overwhelmed was due to the almost unbelievable velocity of the wind. The waves were torn to shreds as they broke so that their force was dissipated, their height diminished. The odd thing was I felt no fear. I remember glancing at Stratton, surprised to find his face calm, almost relaxed. His eyes met mine for an instant, cool and steady. No fear there either. Fear would come later no doubt, as a reaction when the danger had lessened. Fear requires time to infect the system, and we had had no time; it had come upon us too quickly with too much to do. And panic is an instantaneous thing, a nerve storm. Men carrying out the duties for which they have been trained, straining every nerve to meet the situation, their minds entirely concentrated on the work in hand, are seldom liable to panic.

'Have the men put their life-jackets on.' Stratton's voice was barely audible as he shouted the order to Wentworth. 'Everyone. Understand?' He turned to Pinney. 'Go with him. See that every one of your men has his life-jacket on.'

'What about the tiller flat?' Wentworth asked.

'How much water got in?'

'I don't know. It was dark down there and I couldn't see. Quite a bit, I think.'

'Did you fix the hatch?'

'Yes. But it may have got in through the rudder stock housings. It may still be . . .'

'All right, Number One. I'll have a word with Stevens. His engineers will get it pumped out.' He picked up the engine-room phone. 'And have that cut seen to.'

It was after Wentworth had left that I found my bowels reacting and felt that sick void in my guts that is the beginning of fear. If I'd been in control I wouldn't have noticed it. I'd have been too busy. But I was a spectator and what I saw both on the radar screen and through the porthole was the tip of Sgeir Mhor coming closer, a gap-toothed rock half awash and the wicked white of the seas breaking across it. Stratton was keeping the bows head-on to the waves. He had no choice. To sheer away in that sea was impossible—the head of the ship would have been flung sideways by the combined thrust of wind and water and she'd have broached-to and been rolled over. But bows-on we were headed about one-ninety degrees, sometimes nearer two hundred, for the wind was just west of south. We were slowly being forced towards the rocks that formed the western arm of Shelter Bay. Some time back Stratton had realised the danger and had ordered full ahead on both engines, but even at full ahead our progress was painfully slow, the ship labouring to make up against the almost solid wall of the elements. Yard by yard we closed Sgeir Mhor and we kept on closing it. There was no shelter behind those rocks—not enough in that force of wind; our only hope was the open sea beyond.

It was six-ten by the clock above the chart table when we came abreast of Sgeir Mhor and for a full six minutes we were butting our bows into a welter of foaming surf with the last rock showing naked in the backwash of each trough less than a hundred yards on our starboard side. Every moment I expected to feel the rending of her bottom plates as some submerged rock cut into her like a knife gutting a fish. But the echo-sounder clicking merrily away recorded nothing less than 40 fathoms, and at six-sixteen we were clear, clawing our way seaward out of reach, I thought, at last.

North-westward of us now the sheer rock coast of Laerg was opening up, a rampart wall cascading water, its top vanishing into swirling masses of cloud. We were in deeper water then and Stratton was on the phone to the engine-room again, cutting the revolutions until the ship was stationary, just holding her own against the wind. 'If the old girl can just stay in one piece,' he yelled in my ear. I didn't need to be told what he planned to do; it was what I would have done in his shoes. He was reckoning that the storm centre would pass right over us and he was going to butt the wind until it did. Nothing else he could do, for he couldn't turn. When we were into the eye of the storm there would be a period of calm. He'd get the ship round then and tuck himself tight under those towering cliffs. We'd be all right then. As the centre passed, the wind would swing round into the east or northeast. We'd be under the lee of Laerg then. But how long before that happened—an hour, two hours? Out here in the deepest water the waves no longer built up in range upon range of moving hills; they lay flat, cowed by the wind which seemed to be scooping the whole surface of the sea into the air. The noise was shattering, spray hitting the wheelhouse in solid sheets. Visibility was nil, except for brief glimpses of the chaos when a gust died. And then a squall blotting everything out and the Quartermaster quietly announcing that the wind had caught her and she wasn't answering.

'Full astern starboard.'

The ring of the telegraph, faint and insubstantial, the judder of the screws, and the bows steadying. She'd have come back into the wind then, but a sea caught her and she heeled over. If we'd been in the shallow waters of the bay, she'd have rolled right over, but out here it was the wind more than the waves that menaced us; it held her canted at a steep angle and the man who brought Stratton his life-jacket had to crawl on his hands and knees. Stratton tossed it into the corner by the chart table. 'Better get yours, too,' he said to me, 'just in case.' The bows were coming round now, sluggishly. 'Full ahead both. Starboard wheel.' And then she was round with her blunt nose bucking the seas, her screws racing as they were lifted clear in the troughs.

Even head-to-wind again it was a struggle to get down the alleyway to my quarters. McDermott lay on the floor. He had tied himself with a blanket to the bunk support and he'd been sick again, all over himself and the floor. The place was a shambles. 'Was that the power steering packed in?' Wentworth asked me. He was clinging to the desk whilst Fairweather tried to stitch the cut on his head.

'We were blown off,' I said.

But he didn't seem to take that in. 'I tried to tell Stratton. They forgot to close the hatch. To the tiller flat. You remember? I told him . . .'

I did remember and my first reaction was a mental picture of McGregor's corpse being sloshed around in that small compartment above the rudders. My mind must have been sluggish for it was a moment before I realised what was worrying him. If the electric motors shorted . . . The possibility brought the sweat to my palms, a sting to the armpits that I could have sworn I smelt despite the layers of clothing. And then I remembered that the hatch was closed now and the engineers would have disposed of the water. 'They'll have pumped it out by now,' I said.

He nodded. 'Yes. Yes, of course. I remember now.' He seemed dazed, staring at me wide-eyed. 'But that oil. What do you think it was, Mr Ross?' Staring at me like that, the whites of his eyes beginning to show, I began to wonder.

'What oil?' I said.

'It was all round the stern and every time a sea broke ... Look at my hair.' He leaned his head forward, ignoring the Doc's warning. 'See? It's oil. Diesel oil.'

'Don't worry,' I said. 'Another couple of hours ...' I ducked out of the cabin. I wanted fresh air, the confidence that only men doing something to preserve themselves can inspire. Was Wentworth scared, or was it me? All I knew was that something like a contagious disease had touched me in that sour cabin full of the sick smell of vomit. That oil ... I remembered when he'd first come up to the wheelhouse, how his oilskin had been mottled with it, and Stratton asking about it.

The wheelhouse steadied me. There was Stratton smoking a cigarette, the Quartermaster at the wheel, everything going on as before and the bows headed slap into the wind. The radar screen showed Sgeir Mhor dead astern of us less than a mile away. I dropped my life-jacket beside Stratton's. Should I remind him about the oil, or just forget about it? I decided to keep silent. Nothing to be done about it. What was the point? And yet ... I lit a cigarette and saw my hand was trembling. Hell! 'What's under the tank deck?' I heard myself ask. 'Water and fuel oil, I think you said.'

'Yes, fuel oil.' Stratton's voice had an edge to it and he added, 'Something on your mind?' He was staring at me hard and I realised suddenly that he knew—knew we'd damaged the bottom plates getting off.

'No, nothing,' I said, and I left it at that, happier now that the knowledge was shared. Perhaps he was, too, for he smiled. 'Keep your fingers crossed,' he said.

But keeping my fingers crossed doesn't mend steel plates, and it doesn't prevent fuel oil seeping out through the cracks and rents in those battered plates. I stayed with him until I'd finished my cigarette and then I made some excuse and slipped out. There was only one way of finding out. I went down the companion ladder to the deck below, unclamped the steel door leading to the side deck and, leaning out, grabbed hold of the rail. I was just in time, for the force of the wind swept my legs from under me. I was left clinging there, my body flattened along the deck and my lungs filled to bursting with the pressure of air forcing its way into mouth and nostrils.

The power of that wind was demoniac. It forced my eyeballs back against the membranes with a stabbing pain. It tore at my hair and clothing. And the sheet spray flung against my face had the cutting power of sand. Raw and shaken I held on till there was a slight lull, and then I hurled myself back through the door. It took me quite a time to get it shut and the clamps in place. I was wet to the skin and panting with the effort, but I now knew—I had seen the surface of the water sheened with a film of oil, the surface spray held static by the viscosity of it.

When I got back to the wheelhouse Wentworth was there, clinging to the chart table, fresh plaster covering the cut on his forehead. Stratton glanced at me, a slight lift to his brows as he saw the state of my clothes. He knew where I'd been so I just gave a slight confirmatory nod. 'Bad?' he asked.

'Impossible to tell.'

He nodded.

'What's bad?' Wentworth asked. 'Where've you been?' His voice was slightly slurred and the whites of his eyes... I didn't like that tendency for the whites to show.

'I've just been sick,' I said.

He accepted that. 'So've I.' He said it quite cheerfully, the beginning of a smile lighting up his face. He couldn't have been more than twenty-two; much too young, I thought, to face a storm like this. It was the sort of storm you only expect to face once in a lifetime, and then only if you've been all your life at sea. I wondered whether I could paint it. Could any artist get it down on canvas—this soul-destroying, brain-numbing battering, this violence that went beyond the limits of experience?'

216

And the fact that we existed, that the ship still held her blunt bows head-to-wind, battling against the driving planes of water, made it somehow marvellous, the little oasis of the wheelhouse a miracle. In the midst of chaos, here within the tight frame of fragile steel walls, there was the reassurance of familiar things—the radar, the charts, the burly Quartermaster quite unperturbed, orders being given, messages coming in—particularly the messages. L4400 signalling that she was under the lee of Malesgair and riding it out, safe for the moment at any rate. Coastal Command asking us whether we needed assistance, relaying to us the information that the Admiralty tug was now waiting instructions in Lochmaddy. First Braddock and then Standing asking for news of us—how many men had we embarked, what stores and equipment, obviously quite oblivious of the magnitude of the storm. The last contact with Cliff before he went on duty had given the wind locally as south, approximately fifty knots. Fifty knots, when out here it was blowing eighty, ninety, a hundred—God knows what force it was. And at six forty-five the shipping forecast: *A local depression of great intensity may affect parts of sea areas Faeroes, Hebrides ... Winds cyclonic and temporarily reaching hurricane force ...* I think that was the most extraordinary part of it—the sense of still being own world was being blown to bits by the wind, the whole surface of the sea apparently disintegrating and being forced up into the atmosphere.

And then suddenly our little oasis of ordered security crashed about our ears. The engine-room phone had probably been buzzing for some time. But nobody had heard it. The din was too great. It was the ring of the telegraph that informed us and the Quartermaster's voice: 'Port engines losing power, sir.' The spokes of the wheel were turning under his hand, turning until he had full starboard helm on. Again he reached for the brass handle of the port telegraph, gave it two sharp rings and jammed it back at full ahead. Stratton leapt to the engine-room telephone. 'It's all right now, sir.' The Quartermaster was bringing the wheel back amidships. But I was watching Stratton. His face was white, his body rigid. '... Sea water, you say? ... Yes, I knew about the leak ... Well, can't you drain it off? ... I see. Well, that must have happened when we were broadside on in the bay ... All right, Stevens. Do what you can ... Yes, we'll try. But we can't hold her any steadier. There's quite a sea ... Well, give me warning when the other engines start cutting out.' He put the phone back on its hook. His face looked bleak.

'What is it?' Wentworth demanded. 'What's happened?'

'Main tank's leaking and we've been

pumping sea water into the ready-use tank. Only the port engine's affected so far, but ...' He turned to the Quartermaster. 'Think you can hold her on starboard engines alone?'

'I'll try, sir.'

The Cox'n came in then. His flat, broad face was smeared with oil. 'Port outer engine starting to cut out, sir. Chief asked me to tell you he's afraid ... Something in Stratton's face stopped the breathless rush of his words. In a quieter voice he added, 'I was going round the mess decks. I could feel there was something wrong so I slipped down to the engine-room. Chief said he couldn't get you on the phone.'

'Thank you, Cox'n. I've just had a word with him. The starboard engines are all right, I gather?'

'For the moment, sir. But he's afraid the ready-use tank may be ...'

'I've had his report on that.' Stratton's voice, quiet and controlled, stilled the suggestion of panic that had hung for a moment over the wheelhouse.

'There's another thing, sir. The tiller flat. Bilge pumps not working. Chief think's they're choked. Anyway, there's a lot of water ...'

'All right, Cox'n. Have some men closed up on the tiller flat, will you—just in case.'

'Very good, sir.' And as he went out Wentworth, close at my side, said, 'I had a feeling about the tiller flat. Ever since I found the hatch unfastened. We must have taken a

219

hell of a lot of water through it when we were getting off the beach.' His manner was quite different now, almost calm, as though he'd braced himself against the urgency of the situation. He reached for the log book and began entering it up.

Everything normal again, the ship headed into the wind, the beat of the engines steady under our feet. But even with both engines at full ahead she was making little or no headway against the moving masses of air and water that seemed fused into a solid impenetrable wall. The shape of Laerg on the radar screen came and went, fuzzed by the thickness of the atmosphere. The Quartermaster shifted his stance at the wheel, gripped the spokes tighter. And in the same instant I felt it through the soles of my feet, a change of beat, a raggedness. The wheel spun. Full starboard helm and the beat steadier again, but not so strong. 'Port engines both stopped, sir.'

Stratton was already at the phone. He held it to his ear, waiting. 'Good . . . Well, if you can drain off all the sea water . . . Yes, we'll try and hold her bows-on . . . All right. Now what about the tiller flat? . . . You've got a man working on it? Fine . . . Yes, we'll just have to hope for the best.' He put the phone down, glanced at the radar screen and then at me. His lips moved stiffly in a smile. 'Hell of a time you picked to come for a sail with us.' He glanced at the helm. The wheel was amidships again.

'Answering all right, Quartermaster?' he asked.

'Pretty fair, sir.'

But we weren't making headway any longer and Sgeir Mhor a bare mile away, directly down-wind of us. Stratton produced his packet of cigarettes and we stood there, braced against the violence of the movement, smoking and watching the radar screen. And then, suddenly, the Quartermaster's voice announcing that the helm had gone dead. 'Full starboard helm and not answering, sir.'

Wentworth was already at one of the phones. 'Cox'n reports steering motors shorted. There's a lot of water . . .'

'Emergency steering.' Stratton rapped the order out and I saw the Quartermaster lean down and throw across a lever at the base of the steering pedestal.

A sea broke thundering inboard. A solid sheet of spray crashed against the wheelhouse. And as the porthole cleared I saw the bows thrown off and sagging away to leeward. It had taken a bare ten seconds to engage the hand steering, but in those ten seconds the weight of sea and wind combined had caught hold of the bows and flung them off to port.

'Emergency steering not answering, sir.'

The ship staggered to another blow and began to heel as the wind caught her on the starboard bow. She was starting to broach-to. And the Quartermaster's voice again, solid and unemotional: 'Hand steering's all right, sir. But not enough power on the engines.'

Only two engines out of four and the bows swinging fast now. Stratton was at the engine-room phone, but I could see by his face that no one was answering. 'Keep your helm hard a'starboard. You may be able to bring her up in a lull.'

But there wasn't a lull. The ship heeled further and further, and as she came broadside-on to wind and sea we were spilled like cattle down the sloping deck to fetch up half-lying along the port wall of the wheelhouse. 'Any chance,' I gasped, 'of getting the other engines going?' And Stratton looked at me, the sweat shining under the stubble of his beard: 'How can they possibly—do anything—down there?' I realised then what it must be like in the engine-room, cooped up with that mass of machinery, hot oil spilling and their cased-in world turning on its side. 'We're in God's hands now,' he breathed. And a moment later, as though God himself had heard and was denying us even that faint hope, I felt the beat of those two remaining engines stagger, felt it through my whole body as I lay against the sloped steel of the wall.

I have said that panic is a nerve storm, an instinctive, uncontrollable reaction of the nervous system. I had experienced fear before, but not panic. Now, with the pulse of the engines dying, something quite uncontrollable leapt in my throat, my limbs seemed to dissolve and my whole body froze with apprehension. My mouth opened to scream a warning, but no sound came: and then, like a man fighting to stay sober after too much drink, I managed to get a grip of myself. It was a conscious effort of will and I had only just succeeded when the beat of the engines ceased altogether and I felt the ship dead under me. A glance at the radar showed the screen blank, half white, half black, as the sweep light continued to circle as if nothing had happened. We were heeled so far over that all the radar recorded was the sea below us, the sky above.

It was only the fact that we had such a weight of water on board that saved us. If the ship had been riding high, fully buoyant, she'd have turned right over. It was that and the terrific weight of the wind that held the seas flat.

The time was seven twenty-eight and Sgeir Mhor much less than a mile away now, the wind blowing us broadside towards it. Engines and steering gone. There was nothing we could do now and I watched as Stratton fought his way up the slope of the deck, struggling to reach the radio shack. In less than two minutes the operator was calling *Mayday*. But what the hell was the good of that? In those two minutes the velocity of the wind had blown us almost quarter of a mile. And it wasn't a case of the ship herself being blown—the whole surface of the sea was moving down-wind, scooped up and flung north-eastward by the pressure of the air.

Mayday, Mayday, Mayday.

I, too, had scrambled up the slope and into the alleyway. Through the open door of the radio shack I saw the operator clinging to his equipment, could hear him saying that word over and over again into the mike. And then he was in contact, reporting to the world at large that our engines had packed up and we were being driven down on to the southernmost tip of Laerg, on to the rocks of Sgeir Mhor.

The nearest ship was L4400, lying hove-to on the far side of Malesgair, a mere four miles away. But it might just as well have been four hundred miles. She didn't dare leave the shelter of those cliffs. In any case, she'd never have reached us in time. Nothing could reach us. It was pointless putting out a distress call. The ship lurched. I slipped from the supporting wall and was pitched into Stratton's cabin. I fetched up on the far side, half-sprawled across his bunk. A girl's face in a cheap frame hung on the wall at a crazy angle—dark hair and bare shoulders, calm eyes in a pretty face. She looked a million miles away. I don't know why, but I suddenly remembered Marjorie Field's eyes, blue and serious, the wide mouth smiling. And other girls in other lands . . . Would it have made any difference to Stratton that he was married? When it comes to the point you're alone, aren't you, just yourself to make the passage across into the unknown?

224

It wasn't easy, sprawled on that bunk, to realise that in a few short minutes this cabin would be a shattered piece of wreckage tossed in the surf of breaking waves. I closed my eyes wearily. I could hear the wind and the sea, but the full blast of it was muffled, and I couldn't see it—that was the point. It made it difficult to visualise the end; flesh torn to pieces on the jagged rocks, the suffocation of drowning. And yet I knew that was the reality; disembowelment perhaps or going out quickly with the skull smashed to pulp.

Hell! Lie here like a rat in a trap, that was no way to go. I forced myself to my feet, hauled my body up into the alleyway crowded now with men. They lay along the wall, big-chested with their life jackets, their faces white. But no panic, just leaning there, waiting. It was all very ordinary, this moment of disaster. No orders, nobody screaming that they didn't want to die. And then it came to me that all these men saw were the steel walls of the ship. They were wrapped in ignorance. They hadn't seen the storm or the rocks. Exhausted, their senses dulled with sea-sickness, they waited for orders that would never come.

When we struck, the ship would roll over. That's what I figured, anyway. There was only one place to be then—out in the open. In the open there was just a chance. Wentworth had seen that, too. With two of the crew he was struggling to force the door to the deck open. I moved to help him, others with me, and under our combined efforts it fell back with a crash, and a blast of salt air, thick with spray, hit us. The Quartermaster was the first through. 'You next.' Wentworth pushed me through, calling to the men behind him.

Out on the side deck I saw at a glance that we were only just in time. Sgeir Mhor was very close now; grey heaps of rock with the sea slamming against them. Stratton was climbing out of the wheelhouse, the log book clutched in his hand. I shouted to him, and then I went down the ladder to the main deck, my body flattened against it by the wind. It was awkward going down that ladder, my body clumsy in the bulk of my life-jacket. I wondered when I'd put it on. I couldn't remember doing so. The Quartermaster followed me. 'Out to the bows,' he yelled in my ear, and hand over hand, clinging to the rail, we worked our way along the side of the ship. Clear of the bridge housing there would be nothing to fall on us. A big sea struck the ship and burst right over us. It tore one man from the rail and I saw him sail through the air as though he were a gull. And then we went on, working our way out above the tank deck. Only two men followed us. The rest clung in a huddle against the bridge.

Another sea and then another; two in quick succession and all the breath knocked out of me. I remember clinging there, gasping for air. I was about halfway along the ship. I can see

226

her still, lying right over with water streaming from her decks, the sea roaring in the tilted tank hold and all her port side submerged. And broadside to her canted hull, Sgeir Mhor looming jagged and black and wet, an island of broken rock in a sea of foam with the waves breaking, curved green backs that smoked spray and crashed like gunfire exploding salt water fragments high into the air.

And then she struck. It was a light blow, a mere slap, but deep down she shuddered. Another wave lifted her. She tilted, port-side buried in foam, and Sgeir Mhor rushed towards us, lifted skywards, towering black.

I don't remember much after that—the detail is blurred in my mind. She hit with a bone-shaking impact, rolled and butted her mast against vertical rock. Like a lance it broke. Half the bridge housing was concertinaed, men flung to the waves. And then from where I clung I was looking down, not on water, but on bare rock—a spine running out like the back of a dinosaur. It split the ship across the middle; a hacksaw cutting metal couldn't have done it neater. A gap opened within feet of me, widening rapidly and separating us from all the after part of the ship. Rocks whirled by. White water opened up. For a moment we hung in the break of the waves, grating on half-submerged rocks. I thought that was the end, for the bows were smashing themselves to pieces, the steel plates beaten into fantastic shapes. But then

227

the grating and the pounding ceased. We were clear—clear of the submerged rocks, clear of the tip of Sgeir Mhor. We were in open water, lying right over, half-submerged, but still afloat. Buoyed up by the air trapped behind the bulkheads in her sides, she was being driven across Shelter Bay, buried deep in a boiling scum of foam and spray. I didn't think of this as the end, not consciously. My brain, my body, the whole physical entity that was me, was too concentrated on the struggle to cling on. And yet something else that was also me seemed to detach himself from the rest, so that I have a picture that is still clear in my mind of my body, bulky in clothes and life jacket, lying drowned in a turmoil of broken water, sprawled against the steel bulwarks, and of the front half of the shattered ship rolling like a log, with the sea pouring over it.

People came and went in my mind, faces I had known, the brief ephemeral contacts of my life, giving me temporary companionship at the moment of death. And then we grounded in the shallows east of the camp, not far from the ruined Factor's House. But by then I was half-drowned, too dazed to care, mind and body beaten beyond desire for life. I just clung on to the bulwark because that was what I had been doing all the time. There was no instinct of self-preservation about it. My hands seemed locked on the cold, wet steel.

It was a long time before I realised that the

wind had died away; probably because the seas, no longer flattened by its weight, were bigger then. The remains of the bows lay just where the waves were breaking. They beat upon the hollow bottom like giant fists hammering at a steel drum. Boom ... Boom ... Boom—and the roar of the surf. Fifty thousand express trains in the confines of a tunnel couldn't have made so great a noise.

And then that, too, began to lessen. My senses struggled back to life. The wind had gone round. That was my first conscious thought. And when I opened my eyes it was to a lurid sun glow, an orange, near-scarlet gash, like the raw slash of a wound, low down behind Sgeir Mhor. The toppling waves stood etched in chaos against it and all the cloud above me was a smoke-black pall of unbelievable density. There was no daylight on the shore of Shelter Bay, no real daylight; only darkness lit by that unearthly glow. The crofts of the Old Village, the roofless church, the cleits dotting the slopes of Tarsaval high above me—none of it was real. The light, the scene, the crazy, beat-up sea—it was all weird, a demon world.

So my mind saw it, and myself a sodden piece of flotsam washed up on that shore, too battered and exhausted to realise I was alive. That knowledge came with the sight of a fellow creature moving slowly like a spider, feeling his way down the jagged edges of what had been the tank deck.

I watched him fall into the backwash of a wave, beating at the surf with his arms. I closed my eyes, and when I looked again, he was ashore, lying spread-eagled among the boulders.

That was when the instinct for self-preservation stirred in me at last.

I moved then, wearily, each movement a conscious effort, a desperate aching struggle—down the jagged edges of deck plates twisted like tin-foil, down into the surf, falling into it as the other had done and fighting my way ashore, half-drowned, to lie panting and exhausted on the beach beside him.

It wasn't the Quartermaster; I don't know what had happened to him. This was a small man with a sandy moustache and tiny, frightened eyes that stared at me wildly. He'd broken his arm and every time he moved he screamed, a febrile rabbit sound that lost itself in the wind's howl. There was blood on his hair. Blood, too, on the stones where I lay, a thin bright trickle of my own blood, from a scalp wound.

'Shut up,' I said as he screamed again. 'You're alive. What more do you want?' I was thinking of all the others, the picture of the ship crushed against the rocks still vivid in my mind.

My watch had gone, torn from my wrist. How long had it been? I didn't know. Leaning up on one elbow I stared out across the bay.

The orange glow had vanished and Sgeir Mhor was a shadowy outline, a grey blur masked by a rain squall. I forced myself to my feet and was immediately knocked down, beaten flat by a violent down-draught. That was when I realised the wind had gone right round. It was blowing from the other side of the island now, whipping across the Saddle between Malesgair and Tarsaval and down into Shelter Bay, cutting great swathes across it, the water boiling in its wake, a flattened, seething cauldron.

I made the grass above the beach, half crawling, and staggered past the Factor's House, up towards the Old Village and the camp. Daylight was a mockery, drab as a witch, and the wind screamed hell out of the confused masses of cloud that billowed above my head. And when I finally reached the camp I barely recognised it, the whole place laid waste and everything weighing less than a ton whirled inland and scattered across the slopes of Tarsaval. And down on the beach, the trailers we'd off-loaded in haste all gone, the trucks, too—only the bulldozer remained lying in the surf like a half-submerged rock. Wreckage was everywhere. The roof of one of the huts was gone, blown clean away, the walls sagging outwards, and where the latrines had been there was nothing but a row of closets standing bare like porcelain pots.

Pinney's hut was still intact. I turned the handle and the wind flung the door open with a

231

crash, the walls shaking to the blast. It took the last of my strength to get it shut and in the relative peace of the hut's interior I collapsed on to the nearest bed.

How long I lay there I do not know. Time is relative, a mental calculation that measures activity. I was inactive then, my brain numbed, my mind hardly functioning. It might have been only a minute. It might have been an hour, two hours. I didn't sleep. I'm certain of that. I was conscious all the time of the shaking of the hut, of the battering, ceaseless noise of the wind; conscious, too, that there was something I had to do, some urgent intention that had forced me to struggle up from the beach. I dragged myself to my feet, staggering vaguely through the hut until I came to the radio, drawn to it by some action of my subconscious.

I realised then why I'd made the effort. The outside world. Somebody must be told. Help alerted. I slumped into the operator's chair, wondering whether there was any point, still that picture in my mind of the bridge crushed against sheer rock and the waves pounding. Could any of the crew have survived, any of those men huddled like sheep awaiting slaughter in the narrow alleyway out of which I'd clawed my way? But the wind had changed and they'd be under the lee. There was just that chance and I reached out my hand, switching on the set. I didn't touch the tuning. I just sat there waiting for the hum that would tell me the set had warmed up. But nothing happened. It was dead and it took time for my brain to work that out—the generator silent and no current coming through. There were emergency batteries below the table and by following the cables back I was able to cut them in.

The set came alive then and a voice answered almost immediately. It was thin and faint. *'We've been calling and calling. If you're still on Laerg why didn't you answer before?'* He didn't give me a chance to explain. *'I've got Glasgow on the line for you. They've found Mrs McGregor. Hold on.'* There was a click and then silence, and I sat there, helpless, the salt taste of sea water on my mouth. Fifty men battered to pieces on the rocks of Sgeir Mhor and they had to fling Mrs McGregor at me. Why couldn't they have waited for me to tell them what had happened? *'You're through.'* The police first, and then a woman's voice, soft and very Scots, asking for news of her son. I felt almost sick, remembering what had happened, the tiller flat flooded and the poor devil's body tombed up there. 'I'm sorry, Mrs McGregor. I can't tell you anything yet.' And I cut her off, overcome by nausea, the sweat out all over me and my head reeling.

When I got them again, my brother was there. Recognising his voice I felt a flood of instant relief. 'Iain. Iain, thank God!' I was back on Ardnamurchan, crying to my elder brother for help—a rock to cling to in moments of desperation.

But this was no rock. This was a man as sick and frightened as myself. *'Major Braddock here.'* His voice, strained and uneasy, had the snap of panic in it. 'Iain,' I cried again. 'For God's sake. It's Donald.' But the appeal was wasted and his voice when it came was harsh and grating. *'Braddock here. Who's that? What's happened?'*

* * *

The time was then 08.35 and Braddock had been almost six hours in the Movements Office, waiting for news. God knows what he must have been feeling. Flint said he'd paced up and down, hour after hour, grey-faced and silent, whilst the periodic reports came through from our own radio operator and from the man on L4400. Up to the moment when disaster overtook us Movements had a fairly clear picture of what was happening. And then suddenly that Mayday call, and after that silence. 'Get them,' Braddock had shouted at the Signals operator. 'Christ, man! Get them again.' But all the operator could get was L4400 announcing flatly that they were in the storm centre steaming for the shelter of the other side of the island.

'It's Eight-six-one-o I want,' Braddock had almost screamed. 'Get them, man. Keep on

234

trying.'

He'd had far too little sleep that night and the interview he'd had with Standing at two-thirty in the morning cannot have been a pleasant one. Standing had been roused from his bed by a duty driver at twelve-forty, and Ferguson described him as literally shaking with rage when he realised what Braddock had done. The first thing he did was to speak to Stratton on the R/T and then he walked across to the quarters and saw Cliff Morgan. 'White-faced he was, man,' was the way Cliff put it. 'Calling me all sorts of names for interfering. But when I'd explained the situation, he calmed down a bit. He even thanked me. And then he went out, saying it was all Braddock's fault and if anything went wrong he'd get the bloody man slung out of the Service.'

Standing had gone straight to his office and sent for Braddock. There was nobody else present at that meeting so that there is no record of what passed between them. But immediately afterwards Braddock had teleprinted BGS direct, giving his reasons for ordering an immediate evacuation on his own responsibility. And after that he'd remained in the Movements Office waiting for news; and when our Mayday call went out, it was he, not Standing, who had alerted Scottish Command and set the whole emergency machinery in motion. At half past eight he'd walked over to the Met. Office. He was with Cliff Morgan for

235

about ten minutes and it was during those ten minutes that I called Base. A relief operator had just taken over, which was why I was given the Glasgow call instead of being put straight through either to Braddock at the Met. Office or Standing, who was waiting alone in his office.

Probably if I'd got Standing his reaction would have been as slow as my brother's, for neither of them could have any idea of the appalling ferocity of that storm or the magnitude of the disaster. He didn't seem able to understand at first. *'You and one other chap . . . Is that all? Are you certain?'*

I wasn't certain of anything except the memory of the ship on her beam ends and the waves driving her against the rocks. 'If you'd seen the seas . . . It was Sgeir Mhor she hit.'

'Jesus Christ, Donald?' It was the first time he'd used my name and it made a deep impression. *'Jesus Christ! There must be others. There've got to be others.'*

But I didn't think there could be then. 'I've told you, the whole bridge deck was concertinaed in a matter of seconds. They can't possibly . . .'

'Well, have a look. Go and find out.'

'The wind,' I said wearily. 'Don't you realise? You can't stand.'

'Then crawl, laddie—crawl. I must know. I must be certain. Surely to God it can't be as bad as you say.' He was almost screaming at me.

And then his voice dropped abruptly to a wheedling tone. *'For my sake, laddie—please. Find out whether there are any other survivors.'*

His voice. It was so strange—it was Iain's voice now, my own brother's, and the accent Scots. The years fell away . . . 'All right, Iain. I'll try.' It was Mavis all over again—Mavis and all the other times. 'I'll try,' I said again and switched the set off, going down the hut and out into a blast that whipped the door from my hand and knocked me to the ground.

I met the other fellow coming up from the beach, crawling on his hands and knees and crying with the pain of his broken arm. He called to me, but I heard no sound, only his mouth wide open and his good arm pointing seaward. But there was nothing there, nothing but the seething waters of the bay churned by the wind; all the rest was blotted out by rain and Sgeir Mhor a vague blur. 'What is it?' I yelled in his ear and I almost fell on top of him as the wind came down, a solid, breath-taking wall of air.

'The rocks, sir. Sgeir Mhor. I thought I saw . . .' I lost the rest. It was almost dark, a grey gloom with the clouds racing, and so low I could almost have reached up and touched them.

'Saw what?' I shouted. 'What did you think you saw?'

'It was clear for a moment, and there were figures—men. I could have sworn . . .' But he

237

wasn't certain. You couldn't be certain of anything in those conditions. And your eyes played tricks.

I lay there beside him till the rain squall passed. But even then I couldn't see what he still swore he'd seen. Cloud, forced low by the down-draughts, obscured all the upper half of Sgeir Mhor. There was only one thing to do. I told him to go to the hut, and then I started out along the beach road alone. But it was impossible. The weight of the wind was too great. It caught me as I was crossing the Bailey bridge that spanned the burn and it threw me against the girders as though I were a piece of paper. The sheer weight of it was fantastic. If it hadn't been for the girders I think I should have been whirled into the air and flung into the bay. I turned back then, and when I reached the hut I collapsed on Pinney's bed and immediately lost consciousness.

How long I was out I don't know. My whole body ached and there was a pain in my side. The cut in my head had opened again and the pillow was dark with blood. Lying there with my eyes open, slowly struggling back to life, I found myself staring at Pinney's locker. Either my eyes didn't focus immediately or else it took a long time for me to realise that a pair of binoculars might save me the long walk out to Keava and up its steep grass slopes. There they were, lying on a shelf, tucked in between some books and an old khaki jersey. It was much lighter in the hut; quite bright, in fact. And the noise of the wind was less.

I picked up the binoculars and staggered stiffly to the door. And when I opened it I was looking out on to a changed world. The clouds, torn to shreds by the wind, were ragged now. And they had lifted so that all the great spine of Keava was visible and I could see the sheer gap that separated it from Sgeir Mhor, could see all the rocks and caves and patches of grass on Sgeir Mhor itself. The air was clear, washed clean by the rain. Only Tarsaval and the very top of Creag Dubh remained shrouded in gloom, the clouds clinging to their drenched slopes, billowing and swirling among the crags. Seaward, shafts of brighter light showed white water tossed in frightful confusion. I slipped into the lee of the hut and with my back braced against its sodden wall, I focused the glasses on Sgeir Mhor.

Seen suddenly at close vision, isolated like that from the rest of the island, it looked like some massive medieval fortress. All it lacked was a drawbridge spanning the narrow gut that separated it from the Butt of Keava. With the change of wind, the seas no longer exploded against it in plumes of white, but the foam of the waves that had wrecked us lay in banks like snow over all the piled-up battlements of rock. In that clean air I could see every detail and nothing moved. The place was dead; just a great heap of rock and not a living thing. How could there be? Like the cliffs of Keava, it had taken the full brunt of the storm.

I lowered the glasses. Just the two of us. All the rest dead; gone, buried, drowned under masses of water, battered to pulp, their bodies for the fish, for the lobsters and crabs that scuttled in the holes and crevices of submarine rock terraces. Stratton, Wentworth, Pinney— all the faces I had known so briefly on board the ship.

Can you will people alive? Was I God-given that I could stand there and pray so desperately, and then on the instant conjure movement? It seemed like that, for I looked again, hoping against hope, and there in the twin circles of magnification something stirred, a man stood for a moment etched against the luminosity of clouds thinning. Or was it my imagination? Flesh and blood amongst that waste of rock. It seemed impossible, and yet one knows the extraordinary indestructibility of the human body. Countless instances leapt to my mind—things I had read about, things I had been told, things I had actually seen during the war; all things that had really happened, and not so much the indestructibility of the human body as the unwillingness, almost the inability of the human spirit to accept defeat. And here, now, I was gazing at the impossible, and it was no figment of the imagination. This, too, was real; there was a man, off the sky-line now and crawling down the rocks, trying to reach sea level, and another following close behind him.

How many were still alive I didn't know. I didn't care. It was enough that there were survivors on Sgeir Mhor, and I rushed back into the hut and switched on the radio. Base answered my call immediately. *'Hold on.'* And then a voice, not my brother's this time, asking urgently for news.

It was Colonel Standing, and when I told him I'd seen two figures moving on Sgeir Mhor, he said, *'Thank God!'* in a voice that was like a beaten man grasping at the faint hope of recovery. *'If there are two, there may be more.'* He wanted me to find out. But two or twenty— what difference did it make? The problem of rescuing them remained the same. Could I launch a boat? That was his first suggestion and I found myself laughing inanely. I was tired. God! I was tired. And he didn't understand. He'd no idea of the weight of wind that had hit the island. 'There are no boats,' I told him. 'And if there were, there's only myself and a chap with a broken arm.' It was like talking to a child. I found I had to explain in simple terms what the storm had been like—all the trailers gone and a heavy thing like the bulldozer sucked into the sea, the camp a wreck and everything movable shattered or whirled away, the slopes of Tarsaval littered with the Army's debris. I described it all to him—the fight seaward, the engines packing up, the way she'd struck Sgeir Mhor and how the bows had

241

stayed afloat and been driven ashore in Shelter Bay. I talked until my voice was hoarse, my mind too tired to think. Finally, I said. 'What we need is men and equipment—a boat with an outboard motor or rocket rescue apparatus to bridge the gut between Keava and Sgeir Mhor. Where's the other LCT? She could come into the bay now the wind is northerly again.'

But L4400 was twenty miles south-west of Laerg, running before a huge sea, her bridge deck stove in and her plates strained, a wreck of a boat that might or might not get back to port. Weather ship *India* had left her station and was steaming to intercept her. The nearest ship was the Naval tug, but still twenty-four hours away in these conditions. Something my grandfather had told us came sluggishly to the surface of my mind, something about landing on Sgeir Mhor, the sheerness of the rocks. 'I don't think a boat would help,' I said. 'The only landing place on Sgeir Mhor is on the seaward side. And that's not possible except in flat calm weather.'

It took time for that to sink in. He didn't want to believe it. How did I know? Was I absolutely certain? Surely there must be rock ledges up which a skilful climber . . . 'Check with my . . . with Major Braddock,' I said. 'Check with him.' This man arguing, questioning. I wished to God he'd get off the line and give me Iain again. Iain would understand. 'I'd like to have a word with Major

242

Braddock.'

'*I'm handling this.*' The voice was curt. '*Major Braddock's caused enough trouble already.*'

'I'd still like to speak to him.'

'*Well, you can't.*'

'Why not?'

A pause. And then: '*Major Braddock is under arrest.*'

God knows what I said then. I think I cursed—but whether I cursed Standing or the circumstances, I don't know. The futility of it! The one man who could help, who had a grasp of the problem, and this stupid fool had had him arrested. 'For God's sake,' I pleaded. 'Give me Braddock. He'll know what to do.' And sharp and high-pitched over the air came his reply—unbelievable in the circumstances. '*You seem to forget, Mr Ross, that I'm the commanding officer here, and I'm perfectly capable of handling the situation.*'

'Then handle it,' I shouted at him, 'and get those men off Sgeir Mhor.' And I switched off, realising that I was too tired now to control my temper. I just sat there then, thinking of Iain. Poor devil! It was bad enough—the loss of life, the shipwreck, but to be under arrest, sitting inactive with no part in the rescue, with nothing to do but mull over in his mind what had happened. Didn't Standing realise? Or was he a sadist? Whichever it was, the effect on Iain would be the same. The bloody, sodding swine, I thought. The cruel, stupid bastard.

243

'Mr Ross! Mr Ross, sir—you're talking to yourself.'

I opened my eyes, conscious of a hand shaking my shoulder. The fellow with the broken arm was standing there, staring at me with a worried frown. He no longer looked frightened. He even had a certain stature standing there proffering me a steaming mug. 'It's only Bovril,' he said. 'But I fort some'ing 'ot after our bathe . . .' He was Cockney. False teeth smiled at me out of a funny little screwed-up face. 'When you drunk it, you better change them clothes. Catch yer deaf if yer don't. Borrow off of Captain Pinney; 'e won't mind.' This little runt of a man trying to mother me and his broken arm still hanging limp. My heart warmed to him. The lights were on and a new sound—the hum of the generator audible between the gusts.

'You've got the lights going.'

He nodded. ''Ad ter—all electric 'ere, yer see. Wiv'at the generator yer can't cook. I got some bangers on and there's bacon and eggs and fried bread. That do yer?' I asked him his name then and he said, 'Alf Cooper. Come from Lunnon.' He grinned. 'Flippin' long way from Bow Bells, ain't I? Fort I 'eard 'em once or twice when we was in the flaming water, an' they weren't playin' 'ymn toons neither.'

As soon as we'd had our meal I set his arm as best I could, and after that I showed him how to work the radio. I felt stronger now and perhaps because of that the wind seemed less appalling as I tried again to get a closer look at Sgeir Mhor. This time I was able to cross the bridge, but in the flat grassland below the old lazy beds the wind caught me and pinned me down. A bird went screaming close over my head. I crawled to the shelter of a cleit and with my back to the ruins of its dry-stone wall, I focused the glasses on Sgeir Mhor.

Visibility was better now. I could see the rocks falling sheer to the turbulence of the sea, the cracks and gullies, and a figure moving like a seal high up on a bare ledge. There were others crouched there, sheltering from the swell that still beat against the farther side, covering the whole mass with spray. I counted five men lying tucked into crevices, the way sheep huddle for protection against the elements.

Five men. Perhaps there were more. I couldn't see. Just five inert bodies and only one of them showing any signs of life, and now he lay still. I started back then, keeping to the edge of the beach which rose steeply and gave me a little shelter. The burn forced me up on to the bridge and as I entered the camp a blast hit me, flung me down, and a piece of corrugated iron went scything through the air just above my head to hit the sea and go skimming across its flattened surface.

Back in the hut I called Base and was immediately put through to Colonel Standing.

CHAPTER FOUR

RESCUE
(October 22–24)

Long before my first contact with Base, before
even our Mayday call had gone out, all Services
had been alerted and the first moves made to
deal with the emergency. Coastal Command at
Ballykelly had flown off a Shackleton to search
for the *Viking Fisher*; the Navy had dispatched
a destroyer from the Gareloch. Weather ship
India had left her station headed for Laerg, a
fishery protection vessel north-west of the
Orkneys had been ordered to make for the
Hebrides at full speed and a fast mine-layer
was getting steam up ready to sail if required.
By nine o'clock the emergency operation was
being concentrated on L4400, then a battered
wreck running before the storm somewhere to
the west of Laerg. The destroyer was ordered
to close her with all possible speed and either
stand by her to take off survivors or to escort
her to Leverburgh or back to the Clyde if she
could make it. A second Shackleton had taken
off from the Coastal Command base in
Northern Ireland with orders to locate her and
circle her until the destroyer arrived or until
relieved by another aircraft.

That was the situation when I contacted
Base with definite news of survivors from the
wreck of L8610. Neither the Shackletons nor

the destroyer could be of any help to the men on Sgeir Mhor. Both the fishery protection vessel and the mine-layers were too far away to be effective and conditions made the use of Northern Air Sea Rescue's helicopters out of the question. The task was allocated to the Naval tug. Not only was she a more suitable vessel than a destroyer for working close inshore among rocks, she also happened to be much nearer. She sailed from Lochmaddy at 09.17 hours.

In these conditions and in these northern waters the Army was largely dependent on the other Services, and their resources were limited. Standing had to make use of what was available and in the circumstances improvisation was probably justified. When I spoke to him I think his mind was already made up. It's easy to be wise after the event and say that it was a panic decision, but considered from his point of view, he hadn't all that much choice. The tug couldn't possibly reach Laerg before nightfall. In those seas, even allowing for the fact that such a violent storm was bound to die down quickly, it would be good going if she were in Shelter Bay by dawn, and the forecast for dawn next day was not good. The depression, which had been stationary to the west of Ireland, was on the move again and expected to reach the Hebrides within twenty-four hours. Instead of a polar air stream there would then be southerly winds force 6, veering later south-west and increasing to force 7, possibly gale force 8. He had checked with Ferguson and with Field, both officers who knew Laerg well and who had climbed over Sgeir Mhor. They confirmed what I had told him, that the rocks were sheer on the side facing Shelter Bay and that the only possible landing place was on the seaward side. And since that was the side exposed to winds between south and west it was obvious that the forecast not only made it extremely unlikely that any landing could be attempted the following day, but also that there was a grave danger of the survivors being overwhelmed by the force of the waves. That there were any survivors at all was obviously due to the change of wind direction that had occurred almost immediately after the ship had struck, and by dawn they might all be dead of exposure.

Time was, therefore, the vital factor. Moreover, both Ferguson and Field agreed that the only practical way of getting them off was to fire a line to them from the Butt of Keava and bring them over the gut by breeches buoy. That meant a rocket life-saving apparatus. The only equipment of this sort possessed by Guided Weapons had been allocated to the Laerg detachment and nobody was certain whether it had been shipped out or not. Rafferty thought not, but the Movements Officer disagreed and a squad was dispatched to search the stores heaped behind the quay at

Leverburgh. Meantime, Adams had been called in. The wind at Northton was around 35 knots, gusting 40 plus. He refused point blank to fly his helicopter anywhere near Laerg. He had come to Standing's office direct from the Met. Office. He was well aware of the urgency of the situation. He also knew that the turbulence of the air around Laerg made it quite impossible for him to make a landing there.

Time was wasted contacting the two main lifeboat stations. They were standing by, but though they had breeches buoy equipment available, they were even less well placed than the tug for getting it there. There was only one answer, then, to parachute the life-saving gear in. But no Shackleton would dare fly low over the island and a high-level drop would almost certainly result in the parachutes being blown out to sea.

It was Adams who suggested a possible solution. A small aircraft owned by one of the charter companies was waiting at Stornoway for weather clearance back to the mainland. He thought the pilot, a Canadian named Rocky Fellowes who'd done a lot of bush flying in the North West Territories, might have a shot at it. And at Stornoway there was the life-saving gear they needed.

It was then that Ferguson volunteered; if the first drop were successful and the gear landed in a place that was accessible, then he'd make the jump and organise the setting up of the breeches buoy. It faced Standing with a difficult choice. He had now received my second call. He knew there were at least five men marooned on Sgeir Mhor and only seven hours of daylight left. The risk of one man's life against the almost certain death of five; rightly or wrongly, he accepted Ferguson's offer. It was then eleven forty-five. Ten minutes later Ferguson was on his way. Field went with him: also a sergeant and two men, all of whom had completed a parachute course. And while the staff car started its forty-mile dash to Stornoway, Standing got through to the airport and asked them to find Fellowes and have him ring Northton immediately. He also asked them to arrange for the life-saving apparatus to be brought to the airfield and the parachutes to be got ready. Meantime, the tug was ordered to put into Leverburgh in the hopes that the Army's life-saving gear would be located.

This was the situation when I made my next contact with Base. I had found an alarm clock in the remains of the cook-house and the time by this was 12.53. Standing was then able to tell me that Fellows had agreed to attempt the drop. The wind speed at Stornoway was slightly less than the reading shown by Cliff Morgan's anemometer. It was beginning to fall off and he was optimistic. I suppose I should have warned Standing. The wind speed had fallen at Laerg, too. But there is a difference between a drop from around 50 knots and a drop from the fantastic wind speeds we had been experiencing. It was still coming down off the Saddle in gusts of considerable force. Whether it would have made any difference if I had warned him, I don't know. Probably not. Nobody sitting in his office almost a hundred miles away could possibly have any idea of the battering Laerg had received and was still receiving. In any case, I was thinking of those men out on Sgeir Mhor. If the pilot was willing to try it, then it wasn't for me to discourage him. The ETA Standing gave me for the plane's arrival was 14.15 approximate. In an hour's time the wind might have dropped right away. I had known it happen with storms of this intensity. And if it did, then the whole situation would be changed, and a plane overhead could make the difference between life and death to the survivors. It was up to the pilot anyway.

Standing was still talking to me, explaining about the tug and that Adams was standing by in the hope that conditions might improve sufficiently for him to fly the helicopter. Suddenly he stopped in mid-sentence and I heard him say, *'Just a minute.'* And then another voice—a voice I recognised, much fainter, but still quite audible: *'Please. I must see you. You can't do it. If you make Mike jump . . .'*

'I'm not making him. He volunteered.'

'Then stop him. You've got to stop him. He'll

251

kill himself. It's murder expecting him to jump in this wind, just to prove he can do it.'

'For God's sake, Marjorie. Pull yourself together. He's not trying to prove anything.'

'Of course he is. You're taking advantage of him.' She was beside herself, her voice shaken with the violence of her emotions. *'It isn't fair. He'll be killed and . . .'*

I heard the clatter of the phone as he dropped it and his voice was suddenly farther away: *'Look, my dear. Try to understand. This isn't just a question of Mike Ferguson. There are survivors out there and the one chance of getting them off . . .'*

'I don't care. I'm thinking of Mike.'

'Your father's with him. He'll see he doesn't do anything rash.'

But she didn't accept that. *'Daddy and Mike—they're both made the same way. You know that. They've both . . .'* She hesitated, adding, *'He'll jump whatever the conditions.'* And then on a different note: *'Is it true Mr Ross is one of the survivors? Major Rafferty said something about . . .'*

'I'm just speaking to him now.' And then I heard him say, *'Marjorie!'* his voice sharp and angry. She must have grabbed hold of the phone for her voice was suddenly clear and very close to me, trembling uncontrollably so that I caught her mood, the desperate urgency of her fear. She might have been there in the hut with me. *'Mr Ross. Help me—please. Mike*

252

mustn't jump. Do you hear? You've radio. You can contact the plane.' And then, almost with a sob: *'No, let me finish.'* But he'd got the phone away from her. 'Ross? I'll call you back at fourteen hundred hours.' There was a click, and after that silence.

*   *   *

Fellowes took off from Stornoway at 13.40 hours. Conditions had improved slightly with the wind easterly about 30 knots. The overcast, however, had come down again and there were rain squalls. They were in cloud before they'd reached 1,000 feet and they had to climb to more than 6,000 before they were above it. Field was in the co-pilot's seat; Ferguson, the sergeant and the two men back in the fuselage. The plane was an old Consul, the metal of the wings burnished bright by hail and rain, by subjection over many years to the abrasive forces of the elements. They flew for almost forty minutes in watery sunlight across a flat cotton-wool plain of cloud. Airspeed 120, the altimeter steady at 6.5 and towards the end, the pilot searching for an orographical cloud, a bulge in the overcast that would pin-point the position of Laerg. But there was no orographical cloud and at 14.20 they started down through the overcast.

Fellowes' dead reckoning was based on course and speed. He had corrected for drift,

253

but he had no means of telling whether the wind had remained constant and he was doing his sums the way the early fliers did them, his navigational aids on his knee. And all the time he was having to fly his plane in strong winds. He had spoken to me on the radio. But I couldn't even make a guess at the wind speed, for it was broken by Tarsaval and Malesgair and came down from the direction of the Saddle in violent eddies. All I could tell him was that the ceiling was under a thousand. Creag Dubh was just over the thousand and Creag Dubh was blanketed.

Coming down like that through thick cloud couldn't have been very pleasant. Field told me later that he didn't dare look at the altimeter after it had unwound to two thousand. He would like to have been able to shut his eyes, but he couldn't; they remained fixed on the grey void ahead, his body tense and strained forward against the safety belt. The engines made hardly a sound, just a gentle whispering, the wing-tips fluttering in moments of turbulence. Fellowes, too, was strained forward, eyes peering through the windshield. They were both of them waiting for that sudden darkening in the opaque film ahead that would mean hard rock and the end. Theoretically, Fellowes had overshot by five miles and was coming down over empty, unobstructed sea. But he couldn't be certain. Tarsaval was 1,456 feet high.

Five minutes—one of the longest five minutes of his life, Field said. Finally, he tore his eyes away from the empty windshield and glanced at the altimeter. Eight hundred feet. The cloud darkened imperceptibly. His eyes, with nothing substantial to focus on, were playing tricks. He was on the high slopes of a great mountain again, the cloud swirling about him. And then suddenly there was a pattern—streaks of black and white, long foaming lines coming up towards them. The sea, and the long march of the waves had their tops torn from them by the wind.

The aircraft banked sharply, the wing-tip seeming almost to touch the crest of a roller that reared up, curling and then breaking in a great surge of thrusting water. They straightened out, skimming the surface, the black curtain of a rain squall ahead. Bank again to skirt it and then momentarily blinded as water beat against the windshield, driven by the force of the wind into long rivulets that were never still. And on the other side of the squall a dark wall coming to meet them, towering cliffs of black rock sliding back from the starboard wing, the glimpse of two stacs, their tops hidden in cloud. Fladday. Course 280° then and Shelter Bay opening out ahead. Fellowes came right into it, flying at just over 500 feet, and when he turned the wind caught him and flung him like a wounded gull across the top of Sgeir Mhor.

They saw nothing that first run, but when he came in again, slower this time on a course of 020° headed straight into the wind, Field could see men standing amongst the rocks, waving to them. Through his glasses he counted eleven, and when they came in again, slightly lower this time, skimming the tops of the rocks, he made it fourteen. They stood off then, circling the open sea beyond the two arms of the bay whilst Fellowes reported to Base by radio.

Fourteen men still alive. Standing had no choice then. Nor had Ferguson. Nor had Fellowes. He yelled for the men back in the fuselage to get ready and headed back into Shelter Bay. The fuselage door was held open against the slipstream, the two packages poised in the cold blast of the opening. Fellowes raised his hand. 'Let go.' They were flung out. The fuselage door slammed shut. The aircraft banked.

I had left the radio then and was standing in the lee of the hut. I saw the two packages fall—two black dots like bombs dropping from the side of the plane. Twin white canopies blossoming and the plane blown like a leaf towards Sgeir Mhor, losing height, its wings dipping like a bird in flight. It cleared the rocks and vanished into rain. The parachutes moved across the sky above my head, growing larger, but drifting very fast. And then first one and then the other were caught by down-draughts, the nylon canopies half-collapsed. They came

256

down with a rush and then, just before they hit the beach, they each filled with a snap I could almost hear, were whirled upward and then landed gently, almost gracefully, halfway up the slopes of Keava.

I saw what happened to them, but Fellowes didn't. He was too busy fighting his plane clear of Sgeir Mhor. And Field had his eyes on the rocks, not on the parachutes. All they saw when they came out of the rain squall and circled the bay were two parachutes lying side-by-side like two white mushrooms close under the first scree slope on Keava. They didn't realise it was luck not judgment that had put them there. Field signalled back to Mike Ferguson, both thumbs up, and Fellowes took the plane in again. The drill was the same. The two men held the fuselage door open. The sergeant acted as dispatcher. But this time he was dispatching a man, not two inanimate packages. Again Fellowes judged his moment, raised his hand and shouted, 'Jump!'

Whether Fellowes misjudged or whether Mike Ferguson hesitated as the sergeant said he did, nobody will ever know. Field's impression was that he jumped immediately. But in moments like this fractions of a second count and a pilot, tensed and in control of his machine, possesses a sensitivity and a speed of reaction that is much faster than that of the ordinary man. Fellowes thought it was a long time before the sergeant called out that

Ferguson was away. In view of his parachute course record it seems more likely that Ferguson did, in fact, hesitate. If he did, it was a fatal hesitation. He may have felt in those last few moments of the run-in that he was jumping to his death. The sergeant reported that his face was very white, his lips trembling as he moved to the door. But then again, in view of his previous experience, some nervous reaction was inevitable.

In a tragedy of this sort it is pointless to try and apportion the blame. Each man is doing his best according to his lights and in any case it was the wind that was the vital factor. My back was against the hut and at the moment the plane banked and that tiny bundle of human flesh launched itself from the fuselage I felt the whole structure trembling under the onslaught of the wind. I wasn't just a gust. It came in a steady roar and it kept on blowing. I saw the parachute open, his fall suddenly checked. He was then at about 500 feet and right over my head; the plane, still banking, was being flung sideways across Sgeir Mhor.

If the wind had been a down-draught it might have collapsed his parachute momentarily. That was what had happened to the two previous parachutes. He might have landed heavily and been injured, but he would still have been alive. But it was a steady wind. It kept his parachute full. I saw him fighting the nylon cords to partially collapse it, but it was like a balloon, full to bursting and driving towards Keava at a great rate, trailing him behind it. For a moment it looked as though he would be all right. The sloped rock spine of Keava was a good 70 feet high at the point he was headed for, but as he neared it the steep slope facing Shelter Bay produced an updraught. The parachute lifted, soaring towards the clouds. He cleared the top by several hundred feet. For a moment he was lost to sight, swallowed by the overcast. Then I saw him again, the parachute half-collapsed and falling rapidly. It was a glimpse, no more, for in the instant he was lost behind Keava.

Beyond the ridge was sheer cliff, and beyond the cliff nothing but the Atlantic and the gale-torn waves. It was all so remote that it seemed scarcely real; only imagination could associate that brief glimpse of white nylon disappearing with a man dead, drowned in a wet, suffocating world of tumbling water.

The plane stood off, circling by the entrance to the bay. It didn't come in again and nobody else jumped. I went slowly back into the hut and picked up Standing's voice on the radio. It was so shaken that I barely recognised it. He was ordering the pilot to return to Stornoway.

I was glad of that—glad that nobody else was going to be ordered to jump, glad that I didn't have to stand again outside the hut and watch another parachute blown out into the Atlantic. I found I was trembling, still with that picture in my mind of a man dangling and the white envelope coming out of the clouds, half-collapsed, and the poor fellow falling to a cold death in the Atlantic. I had liked Mike Ferguson. He'd a lot of guts to face that jump. And then I was thinking of Marjorie Field and of that interview she'd had with Colonel Standing when I had been an involuntary eavesdropper. Somebody would have to tell her and I was glad I wasn't her father. The dead have their moment of struggle, that brief moment of shock which is worse than birth because the ties with this world are stronger. But for the living, the pain does not cease with death. It remains till memory is dull and the face that cased the loved one's personality has faded.

I was still thinking of Marjorie when Standing called me, demanding estimates of wind speed, force of down-draughts, height of ceiling. I went to the door of the hut. The wind's roar had momentarily died away. Nothing stronger now than 40 knots, I thought. My eyes went involuntarily to the sloping back of Keava. If only Mike had waited. He would have had a chance now, but it was done. He'd jumped and he was gone. The sky to the south, by the bay entrance, was empty, the plane gone.

I went back and reported to Standing. He asked particularly about down-draughts and I told him they were intermittent, that at the moment they had lost much of their force.

There was a long pause and then he said they'd try and make a helicopter landing. I didn't attempt to discourage him. Those men were still on Sgeir Mhor and I was tired. Anyway, it was quieter now. How long it would last I didn't know. I just wished to God they'd flown the helicopter instead of trying to parachute men in. I wondered whether it was really Adams who had refused to fly or whether Standing's cold mathematical mind had been influenced by the high cost of these machines. That was a thought that made me angry. When you consider how the Services waste the taxpayers' money, millions stupidly spent, and here perhaps a decent man had been sent to his death for fear of risking a few thousands. 'About bloody time,' I said angrily. 'If you'd used the helicopter in the first place . . .'

I let it go at that. The poor bastard! It wasn't his fault. Decisions have to be made by the men in command and sometimes, inevitably, they're the wrong decisions. It was something that he'd tried to get help to the survivors before nightfall. I wondered what my brother would have done. With all his faults, Iain was a man of action. His behaviour in an emergency was instinctive. 'A pity you didn't leave it to Major Braddock.' I'd said it before I could stop myself. I heard his quick intake of breath. And then, in a stiff, cold voice, he said, *'We'll be with you under the hour.'*

We! I remember thinking about that, sitting

261

there, dazed with fatigue. What Standing coming himself? But it didn't seem to matter—not then. The life-saving gear was up there on the slopes of Keava and all we needed were the men to collect it and set it up. Men who were fresh and full of energy. I was tired. Too tired to move, my aching body barely reacting to the orders of my brain. Nerves, muscles, every part of my anatomy cried out for rest.

I woke Cooper, told him to keep radio watch and wake me in forty minutes' time. Then I fell on to Pinney's bed, not bothering to undress, and was instantly asleep.

'Mr Ross. Wake up.' The voice went on and on, a hand shaking my shoulder. I blinked my eyes and sat up. 'Gawd Almighty! Yer didn't 'alf give me a turn. Thought you'd croaked. Honest I did.' Cooper bending over me, staring at me anxiously. 'You orl right, sir?' And then he said, 'They're on the air now. Want ter know what conditions are like. I told 'em: still blowing like 'ell, but it's clearer—only the top of Tarsaval's got cla'd on it now.'

I got up and went to the radio. The time was twelve minutes to four. Adams' voice came faint and crackling. He wanted an estimate of the wind speed, its direction, the strength of the down-draughts. I went to the door of the hut. It was certainly much clearer now; quite bright, in fact. The overcast was breaking up, torn rags of clouds hurrying across a cold blue sky and the broken water seaward shining white in patches

262

of slanting sunlight. Keava and Malesgair, the two arms that enclosed Shelter Bay, were clear of cloud. So was Creag Dubh. For the first time I could see the Lookout where the tracking station radar had been housed. Only the summit of Tarsaval was still obscured, a giant wearing a cloth cap made shapeless by the wind. It was blowing harder, I thought, and the down-draughts were irregular. Sometimes there was a long interval in which the wind just blew. Then suddenly it would wham down off the heights, two or three gusts in quick succession.

I went back to the radio and reported to Adams. He said he could see Laerg quite plainly and estimated that he had about seven miles to go. *'I'll come in from the south at about four hundred,'* he said. *'You know where the landing ground is—down by the Factor's House. I'll watch for you there. I'm relying on you to signal me in. I'll need about sixty seconds clear of down-draughts. Okay?'* I don't think he heard my protest. At any rate, he didn't answer, and I went out, cursing him for trying to put the onus on me. Did he think I could control the down-draughts? There was no pattern about them. They came and went; one minute I was walking quite easily, the next I was knocked flat and all the breath pushed back into my throat. Damn the man! If I signalled him in it would be my responsibility if anything went wrong.

But there wasn't time to consider that, I'd

barely reached the beach when I saw the helicopter, a speck low down over the water beyond the entrance to the bay. It came in fast and by the time I'd reached the Factor's House I could hear its engine, a buzz-saw drone above the suck and seethe of the surf. A down-draught hit, beating the grasses flat and whistling out over the bay, the surface boiling as though a million small fry were skittering there. It was gone almost as soon as it had come. Another and another hit the ground, flattening the long brown wisps of grass, whirling the dried seaweed into the air. They came like sand devils, spiralling down. The helicopter, caught in one, slammed down almost to sea level and then rocketed up. It was very close now and growing bigger every minute, the sound of its engine filling the air. In the sudden stillness that followed that last gust I thought I could hear the swish of its rotor blades.

No point in waiting, for every second he hovered there he was in mortal danger. I waved him in, praying to God that he'd plonk himself down in one quick rush before the next blast struck. But he didn't. He was a cautious man, which is a fine thing in a pilot; except that this was no moment for caution. He came in slowly, feeling his way, and the next gust caught him when he was still a hundred feet up. It came slam like the punch of a fist. The helicopter, flung sideways and downwards, hit the beach;

the floats crumpled and at the same instant, with the rotor blades still turning, the whole machine was heaved up and flung seaward. It touched the water, tipped, foam flying from the dripping blades, and then it sank till it lay on its side, half-submerged, a broken float support sticking stiffly into the air like the leg of some bloated carcase.

Stillness then, the wind gone and everything momentarily quiet. A head bobbed up beside the floating wreck. Another and another. Three men swimming awkwardly, and then the tin carcase rolled its other splintered leg into the air and sank. Air came out of it, a single belch that lifted the surface of the water, and after that nothing; just the flat sea rippled by the wind and three dark heads floundering in to the beach.

Fortunately there was little surf. One by one they found their feet and waded ashore, drowned men gasping for air, flinging themselves down on the wet stones, suddenly exhausted as fear gripped them. I ran down to them, looking at each face. But they were men I didn't know. They were alive because they'd been in the fuselage within reach of the door. Standing had been sitting with Adams up by the controls. They'd both been trapped.

It was only minutes before, a few short minutes, that I'd been talking to Adams. It didn't seem possible. One moment the helicopter had been there, so close above my head that I'd ducked involuntarily—and now it was gone. I stood there with those three men moaning at my feet staring unbelievingly at the waters of the bay. Nothing. Nothing but the steel-bright surface exploding into spray and beneath it Standing and Adams still strapped into their seats, eyes already sightless . . . Was it my fault? I felt sick right through to my guts, utterly drained.

'Christ, man. What are you staring at?'

One of the figures, a sergeant, had staggered to his feet and was staring at me, wild-eyed, his hair plastered limp across his head.

'Nothing,' I said. It was nothing that he could see. The two dead men were in my mind and he wasn't thinking of them, only of the fact that he was alive.

'Jesus! It was cold.' He was shivering; moaning to himself. But then habit and training reasserted itself. He got his men to their feet and I took them up to the camp.

It was, I thought, the end of all hope for the survivors on Sgeir Mhor; three men killed and nothing achieved. Standing's death had a numbing effect on the rescue operation. It was not so much the man himself as the command he represented. It left a vacuum and there was only one man in Northton with the experience to fill it; that man was lying on his bed, nursing a hatred that no longer had any point. In the midst of the flood of teleprints back and forth nobody thought of informing him that Standing was dead. He heard about it from his escorting officer who had got it from the orderly who brought them their tea. It took time for the implications to sink in and it wasn't until almost five-fifteen that he finally stirred himself, got to his feet and ordered Lieutenant Phipps to accompany him to the Movements Office. There he sent off a teleprint to Brigadier Matthieson: *In view of Colonel Standing's death presume I have your authority to take over command. Please confirm so that I can organise attempt to rescue survivors dawn tomorrow.* This was dispatched at 17.23 hours.

Brigadier Matthieson, who admitted later that he considered Standing's action in placing his second-in-command under close arrest ill-advised, immediately signalled back: *Your temporary command Northton confirmed. Advise action planned for getting survivors off.*

Queen's Regulations are not very specific on the subject of an arrested officer assuming command and Matthieson's signal carefully avoided reference to the matter. He had, in fact, very little alternative. There was no other officer at Northton competent to take control in a situation like this and to fly a replacement CO in would take time. Moreover, Braddock had the confidence of his superiors at the War Office. There was another factor, too. The Press were now alerted to what was happening up in the Outer Hebrides. The Press Officer at Scottish Command had, during the past hour

267

or so, faced a barrage of demands for information from London as well as Scottish newspaper offices. They knew about the trawler that had disappeared. They knew that a landing craft was in difficulties to the west of Laerg. They also knew that another LCT had been shipwrecked on the island and that there were survivors. No doubt they had been briefed by amateur radio operators—either Scottish 'ham' operators monitoring my radio contacts with Base or Irish radio enthusiasts picking up the signals passing between Coastal Command and their two Shackletons.

Whatever the source of their information the effect was the same; it convinced Matthieson that this was no longer a strictly Army affair but had become something much bigger. Like a submarine disaster, it had all the dramatic qualities to capture the imagination of the British public. From tomorrow morning onwards the whole country would be waiting for news of the survivors, and if the news were bad ... Well, he certainly didn't intend to be blamed for it, not with only a few months of his time to go. In confirming my brother as temporary Base Commander, he was clutching at a straw. If things went right then he could take some credit. And if things went wrong then he had his scapegoat. I'm convinced that that was the way his mind was working when he made the decision.

At approximately five-thirty when my

brother officially took command the position was this: Two relief Shackletons had been flown off, one to continue the search for the missing trawler, the other to watch over L4400 until the destroyer, now little more than 100 miles away, reached her. *W/S India* had been ordered back on to station. The Naval tug was still snug against the quay at Leverburgh.

Apart from shore-based aircraft, there was nothing else available in the area to assist in the rescue operation. True, the destroyer would pass quite close to Laerg, but L4400 urgently needed her. The landing craft was barely afloat. Almost half her crew were casualties, the bridge deck ripped to pieces, mast and funnel gone, the tank hold full of water and the pumps barely capable of holding in check the sea pouring in through her strained and buckled plates.

And since conditions made the use of aircraft impracticable, the tug remained the only hope.

In the uncertainty that followed immediately on Standing's death, nobody had apparently thought of informing the skipper of the changed situation. That his vessel was still tied up in Leverburgh was not due to any lack of initiative on his part. He was waiting for conditions to improve, knowing that he needn't sail until six at the earliest to reach Laerg by first light.

Braddock's immediate reaction to the

situation was to send out three signals in quick succession—to Command, demanding the instant dispatch of two helicopters; to Coastal Command requesting that a further Shackleton be held fuelled and ready for immediate take-off should he require it; to the destroyer urging her captain to close Sgeir Mhor on his way out to L4400 and endeavour to float off supplies to the survivors, or if that were not possible, to signal them by lamp that help was on its way. Then he went to see Cliff Morgan.

Captain Flint, who was in Movements at the time, said he personally felt a great lift when Braddock took command. If any man could get the survivors off, he thought Braddock would.

Cliff Morgan's reaction, on the other hand, was very different. Like Standing, he regarded Braddock as responsible for what had happened. He was appalled when Braddock came into his quarters—'Bold as brass, man,' was the way he put it. ' "Colonel Standing's dead and I've taken over command. Now, Morgan, let's have your ideas of the weather for the next twelve hours." Just like that. And when I told him it was a pity it was Standing who'd gone and not him he laughed in my face; told me to mind my own bloody business and stick to the weather which he thought perhaps I understood. I was in radio contact with a "ham" over in Tobermory at the time and when I started to finish the conversation, he put his big hand over the key. "You take your fat arse off that chair," he told me, "and come over to the Met. Office or I'll take you there by the scruff of your neck." '

Over in the Met. Office Cliff had given him a forecast that he admitted was enough to daunt any man planning a rescue operation on an island a hundred miles out in the Atlantic. The effect of the local depression that had caused all the havoc would die out entirely within the next hour or so—probably it had died out already. For a time then the island would come again under the influence of the polar air stream with winds northerly between thirty and forty knots. Later those winds would decrease and perhaps die out for a while as the polar air stream was gradually dominated by the new depression moving in from the Atlantic. The period of relative calm would be followed by winds of rapidly increasing strength as the depression built up and spread over the area. Southerly at first, the winds would veer south-westerly increasing to gale force.

'When?' Braddock had asked. 'When will that happen?' And Cliff had shrugged.

'You're asking me how fast that depression is moving? I don't know.'

'Then contact somebody who does. There are more than a dozen men on that bloody rock and when this depression hits . . .' Braddock checked himself. He even patted Cliff on the shoulder. 'Just tell me when. Better still, tell me when that period of calm will be.'

Cliff says he hesitated, unwilling to commit himself. He was staring at the map he'd drawn. Sykes came in with another sheet from the teleprinter, more barometric pressure figures. He entered them in, connected them up, scoring the isobars with a red pencil. One of those figures represented a report from the Shackleton circling L4400. It showed a drop of two millibars in the past hour. 'The calm will be just about there; within the hour, at any rate.'

'Goddammit!' Braddock said. 'An hour. Are you certain?' And when Cliff nodded, he said, 'How long will it last? Listen. In an hour and a half perhaps I could have helicopters here. Say three hours by the time they're refuelled and have reached Laerg. I need four hours. Can you give me four hours?'

'No.' Cliff shook his head, quite definite now. 'You can see for yourself.' He was pointing to the red lines he'd drawn. The nearest was almost touching Laerg, coming down in a broad sweep from Iceland and running away westward just north of Ireland. 'Two hours I'd give it; no more. Two hours from now and the wind will begin blowing from the south. It must do.'

'Then God help them,' was all Braddock said and he turned and went out, walking swiftly through the fading light. Cliff called after him that there was a warm front associated with the depression. There would probably be heavy rain accompanied by low ceiling and poor visibility. Braddock didn't answer. He made no acknowledgment that he'd heard, but walked straight on, shoulders very square, head held well back on the short, thick neck—a man bracing himself for a fight, Cliff thought. And overhead the clouds gathering again, aerial cavalry of a new enemy onslaught forming themselves into dark ranks, galloping eastward and rolling up the blue-green late afternoon canopy that, though cold, had the bright promise of hope. Now hope was fallen victim to the gathering clouds and my brother, alone in the loneliness of command, had to decide what further lives, if any, should be risked to attempt to save men doomed to face a night of terror, exposed again to the fury of the elements.

Field was back when he reached the Movements Office—Charles Field, looking old and grey and stooped, the lines of his face etched deeper than ever and an uneasy, shifting light in his steel-blue eyes. He said what he had to say, adding, 'It was nobody's fault. Nobody's fault at all. I'll write a full report, of course.' He was edging towards the door. 'Think I'll go over to the Mess now.'

'The Mess?' Braddock stared at him, saw the lips twitching, the slight blink of the eyes, that shifting look. 'For a drink?'

Field nodded unhappily. 'I thought just one. Just a quick one, to steady me. A shock, you know. A most frightful shock.' And he added, justifying himself, 'I hope you realise, I don't normally drink. But on this occasion. You understand . . .'

Braddock reached him in two quick strides, seized hold of him by the arm. 'Sure. I understand. Just one, and that'll lead to another. You're the one man I want sober. So you stay here. Okay?' And he pushed him into a chair. 'You're going back to Laerg—tonight.'

'No.' Field was up from the chair, his eyes overbright. 'No. I absolutely refuse.'

'Then I'll place you under arrest and have you escorted on board.' He patted his arm as though comforting a child. 'Don't worry. I'll be with you. We're going out there together.' And he sent Phipps for the long wheel-base Land-Rover and dictated a signal to Brigadier Matthieson: *Weather forecast suggests quite impracticable attempt lift survivors out by helicopter. Am proceeding to Laerg by Naval tug. Will personally direct rescue operations on arrival dawn tomorrow.* It was sent out signed: *Braddock, Commanding Officer Guided Weapons, Northton.*

In taking Field with him my brother was instinctively seeking the support of the one man whose experience and background could help. He also took the MO, Lt. Phipps, a Sergeant Wetherby and four men, all hand-picked for their toughness and their known ability in the water and on the Laerg crags. Flint went with them. It took almost half an hour to gather them and their kit and the necessary equipment—climbing ropes, inflatable dinghy, aqualung cylinders and frogmen's suits, everything that might possibly be of use. Meantime, radio contact had been established with the tug and the skipper requested to stand by to sail immediately they arrived on board.

They left the Base at ten to six. Unfortunately, the clothes Field needed were at his croft. It was only a few minutes' drive from Leverburgh, but Marjorie was there. For the past two hours she had been with Laura Standing. She knew what had happened. She was white-faced, on the verge of hysteria. 'Why did you let him jump?' she demanded of her father. 'Why in God's name did you let him?' And he stood there, not saying a word, because there was nothing to say, whilst his own daughter accused him of being responsible for Mike's death.

Braddock got out of the Land-Rover. 'Hurry up, Field. We've no time to waste.'

Marjorie was still pouring out a flood of words, but she stopped then, staring at the Land-Rover, the significance of it standing there full of men slowly dawning on her. She doesn't remember what she said or what she did, but Flint described it to me: 'Moments like that, when you're headed for trouble an' you don't know how bad it's going to be, you don't want a girl around then, particularly a girl

275

who's just lost somebody she cared about. One moment she was giving her father hell, saying it was all his fault, and then all of a sudden she switched her attention to Major B. That was when she realised he was taking her father out to Laerg. "You can't do it," she said. "He's not a young man. He hasn't climbed in years." She knew what it was all about. She'd broken the news of Standing's death to his wife. She knew what had happened. She knew the sort of man Braddock was—guessed he'd stop at nothing, risk anything to get those men off. She went for him like a bitch defending her last remaining puppy, screaming at him that it was all his fault, that he'd killed Mike, killed Simon Standing; it was plain bloody murder, she said, and she wasn't going to let him kill her father. Braddock tried soothing her with logic—her father was in the Army, there was a job to do and that was that. But reasoning with a girl who's scared out of her wits, whose emotions are tearing her nerves to shreds, is like pouring water on a high voltage short—it just doesn't make a damn bit of difference. In the end he slapped her. Not hard. Just twice across the face and told her to pull herself together and not disgrace her father. It shut her up, and after that she just stood there, white an' trembling all over.'

It was just after six-fifteen when they boarded the tug. The warps were let go immediately and he steamed out into the

276

Sound of Harris, heading west. We were then experiencing the lull Cliff had forecast. It was so still in the hut that I went out to see what was wrong. After hours of battering the sudden quiet seemed unnatural. Darkness was closing down on Laerg, the clouds low overhead and hanging motionless. I could see the outline of Sgeir Mhor, the sloping spine of Keava disappearing into the blanket of the overcast, but they were dim, blurred shapes. The air was heavy with humidity, and not a breath of wind.

I got a torch and signalled towards Sgeir Mhor. But there was no answering flash. It meant nothing for it was unlikely that any of the survivors had got ashore with a torch. I tried to contact Base, but there was other traffic—Rafferty talking to the destroyer, to the tug, finally to Coastal Command. And then the destroyer to me: ETA Laerg 01.25 hours. Would I please stand by the radio as from 01.00. Base came through immediately afterwards: The tug's ETA would be about 04.30 dependent on conditions. I was requested to keep radio watch from four-thirty onwards. Roger. I had six hours in which to get some rest. I arranged with Cooper for a hot meal at one o'clock, set the alarm, undressed and tumbled into bed.

I must have recovered some of my energy, for it wasn't the alarm that woke me. I reached out and switched on the light. A mouse was sitting up by the edge of my empty plate, sitting

277

on its haunches on the bedside table cleaning its whiskers with its forepaws. It was one of the breed peculiar to Laerg, a throw-back to pre-glacial life, to before the last Ice Age that covered the British Isles anything up to ten thousand years ago. It was larger than the ordinary British field-mouse, its ears were bigger, its hind-legs longer and the tail was as long as its body; the brown of its coat had a distinctly reddish tinge brightening to dull orange on the under-belly. It sat quite still, two shiny black pin-head eyes staring at me. It seemed possessed of curiosity rather than fear, and after a moment it resumed its toilet, cleaning its whiskers with little stroking movements of its paws. The time was eleven minutes past midnight. The wind was back, beating round the corners of the hut in a steady roar that drowned the sound of the generator. And behind the wind was another, more sinister sound—one that I hadn't heard for some time; the crash and suck of waves breaking on the beach. I thought it was this sound rather than the mouse that had woken me.

There was something about that little morsel of animal life that was infinitely comforting; a sign perhaps of the indestructibility of life. The mouse in that moment meant a lot to me and I lay there watching it until it had finished its toilet and quietly disappeared. Then I got up and dressed and went to the door of the hut. It was a black night, the two lights Cooper had left on in the camp shining in isolation. The wind was from the south, about force 7. The waves, coming straight into the bay, broke with an earth-shaking thud. The sound of the surf was louder than the wind, and as my eyes became accustomed to the darkness, I could see the ghostly glimmer of white water ringing the beach; just the glimmer of it, nothing else. It was a wild, ugly night, the air much warmer so that I thought I could smell rain again, the warm front moving in.

At one o'clock I contacted the destroyer. She had Laerg clear on the radar at thirteen miles range. ETA approximately, one-thirty. Alf Cooper appeared at my side, a khaki gnome, his head encased in a woolen balaclava. 'Grub up.' He put the tray down on the table beside the radio—a Thermos flask of oxtail soup and two mess tins full of corned beef and potato hash all steaming hot. 'A night for the flippin' bears, ain't it. 'Ibernation, that's my idea o' paradise this time of the year. You reck'n that destroyer'll be able to do any good?'

'No,' I said.

He nodded, sucking at his soup. 'That's wot I fort. Ruddy waves must be breaking right over the poor bastards.' I asked him about the men from the helicopter. 'Sleepin' their ruddy heads orf,' he said. 'Orl right for them. They got full bellies. Me, I'm fair famished.' He reached for one of the mess tins. "Ope yer don't mind bully. Easy ter make, yer see. Fillin' too.'

At one-thirty we went out of the hut and stood in the teeth of the wind staring into the black darkness that hid Sgeir Mhor. It was drizzling, a wet, driving mist. Suddenly light blazed, the pencil stab of a searchlight that threw the blurred shape of Sgeir Mhor into black relief. It probed the mist, producing strange halos of light in the damp air. A gun flashed, a small sound against the thunder of breaking waves. The overcast glimmered with light as the star shell burst. It was a minute or two before it floated clear of the clouds over Keava; for a moment the bay and the surrounding rocks were bathed in its incandescent glare. It was an unearthly sight; the waves marching into the bay, building up till their tops curled and broke, roaring up the beach in a welter of foam, and all around the horseshoe curve of breaking water, the rocks standing piled in ghostly brilliance. Rock and cliff and sodden grass slope all looked more hellish in that macabre light. I saw the spume of waves breaking over the lower bastions of Sgeir Mhor. Then the flare touched the sea and was instantly extinguished, and after that the night was blacker, more frightening than before.

A signal lamp stabbed its pin-point of light just beyond the tip of Sgeir Mhor: *Help arriving first light. Stick it out four more hours and . . .* That was all I read for the destroyer was steaming slowly westward and the stab of her

280

signal lamp was obscured by the rocks. The searchlight probed again, searching the far side of the rock promontory as though trying to count the survivors. And then that too went out and after that there was nothing but the pitch-black night.

I re-set the alarm and lay down again on Pinney's bed, not bothering this time to undress. Time passed slowly and I couldn't sleep. The mouse came back. I could hear its claws scratching at the aluminium of the mess tins, but I didn't switch the light on. I lay there with my eyes closed waiting for the alarm, thinking of those men out on the rocks drenched by the mist and the spray, wondering whether it would be possible to get them off.

At four-thirty I was at the radio and the tug came through prompt on schedule, my brother's voice requesting information about sea and landing conditions. I was able to tell him that the wind was now west of south. But it had also increased in strength. It was definitely blowing a gale now and it was raining heavily. However, if the wind veered further, as seemed likely, there was a chance that a landing could be made in the western curve of the bay, close under Keava where there would be some shelter. *'Okay,'* he said. *'We'll recce the lee side of Sgeir Mhor first and if that's no good, we'll anchor and attempt to make the beach on inflatable rafts.'*

It was still dark when they came into the bay

281

and all I saw of the tug was the two steaming lights, one above the other, swinging and dipping. She came right into the bay, almost to the break of the waves, and then the lights moved apart and the distance between them increased as she turned westward. The green of her starboard navigation lights showed for a while, still half-obscured by rain. And then that vanished, together with the steaming lights, and I caught glimpses of her stern lights as she browsed along the western arm of the bay, the will-o'-the-wisp bounced from wave-top to wave-top. A searchlight stabbed a brilliant beam, iridescent with moisture, and the rocks of Sgeir Mhor showed ghostly grey across tumbled acres of sea; columns of spray like ostrich feather plumes waved behind it, sinking and rising with the surge of the Atlantic.

Dawn came slowly and with reluctance, a sheathed pallor stealing into the curve below the encircling hills. The tug lay close under Keava, just clear of the narrow, surf-filled gut that separated it from Sgeir Mhor. She didn't anchor, but stayed head-to-wind under power, and they came ashore in rubber dinghies where the surf was least.

I was coming along the foreshore when my brother staggered dripping out of the suck of the waves, dragging a rubber dinghy after him. He was dressed like the others in a frogman's suit and I can see him still, standing there in that twilit world that was the dawn, finned feet straddled at the surf's edge, not looking at that moment at his companions, but staring up at the cloud-hidden heights. There was a stillness about him, an immobility—he seemed for an instant petrified, a part of the landscape, his body turned to stone, statuesque like a rock.

Then the others piled in through the surf and he was a man again, moving to help them, going back into the waves to pull two more rubber dinghies ashore.

I met them on the beach. 'Thank God you made it,' I yelled to him above the wind.

He stared at me. His face looked haggard, his eyes wild. I swear he didn't recognise me.

'Iain. Are you all right, Iain?'

For a moment his face stayed blank. Then his eyes snapped. 'Ross.' He glanced quickly at Field standing at the surf's edge. Then he came towards me, gripped my shoulder. 'The name's Braddock, damn you,' he hissed, his fingers digging a warning into my flesh. His mouth had hardened and his eyes blazed black. He'd have seen me dead and drowned before he'd have admitted to his real name.

Field wiped a smear of phlegm from below his nose. 'We saw several men clinging to the rocks.' His eyes looked dead and tired, bloodshot with the salt. 'Where are the parachutes—the live-saving gear you dropped?' Braddock asked.

'Up there.' Field nodded to the heights of Keava, the long slope leading to the spine.

'Yes, up there,' I agreed. But the rain-dimmed dawn showed nothing on the slopes—only the clouds writhing in white pillars.

Their clothes, tied in plastic bundles in the dinghies, were safe and dry. They changed in the bird-oil stench of an old cleit, and then we climbed, strung out across the slopes, climbed until we met the clouds, gasping wet air. The daylight had strengthened by then and ragged gaps in the overcast showed the slopes of Keava bare to its spine and to the cliffs beyond. The parachutes had gone. Some time during the night, I suppose, a gust had filled the nylon canopies and carried them over the top and far out into the sea beyond.

Braddock shook Field's arm. 'Are you sure that's where you dropped them?'

Field nodded.

'Then they're gone.'

Field's face was set in a wooden look as he agreed they'd gone. Up there in the wind and the driving clouds, with the thunder of the waves breaking at the foot of the cliffs, he and I, we could both recall the solitary parachute lifting and sailing out into the Atlantic. 'Wasted. All wasted.' There were tears in his eyes, but it may have been the wind.

'Okay. Well, there's only one way to get a line across.'

Field nodded absently.

'We'll have to take it ourselves. Swim it across the gut, and then climb with it.'

Easy to say; not so easy to do. The drop from the Butt of Keava was possible, the 350-foot cliff went down in a series of ledges. It was the gut between and the sheer cliff beyond. The gut was 50 yards at its narrowest and the seas were breaking there in a welter of foam; the cliffs of Sgeir Mhor were black volcanic gabbro, hard as granite, smooth and unbroken for long stretches.

'Well?' Braddock stared at Field. 'I swim it, you climb it, eh?' And his face cracked in a grin. It was a dare. This was the sort of thing he loved—physical action spiced with danger. And if the other man cracked . . . Poor Field's face was ashen, his eyes staring at the smooth black panels of wet rock beyond the maelstrom of the chasm.

I think my brother had watched quite a few men crack. I don't say it gave him pleasure, but it may well have been something he needed, a bolster to his own morale. His world had always been a physical one. Mentally and emotionally he was something of a child; or that was how he had often seemed to me; which was why, I suppose, our relationship, so inimical at times, had been at others so strangely close; we had each supplied what the other lacked.

Now, he didn't hesitate. He didn't even watch for Field's reaction. He caught the man's fear at a glance and overlaid it with his own determination, the quick positiveness of his orders. He led us pell-mell back down the slope, back to the beach and the dinghies laden with rope and all the things he'd feared they might need. And then, in his frogman's kit again, up the sloping shoulders of the rocks to the wet thunder of the surf breaking through the gut.

The sergeant and I, with two men, were ordered to the top of the cliff with one end of the nylon climbing rope. Down at the bottom he and Field, together with Lieutenant Phipps and the two other men, manoeuvred one of the rubber dinghies.

Flat on my stomach at the cliff's edge I watched Iain working his way along the ledges westward through the gut. He was alone and his thick, powerful body in its black rubber suit looked like a seal's as it flattened itself against the rocks to meet each wave as it broke foaming across the ledges—a baby seal from that height, the rope around his waist and trailing white behind him like an umbilical cord. And then from the farthest point west that he could fight his way, he suddenly stood on a sheer-edged shelf of rock and dived.

He dived into the back-surge of a big wave and went deep, his fins beating furiously, drumming at the surf. It looked so easy. One moment he was diving and the next he had bobbed up on the back of a breaker on the far side, a black head with black arms paddling. A quick look round, then down again as the next comber broke, and as it spent its energy, he rode its back on to a long, sloped ledge, and pulled himself up.

Now, with the dawn light stronger, I could see two figures prone among the rocks on the far side, peering down. I thought I recognised Wentworth, but I couldn't be sure. The face was a dim blur in the rain and the flying spray.

Iain was clear of the water now, clear of the surge of even the biggest waves, curled up at the farthest end of that sloped ledge and pulling on the rope. Below me I saw Field hesitate. The rope came taut on the rush of a wave. The rubber dinghy shifted on the rocks. And then it was in the water, and he was in it, head down, hands gripping the gunnels as it was pulled across. Once I thought he was lost. The dinghy reared on a curling crest, turned half over it as it broke. But then it righted itself, lifted on the backwash from the far side, and in one buoyant rush came to rest on the ledge where Iain crouched.

I saw arms wave on the cliff opposite. There were three bodies there now, all waving in the excitement of imminent rescue. But there was still that sheer cliff and the men on the top could do nothing to help. It was up to Field now. Field alone could lift the end of that rope the 300 feet that would transform it from just the tail-end of a line into a connecting link, a bridge between the two masses of rock—a bridge that could act as a means of escape.

Field had crossed the gut barefooted, but in

287

his battledress. Now, soaked to the skin, he leaned against the vertical rock and put on his climbing boots. That done, he fastened a belt round his waist that was stuffed with rock pitons like steel dog's teeth. An ice hammer looped by its thong to his wrist, the rope fastened around his waist, and he was ready. But then he stood for a long time with his head thrown back, gazing up at the cliff above him.

He stood like that for so long that I thought he was held fast by the sheer impossibility of it. Perhaps by fear, too. And I for one wouldn't have blamed him. Those shining panels of rock, trickling water—a spider would have its work cut out to find a footing. There were ledges and crevices, it was true. There are in almost any rock. But they were so minute and spaced so far apart. And all the time the sea swirled about his legs. The din of it was incessant, the gut streaming with wind-blown spray, gusts of spume, spongy masses of it flying through the air.

At last he moved; a flick of the hand holding the rope. Iain squatted tighter into his niche, waiting, both hands on the rope. The three men on the cliff-top opposite me leaned out and waved. Field saw them, for he lifted his hand. And then at last he began to climb, traversing out along a toe-hold crack that was a fractured continuation of the ledge on which he had stood.

It was fascinating to watch him. He must

have been over fifty and out of practice, yet he balanced himself like an acrobat, hanging in space and moving steadily upwards, his feet doing the work, the rest of his body still and quiet. To the left at first, a long traverse, and then a quick gain of perhaps fifty or sixty feet up toe and finger holds I couldn't see; a short traverse right and then a pause. The pause lengthened out, his hands reaching occasionally and drawing back. Then for a long time he hung there quite motionless.

Had his nerve gone? I don't know. I asked him once, but he only smiled and said, 'It was an ugly place. I thought it better to start again.'

I didn't see him jump. One moment he was there, and the next he was in the sea, and Iain was hauling him back to the ledge where he lay for a while getting his breath. Then he started up again.

The same route, but a left traverse at the top and then he was hammering a piton into a crevice, snapping on a hook for the rope, and up again using pitons from the clanking string of them around his waist, one after another. He must have hammered in about two dozen of them before he reached the overhang, and there he stuck with less than fifty feet to go—a fly on wet slate with the spume curling up like smoke from the cauldron below him.

He got round it eventually by going down about half the distance he'd climbed and working another crevice line to the right. This brought him almost opposite me, and right below him then was a deadly mass of rocks awash. He looked down once and I could imagine how he felt with only the rope running now through three pitons to hold him. The last 50 ft. seemed to take him almost as many minutes. The crevices were too shallow for the pitons and he was white with cold, his clothes heavy with water. But he did it.

His head came level with the cliff-top. Hands reached down and he went over the top on his belly. Then he suddenly passed out, lying there, limp. But the rope was there and that was life to those who'd survived. The tail-end, passed back down the cliff to Iain, was made fast to a heavier line, and so, with many goings back and forth to the camp, we rigged up a makeshift breeches-buoy.

It took us all morning in the teeth of the gale with five of the tug's crew and the Doc and the men who had survived the helicopter crash. Baulks of timber had to be brought up, heavy hawsers, block and tackle, and everything rigged by trial and error. Just after midday we managed to get food and clothing across to them. But it wasn't until almost 2 p.m. that we got the first man over the gut and safe on to Keava. And after that it was slow, back-breaking work, for many of them were stretcher cases, who, when they reached Keava, had to be carried down the slopes and along the beach to the camp. There was no vehicle, no means of transporting them other than by hand.

We took altogether twenty-three men off Sgeir Mhor, five of them unconscious, and several badly injured. All were suffering from exposure, their skin a leprous white from constant immersion in salt water. Wentworth was the last to come across, a different man now, burned up by the twenty-four hours he'd been in command. Stratton was dead—with the Cox'n he'd been getting the men out of the mess deck when the whole bridge structure had been crushed like a biscuit tin; and Pinney, who'd thought Laerg the best posting he'd had. Four men had died during the night, including the young steward, Perkins, whose ribcage had been stoved in by the slam of the water-tight doors. Field said there was no sign of the landing craft, only bits and pieces of metal scattered among the rocks.

The wind went round that night into the northwest and the tug came close inshore. By midnight everybody had been embarked. Everybody except my brother. It was the Doc who discovered he wasn't on board. He'd had a list made and a roll called, for the confusion on the tug was indescribable—thirty-five extra men, many of them casualties.

'Where's Major Braddock?' I heard the question passed along the deck. 'Anybody seen Major Braddock?' Voices calling in the darkness of the decks. And then the Skipper giving orders. Sergeant Wetherby piling into the boat again, the outboard motor bursting into life. I jumped in beside him and we shot away from the tug's side, slapping through the shallows over the low tide sand bar.

The outboard died as the bows grated and the boat came to a sudden halt. We scrambled out into a foot or more of water and ploughed over the sands to the beach. Wetherby thought he might have gone to check the remains of the transport that lay, battered and derelict, among the rocks behind the loading beach. He was an MT sergeant. Whilst he went towards the dim shape of the bulldozer, now standing high and dry on the sands, I hurried to the camp. Every now and then the wind brought me the sound of his voice calling: 'Major Braddock! Major Braddock!'

The lights were out in the camp now, the generator still. I stumbled about in the darkness, calling. At first I called his Army name, but then, because it didn't seem to matter here alone, I called: 'Iain! Iain—where are you?' I reached the hut and, fumbling in the dark, found the torch I'd used. The place was empty; the radio still there and all the mess and litter of its temporary use as a casualty clearing station. I went outside then, probing and calling.

I'd never have found him without the torch. He was standing in the lee of the cookhouse, quite still, his back turned towards me as though afraid his face might catch the light: 'What the hell are you playing at?' I demanded. 'Why didn't you answer?'

He stared at me, but didn't say anything for a moment. There was a twitch at the corner of his mouth and his face was deathly pale. 'Are you ill?' I asked.

He moved then, came closer to me and reached for my arm. 'Donald.' His voice was hoarse, little more than a whisper against the blatter of the wind. 'Go back. Go back to the ship. You haven't seen me. Understand?' The urgency of his request was almost as startling as the request itself. He jerked at my arm. 'Go—back.' Behind the hoarseness of his voice, I caught the tremor of his mood, something deep that he couldn't control. 'As you love me, Donald, go back.'

'But why? What's wrong? Is it Lane?' I asked. 'Has he been worrying you?'

'He's been on to me—twice from the mainland. But it isn't that.' His grip tightened on my arm. 'Leave me now, will you?'

'But why?'

'Damn you, Donald! Can't you do what I ask?' And then, his voice more controlled: 'Something I have to do. We left in a hurry— the tide and a change of wind. No time . . . and Leroux half dead, too weak to do anything. It was either that or be trapped.' His voice had died to a whisper.

'You mean you were here?' I asked. 'After

the *Duart Castle* ...'

'Try to understand, can't you? Just leave me here and no questions.'

I hesitated. The torch on his face showed his mouth tight-set, his eyes urgent. 'All right,' I said. 'If that's what you want ...'

But I was too late. As I switched off the torch and turned to go, a voice spoke out of the darkness behind me: 'You've found him then?' It was Sergeant Wetherby. His jacketed figure loomed bulkily from the direction of the generator. And to Iain, he said, 'Major Braddock, sir. The tug's all ready to go—everybody on board. Only yourself, sir. They're waiting for you.'

I heard Iain's muttered curse. And then in a flat voice: 'Very good, Sergeant. Sorry if I held things up—just a last check round.' He came with us then. There was nothing else he could do for he couldn't hope to persuade the sergeant to let him stay. And so we embarked and at 01.15 hours on the morning of October 24, the tug steamed out of Shelter Bay with the last remnant of the Army Detachment.

The evacuation was complete at a cost of fifty-three lives, the loss of one landing craft, a helicopter and a great deal of equipment.

PART THREE

AFTERMATH OF DISASTER

WITCH-HUNT
(October 24–February 28)

Press reaction to the news of the disaster was immediate. The first scattered fragments had begun coming through within hours of our landing craft being wrecked. Radio and TV put it out in their newscasts as it filtered through and during the day the story moved from the Stop Press of the evening papers to the front page. The main body of the Press, however, had almost twelve hours in which to build the story up; and because it involved the out-islands, ships, the sea, the weather, they knew the impact it would have on the public. All that day telephones rang continuously in the press offices of the three Services and in the Meteorological Office in Kingsway. The Admiralty and the Air Ministry were helpful; the Army less so for they were inhibited by the knowledge that a commanding officer had ordered the arrest of his second-in-command. In an attempt to avoid this becoming known to the Press, they clamped down on all comment, closed the military line to Northton to all but official calls and confined their press releases to the facts of the situation. The effect was to make the Press suspicious.

An enterprising reporter on the local Stornoway paper got hold of Fellowes. His story of the flight to Laerg and Mike Ferguson's death was scooped by a popular daily. A Reuter's man, who had flown north from Glasgow that morning, reached Northton in time to get the news of Standing's death and watch the tug leave from Leverburgh quay. His dispatches went out on the Reuter teleprint service to all newspaper offices.

By that night the full extent of the disaster was known, the presses of the national dailies were rolling out the story and reporters and photographers were hurrying north. So many took the night train to Glasgow that BEA, who had cancelled the morning's flight to Stornoway, had second thoughts. The newspaper men had a rough flight, but by midday they were piling into Northton and Leverburgh. Others, mainly photographers with specially chartered planes, stood by at Stornoway from dawn onwards to take pictures of Laerg. Fellowes found his plane in great demand.

The fact that there were survivors gave a dramatic quality to the news and most of Britain had the story on their breakfast tables, front-paged under flaring headlines—a story of storm and disaster, of a colonel and his adjutant killed in the attempts to rescue men trapped on a gale-torn rock in the North Atlantic. And to add to the drama was the suggestion that the Army had something to hide. Editors' instructions were to get at the truth.

Two reporters in search of a drink landed up at the hotel at Rodil. They got hold of Marjorie. She was in a highly emotional state and prepared to talk. If Standing had been alive, she might have blamed him on account of Mike Ferguson's death. But Standing was dead, and because she was frightened for her father, she put the blame for everything on Major Braddock, and in attacking him, she revealed that he had been placed under arrest for ordering the LCT in to the beach. For those two reporters she was worth her weight in gold.

Other reporters, casing the Northton HQ and getting no change out of the Army personnel who had all been instructed to have no contact with the Press, transferred their attention to the Met. Office. They, too, struck gold. Cliff was a story in himself and nothing would have stopped that little Welshman from talking. He gave it to them, blow by blow, as seen from the weather man's point of view. One correspondent, reporting him from a tape-recorded interview, gave his words verbatim: 'I tell you, the man must have been off his bloody nut, ordering a landing craft into the beach on a night like that. Oh yes, the wind was north then and they were under the lee of the island

299

in Shelter Bay. But aground like that, she was at the mercy of the elements, you see, and when the wind swung into the south . . .'

There was more in the same vein and it all went south by wire and phone to the waiting presses in London. And by the following morning the public was convinced that the man responsible for this appalling loss of life was Major Braddock. They weren't told that in so many words, but it was implied, and this before he had had a chance to defend himself, when he was, in fact, still on Laerg organising the rescue operations.

Once the survivors had been reported safe, the excitement of the story dwindled and news-hungry reporters, looking for a fresh angle, began delving into the relations between Braddock and his Commanding Officer. What had happened at that interview in Standing's office in the early hours of the morning of October 22? Why had he placed Braddock under arrest? Cliff was interviewed on TV and radio. So was Marjorie. Laura Standing, too, and Fellowes. The evidence piled up and all this canned material was being rushed down to London whilst the tug was still battling its way through the aftermath of the gale.

We steamed into Leverburgh just after four-thirty in the afternoon. We had been hove-to twice for the MO to carry out minor operations. The rest of the time we had managed little more than seven knots. The tug's internal accommodation was sufficient only for the serious casualties. The rest—men suffering from exposure and extreme exhaustion—had to be left out on the open deck. Anything over seven knots and the tug would have been shipping water in the heavy seas. As a result the voyage took almost fourteen hours and during all that time the men were exposed to wind and spray. One man died during the night and there were several showing symptoms of pneumonia by the time we docked.

The quay was packed as we came alongside, packed solid with men whose dress proclaimed them foreigners to the Hebrides. Army personnel in charge of the vehicles to take the survivors to Northton tried to hold them back, but as the tug's side touched the quay they swarmed on board. They were all after one man. 'Where's Braddock? Which is Major Braddock? Where is he—in the Captain's cabin?'

In fact, Iain had been sleeping in the scuppers on the port side. 'I don't think he'll see anybody. He's very tired.'

'I can't help that. He's news.' He told me the paper he represented and thrust a note into my hand. 'Here's a five. Just point him out to me, that's all.' And when I told him to go to hell, he tried to make it a tenner.

They found him in the end, of course. They brought him to bay like a pack of hounds in a corner under the bridge housing and he stood there, facing them, his battered face grey with fatigue, his voice hoarse with shouting above the wind. They were all round him, their notebooks out, firing questions. And all he said was, 'No comment.'

He didn't realise that this was his one opportunity to defend himself—that he'd never get another. He stuck to the letter of QRs and refused to make a statement, relying on his superiors to back him up. Relying, too, on the fact that without his efforts the survivors would never have been got off Sgeir Mhor alive. He didn't know then that his superiors were going to throw him to the wolves, that he was to be the scapegoat. How could he? For the last thirty-six hours he'd been involved in physical action, body and mind devoted to one thing alone—getting those men off. He didn't understand that these reporters couldn't visualise the circumstances. He was dead tired and his own mind was incapable at that moment of making the leap from individual effort to the broader aspects of the affair. No comment! A statement will be issued in due course. His Army training overlaid whatever personal inclination he had. He behaved, in fact, with perfect correctness and in doing so he damned himself before that most violent and blind of all judges—the public.

I saw the faces of the reporters harden. Frustration developed into anger. One man, snapping his notebook shut, seemed to speak for the rest: 'Okay, Major, have it your own way. But don't blame us if the public forms its own opinion of your evacuation order.'

Other notebooks snapped. The circle broke up and Iain stood there, tight-lipped and with a baffled look on his face, as they suddenly abandoned him to move amongst the survivors in search of personal, human interest stories. There was no shortage of these. The struggle to get the landing craft off the beach, the fight to get her out of Shelter Bay and clear of the rocks of Sgeir Mhor in the teeth of the hurricane, the failure of the engines, the scene of utter confusion as she struck with the bridge deck concertinaed against the fortress mass of Sgeir Mhor; how for a short while the up-lifted stern section had acted as a sort of ramp, enabling those that were still alive to scramble ashore, the desperate hours of waiting through that ghastly night and the rising seas and the new storm breaking over them.

There was so much of human interest. In particular, there was Field. They got the story of his climb from Sergeant Wetherby and a bunch of them crowded round him. 'Tell me, Mr Field—how did you feel? Were you scared?' He tried to tell them about Braddock's crossing of the gut between the Butt of Keava and Sgeir Mhor, but they weren't interested in that now. Reporters in London, working on the background of the officers involved, had interviewed Field's wife. As a result they knew who he was. 'Could you give us your reactions please? ... How did it feel climbing that sheer cliff face? ... Was it as stiff as the climbs you faced in the Himalayas?' Cameras clicked, the TV men closed in.

And all the time Captain Flint with a squad of men was trying to get the injured off the ship and into the waiting vehicles. 'Get the hell out of it, you bloody blood-sucking bastards.' His Cockney humour had deserted him. The essential warmth of his nature was revolted by this spectacle of news-hungry men milling around amongst injured and exhausted survivors, fighting to get to grips with their stories. I saw him take a camera out of one photographer's hand and throw it over the side. The man had been trying to get a close-up of some poor devil with his face smashed in. 'The next one of you ghouls that tries that I'll 'eave the beggar over the side, camera an' all.'

I found Marjorie struggling to get near her father—shut out by the ring of men surrounding him. 'Oh, thank God!' she said when she saw me. 'What happened? Why are they all crowding round him?' The bloom was gone from her face, all the vitality knocked out of her. 'I can't get near him.' The pupils of those strangely blue eyes were dilated and the words came in a panic rush, almost a sob.

Briefly I told her what her father had done, and all the time she had hold of my hand,

304

clinging to it as though I were the one stable thing left to her. But as I talked I saw a change come over her. She seemed gradually to come alive. 'Then perhaps it's all right,' she breathed. 'Perhaps this is the end of it then.' It was extraordinary—the recuperative power of youth. Her eyes were suddenly shining, bright with hope, and then she kissed me full on the mouth for no apparent reason that I could see except that she needed to express her joy, her sense of relief that her father was safe and she didn't have to worry about him any longer. 'And what about you? All those hours alone on Laerg. You must be exhausted.' And she suggested that I come up to the croft with her father. 'It'll be better than going to the camp.' And with an understanding that surprised me because I'd never had anybody who'd cared a damn how I felt, she said, 'You'll need to unwind—slowly.'

I knew she was right. I was still extraordinarily keyed up. And yet at the same time I was utterly exhausted—a state of complete nervous fatigue. I did need to unwind, and I was grateful to her.

'If you'll just try and extricate my father . . .'

And so I left with them in the little estate car and I didn't see my brother again for a long time.

The next day's papers were full of the story of the disaster, pages of it—eye-witness accounts and personal stories, timetables of the events leading up to the rescue and Field's climb. Charles Field was suddenly a hero again. There were pictures of him. Pictures of the survivors. But reading the papers with the whole story written up like a thrilling serial, the blow-by-blow account of a great storm with human courage surmounting disaster, I detected an ominous note. There were leaders implying that men had died unnecessarily. There were feature articles that showed the whole course of that intense local depression— some gave the wind speed as high as 150 knots, though they had no means of knowing since there were no anemometers to record it—and here the implication was that if the officer in charge (meaning my brother) had taken the advice of the local Met. Officer, no lives need have been lost. They completely ignored the fact that Cliff's warning had come too late, almost three hours after the order to evacuate had been given.

Throughout every paper there was the same searching, angry note of inquiry. Somebody was responsible, and with Standing dead that man could only be Braddock. The order to evacuate, taken on his own responsibility, and his subsequent arrest, damned him utterly. There were questions asked about it in the House. The Secretary of State for War promised a full-scale inquiry.

It was a witch-hunt, nothing less, and my brother was the man they were all gunning for.

The people responsible for his appointment to the Hebrides did nothing to demonstrate their confidence in him. The reverse, in fact. They relieved him of his temporary command and sent him on indefinite leave pending the results of the Inquiry. No doubt this action was intended to relieve him of the pressure of phone calls, but its effect, inevitably, was to confirm the Press in their condemnation of his conduct.

I only heard that he'd been ordered away on leave two days later when I felt sufficiently recovered to visit Northton. Marjorie drove me to the camp. With her father and myself to look after, the croft to run and reporters to keep at bay, she was out of touch with camp affairs. I went straight to the Admin. block. There was a new adjutant, a Captain Davidson, short and dapper with a little moustache. 'Major Braddock? I'm sorry, he's away on leave. Colonel Webb's in command here now.' And he added, 'I'm afraid I can't give you Braddock's address. I don't think we've been notified where he's staying.'

And that was that. I saw Rafferty and Flint. Nobody had Iain's address. The slate had been wiped clean, my brother expunged as though he'd never existed. Whether they acted under orders, I don't know. The effect, at any rate, was the same. He was gone and nobody would, or could, tell me where. I returned to Marjorie waiting in the car and all the way back to Rodil

I was thinking of Iain, somewhere in the British Isles, a man condemned without a hearing. They hadn't even been able to tell me when the Inquiry would be held. 'You'll be notified in due course, Mr Ross,' the dapper little adjutant had said. 'At least, I imagine you will, since I gather you're a vital witness.'

A witness! I hadn't thought of that. A witness against my own brother. And Iain wandering lost and alone with nobody to turn to. If he hadn't been separated from his wife, if he'd been able to draw on the strength of his family ... But life had kicked even that support from under him.

'He's alone,' I said, not realising I was speaking aloud. 'Absolutely alone.'

Marjorie braked, glancing at me quickly. 'Who? Major Braddock?' And then, in a quiet voice, she said, 'Donald, I've been wondering— we've both been wondering ... What is your connection with Major Braddock?' She was staring straight ahead of her then, her eyes fixed on the road. 'There is a connection, isn't there?'

So they'd noticed. I didn't say anything for a moment. 'If you don't want to talk about it . . . I thought perhaps it might help.'

I had to think about this, about whether it was fair to Iain. But I, too, was alone. And they'd been kind to me. Friendship, understanding ... I suppose even then I was aware of the attraction of this girl, a growing

308

closeness between us that wasn't only physical. And to share my fears . . .

But remembering the haunted look on his face, I shook my head. 'Not now,' I said. 'Later perhaps . . .'

She touched my hand, a gesture of sympathy. 'If I'd known . . .' But then she shook her head. 'No, I'd still have felt the same. He did give the order, you know.' And she added, 'Why? Why was he so determined to get them away on that last LCT?'

Why indeed? With a woman's intuition she had hit on the real point, the basic fact that made my brother guilty. But I couldn't see it then. I was thinking only of the disaster, not of what might have gone before when he cloaked himself in another man's identity, and I said, 'It was because he knew if he didn't get them off then, they'd have been stuck there for the winter with insufficient supplies.' I was quoting Field, who'd had it from Rafferty, and all the time the thing was there, staring me in the face.

But Lane, his mind concentrated on his own monetary affairs, unclouded by all the details of the disaster, had seen it. I had a phone call from him within an hour of my return to London. 'That you, Ross? Glad to know you're back at last. Where's your brother?' I tried to deny that he was my brother, but he ignored that. 'I want a word with that guy. Now you just tell me where he is or I'm going to pass this whole story over to the Press. After what's

309

happened, they'll just lap it up.'

'I don't think so,' I said.

'And why not?'

'In this country the law of libel is still very—'

'Libel!' His soft voice was suddenly tough. 'You talk about libel when the man may prove to be a murderer. Yeah, a murderer.' I thought he was referring to the men who'd been drowned. But it wasn't that. His one-track mind was making a much more specific charge. 'Have you considered, Mr Ross, what happened to the original Braddock—the young George Braddock, aged twenty and just commissioned, afloat on that life-raft with this monster of a brother of yours? Have you considered that?'

It came as a shock. And yet it had been at the back of my mind ever since I'd seen Iain standing with his finned feet in the surf, staring up at the hidden heights of Laerg; ever since that moment when I'd come ashore to find him waiting up in the camp, desperate to be left alone there. 'I think,' I said, trying to keep control of my voice, 'you'd better not repeat that. Major Braddock may be facing an Inquiry, but that doesn't mean you can make wild accusations . . .'

'Major Braddock!' There was anger and contempt in his voice. 'His name's Iain Ross. It's Iain Ross we're talking about, and you know it. Why else did you go north to the

310

Hebrides? How else could you have managed to get on that landing craft and finish up in Laerg? Both of you, there on your own island together. Now you just tell me where I'll find the son-of-a-bitch. That's all I want from you—for the moment.' And when I told him I didn't know, he said, 'All right, Ross. You stick by him. Very admirable of you—very fraternal. But you won't fob me off as easily as that. I'll just stay on here in England. I can wait. They'll produce him when the Board of Inquiry sits. And then I'll get him. I'll get the truth out of him then, so help me God, and if it's what I think it is, I'll brand him for the Goddamned murdering bastard he is. Goo'bye.' And he slammed the phone down.

I didn't see my brother again until the Board of Inquiry, which was held at Scottish Command on November 2. He had, however, been in touch with me once, very briefly, during the intervening ten days. It was a phone call late at night, about eleven-fifteen. I recognised his voice at once for he made no pretence of concealing his natural accent. 'Donald? Is that you, Donald?'

'Where are you?' I said. 'In London?'

'Aye, in some bluidy nightclub—I forget the name. I must ha' a wee talk wi' you, Donald. Can you come down here? Right away. I must ha' a talk wi' ye.'

'Of course.' And I added, 'Are you all right, Iain?' His voice sounded thick and slurred. I thought he'd been drinking.

'Yes, I'm all right, laddie. It's just that I've made up my mind. I must talk to somebody. I'm all alone, you see. An' I thought maybe if you'd nothing better to do . . .'

'Whereabouts are you?' I said. I didn't want to lose him. 'I'll come right down. Just tell me where to meet you.'

'Aye, weel—I'm somewhere doon Curzon Street way.' The accent was very broad and getting more slurred. 'What aboot Cook's now, meet me outside Cook's in Berkeley Street.'

'Okay, I'll be there at midnight,' I said.

'Fine, fine, that'll do fine. We'll ha' a wee drink together, eh? Like old times. Only hurry. I canna stand my own company much longer.' And he'd hung up.

I'd just gone to bed, so that I had to dress, and then there was the problem of transport. Fortunately I had enough money in the studio for a taxi and I found one on the rank outside Aldgate East Station. I was at Cook's by five to twelve. But he wasn't there, and though I hung around until 2 a.m., he never showed up.

He didn't ring me again and that was my only contact with him until I saw him in Service dress walking out of the Conference Room where the Board of Inquiry was being held. I was shocked at the change in him. The twitch at the corner of his mouth had become much more marked, the lines of his face deeper. There were bags under his eyes, and above

312

them the eyes themselves stared weary and lack-lustre out of darkened sockets. He'd obviously been drinking heavily. His hands were trembling. He passed me without a flicker of recognition.

Shortly afterwards I was called to give evidence. The Inquiry was being conducted by a colonel. He sat at a mahogany table with a major on one side and a captain on the other. None of these officers was connected with Northton. They were taking depositions and by the way they questioned me I was certain it was merely the prelude to a court martial.

They took my evidence under oath. To some extent it was a cross-examination, with the Major making notes of my replies. They went over the whole sequence of events and my part in them. And when I had told them all I knew, the Major laboriously wrote out a summarised version in longhand. Then he read it through to me and when I had agreed that it was a fair statement of what I'd told them, I was asked to sign it.

I thought that was the end of it and was just getting up to leave, when the Colonel said, 'One moment, Mr Ross.' He searched through the folder in front of him and produced a letter. 'D'you know anything about a Mr Edward William Lane of Vancouver, a Canadian businessman?' I'd been expecting this and I was prepared for it. 'Yes,' I said. 'He visited me in London on October 15. My brother Iain was among those missing when the *Duart Castle* was torpedoed in 1944. Lane had a theory that he was still alive.'

'In fact, he thought Major Braddock might be your brother. Correct?'

I nodded.

'The next day you left London for the Outer Hebrides. You landed at Rodil in the Island of Harris on October 18 and I understand you saw Major Braddock the following day.'

'Yes.'

'Had you ever visited the Outer Hebrides before?' And when I admitted I hadn't, he said, 'I take it then that you went up there for the express purpose of checking on Major Braddock's identity? In other words, you thought there was a possibility that he might be your missing brother?'

'It was partly that,' I agreed. 'Lane had convinced me that my brother could have been with Braddock on that life-raft and I thought he might be able to tell me what had happened. Also,' I added, 'there seemed a possibility that I might be able to get out to Laerg.' I started to explain to him then about my connection with the island and my desire to paint the scenes that my grandfather had described, but he cut me short.

'We are only concerned here with your visit as it affected Major Braddock. Now then, is there any truth in Lane's suggestion?'

I didn't give him a direct answer. Instead, I

314

said, 'I understand that you've already taken evidence from the Senior Meteorological Officer at Northton. My first meeting with Major Braddock took place in the Met. Office. I imagine you have already asked Cliff Morgan whether Braddock and I recognised each other.'

He nodded.

'What did he say?' I asked.

'That as far as he can remember there was no indication that you had ever met each other before.'

It was a great weight off my mind to know that. 'Then that surely is your answer, sir,' I said. 'If Braddock had, in fact, been my brother, then I would hardly be a reliable witness. At the same time, it would have shown in our reaction to each other at that first meeting. You can have my word for it, if you like, but I think you will agree that the best evidence you have that there is no connection between us is Morgan's.' And I added, 'Perhaps you haven't appreciated this point. I don't know whether Lane explains it in that letter, but he's now over here in an attempt to prove that Major Braddock is not entitled to a fortune of some quarter of a million dollars left him by his aunt. From what Lane told me, I got the impression that he was prepared to go to almost any lengths to upset the Will and get the money for his wife's family.'

'I see. No, he doesn't mention that here.'

The Colonel hesitated. Finally he said, 'It puts rather a different complexion on the whole business.'

For Iain's sake I'd been prepared to lie, but after that it wasn't necessary. The Colonel was faced with an unpleasant enough task as it was. He'd no wish to become involved with something that had happened more than twenty years ago. 'Very well, I agree. That settles it. And I'm glad, for if there'd been any truth in it, then it would have raised the question of what had happened to the real George Braddock.' He gave a little sigh and pushed the letter back into the folder. 'Extraordinary what people will do for money. I'm sorry I've had to raise the matter . . . most unpleasant for you.' And he smiled his relief and said, 'That's all, Mr Ross. Thank you for coming to the evidence. I am also asked by my superiors to thank you for all you did on Laerg to assist in the rescue of the survivors.'

'I didn't do much,' I said. 'Braddock's the man to whom the survivors owe their lives. Field would never have made that climb if it hadn't been for Braddock. He organised the whole thing.'

The Colonel's sharp little eyes stared at me hard and I wondered for a moment if I'd said too much. But it was true and I was damned if I was going to leave the Inquiry without making the point. If they were going to blame him for what had happened, at least they ought to

316

realise that without the driving force of his personality nobody would have been saved and the loss of life would have been that much greater.

Probably they knew that already. But it made no difference.

After hearing over a dozen witnesses they passed the depositions to the Director of Army Legal Services and in due course the next step towards Court Martial proceedings was taken. This was a Summary of Evidence and again I was called. Iain was present throughout the examination of witnesses, and this, more than anything else, seemed to emphasise the seriousness of his situation.

I understand he had the right to question witnesses. Whether he availed himself of this right I do not know; in my case he certainly did not, sitting tense and very still, his eyes never raised to my face. I was in the room almost two hours and all the time I was conscious of the nervous tension in him, could literally feel it. And he looked desperately ill.

I thought perhaps he would contact me afterwards, but he didn't, and though I stayed the night in Edinburgh just in case, I had no word from him. Perhaps he thought it would be unwise. In any case there was nothing I could have done—only given him moral support. Back in London I wrote him a carefully worded letter beginning *Dear Major Braddock* and inquiring whether there was anything I could do to help. I received no reply.

The waiting I knew would be hard on him, a nervous strain. The loneliness, too. This worried me as much as anything else, and in desperation I went and saw his wife.

I'd kept a newspaper cutting that gave her address and I found her living in one of the back streets of Hertford, a small woman with doe-like eyes and a will that was hard as iron. I went in the evening with the story that I was a welfare worker for SAAFA, but nothing I could say would induce her to visit her husband. She got the Army allowance, and that was all she wanted of him. And the only clues she gave me to why they had parted was when she said, 'I had five years of it.' And added, 'Nerves are one thing, but nerves and drink . . . No, I don't want to see him again.'

Yet she still had his photograph in a silver frame standing on a table beside the TV set—aged about thirty, I thought, and much as I remembered him in the Glasgow days, the lines of his face barely showing, but still that scar above the bridge of the nose. 'If it's any comfort to him in his present circumstances,' she said as she showed me to the door, 'you can tell him both the girls are well and pray for him nightly.' And she added, her lips tight and no tenderness in her eyes, 'I told them he'd been killed—and then this business with reporters coming here and the news of it on the telly, you can imagine the shock it was—how I felt.'

Christmas came and went, the New Year. Marjorie wrote from Rodil that Iain was in hospital. 'My father says they think Major Braddock is suffering from some sort of nervous breakdown. It's not serious apparently, but I thought you'd like to know. It's the waiting, of course. And now I can't help feeling sorry for him.'

There was nothing I could do about it. I couldn't very well write to him again, and if I tried to visit him the authorities would wonder at my interest. I was working all the time and so January slipped into February with news from Marjorie that he was out of hospital. The rest of her letter was about the fishing and how the solan geese were starting to come back. 'Soon there'll be all manner of birds and it'll be warmer with clear skies. Come back then and paint. It's so beautiful in the spring . . .'

And then at last the official letter notifying me that Major Braddock's Court Martial would be held in Edinburgh on February 24, starting at 10 a.m.: *You are pursuant to Section 103 of the Army Act, 1955, and Rule 91 of the Rules of Procedure (Army), 1956, made thereunder, hereby summoned and required to attend at the sitting of the said court . . . and so to attend from day to day until you shall be duly discharged; whereof you shall fail at your peril.*

Four days later I got an airmail letter from Lane in Vancouver. Obviously he was paying somebody to keep him posted. 'Tell your brother that I'm flying over immediately and will be in Edinburgh on the 24th. Tell him also that I have some fresh evidence. My agents have located one of the Military Policemen acting as his escort on the *Duart Castle*. This man survived on one of the boats that reached Ireland and he is prepared to swear that Sergeant Iain Alasdair Ross was on that life-raft. He also saw Second-Lieutenant George Braddock clinging to it. Furthermore, he says he would recognise your brother . . .'

The Court Martial was held at Dreghorn Camp just outside Edinburgh. It opened prompt at ten o'clock with the swearing in of the Court. For this ceremony the witnesses were present, all of us standing at the back of the court. It was a bare, rather bleak room, but the arrangement of the desks and tables and the grouping of the officers transformed it, and the colour of the uniforms made it impressive so that I was conscious of the atmosphere, the sense of being caught up in the Military legal machine. Instead of a judge with his wig and scarlet robes, five officers sat in judgment. And in the body of the court—the accused, the officer defending him, the Prosecuting Officer, all the various officials, even to the NCOs on duty, in full dress. The effect was overpowering and I wondered how my brother felt as the doors closed and quiet descended. The Judge Advocate, seated on the President's right hand, read the convening order.

From where I stood I could see only the back of Iain's head, hunched down into his shoulders, which sagged slightly as he sat slumped in his seat, staring down at the table in front of him. He seemed quite passive, almost dazed, and when he was asked if he objected to being tried by the President or any of the other members of the Court his reply was inaudible. And then the Judge Advocate's voice, clear and crisp: 'Everybody will stand uncovered whilst the Court is sworn.' A shuffle of chairs and the court-room rose to its feet as he faced the President. 'Please repeat after me—' The Brigadier spoke the words he knew by heart in a clipped, very clear voice: 'I swear by Almighty God that I will well and truly try the Accused before the Court according to the evidence and that I will duly administer justice according to the Army Act, 1955, without partiality, favour or affection . . .'

The four other officers who constituted the Court were sworn and then the President swore in the Judge Advocate himself. After that the witnesses were ushered out into an adjoining room. There were altogether twenty-seven witnesses. Most of them were from Northton—Field, Rafferty, Flint, the MO, Phipps, Sergeant Wetherby and several other ranks I'd never seen before, including the Signals NCO who'd been on duty when the fatal order was given. Cliff was there and another civilian who turned out to be Fellowes, the pilot who had flown the plane from which Mike Ferguson had jumped to his death. Wentworth, too, and a young Captain who, Field told me, was the Commander of L4400. Both Brigadier Matthieson and the BGS from the War Office had also been called, but their rank enabled them to avoid the tedium of waiting in the confines of that small room.

There was a Military Policeman on the door to see that we didn't discuss the case, nothing to do but sit and smoke, and I had ample opportunity to consider what my brother must be going through in the next room. Occasionally we could hear the murmur of voices, the stamp of boots as some NCO moved, the scrape of chairs, the sound of coughing.

The preliminaries took just over an hour— the reading of the charges and the Prosecuting Officer's speech in which he put his case. We could just hear the murmur of his voice. The first witness was called shortly after eleven-thirty. This was the Signals NCO. He was followed by the duty driver, then Flint, then Wentworth. Wentworth was still giving evidence when the Court adjourned for lunch. The order in which the witnesses had been called was our only indication of the course the case was taking. Clearly the Prosecuting Officer was establishing the fact of the order to evacuate having been given.

Field was called during the afternoon and

when the Court finally rose, he was waiting for me outside. 'Marjorie asked me to give you her love.' He smiled. He was looking younger, more buoyant, and his eyes had lost that nervous blink.

'How was Braddock?' I asked.

He hesitated then shook his head. 'Not good, I'm afraid. Very nervy-looking; at times I wondered whether he understood what was going on. He's still a sick man, I'm afraid.'

I asked him about the nervous breakdown, but he didn't know the details. 'The strain of waiting, I imagine. Three months almost. It's a long time. Too long. But once it's over, probably he'll be all right then.'

'What are the chances?' I asked.

He shrugged. 'Hard to say. He's got a good man defending him, good enough at any rate to handle the two brigadiers. But even if he gets them to say they had every confidence in the accused, it won't outweigh the fact that Standing had him arrested. If Standing were here to be cross-examined . . .' Again that little shrug. 'But he isn't, you see, and dying like that he's something of a hero. That counts for a lot in a case like this. And there's all the publicity. The Judge Advocate may tell them what the law is, but the Court is human; they can't help being influenced by it. And the size of the disaster. Fifty-three men dead. Who's to be blamed if Braddock is acquitted? The Press will say the Army is covering up and there'll be more questions in the House.'

'So you don't think he's got a chance?'

He hesitated. And then he said, 'No. Frankly, I don't.'

I was called the following afternoon, immediately after Cliff Morgan had given evidence. When I took my place at the witness table I was shocked to see how ill Iain looked, his eyes wandering vacantly, his big, powerful hands never still—plucking at the buttons of his uniform, toying with his pencil, sometimes brushing over his face and up through his hair with a quick, nervous gesture. I don't think he once looked directly at me all the time I was being questioned. As Field had said, he still seemed a sick man—all his intense nervous energy beaten down, as though something had destroyed his will to fight back. I had that feeling very strongly, that his strength was being sapped from within, and I wondered to what extent he had been affected by the fact that Lane was in Edinburgh. I had seen Lane that morning, just a glimpse of him as I was entering the main gate of the camp. He was sitting there in a car with another man.

'Will the witness please answer the question.' The President's voice, kindly but firm, brought me back to the stillness of the court-room and the rather bland-looking major who was defending Iain standing facing me, waiting patiently for my answer.

'I'm sorry,' I said. 'Perhaps you would repeat

324

the question.'

'I asked you, Mr Ross, whether you could recall the time at which Major Braddock gave the order to evacuate the island?'

'Yes,' I said. 'Or rather, I can remember when the landing craft came into the beach. She grounded at nine forty-eight.'

'And Major Braddock's order?'

'About ten minutes earlier. The landing craft was coming into the beach as we left the hut. Say, nine-thirty.'

'Now I want the Court to understand the circumstances in which that order was given. What was the direction of the wind at that time?'

'Northerly. It had been northerly all day.'

'And no indication of a change?'

'No.'

'After the landing craft beached you went on board?'

'Yes.'

'Where were you then?'

'I was helping on the tank deck until nearly midnight. After that I went to the wardroom.'

'Where you found Lieutenant Wentworth talking to Captain Stratton?'

'Yes.'

'What were they discussing?'

'A radio message they had received from the Met. Officer at Northton.'

'Do you know when that message was received?'

'It had just come in so it would have been shortly after midnight.'

'Two and a half hours after Major Braddock had given the order.'

'Yes.'

'And the wind at Laerg was still northerly then?'

'Yes.' I saw the point he was trying to establish and I added, 'It remained northerly for another four and a half hours.'

The Major reached for his glasses and glanced at his notes. 'Mr Morgan in his evidence said that he was in contact with the *Viking Fisher* at twenty-three forty-seven. That's the trawler that was finally lost with all hands. Thirteen minutes to midnight. In your opinion was there any way in which Major Braddock could have foreseen how circumstances were going to change?'

'No,' I said. 'Definitely not.' I glanced at Iain as his Defending Officer said, 'Thank you, Mr Ross,' in a satisfied tone. I was surprised to see him running his pencil back and forth across the table in front of him, apparently taking no interest in the proceedings.

The Defending Officer turned to the President of the Court. 'That is the point I wish to establish.' And then to me: 'You have some experience of the sea, I believe. A year in the Navy and ten in the Merchant Service as a deck officer. Correct?'

'Yes.'

'You were on the bridge with Captain Stratton part of the time during the crossing to Laerg and throughout the events that led up to the loss of the ship. Would you say he was a capable seaman?'

'Very capable.'

'So that in coming in to the beach you would say, would you not, that it was the action of a capable seaman?'

'Yes,' I said. 'I'm certain Captain Stratton would never have brought his landing craft in to the beach if he had thought there was any danger.'

'And he was in a much better position than Major Braddock to assess the local weather situation?'

'I think you have made your point, Major Selkirk,' the President said.

The Major gave a nod and a quick smile. 'I just wanted to make it quite clear, sir.' He glanced down at the papers on his desk. 'Lieutenant Wentworth in his evidence has said that after the ship was unloaded Captain Pinney refused to take his men ashore. Can you confirm that?'

'Yes. I was in the wheelhouse at the time.'

'When was this?'

'Between two-thirty and three, I should say.'

'Can you recall the conversation?'

'It was hardly a conversation,' I said.

'A row?'

'No, not a row.' Briefly I told them what

327

Pinney's attitude had been.

'So even then, somewhere between two-thirty and three, there was doubt about the wind shifting from the north?'

'Yes.'

'Not only in Pinney's mind, but in Stratton's as well?'

I nodded.

'Thank you.' He shifted his stance, glanced at my brother who was still fiddling around with that damned pencil, and then his gaze came back to me. 'You remember that Captain Stratton asked his radio operator to contact Colonel Standing. About what time would that have been?'

'Around twelve-thirty. We were in the wardroom then. He wanted to talk to Colonel Standing personally and he told the operator that the Colonel was to be got out of bed if necessary.' And I added, 'He said something about it being time the men who gave the orders lost a little sleep on our account.'

Quick as a flash he said, 'Are you implying that he knew Colonel Standing had gone up to his house, which was a mile from the camp—that he had, in fact, retired to—'

But the President interrupted him. 'Major Selkirk. I must remind you again that Colonel Standing is dead. References to him should be confined to facts. You must not include vague statements about him or expressions of opinion or the comments of other officers.'

328

'I quite understand, sir.' The Defending Officer's face was wooden and he rustled the papers in his hand as he faced the Court. 'I will endeavour to follow your ruling, but I must point out that the officer I am defending faces very serious charges and my case rests to some extent on the clash of personalities that, I submit, was the direct and inevitable result of this somewhat, shall I say, unusual appointment. You have heard the evidence this morning of two brigadiers, both of whom briefed the accused following his appointment. Both have admitted that their instructions could be interpreted as making Major Braddock directly responsible for the success of the operation. However, if Colonel Standing's behaviour is not to be referred to . . .' He flung his papers on to the desk. 'Mr Ross, you will now tell the Court what Captain Stratton said after he'd spoken to Colonel Standing.'

I hesitated, for I didn't see how this could help Iain. But the Court was waiting and I said, 'He didn't say very much—just that Colonel Standing hadn't known about the order and was angry.'

'Angry? Because he'd been got out of bed in the middle of the night?' I saw the President lean forward, but Selkirk was too quick for him. 'Or was it because he didn't know, at that time, that there was a landing craft grounded on the beach in Shelter Bay?'

'I think it was because he didn't know about the evacuation.'

'Did he know there was a landing craft on the beach or not?'

'He couldn't have done.'

'Did he know about the Met. Officer's latest forecast?'

'I don't think so.'

'In other words, he was completely out of touch with the situation and it was Major Braddock—'

The Prosecuting Officer was on his feet, but the President forestalled him: 'I must insist that you confine yourself to questions of fact and refrain from putting opinions of your own into the witness's mouth.'

'Very well, sir. But I would ask the Court's indulgence. It is a little difficult to know who exactly was in command.' Again he adjusted his glasses, leaning down to check his notes. 'Now, about radio contact. In your deposition which I have here, you say you spoke to Mr Morgan yourself on R/T. What was the reception like?'

'Very poor,' I told him. 'And Stratton said it was bad when he was talking to Colonel Standing.'

'Was that the reason, do you think, that Captain Pinney wasn't given a direct order by his superiors to get his men off the ship?' And before I could reply, he went on, 'Or would you say, from your own experience, that in a situation like this Major Braddock would be fully justified in leaving any decision like that to the men on the spot?'

'I think by then,' I said, 'the situation was beyond the control of anybody at Base.'

He nodded, and after that he stood for a moment reading through his notes. I saw my brother's attention wander to the door at the back of the court. He had done that several times. Major Selkirk had stepped back from his desk, head thrown up and his eyes fixed on me again. 'Now we come to the loss of L8610 ... the cause, or rather the twin causes, for there were two, weren't there?' And when I nodded, he went on, 'These were covered very fully by Lieutenant Wentworrh in his evidence, but I would like to confirm one point with you—the failure of the steering. Do you remember Lieutenant Wentworth making a comment about the tiller flat? He says he told Captain Stratton that it was being flooded. Do you recall him making that report?'

'Yes.'

'And did he give a reason?'

I told them then how the stretcher party had taken McGregor's body to the tiller flat and had failed to secure the hatch on leaving. 'That was what caused the flooding.'

'And it was the failure of the steering, was it not, that threw the ship on her beam ends and made it impossible to deal with the sea water in the ready-use tank?'

'Yes.'

'And that again was something that Captain Stratton couldn't have foreseen?'

'Nobody could have foreseen it,' I said.

'And certainly not Major Braddock, back at Base?'

'No.'

And on that he sat down. There was a moment of shuffling relaxation in the court-room, and then the Prosecuting Officer rose to cross-examine me. He was a large, quiet man with a soft voice and a manner that was easy, almost friendly. 'One or two small points, Mr Ross. We know that Captain Pinney virtually refused to take his men off the ship. But later, just before you got off the beach, I think I'm right in saying that Colonel Standing spoke to him on the R/T. Am I also right in saying that the result of that talk was a direct order from his Colonel to get his men disembarked?'

'I believe so, but by then it was quite impossible.' I knew what he was after. He wanted to show that Standing had not only countermanded the order, but had come very near to saving the situation. He was going to try and show Standing as a decisive man whose subordinate had let him down and who was making a last-minute effort to rectify the damage that had been done. I glanced at my brother, but his head was again turned towards the door, which was half-open. A sergeant had come in and was just closing it. I turned to the President, determined not to have this point twisted to the advantage of the Prosecution. 'The first contact Colonel Standing had with the ship was when he spoke to Captain Stratton. My impression is that he had already taken personal command; yet he gave no order for the disembarkation of the Laerg detachment. I agree he did eventually give the order to Pinney, but by then it was at least two hours too late.'

The President nodded. 'And in your view the accused officer was not responsible at that time?'

'That's my impression—that Colonel Standing was in control.'

The Prosecuting Officer continued: 'You mentioned that radio conditions were bad . . .' He was shifting his ground, but at that moment the sergeant came down the room, his footsteps loud on the bare boards. He handed the President a note. When he had read it, the President glanced quickly at me, and from me to Iain. He didn't say anything, but after consultation with the Judge Advocate he cleared the Court.

Nobody has ever told me what was in that note. But I can guess, for Lane made a statement to the Court and this was supported by the man he had brought with him. After we had been kept waiting about half an hour, it was announced that the Court was adjourned until the following day.

Knowing what Lane would have told the

Court, I was expecting every moment to be called to an interview. But nothing happened. Instead a rumour circulated that Major Braddock had collapsed and had been rushed unconscious to the Medical Reception. This proved correct. A statement was issued to the Press that night and the following morning my newspaper carried the story under the headline: ACCUSED MAJOR BREAKS DOWN— LAERG COURT MARTIAL POSTPONED.

I read it over my breakfast and I was still drinking my coffee and wondering about it when the hotel receptionist came in to tell me there was an Army officer waiting to see me. He was a young second-lieutenant and he had orders to take me to the hospital. It is not clear to me even now whether the Army had accepted the fact that Major Braddock and I were brothers. I think probably they had— privately. But the Army, like any other large organisation, is a community in itself with its own code of behaviour. As such it closes its ranks and throws a protective cloak over its members when they are attacked by the outside world. I suspect that Lane's accusation was not accepted by the Court—officially, at any rate. In any case it was quite outside the scope of their proceedings.

To Lane it must have seemed nothing less than a conspiracy of silence. First the Army, and then the Press. I know he approached several newspapers, for they dug up the *Duart*

334

Castle story, and in addition they wrote up Lane himself—not very kindly. But none of them referred to his accusations, other than obliquely. The law of libel made that too hot a story. There was another factor, too. Braddock's collapse had to some extent swung public feeling. The disaster was now past history. It had happened more than three months ago and here was this man being hounded into a nervous breakdown.

A RAMC Colonel and a psychiatrist were waiting for me at the MR Station. Possibly they thought my presence might jerk Braddock's mind back into awareness of the world around him. In fact, he stared at me without a flicker of recognition or even interest, face and eyes quite blank. He had a room to himself and was lying in bed, propped up on pillows. The lines of his face seemed smoothed out so that he looked much younger, almost like the youth I had known. He could talk quite lucidly, but only about the things going on around him. He appeared to remember nothing of the Court Martial or of the events on Laerg. At least he didn't refer to them. 'Do I know you?' he asked me innocently. 'We've met before, I suppose, but I'm afraid I don't remember. They say I've lost my memory, you see.'

'Talk to him about Laerg,' the psychiatrist whispered to me.

But Laerg meant nothing to him. 'You were there,' I said. 'You saved the lives of twenty-three men.'

He frowned as though making an effort to remember. And then he smiled and shook his head. There was a vacant quality about that smile. 'I'll take your word for it,' he said. 'I don't remember. I don't remember a damn' thing.'

I was there nearly an hour and all the time, at the back of my mind, was the question—was this a genuine brainstorm or was he pretending? There was that smoothed-out quite untroubled face, the vacant, puzzled look in his eyes. And in a case of this sort where is the borderline between genuine mental illness and the need to seek refuge from the strain of events? One leads to the other and by the time I left I was convinced that even if he had deliberately sought this refuge, there was now no doubt that he had willed himself into a state of mental blackout.

'Kind of you to come and see me,' he said as I was leaving. He spoke quite cheerfully, but his voice sounded tired as though talking to me had been a strain.

Outside, the psychiatrist said, 'Afraid it didn't work. Perhaps in a few weeks' time when his mind's rested, eh?' No reference to the possibility that we might be related. But it was there all the same, implicit in his assumption that I'd be prepared to come all the way up from London at my own expense to visit him again.

This I did about two weeks later at their request. By then my brother had been moved to a civilian institution and he was up and dressed. On this occasion they left us alone together. But it made no difference. His mind was a blank, or it appeared to be—blank of everything he didn't want to remember. And if he recognised me, he didn't show it. 'They've got microphones in the walls,' he said. But whether they had, I don't know. The psychiatrist said no. They'd been giving him treatment, electric shock treatment. 'This place is like a brain-washing establishment. Refinements of mental cruelty. They think I'm somebody else. They keep trying to tell me I'm somebody else. If I'll admit it, then I needn't have shock treatment. And when I say I know who I am, they put the clamps on my head and turn up their rheostats full blast. Ever had shock treatment?' And when I shook my head, he grinned and said, 'Lucky fellow! Take my advice. Don't ever let them get their hands on you. Resist and you're in a strait-jacket and down to the torture chamber.'

There was a lot more that I can't remember and all of it with a thread of truth running through the fantasy. 'They think they'll break me.' He said that several times, and then words tumbling out of his mouth again as though he were afraid I'd leave him if he didn't go on talking—as though he were desperate for my company. 'They want me to admit that I'm responsible for the death of a lot of men. Well, old man, I'll tell you. They can flay me alive with their damned machines, but I'll admit nothing. Nothing, you get me. I've even had a lawyer here. Wanted to give me some money— ten thousand dollars if I'd say I'm not George Braddock. But they won't catch me that way.' He had fixed me with his eyes and now he grabbed hold of my arm and drew me down. 'You know they've got a Court sitting, waiting to try me.'

All right,' I said. My face was so close to his nobody could possibly overhear. 'Then why not tell them: Why not tell them what happened out there in the Atlantic? Get it over with.' All the way up in the train I'd been thinking about it, certain that this was the root of the trouble.

But all he said was, 'Somewhere in the basement I think it is. And if I admit anything . . .'

'It's a long time ago,' I said. 'If you just tell them what happened.'

But it didn't seem to get through to him. '. . . then they're waiting for me, and I'll be down there, facing a lot of filthy accusations. I tell you, there's nothing they won't do.' And so it went on, the words pouring out to reveal a mental kaleidoscope, truth and fantasy inextricably mixed.

Mad? Or just clever simulation? I wondered, and so apparently did the psychiatrist. 'What do you think?' he asked me as I was leaving. It was the same man, thick tortoise-shell glasses and the earnest, humourless air of one who believes that the mystery of his profession elevates him to a sort of priesthood. 'If we let him out, then he's fit and the Court Martial will have to sit again. He's not fit—or is he?' He stared at me, searchingly. 'No, of course—not your department. And you wouldn't admit anything yourself, would you?'

Veiled accusations like that. And the devil of it was there was nothing I could do to help Iain.

A week later they had another attempt at shock treatment—mental, not electrical this time. They brought Lane in to see him and before the wretched man had been in there five minutes, they had to rush in and rescue him. Iain had him by the throat and was choking the life out of him.

After that they left him alone.

Two days later the police came to my studio. It was just after lunch and I was working on a canvas that I was doing entirely for my own benefit—a portrait of Marjorie, painted from memory. I hadn't even a photograph of her at that time. I heard their footsteps on the bare stairboards, and when I went to the door a sergeant and a constable were standing there. 'Mr Ross?' The sergeant came in, a big man with a flattened nose and small, inquisitive eyes. 'I understand you're acquainted with a certain Major Braddock who is undergoing treatment in the James Craig Institute,

Edinburgh?' And when I nodded he said, 'Well now, would it surprise you, sir, to know that he's escaped?'

'Escaped—when?' I asked.

'Last night. He was discovered missing this morning. I've been instructed to check whether he's been seen in this neighbourhood and in particular whether he's visited you.'

'No,' I said. 'Why should he?'

'I'm given to understand you're related. They seemed to think he might try to contact you.' He stood staring at me, waiting for me to answer. 'Well, has he?'

'I'm afraid I can't help you. He certainly hasn't been here.'

I saw his eyes searching the studio as though he wasn't prepared to take my word for it. Finally he said, 'Very good, Mr Ross. I'll tell them. And if he does contact you, telephone us immediately. I should warn you that he may be dangerous.' He gave me the number of the police station and then with a jerk of his head at the constable, who had been quietly sniffing round the studio like a terrier after a bone, he left.

Their footsteps faded away down the stairs and I stood there without moving, thinking of Iain on the run with the police as well as the Army after him. Where would he go? But I knew where he'd go—knew in the same instant that I'd have to go there, too. Everything that had happened, his every action ... all led

340

inevitably back to Laerg.

I lit a cigarette, my hands trembling, all my fears brought suddenly to a head. Twenty-two days on a raft in the North Atlantic. Sooner or later they'd guess—guess that no man could have lasted that long, not in mid-winter; and Laerg on his direct route. They'd work it out, just as I had worked it out, and then... I turned to the window; drab vistas of grey slates, the mist hanging over the river, and my mind far away, wondering how to get there—how to reach Laerg on my own without anybody knowing? I hadn't the money to buy a boat, and to charter meant involving other people. But I could afford a rubber dinghy, and given twenty-four hours' calm weather... I thought Cliff Morgan could help me there. A radio to pick up his forecasts, a compass, an outboard motor—it ought to be possible.

I was up half the night working it out, making lists. And in the morning I drew all my cash out of the bank, booked a seat on a night train for Mallaig and began a hectic six hours, shopping for the equipment I needed.

CHAPTER TWO

LONE VOYAGE
(March 1–6)

There was news of Iain in the papers that night. It was in the Stop Press—MISSING MAJOR SEEN AT STIRLING. A motorist had given him a lift to Killin at the head of Loch Tay. And in the morning when the train pulled into Glasgow I found the Scottish papers full of it, his picture all over the front pages. He'd been seen on the railway station at Crianlarich and again at Fort William. A police watch was being kept on the quay at Mallaig in case he tried to board the steamer for the Western Isles and all the villages along the coast had been alerted. The net was closing in on him and in that sparsely populated district I didn't think he had a chance.

A man who boarded the train at Arisaig told me a stranger had been seen walking the coast towards Loch Moidart, and with Ardnamurchan so close, I toyed with the idea that he might be making for our old croft. But at Mallaig there was more definite news, a lobster boat stolen during the night from a cove in Loch Nevin. The whole town was talking about it and an old man on the quay told me it was an open boat, 30 feet long with a single screw and a diesel engine. 'An oldish boat, ye ken, but sound, and the bluidy man will wreck her for sure.' I was certain he was wrong there; just as I was certain now that Iain was making for Laerg. He'd push across to Eigg or Rum or one of the smaller islands and lie up in the lee. But to cross The Minch and cover the eighty-odd miles of Atlantic beyond he'd need better weather than this; he'd also need fuel. By taking the steamer I'd be in the Outer Hebrides before he'd even left the mainland coast.

It was late in the afternoon of the following day, March 3, that I reached Rodil. The passage across The Minch had been bad—the steel-grey of the sea ribbed with the white of breaking waves, the sky a pale, almost greenish-blue with mares' tails feathering across it like vapour trails. Later the black outline of the Western Isles had become blurred by rain.

I had planned to pitch my tent at the head of Loch Rodil, well away from the hotel, but the boatman refused to attempt it and landed me at the jetty instead, along with my gear and two other passengers. 'Will you be staying long this time, Mr Ross?' He eyed me doubtfully. 'Last time you were here . . .' He shook his head. 'That was a tur-rible storm.' The two passengers, Army officers in civilian clothes, regarded me with interest.

I dumped my gear and got hold of Marjorie. I was in too much of a hurry to consider how she would react to my sudden unexpected appearance. All I wanted was to contact Cliff

343

and get away from Rodil before the Army discovered I was there.

As she drove me in to Northton, she said, 'It's true, then, that Major Braddock has stolen a Mallaig boat. That's why you're here, isn't it?'

I didn't want to be questioned and when I didn't answer she gave me a wry grin. 'For one wild moment I thought you might have come to see me.'

'I'm sorry.' I ought to have managed this meeting better, but it couldn't be helped. She was wearing the faded anorak she'd had on when I'd first seen her. Wisps of her black hair escaped the hood, glistening with moisture. She looked very attractive and at any other time . . .

'That rubber dinghy, the outboard, all that gear on the jetty—it's yours I take it.' And when I nodded, she said, 'I'm afraid you haven't chosen a very good time. It's been like this for almost a fortnight, nothing but rain and wind.' She meant it as a warning. And she added, 'It's Laerg, isn't it? You're going to Laerg.'

'Yes,' I said. 'I'm going to Laerg.' No point in denying it when she'd known it instinctively. 'But please don't tell anybody. I'm hoping Cliff will give me the local forecasts and then I'll get away from here just as soon as I can.'

We were driving into the camp then and she stopped at the main gate. 'I'll wait for you here. I have to pick my father up anyway.'

My luck was in. Cliff was on the afternoon shift and he was still there, standing by the sloped desk, checking through a teleprint sheet. 'Ross.' He put down the teleprint sheets. 'Damn it, man, what are you doing here?' He hadn't changed—still the same old cardigan, the open-necked shirt, the quick, volatile manner.

'I want your help,' I said. And I told him about my plan to go to Laerg.

'Good God! I should have thought you'd have had enough of the place after what you went through there.' The quick brown eyes stared at me curiously from behind their thick-lensed glasses. 'What makes you want to go back?'

'You forget I'm an artist,' I said. 'And my father was born on Laerg. Now that the Army's evacuated, it's an opportunity to be there alone. The birds will be back now. I want to paint.'

He nodded and I thought he'd accepted my explanation. But he was still looking at me curiously. 'Have you got the Army's permission?'

'No.'

'What about Nature Conservancy then?'

'I haven't got anybody's permission,' I said. 'I'm just going to go there.' And I explained what I wanted from him; a weather clearance at the first possible moment, the certainty of at least twenty-four hours of light winds; and one,

345

preferably two, personal weather forecasts during the voyage. 'I want to sail as soon as possible and it's essential that I have calm conditions on arrival at Laerg.'

He asked then about the sort of boat I'd got, and when I told him, he reached for his cigarettes. 'You know what you're doing, I suppose.' He didn't expect an answer to that, but went on to inquire about my radio. Could I take Morse? What speed?

'Fast enough,' I said.

'And you'll be on your own?'

'Yes.'

He lit his cigarette, staring thoughtfully out of the window.

'Well,' I said, 'will you do it?'

'And you need calm weather at the other end.' He seemed to be thinking aloud. 'That means you're not planning to land in Shelter Bay.' I thought he was much too shrewd where weather was concerned. But instead of pursuing the matter, he turned abruptly to the maps on the wall. 'Well, there's the situation.' The lower one showed a low pressure area south-east of Iceland and another Low coming in from the Atlantic. But it was the upper one that interested me, the one that gave his forecast for midnight. It showed that second Low just west of the Hebrides. 'A southerly air stream, you see, with the wind veering south-westerly some time during the night.' Behind the depression with its wedge-shaped lines marking the warm and cold fronts was a shallow ridge of high pressure. Beyond that, farther out in the Atlantic, another Low.

'It doesn't look very promising,' I said.

He had walked over to the map and was standing there, staring up at it. 'No. Fine tomorrow with the wind falling fairly light, and after that high winds again. But it's not quite as bad as it looks. The Azores High is strengthening—I was just looking at the figures when you came in. Maybe in a couple of days . . .'

And then without a change in his voice: 'You know Braddock's been seen on the mainland.' He turned abruptly and faced me. 'There's talk in the Mess that he's stolen a boat—one of those lobster boats. He could reach Laerg in a boat like that.' He was staring at me, his gaze fixed on my face. 'The last time you were in this office, Braddock came in. Remember? They questioned me about that at the Inquiry. They asked me whether you'd recognised each other. Did you know that?' And when I nodded, he added, 'I told them no.' He hesitated. 'You're not being quite frank with me now, are you? It's because of Braddock you're going to Laerg.'

It was no good denying it. I needed his help. 'Yes,' I said. 'But I'd rather not talk about it now.'

To my relief he seemed to accept that. 'Well, it's your own business, nothing to do with me. I don't give a bloody damn about Braddock. He cost a lot of men their lives and if he'd bothered to consult me first . . . However—' He shrugged. 'It's done now and I don't like to see a man hounded out of his wits. Did you know they'd got an aircraft up looking for him?' He stood there a moment, thinking it out. 'Suppose I refuse to give you the local forecast—what then, would you still go?'

'Yes. I'd have to rely on the BBC shipping forecasts, and that wouldn't be the same as having the local weather from you. But I'd still go.'

He nodded. 'Okay. That's what I thought.' And he added, 'I don't know what your connection with Braddock is or what you hope to achieve by going to Laerg, but nobody would undertake a trip like that unless they had very strong reasons for doing so. I accept that, and I'll do what I can to help you.' He stubbed out his cigarette. 'The weather's been bloody awful these last few weeks and that Low that's coming in from the Atlantic—' he nodded to the weather map—'it's still intensifying. The new figures just came in over the teleprinter. Pressure at the centre is nine-seven-two falling and unless the ridge of high pressure in front of it builds up—and I don't think it will—that next Low will start coming through some time tomorrow night. After that . . . well, this is just guesswork, but we might get a fine spell. It's about time, you know.' He went back to the desk. 'I'll give you my call sign and the frequency you have to listen on.' He wrote it down for me and suggested I tuned in to his net at 22.00 hours. 'Just to check that you're picking me up all right. Phone me at nine o'clock tomorrow morning here. I usually look in about that time if I'm not on the morning shift.'

I thanked him, but as I turned to go he stopped me, 'Take my advice, Ross, and keep clear of the Military. It's not only Braddock they're worried about. There's a report of a Russian trawler in the area, and this new chap, Colonel Webb—very cautious he is. Can't blame him after what's happened. And a fellow alone in a rubber dinghy, you see . . . thought I'd better warn you.'

I left him then. It was just after six-thirty. The car was waiting for me at the main gate and there was an officer leaning against it, talking to Field. It was the dapper little captain who had replaced Mike Ferguson as Adjutant. He watched as I climbed into the back of the car and I thought he recognised me.

'Marjorie tells me you're going to Laerg,' Field said as we drove off. 'Alone?'

'Yes.'

'Well, I hope Cliff Morgan was able to offer you the prospect of some better weather.' He didn't ask me why I was going.

But later that evening, sitting by the peat fire in their croft, it was obvious he had guessed.

'The air search is being stepped up tomorrow—two helicopters and a Shackleton. They'll be concentrating on The Minch and the Inner Hebrides, and every fishing vessel will be on the lookout for him.'

'He hasn't been seen then?'

'No. But it's just a matter of time.' And he added, 'I gather he was under treatment. It's possible he said things . . .' He didn't look at me, but sat staring into the fire, his long, beaked face in silhouette against the lamplight. 'These truth drugs, they quite often work, you know.' And then he gave me the same advice that Cliff had given me. 'If you don't want the Army bothering you, I should get away from here just as soon as you can. The North Ford, between North Uist and Benbecula, is as good a jumping-off place as any. Nobody will bother you there, and when you do sail you'd have the Monach Isles to land on if the wind got up.' He turned his head suddenly and looked at me. 'I wonder what makes you so certain Braddock is heading for Laerg?' And when I didn't say anything, he added, 'That night when we were leaving, he wanted the tug to go without him, didn't he?' I hadn't expected him to have guessed that. His gaze returned to the fire. 'A strange man. Quite ruthless. But a great deal of courage. And with a drive . . . I think that's what one most admired, that driving energy of his.' And after a moment he added, 'For your sake I hope the end of it all isn't—' he

350

hesitated—' some ghastly tragedy.'

Marjorie came in then with supper on a tray. We ate it there by the fire. It was a cosy, pleasant meal, and for a while I was able to forget the weather and the sense of loneliness, almost of isolation, that had been growing in me ever since I'd returned to the Hebrides.

I had to leave at nine-thirty in order to be back in time to pick up Cliff's transmission and test reception. 'I'll walk down with you,' Field said. Marjorie came to the door with us. 'I'll see you in the morning,' she said. 'I hope you don't have too unpleasant a night.'

Outside the rain had ceased, but it was blowing harder than ever. Field didn't say anything until we had passed the church. 'I wanted to have a word with you alone.' His voice was hesitant. 'About Marjorie. You realise she's in love with you?' And he went on quickly. 'She's Celt—both sides. She's the sort of girl who'd break her heart over somebody.' He stopped and faced me. 'I wouldn't be talking to you like this if you were an ordinary fellow. But you're not. You're an artist. I don't know why that makes a difference but it does.'

I didn't know what to say, for I hadn't given much thought to the way the relationship between us had been developing, and now . . . 'Probably it's just the reaction . . . I mean, she was fond of Ferguson.'

'Fond, yes. But nothing more. You're an older man . . .' He hesitated. 'Not married, are

351

you?'

'I was—for a few months. But that finished years ago.'

'I see. Well . . .' He sounded awkward about it now. 'We're very close, Marjorie and I—always have been since her mother died. And now she's grown up . . .' He started walking again, his head down. 'Not your fault, perhaps, but don't make a fool of her. I couldn't bear that—and nor could she.' And he added, 'Well, there it is . . . just so that you understand.' He didn't give me a chance to say anything, but switched abruptly to the subject of my voyage to Laerg. 'I don't like it,' he said. 'The weather up here can change very quickly. Right now there are half-a-dozen lobster fishermen marooned on the Monachs. Been there almost a fortnight.'

'I'll be all right,' I said. 'Cliff's giving me the local forecasts.'

'If I weren't tied up here, I'd offer to come with you. I don't like the idea of your doing it alone. Nor does Marjorie.' We had reached the dip in the road that led down to the hotel and he stopped. 'Well, you know what you're doing, I suppose.' And he added, 'I'll let you know if there's any further news of Braddock.' He left me then, going back up the road, the darkness swallowing him almost at once.

I had pitched my tent on the same grass slope just beyond the small boat harbour and I got back to it just in time to pick up Cliff's

352

transmission. He gave me his call sign first— GM3CMX, repeated several times; then the weather forecast, keyed much slower than he would normally send. Reception was good, loud and clear with no interruption. He followed the forecast with a brief message: *Your arrival commented on. Remember my advice and clear out tomorrow.* He ended his message with the letters *CL*, which meant that he was closing down his station.

I lit the pressure lamp and got out my charts, starting with 2508 which covered the whole hundred miles of the Outer Hebrides chain and included all the out-islands. Laerg stood solitary and alone on the very edge of the chart, a tiny speck surrounded by the blank white of ocean, with only scattered soundings. The shortest line from Laerg to the Hebrides touched North Uist at its westernmost point, Air-an-Runair. The distance was eighty-three nautical miles.

But now that I had disembarked my gear and contacted Cliff, I was no longer tied to Rodil and could shorten the voyage by crossing the Sound of Harris. The west coast of North Uist was too exposed, but remembering what Field had said, my eyes were drawn to the North Ford and to a straggle of islands shaped like the wings of a butterfly that lay barely a dozen miles to the west. These were marked on the chart—'Heisker (The Monach Islands.')

I lit a cigarette, got out chart No. 3168 and

353

began to examine the North Ford in detail. It would be low water before I got there and I saw at a glance that the narrow channels through the sand would make it possible for me to go through whatever the tide. And at the western end, beyond the causeway that joined North Uist to Benbecula, the island of Baleshare stretched a great dune tongue down from the north, a bare waste devoid of any croft. I pencilled a circle round it, let the pressure out of the lamp and lay down with a sense of satisfaction. From Baleshare to the Monachs was about nine miles. From the Monachs to Laerg seventy-six miles. This way I should reduce the open sea passage by at least thirteen miles.

I left the following morning immediately after phoning Cliff. A cold, clear day with the wind fallen light and the clouds lifted to a thin-grey film of cirrostratus high in the sky. And late that afternoon I pitched my tent against a background so utterly different that I might have been in another country. Gone were the lofty hills of Harris, the sense of being shut in, pressed against the sea's edge by sodden heights. Gone, too, was the brown of the seaweed, the sombre dark of rocks. Here all was sand, great vistas of it, golden bright and stretching flat to the distant hump of a solitary, purpling peak. My camp faced east and the tide was out. The peak was Eaval. Behind me were the dunes of Baleshare. All the rest was sky, thin mackerel scales of cloud, silver-grey and full of light. And not another soul to be seen, only the distant outline of solitary crofts, remote on islands in the Ford.

From the top of the dunes I could see the channelled entrance to the Ford, marked out for me by the white of waves breaking on the sand bars. A mile or more of broken water, and beyond that, low on the western horizon, the outline of the Monachs, the pointed finger of the disused lighthouse just visible.

The sun set and the heavens flared, a fantastic, fiery red. From horizon to horizon the sky blazed, a lurid canopy shot through with flaming wisps of cloud. It was a blood-bath of colour, and as I watched it, the red gradually darkening to purple, the whole vast expanse of sky was like a wound slowly clotting. Darkness fell and the tide rose; the dinghy floated closer until it rested just below my tent.

Cliff came through prompt at ten o'clock. The weather pattern was unchanged. I had some food then and went to bed and lay in the dark, thinking of Laerg—out there to the westward, beyond the break of the sand bar surf, beyond the dim-seen shape of the Monachs, hidden below the horizon.

If, when I had left Rodil that morning, the engine had failed to start, or I had found an air leak in the dinghy, or anything had gone wrong, then I think I should have regarded it as an omen. But across the Sound of Harris, and all the way down the coast of North Uist, the engine had run without faltering. The speed, measured between identified islands, had been just over 3½ knots. Even in the North Ford, where it was wind against tide and quite a lop on the water, I hadn't experienced a moment's uneasiness. The craft was buoyant, despite her heavy load. She had shot the rapids under the Causeway bridge without taking any water, and though the tide was falling then and the channel tortuous, she had only twice grounded, and each time I had been able to float her off.

I was sure, lying in my tent that night, that I could make Laerg. But confidence is not easily maintained against such an elemental force as the sea. The break of the waves on the bar had been no more than a murmur in my ears when I had gone to sleep. When I woke it was a pounding roar that shook the dunes and the air was thick with the slaver of the gale; great gobs of spume, like froth, blown on the wind. Rain drove in grey sheets up the Ford and to stand on the dunes and look seaward was to face layer upon layer of rollers piling in, their creaming tops whipped landward by the wind.

It lasted a few hours, that was all, but the speed with which it had arrived and the suddenness of those big seas was disturbing.

The synopsis at the beginning of the one-forty forecast confirmed the pattern transmitted to me by Cliff the previous night; the depression centred over Scotland moving away north-eastward, and a high pressure system building up behind it and covering the Eastern Atlantic from the Azores to approximately latitude 60° North. Outlook for sea area Hebrides was wind force 6, veering north-westerly and decreasing to light variable; sea moderating, becoming calm; visibility moderate to good, but chance of fog patches locally.

I moved fast after that. The gale had lost me half the day and now the tide was falling. Where I was camped on the southern tip of Baleshare the deep water channel swung close in to the dunes, but on the other side, towards Gramisdale, the sands were already beginning to dry. My most urgent need was petrol. I had used over eight gallons coming down. I filled up the tank of the outboard, slid my ungainly craft into the water and pushed off with the two empty jerricans, following the channel north-east past the tufted grass island of Stromay towards the village of Carinish.

Beyond Stromay the deep water channel forked. I took the right fork. It was still blowing quite hard and by keeping to the roughest water I avoided the shallows. I beached just south of the village, tied the painter to a stone and hurried up the track, carrying the jerricans. There was no petrol pump at Carninish, but the chart had marked a Post Office and as I had expected it was the centre of village information. There were about half a dozen

357

women gossiping in the little room and when I explained what I'd come for, one of them immediately said, 'There's Roddie McNeil now. He runs a car. D'ye ken the hoose?' And when I shook my head, she said, 'Och weel, I'll get it for you myself.' And she went off with my jerricans.

I asked if I could telephone then and the post mistress pushed the phone across the counter to me. 'You'll be the pairson that's camped in the dunes across the water to Eachkamish,' she said. Eachkamish was the name of the southern part of Baleshare. 'Would you be expecting somebody now?'

'No,' I said, thinking immediately of the Army.

'A lassie, maybe?' Her eyes stared at me, roguish and full of curiosity. 'Weel noo, it'll be a pleasant surprise for ye. She came in by the bus from Newton Ferry and now she's away to the Morrisons to inquire aboot a boat.'

'Was it a Miss Field?'

She shook her head, smiling at me. 'I dinna ken the name. But she was in a turrible hurry to get to ye.' And she turned to a young woman standing there and told her to go down to the Morrisons and bring the lassie back.

I picked up the phone and gave the exchange the number of the Met. Office at Northton. It couldn't be anyone else but Marjorie and I wondered why she'd come, for it wasn't an easy journey from Rodil. There was a click and a

358

voice said, 'Sykes, Met. Office Northton, here.' Apparently Cliff had been called down to the camp. 'Will you give him a message for me,' I said. 'Tell him I'll be leaving first light tomorrow. If there's any change in the weather pattern he must let me know tonight.' He asked my name then and I said, 'He'll know who it is,' and hung up.

Five minutes later Marjorie arrived, flushed and out of breath. 'We'd almost got the boat down in the water when I saw the dinghy there. If I hadn't gone in for a cup of tea with the Morrisons, I'd have seen you coming across.'

'How did you know where I was?'

'Daddy was sure you'd be somewhere in the North Ford and this seemed the most likely place.' She glanced round at the faces all eagerly watching us. 'Walk down the road with me, will you. We can't talk here. What with that odd craft of yours and me coming here asking for a man camped in the dunes—it'll be all over North Uist by this evening.' She gave me a quick little nervous smile. 'I didn't give your name.' And then, when we were clear of the Post Office, she said, 'The boat's been seen at Eriskay, on the east. Colonel Webb was notified this morning and Daddy rang the hotel. He thought you'd want to know.' And she added. 'A crofter saw it there last night. They're not sure it's the one Major Braddock took, but it's a lobster boat and it doesn't belong to any of the local fishermen.'

So he'd crossed The Minch and was waiting like me for the expected break in the weather. I was quite sure it was Iain. The island of Eriskay was immediately below South Uist and right opposite Mallaig. 'What are they doing about it?' I asked.

'They've sent out a plane to investigate.'

'A helicopter?'

'No. A plane, Daddy said.'

A wild coast and no place to land. A plane wouldn't stop Iain. And for me to try and intercept him was out of the question. He'd shift to the little islands in the Sound of Barra and by tomorrow he'd be gone.

'It's what you were expecting, isn't it?' She had stopped and was standing facing me, the wind on her face.

'Yes.' And I added, 'It was good of you. To come all this way.'

'I suppose you'll go now.'

'Tomorrow morning.'

'He's got a much bigger boat than you. If anything happened . . . I mean, you ought to have somebody with you—just in case.'

'In case I fall overboard?' I smiled. 'I wouldn't have far to fall—a few inches, that's all.'

'It's nearly a hundred miles to Laerg, and that wretched little dinghy . . .' She was staring at me, her eyes wide. 'I realise you can't take anyone—anyone who wouldn't understand. But—' she hesitated, her gaze, level and direct,

360

fixed on me. 'I've brought cold weather clothing and oilskins. I thought if you wouldn't take anyone else...' Her hand touched my arm. 'Please. I want to come with you.'

I didn't know what to say, for she wasn't a fool; she knew the danger. And she meant it, of course. 'Don't be silly,' I said. 'Imagine what your father would say.'

'Oh, Daddy knows.' She said it quite gaily and I knew she really had settled it with him. And when I said, 'You know it's out of the question,' her temper flared immediately. 'I don't know anything of the sort. You can't go alone...'

'I've got to,' I said.

She started to argue then, but I cut her short. 'It's no good, Marjorie. You can't help me. Nobody can. In any case, there isn't room. When the stores are in it, that rubber dinghy is full—there's barely space for me.'

'That's just an excuse.'

I took her by the shoulders, but she flung me off. She was angry now and her eyes blazed. 'You're so bloody pig-headed. Just because I'm a girl...'

'If you'd been a man,' I told her, 'the answer would have been the same. There's no room for anybody else. And to be perfectly honest, I don't want anyone. This is something I've got to do alone.'

'But why? Why do you have to?'

'He's my brother,' I said. No point in

361

concealing it from her now.

'Your brother?' She stared at me, and I could see her thinking it out and going over it in her mind.

'Now do you understand? This is something I've got to work out for myself. Perhaps for Iain, too.' I took her by the shoulders and this time she didn't draw away.

'It's settled then. You're going—tomorrow.'

'Yes.'

She didn't argue any more and when I drew her to me, she let me kiss her. 'Thank you,' I said. 'Thank you for coming, for offering to go with me.' Her lips were cool with the wind. 'That's something I'll always remember. And when I get back . . .' I felt her body come against me, the softness of it and her arms round my neck, her mouth on mine; and then she had drawn away. 'I'll see you off, anyway.' She was suddenly practical and we walked back in silence.

The woman who had gone off with the jerricans was waiting for me outside the Post Office. 'Ye'll find Roddie McNeil wi' your petrol doon by the landing place.' I thanked her. 'It's nae bother. And there's nae call for ye to be thanking Roddie. He'll be charging ye for his time as well as the petrol, ye ken.'

McNeil was waiting for me on the sands, a small, dour man with sandy hair. 'There's a wee bit extra for the cartage,' he said. I paid him and he helped me launch the dinghy and stow the jerricans. 'Is it long ye'll be camped over to Baleshare?' And when I told him I'd be gone in the morning if the weather were fine, he said, 'Aye, weel . . .' And he sniffed at the breeze like a sheltie. 'It'll be fine weather the noo, I'm thinking.'

He held the boat whilst I started the engine, and then I looked back at Marjorie. There was something almost boyish about her, standing there alone on the sands, the faded anorak and the green cord trousers tucked into gum boots, her head bare and her hair blown across her face. And yet not boyish; more like an island woman, I thought, her body slim and erect, her face clouded—and she'd been quite prepared to come to sea. The noise of the engine drowned all possibility of speech. I waved and she waved back, and that was that, and a feeling of sadness enveloped me as I motored down the channel. I didn't look back and in less than twenty minutes I had beached the dinghy below my tent. I was on my own again with the surface of the dune sand dried now and the wind sifting it through the wiry grass stems.

I began loading the dinghy ready for the morning. Reed's Nautical Almanac gave time of sunrise as 06.43. There was no moon. I thought I should have sufficient light to cross the bar just before five. And once out beyond the bar I should be stuck at the helm hour after hour with no chance to change the stowage or search for things. Everything I needed had to

363

be ready to hand.

There was another problem, too. At five o'clock in the morning the tide would be almost low. If I left the dinghy where it was, moored to the shore, it would be high and dry when I wanted to leave, and loaded it would be much too heavy to drag into the water. The only alternative was to anchor off in deep water and sleep aboard.

I stowed everything in its place except the tent and the radio set, and by the time I had finished the sun was shining, the wind no more than a rustle in the grasses. It was a calm, clear evening with Eaval standing out brown and smiling against the black storm clouds still piled against the mainland hills. I climbed to the top of the dunes, and all to the west the sky was clear, a pale pastel shade of blue, with the seas white on the bar, but breaking lazily now and without much force.

There was nothing more I could do and I got my sketchbook out. The two drawings I did show the loaded dinghy lying like a basking shark stranded at the water's edge, the tent snugged in its hollow against the dunes, and that flat world of sand and water stretching away to the sunken hulks of the distant hills. They set the scene, but they miss the bright calm of that suddenly cloudless sky, the curlews piping to the more anxious note of the oyster-catchers, the flight of the grey plover and the laboured strokes of a heron. The sun set, an orange ball that turned the Monachs black like a ship hull-down, and as twilight fell, the darkening world seemed hushed to a sort of sanctity so that I felt I understood what it was that had drawn the early Christians to these islands.

Cliff Morgan's transmission came through very sharp that night, with almost no interference. *Message received. Weather set fair for 24 hours at least, possibly 48. Fog your chief hazard. Future transmissions twice daily at 13.30 and 01.00 continuing for 3 days. Thereafter 22.00 as before for 4 days. If no message received by March 10 will presume you are in trouble and take appropriate action.* He repeated the message, the speed of his key steadily increasing. Finally: *Bon voyage CL.*

I marked the times of his transmissions on the chart and checked once again the course I should have to steer. He had given me seven clear days in which to get a message through to him. Time enough to worry how I was going to do that when I reached Laerg. I wished Iain could have heard that forecast. Fog was just what he wanted now.

I checked the tides given on the chart for every hour before and after high water Stornoway, pencilling in the direction and speed for the twenty-four hours commencing 05.00. I also made a note of the magnetic variation—13° West—and my compass deviation which I found to be a further 4° West with all my gear stowed. Taking these factors into account the compass course I should have to steer after clearing the Monachs was 282°.

Having satisfied myself that all the navigational information I required was entered on the charts, and having checked through again for accuracy, I folded it and slipped it into its spray-proof case. Together with the radio, I stowed it in the dinghy within reach of the helm. Then I struck the tent and when that was loaded and the camp entirely cleared, I waded into the water, pushed off and clambered in. I moored out in the channel, a stone tied to the painter, and went to sleep under the stars, clad in my oilskins, lying crossways, my feet stuck out over the side and my head cushioned on the far curve of the tight-blown fabric.

It was cold that night and I slept fitfully, conscious of the yawing of the dinghy, the ripple of the tide tugging at the mooring. I had no alarm clock, but it wasn't necessary. Seabirds woke me as the first glimmering of dawn showed grey in the east, silhouetting the dark outline of Eaval. I dipped my face in salt water, conscious now of a feeling of tension; eyes and head were sluggish with the night and the cold had cramped my bones. I drank the tea I had left in the Thermos, ate some digestive biscuits and cheese, and then I pulled up the mooring, untying the stone and letting it fall back into the water. The outboard engine started at the second pull and I was on my way, circling in the tide run and heading down the centre of the pale ribbon of water that ran between the sands towards the open sea.

The light in the east was pale and cold as steel; the stars overhead still bright. The speed of my passage made a little wind, and that too was cold, so that I shivered under my oilskins. All ahead was black darkness. I had a moment of panic that I should lose the channel and get stranded among the breakers on the bar. Passing through the narrows between Eachkamish and the northern tip of Benbecula—the channel marked on the chart as Beul an Toim—the broken water of the bar showed in a ghostly semi-circle beyond the piled-up bulk of my stores. Even when I could see the breaking waves, I could not hear them. All I heard was the powerful roar of the outboard. I steered a compass course, running the engine slow, and as the dunes slid away behind me, my craft came suddenly alive to the movement of the waves.

Breaking water right ahead and no gap visible. The light was growing steadily and I jilled around for a moment searching the line of breakers. A darker patch, further south than I had expected . . . I felt my way towards it, conscious of the tug of the tide under the boat, noting the sideways drift. And then suddenly my eyes, grown accustomed to the light, picked out the channel, a narrow highway of dark

367

water, growing wider as I entered it. The swell was bad here out on the bar, the waves steep but only occasionally breaking. The dinghy pitched wildly, the engine racing as the prop was lifted clear of the water.

There was a moment when I thought I'd missed the channel, the waves higher than my head and starting to curl at the top. I wanted to turn back then, but I didn't dare for fear the dinghy would overturn. The jerricans were shifting despite their lashings and I had to grip hold of the wooden slats at my feet to prevent myself from being thrown out. This lasted for perhaps a minute. Then suddenly the waves were less steep. A moment later, and I was motoring in calm water and the sea's only movement was a long, flat, oily swell. I was over the bar, and looking back I could scarcely believe that I had found a way through from landward, for all behind me was an unbroken line of white water, the confusion of the waves showing as toppling masses against the dawn sky, the low land surrounding the Ford already lost in the haze of spray that hung above the bar. I set my course by the compass, took a small nip from the flask I had kept handy and settled down to the long business of steering and keeping the engine going.

Shortly before seven the sun rose. It was broad daylight then and the Monachs clearly visible on the port bow. At 06.45 I had tuned in to the BBC on 1500 metres. There was no change in the weather pattern and the forecast for sea area Hebrides was wind force 1 to 2 variable, good visibility, but fog locally. Shortly after nine the Monachs were abeam to port about two miles. They were flat as a table and at that distance the grass of the *machair* looked like a lawn. My compass was one of those which could be taken out of its holder and used as a hand-bearing compass. I took a bearing on the disused lighthouse, and another on Haskeir Island away to the north. These, together with a stern-bearing on the top of Clettraval on North Uist, gave me a three-point fix. I marked my position on the chart and checked it against my dead reckoning, which was based on course and speed, making due allowance for tide. The difference was 1.4 miles at 275°. That fix was very important to me, for thereafter I was able to base my dead reckoning on a speed of 3.8 knots.

The sun was warm now, shimmering on the water, a blinding glare that made me drowsy. The one thing I hadn't thought of was dark glasses. I had taken my oilskin jacket off some miles back. Now I removed the first of my sweaters and refilled the tank with the engine running slow. In doing so I nearly missed the only ship I was to sight that day—a trawler, hull-down on the horizon, trailing a smudge of smoke.

Every hour I wrote up my log and entered my DR position on the chart, just as I had always done back in the old days on the bridge of a freighter. The engine was my main concern, and I was sensitive to every change of note, real or imagined. All around me, the sea was alive, the movement of the swell, the flight of birds; and whenever I felt the need, there was always the radio with the Light Programme churning out endless music.

Just after eleven I ran into a school of porpoise. I thought at first it was a tidal swirl, mistaking their curving backs for the shadow cast by the lip of a small wave breaking. And then I saw one not fifty yards away, a dark body glinting in the sun and curved like the top of a wheel revolving. The pack must have numbered more than a dozen. They came out of the water three times, almost in unison and gaining momentum with each re-entry. At the final voracious plunge, the whole surface of the sea ahead of me seethed; from flat calm it was suddenly a boiling cauldron as millions of small fry skittered in panic across the surface. For an instant I seemed to be headed for a sheet of molten silver, and then the sea was oily smooth again, so that I stared, wondering whether I had imagined it.

A flash of white from the sky, the sudden splash of a projectile hitting the water . . . this new phenomenon thrilled me as something dimly remembered but not seen in a long while. The gannets had arrived.

There were a dozen or more of them,

wheeling low and then hurling themselves into the sea with closed wings and out-thrust head, a spear-beaked missile diving headlong for the herring on which the porpoise were feeding and which in turn were attacking the small fry. I could remember my grandfather's words before I had ever seen a gannet dive: 'Aye,' he'd said, his thick, guttural voice burring at us, 'ye'll no' see a finer sight of heaven, for there's nae muckle fowl (he pronounced it the Norwegian way—*Fugl*) can dive like a solan goose.'

Where the gannets came from I don't know, for until that moment I had seen none. They appeared as though by magic, coming up from all angles and all heights and the little bombplumes of their dives spouted in the sea all round me. My presence didn't seem to disturb them at all. Perhaps it was because the dinghy was so different in shape and appearance to any boat they had encountered before. Three of them dived in quick succession, hitting the water so close that I could almost reach out and touch the plumes of spray. They surfaced practically together, each with a herring gripped in its long beak. A vigorous washing, a quick twist to turn the fish head first and then it was swallowed and they took off again, taxiing clumsily in a long run, wings and feet labouring at the surface of the water. Other birds were there—big herring gulls and black-backs; shearwaters and razorbills too, I think, but at that time I was not so practised at bird recognition. The smooth-moving hillocks of the sea became littered with the debris of the massacre; littered, too, with porpoise excreta—small, brown aerated lumps floating light as corks.

It was over as suddenly as it had started. All at once the birds were gone and I was left alone with the noise of the engine, only then realising how the scream of the gulls had pierced that sound. I looked at the Monachs and was surprised to find they had scarcely moved. There was nothing else in sight, not even a fishing boat, and the only aircraft I saw was the BEA flight coming into Benbecula, a silver flash of wings against the blue of the sky.

Though less than four miles long from Stockay to the lighthouse, the Monachs were with me a long time. It was not until almost midday that they began to drop out of sight astern. Visibility was still very good then. The stone of the lighthouse stood out clear and white, and though the North Ford and all the low-lying country of Benbecula and the Uists had long since disappeared, the high ground remained clearly visible; particularly the massive brown bulk of the Harris hills.

It was about this time that I thought I saw, peeping up at me over the horizon ahead, the faint outline of what looked like a solitary rock. The peak of Tarsaval on Laerg? I couldn't be certain, for though I stared and stared and blinked repeatedly to re-focus my eyes, it remained indefinite as a mirage, an ephemeral shape that might just as easily have been a reflection of my own desire; for what I wanted most to see—what any seaman wants to see—was my objective coming up right over the bows to confirm me in my navigation.

But I never had that satisfaction. It was there, I thought, for a while; then I couldn't be certain. Finally I was sure it wasn't, for by that time even the Harris hills had become blurred and indistinct.

I was conscious then of a drop in temperature. The sun had lost its warmth, the sky its brilliance, and where sky met sea, the pale, watery blue was shaded to the sepia of haze. Where I thought I had glimpsed Laerg there was soon no clear-cut horizon, only a pale blurring of the light like refraction from a shallow cloud lying on the surface of the sea.

Fog! I could feel it in my bones, and it wasn't long before I could see it. And at 13.30 Cliff Morgan confirmed my fears. After giving me a weather forecast that was much the same as before, he added: *Your greatest menace now is fog. Weather ship 'India' reports visibility at 11.00 hours 50 yards*. The BBC forecast at 13.40 merely referred to *Chance of fog patches*.

I had already put on my sweaters again; now I put on my oilskin jacket. Within minutes the atmosphere had chilled and thickened. A little wind sprang up, cats' paws rippling the oily surface of the swell. One moment the hills of

Harris were still there, just visible, then they were gone and the only thing in sight, besides the sea, was the tower of the Monachs lighthouse iridescent in a gleam of sun. Then that, too, vanished, and I was alone in a world where the sky seemed a sponge, the air so full of moisture that the sun scarcely percolated through it.

Half an hour later I entered the fog bank proper. It came up on me imperceptibly at first, a slow darkening of the atmosphere ahead, a gradual lessening of visibility. Then, suddenly, wreathing veils of white curled smoky tendrils round me. The cats' paws merged, became a steady chilling breeze; little waves began to break against the bows, throwing spray in my face. Abruptly my world was reduced to a fifty-yard stretch of sea, a dank prison with water-vapour walls that moved with me as I advanced, an insubstantial, yet impenetrable enclosure.

After that I had no sense of progress, and not even the sound of the engine or the burble of the propeller's wake astern could convince me that I was moving, for I took my grey prison with me, captive to the inability of my eyes to penetrate the veil of moisture that enclosed me.

Time had no meaning for me then. I nursed the engine, watched the compass, stared into the fog, and thought of Laerg, wondering how I was to find the entrance to the geo—wondering too, whether I should be able even

374

to locate the island in this thick wet blanket of misery that shut out all sight. It would be night then, and the slightest error in navigation . . .

I checked and re-checked my course constantly, the moisture dripping from my face and hands, running down the sleeves of my oilskin jacket on to the Celluloid surface of the chart case. Tired now and cold, my limbs cramped, I crouched listless at the helm, hearing again my grandfather's voice; stories of Laerg and his prowess on the crags. He had claimed he was fleeter than anyone else. Even at sixty, he said, he'd been able to reach ledges no youngster dare visit. Probably he was justified in his claims. At the time the islanders left Laerg there were only five men left between the ages of fifteen and twenty-five, and remembering those long, almost ape-like arms, those huge hands and the enormous breadth of his shoulders, I could well imagine the old devil swinging down the face of a thousand-foot cliff, his grizzled beard glistening with the vapour that swirled about him as he sought some almost invisible ledge where the guillemots or solan geese were nesting.

In just such a fog as this he had gone down the face of the sheer cliffs on the north side of the island, below Tarsaval, lowering himself on the old horse-hair rope that had been part of his wife's dowry when they married at the turn of the century. Those cliffs were over 1,300 feet

375

high, the most spectacular volcanic wall in the British Isles. He was on his own and he had missed his footing. His hands had slipped on the wet rope and he had fallen fifty feet, his foot catching in the loop at the end. They had found him hanging there head-downwards in the morning. He had been like that most of the night, a total of five hours, but though he was frozen stiff as a board and his joints had seized solid, he nevertheless managed to walk down to his cottage. He had been fifty-two years old then.

These and other stories came flooding back into my mind; how when he had married my grandmother he had had to undergo the ordeal of the Lovers' Stone. That sloped crag, jutting out high over the sea where it boiled against the base of the cliffs, had made an indelible impression on my young mind. He had told us that all bridegrooms had had to pass this test, walking out along the tiled stone to stand on the knife-edge, balanced on the balls of their feet and reaching down to touch their toes. It was a test to prove that they were competent cragsmen, men enough to support a woman on an island where the ability to collect eggs and birds from their nesting places could make the difference between a full belly and starvation in winter. 'Aye, and I was fool enough to stand first on one foot and then on the other, and then put my head down and stand on my hands—just to prove I wasna scared of anything at all in the whole wide wor-rld.' The old man's voice seemed to come to me again through the roar of the engine.

I was tired by then, of course, and I had the illusion that if only I could penetrate the grey curtain ahead of me, I should see the towering cliffs of Laerg rising out of the sea. At moments I even imagined there was a sudden darkening in the fog. But then I reached for the chart and a glance at it confirmed that my imagination was playing me tricks. At five o'clock the island was still almost thirty miles away. I had most of the night ahead of me before I reached it. Then, if the fog held, the first indication would not be anything seen, but the pounding of the swell at the base of the cliffs, perhaps a glint of white water.

And that was presuming my navigation was accurate.

It was just after the six o'clock weather forecast, in which the BBC admitted for the first time the whole Eastern Atlantic was enveloped in fog, that the thing I had most feared happened. There was a change in the engine note. The revolutions fell off and it began to labour. I tried it with full throttle, but it made no difference. I adjusted the choke, giving it a richer mixture, but it still continued to labour. The water cooling outlet thinned to a trickle and finally ceased. The engine was beginning to pound as it ran hot. In the end it stopped altogether.

The sudden silence was frightening. For more than twelve hours I had had the roar of the engine in my ears to the exclusion of all other sounds. Now I could hear the slap of the waves against the flat rubberised gunnels. I could hear the little rushing hisses they made as they broke all round me. There wasn't anything of a sea running, but the swell was broken by small cross-seas. The wind was about force 3, northerly, and in the stillness I could almost hear it. Other sounds were audible, too—the slop of petrol in a half-empty jerrican, the drip of moisture from my oilskins, the rattle of tins badly stowed as the dinghy wallowed with a quick, unpredictable movement.

My first thought was that the engine had run out of fuel, but I had refilled the tank less than half an hour ago, and when I checked it was still more than half-full. I thought then that it must be water in the petrol, particularly when I discovered that the jerrican I had last used was one of those that had been filled by the crofter at Carinish. Rather than empty the tank, I disconnected the fuel lead, drained the carburettor and refilled it from another jerrican; a difficult and laborious business, cramped as I was and the motion at times quite violent.

The engine started first pull and for a moment I thought I had put my finger on the trouble. But no water came out of the cooling outlet and though it ran for a moment quite normally, the revolutions gradually fell off again and for fear of permanent damage due to overheating, I stopped it.

I knew then that something must have gone wrong with the cooling system. The outlook was grim. I was not a mechanic and I had few spares. Moreover, the light was already failing. It would soon be dark, and to strip the engine down by the light of a torch was to ask for trouble with the dinghy tossing about and all available space taken up with stores. The wind seemed to be rising, too; but perhaps that was my imagination.

I sat there for a long time wondering what to do—whether to start work on it now or to wait until morning. But to wait for morning was to risk a change in the weather conditions and at least there was still light enough for me to make a start on the job. First, I had to get the engine off its bracket and into the boat. It was a big outboard, and heavy. For safety, I tied the painter round it, and then, kneeling in the stern, I undid the clamp and with a back-breaking twist managed to heave it on to the floor at my feet.

It was immensely heavy—far heavier than I had expected. But it wasn't until it was lying on the floor at my feet that the reason became apparent. The propeller and all the lower part of the shaft, including the water-cooling inlet and the exhaust, was wrapped and choked with seaweed. I almost laughed aloud with relief.

379

'You silly, bloody fool.' I had begun talking to myself by then. I kept repeating, 'You bloody fool!' for I remembered now that as I had sat with the earphones on, listening to the forecast, I had motored through a patch of sea that was littered with the wrack of the recent gale—dark patches of weed that produced their own calm where the sea did not break.

Cleared of weed and refastened to its bracket, the engine resumed its purposeful note and the sound of the sea was lost again. Lost, too, was that sense of fear, which for a moment had made me wish Cliff Morgan had allowed less than seven days before presuming I was in trouble.

I switched on the compass light and immediately it became the focus of my eyes, a little oasis of brightness that revealed the fog as a stifling blanket composed of millions upon millions of tiny beads of moisture. All else was black darkness.

It became intensely cold. Surprisingly, I suffered from thirst. But the little water I had brought with me was stowed for'ard against an emergency—and in any case, relieving myself was a problem. I suffered from cramp, too. Both feet had gone dead long ago due to constriction of the blood circulation.

My eyes, mesmerised by the compass light, became droop-lidded and I began to nod. I was steering in a daze men, my thoughts wandering. 'You'll go to Laerg, and I'll go to my grave fighting for the mucking Sassenachs.' That was Iain, ages and ages ago, in a pub in Sauchiehall Street. What had made him say that, standing at that crowded bar in his new battledress? I couldn't remember now. But I could see him still, his dark hair tousled, a black look on his face. He was a little drunk and swaying slightly. Something else he'd said ... 'That bloody old fool.' And I'd known whom he meant, for the old man had both fascinated and repelled him. 'Dying of a broken heart. If he'd had any guts, he'd have stuck it out alone on the island, instead of blethering about it to the two of us.' But that wasn't what I was trying to remember. It was something he'd said after that. He'd repeated it, as though it were a great truth, slurring his words. 'Why die where you don't belong?' And then he'd clapped me on the back and ordered another drink. 'You're lucky,' he'd said. 'You're too young.' And I'd hated him as I often did.

Or was that the next time, when he'd come swaggering back, on leave after Dieppe? Too young! Always too young where he was concerned! If I hadn't been too young, I'd have taken Mavis ...

The engine coughed, warning that the tank was running dry. I refilled it, still seeing Iain as I had seen him then, cock-sure and getting crazy drunk. Another pub that time, his black eyes wild and lines already showing on his face, boasting of the girls he'd ploughed and me saying, 'She's going to have a baby.'

'Yours or mine?' he said with a jeering, friendly grin.

I came near to hitting him them. 'You know damn well whose it is.'

'Och well, there's a war on and there's plenty of lassies with bairns and no father to call them after.' And he'd laughed in my face and raised his glass. 'Well, here's to them. The country needs all they can produce the way this bloody war is going.' That was Iain, living for the moment, grabbing all he could and to hell with the consequences. He'd had quite a reputation even in that Glasgow factory, and God knows that was a tough place to get a reputation in. Wild, they called him—wild as a young stallion, with the girls rubbing round him and the drink in him talking big and angry.

And then that last evening we'd had together . . . he'd forgotten I was growing up. It had ended in a row, with him breaking a glass and threatening to cut my face to ribbons with the jagged edge of it if I didn't have another drink with him—'One for the road,' he'd said. 'But not the bloody road to the Isles.' And he'd laughed drunkenly. 'Donald my Donald, my wee brother Donald.' I'd always hated him when he'd called me that. 'You've no spunk in your belly, but you'll drink with me this once to show you love me and would hate to see me die.'

I'd had that last drink with him and walked

with him back to his barracks. Standing there, with the sentry looking on, he'd taken hold of me by the shoulders. 'I'll make a bargain wi' ye, Donald my Donald. If ye die first, which I know bloody well ye'll never do, I'll take your body to Laerg and dump it there in a cleit to be pickled by the winds. You do the same for me, eh? Then the old bastard can lie in peace, knowing there's one of the family forever staring with sightless eyes, watching the birds copulate and produce their young and migrate and come again each year.' I had promised because he was tight and because I wanted to get away and forget about not being old enough to be a soldier.

Damn him, I thought, knowing he was out there somewhere in the fog. He wouldn't be thinking of me. He's be thinking of the last time he was in these waters—a Carley float instead of a lobster boat and men dying of exposure. All those years ago and the memory of it like a worm eating into him. Had Lane been right, making that wild accusation? Quite ruthless, Field had said. I shivered. Alone out here in the darkness, he seemed very close.

CHAPTER THREE

ISLAND OF MY ANCESTORS
(March 7)

Thinking of him, remembering moments that I'd thought obliterated from my mind, the time passed, not quickly, but unnoticed. I got the weather forecast just after midnight—wind north-westerly force 3, backing westerly and increasing to 4. Fog. Cliff Morgan at 01.00 was more specific: *Fog belt very extensive, but chance of clearance your area mid-morning.* The wind was westerly force 4 already and my problem remained—how to locate the island.

Between two and three in the morning I became very sleepy. I had been at the helm then for over twenty hours and it was almost impossible for me to keep my eyes open. The engine noise seemed to have a brain-deadening quality, the compass light a hypnotic, sleep-inducing effect. Every few moments I'd catch my head falling and jerk awake to find the compass card swinging. This happened so many times that I lost all confidence in my ability to steer a course, and as a result began to doubt my exact position.

It was a dangerous thing to do, but I took a pull at the flask then. The smell of it and the raw taste of it on my dried-up tongue, the trickle of warmth seeping down into my bowels—I was suddenly wide awake. The time was 02.48. Was it my imagination, or was the movement less?

I picked up the chart, marked in my DR position for 03.00 and then measured off the distance still to go with a pair of dividers. It was 4.8 miles—about an hour and a half.

I hadn't noticed it while I had been dozing, but the wind had definitely dropped. I could, of course, already be under the lee of Laerg if my speed had been better than I'd reckoned, but I'd no means of knowing. The fog remained impenetrable. I switched off the compass light for a moment, but it made no difference—I was simply faced with darkness then, a darkness so absolute that I might have been struck blind.

With my ETA confirmed now as approximately 04.30, I no longer seemed to have the slightest inclination to sleep. I could easily be an hour, an hour and a half out in my reckoning. At that very moment I might be heading straight for a wall of rock—or straight past the island, out into the Atlantic.

I topped up the tank so that there would be no danger of the engine stopping at the very moment when I needed it most, and after that I kept going. There was nothing else I could do—just sit there, staring at the compass.

Four o'clock. Four-fifteen. And nothing to be seen, nothing at all. If this had been a night like the last, the bulk of Tarsaval would be standing black against the stars. There would have been no difficulty at all then.

At four-thirty I switched off the engine and turned out the compass light. Black darkness and the boat rocking, and not a sound but the slop and movement of the sea. No bird called, no beat of waves on rock. I might have been a thousand miles from land.

I had only to sit there, of course, until the fog cleared. But a man doesn't think that rationally when he's bobbing about in a rubber dinghy, alone in utter darkness and virtually sitting in the sea. My grandfather's voice again, telling us of fogs that had lasted a week or more. I switched on the torch and worked over my figures again, staring at the chart. Was it the tide, or an error in navigation or just that, dozing, I had steered in circles? But even a combination of all three wouldn't produce an error of more than a few miles, and Laerg was a group of islands; it covered quite a wide area. The only answer was to cast about until I found it. The search pattern I worked out was a simple rectangular box. Fifteen minutes on my original course, then south for half an hour, east for fifteen minutes, north for an hour. At four forty-five I started the engine again, holding my course until five o'clock. Stop and listen again. Steering south then, with the grey light of dawn filtering through and the sea taking shape around me, a lumpy, confused sea, with the white of waves beginning to break.

The wind was freshening now. I could feel it on my face. At five-fifteen I stopped again to listen. The waves made little rushing sounds, and away to my left, to port, I thought I heard the surge of the swell on some obstruction—thought, too, I could discern a movement in the fog.

It was getting lighter all the time, and I sat there, the minutes ticking by, straining to listen, straining to see. My eyes played tricks, pricking with fatigue. I could have sworn the clammy curtain of the mist moved; and then I was certain as a lane opened out to starboard and the fog swirled, wreathing a pattern over the broken surface of the sea. Somewhere a gull screamed, but it was a distant insubstantial sound—impossible to tell the direction of it.

I continued then, searching all the time the shifting wraith-like movements of the fog. A gust of wind hit me, blattering at the surface of the sea. A downdraught? I was given no time to think that out. A sudden darkness loomed ahead. A swirling uplift of the fog, and there was rock, wet, black rock ahead of me and to port.

I pulled the helm over, feeling the undertow at the same instant that I saw the waves lazily lifting and falling against a towering crag that rose vertically like a wall to disappear in white, moving tendrils of mist. Laerg, or Fladday, or one of the stacs—or was it the western outpost reef of Vallay? In the moment of discovery I didn't care. I had made my land-fall, reached my destination.

I celebrated with a drink from my flask and ate some chocolate as I motored south-west, keeping the cliff-face just in sight.

It wasn't one of the stacs, that was obvious immediately. That darkening in the fog remained too long. And then it faded suddenly, as though swallowed by the mist. I steered to port, closing it again on a course that was almost due south. The wind was in front of me, behind me, all round me; the sea very confused. Then I saw waves breaking on the top of a rock close ahead. I turned to starboard. More rock. To starboard again with rocks close to port.

A glance at the compass told me that I was in a bay, for I was steering now north-west with rock close to port. The rocks became cliffs again. Four minutes on north-west and then I had to turn west to keep those cliffs in sight. I knew where I was then. There was only one bay that would give me the courses I had steered— Strath Bay on the north side of Laerg itself.

I checked with the survey map, just to be certain. There was nowhere else I could be. Confirmation came almost immediately with a ninety-degree turn to port as I rounded the headland that marked the northern end of Aird Mullaichean. Course south-west now and the sea steep and breaking. I hugged the cliffs just clear of the backwash and ten minutes later the movement became more violent.

I was in a tide-rip, the sound of the engine beating back at me from hidden rock surfaces.

An islet loomed, white with the stain of guano, and as I skirted it, the wind came funnelling down from the hidden heights above, strong enough to flatten the sea; and then the downdraught turned to an updraught, sucking the fog with it, and for an instant I glimpsed a staggering sight—two rock cliffs hemming me in and towering up on either side like the walls of a canyon.

They rose stupendous to lose themselves in vapour; dark volcanic masses of gabbro rock, high as the gates of hell, reaching up into infinity. *Sheer adamantine rock.* Wasn't that how Milton had described it? But before I could recall the exact words, I was through, spewed out by the tide, and Eileann nan Shoay had vanished astern, mist-engulfed as the fog closed in again.

I had marked the geo on the survey map, guessing at the position from the stories my grandfather had told of how he had stumbled on it by accident and as a result had sometimes been able to bring in lobster when the waves were so big in Shelter Bay that nobody dared put to sea. 'I didna tell them, ye ken. A tur-rible thing that in a community as close as ours.' And his eyes had twinkled under his shaggy brows. 'For ken it was a secret and I'm telling it to ye the noo so it willna die wi' me. There'll come a day mebbe when ye'll need to know aboot that geo.'

For me, that day was now. I closed in to the

cliffs, the engine ticking over just fast enough to give me steerage away. South of Eileann nan Shoay he'd said, about as far as it is from the Factor's House to the old graveyard. Measured on the map that was just over six hundred yards. The middle one of the three—he had described the other two as full of rock and very dangerous to enter.

I saw the first of the gaping holes, black with the waves slopping in the entrance. It was a huge yawning cavity. The other two were smaller and close together, like two mine adits driven into the base of the cliffs.

Geo na Cleigeann, the old man had called it. 'And a tur-rible wee place it looks from the water wi' a muckle great slab hanging over it.' I could hear his words still and there was the slab jutting out from the cliff face and the black gap below about as inviting as a rat hole with the sea slopping about in the mouth of it. It took me a moment to make up my mind, remembering the old devil's dour sense of humour. But this was no place to hang about with the wind whistling down off the crags above and the tide sweeping along the base of those fog-bound cliffs.

I picked up the torch, put the helm hard down and headed for the opening. A gull shied away from me and was whirled screaming up the face of the cliffs like a piece of wind-blown paper. The fog, torn by an up-draught, revealed crag upon crag towering over me. I had a fleeting impression of the whole great mass toppling forward; then the overhanging slab blotted it out and I was faced with the wet mouth of the cave itself, a grey gloom of rock spreading back into black darkness and reverberating to the noise of the engine.

The hole was bigger than I had first thought—about fifteen feet wide and twenty high. The westerly swell, broken on the skerries of Shoay Sgeir that jutted south from Eileann nan Shoay, caused only a mild surge. Behind me the geo was like a tunnel blasted in the rock, the entrance a grey glimmer of daylight.

I probed ahead with the beam of my torch, expecting every moment to see the shape of the lobster boat. I was so certain Iain must be ahead of me, and if I'd been him I thought I'd make for the geo rather than Shelter Bay. The surface of the water was black and still, and falling gently; rock ahead and I cut the engine. The roof was higher here, the sides further away. I was in a huge cavern, a sort of expansion chamber. No daylight ahead, no indication that there was a way out. The bows touched the rock and I reached out to it, gripping the wet surface with my fingers and hauling myself along.

In a westerly, with the waves rolling clean across the reef of Shoay Sgeir, this place would be a death trap. The rock round which I hauled myself had been torn from the roof, now so high that my torch could barely locate it. I probed with an oar. The water was still deep. Beyond the rock I paddled gently. The walls closed in again. The roof came down. And then the bows grounded on a steep-sloped beach, all boulders. I was ashore in the dark womb of those gabbro cliffs and no sign of Iain.

In the tension of the last hour I had forgotten how stiff and cramped I was. When I tried to clamber out I found I couldn't move. I drank a little whisky and then began to massage my limbs. The enforced wait made me increasingly conscious of the eeriness of the place, the slop of the sea in the entrance magnified, and everywhere the drip, drip of moisture from the roof. The place reeked of the sea's salt dampness and above me God knows how many hundred feet of rock pressed down on the geo.

As soon as I was sure my legs would support me, I eased myself over the side and into the water. It was knee-deep and bitterly cold; ashore I tied the painter to a rock, and then went up, probing with my torch, urgent now to discover the outlet to this subterranean world. It was over thirty years since my grandfather had been here; there might have been a fall, anything.

The beach sloped up at an angle of about twenty degrees, narrowing to a point where the roof seemed split by a fault. It was a rock cleft about six feet wide. The boulders were smaller here, the slope steeper. I seemed to cross a divide with mud underfoot and I slithered down into another cave to find the bottom littered with the same big rounded boulders.

It took me a little time to find the continuation of the fault, and it wasn't the fault I found first, but a rock ledge with the remains of some old lobster pots resting on a litter of rotted feathers. On the ground below the ledge was a length of flaking chain half-buried amongst the skeletal remains of fish. All the evidence of the old man's secret fishing, all except the boat he'd built himself and had abandoned here when he'd left with the rest of the islanders. And then, probing the farther recesses of the cavern, I saw a blackened circle of stones and the traces of a long-dead fire. Though the planking had all gone, the half-burnt remains of the stern and part of the keel were still identifiable, rotting now amongst a litter of charred bones.

I was too tired then, too anxious to locate the exit to the geo to concern myself about the wanton destruction of the boat, vaguely wondering who had made that fire and when, as I scrambled up the last steep slope to see a gleam of sunlight high above me. The slope was almost vertical here and slabs of stone had been let into the walls to form a primitive staircase, presumably the work of some long-dead generation of islanders.

The cleft at the top was wet and grass-choked, the crevices filled with tiny ferns; a small brown bird, a wren, went burring past me. And then I was out on a steep grass slope, out in the sunlight with the fog below me. It lay like a milk-white sea, lapping at the slopes of Strath Mhurain, writhing along the cliff-line to the north of Tarsaval, and all above was the blue of the sky—a cold, translucent blue without a single cloud. The sun had warmth and the air was scented with the smell of grass. Sheep moved, grazing on the slopes of Creag Dubh, and behind me white trails of vapour rose and fell in strange convoluted billows above the cliff-edge where fulmars wheeled in constant flight, soaring, still-winged on the up-draughts.

I stood there a moment filling my lungs with the freshness of the air, letting the magnificence of the scene wash over me— thanking God that my grandfather hadn't lied, that the exit from the geo had remained intact. I thought it likely now that Iain had landed in Shelter Bay and because I was afraid the fog might clamp down at any moment, I stripped off my oilskins and started out across the island. I crossed the top of Strath Mhurain, skirting black edges of peat bog, and climbed into the Druim Ridge with the sun-warm hills standing islanded in fog and the only sound the incessant wailing of the birds.

From the Druim Ridge I looked down into the great horseshoe of Shelter Bay. The Military High Road was just below me, snaking down into the fog. To my left Creag Dubh, with the pill-box shape of the Army's lookout, rising to Tarsaval; dark scree slopes falling to the dotted shapes of cleits and, beyond, the long ridge of Malesgair vanishing into the milk-white void. To my right the High Road spur running out towards the Butt of Keava, the rocky spine of the hills piercing the fog bank like a jagged reef. It was a strange, eerie scene with the surge of the swell on the storm beach coming faint on puffs of air; something else, too—the sound of an engine, I thought. But then it was gone and I couldn't be sure.

I hurried on then, following the road down into the fog, iridescent at first, but thickening as I descended until it was a grey blanket choked with moisture. Without the road to follow the descent would have been dangerous, for the fog was banked thick in the confines of the hills and visibility reduced to a few yards. It lifted a little as the road flattened out behind the beach. I could see the swell breaking and beyond the lazy beds the outline of the first ruined cottage, everything vague, blurred by the dankness of the atmosphere. And then a voice calling stopped me in my tracks. It came again, disembodied, weird and insubstantial. Other voices answered, the words unintelligible.

I stood listening, all my senses alert, intent on piercing the barrier of the fog. Silence and the only sounds the surge of the waves, the cries of the gulls. Somewhere a raven croaked, but I couldn't see it. Ahead of me was the dim outline of the bridge. And then voices—again, talking quietly, the sound oddly magnified. The fog swirled to a movement of air from the heights. I glimpsed the ruins of the old jetty and a boat drawn up on the beach. Two figures stood beside it, two men talking in a foreign tongue, and out beyond the break of the waves I thought I saw the dark shape of a ship; a trawler by the look of it. Two more figures joined the men by the boat. The fog came down again and I was left with only the sound of their voices. I went back then, for I was cold and tired and I'd no desire to make contact with the crew of a foreign trawler. Looting probably, and if Iain had landed in Shelter Bay he'd have hidden himself away in one of the cleits or amongst the ruins of the Old Village. Wearily I climbed the hairpin bends, back up to the Druim Ridge and the sunlight, nothing to do now but go back down into the bowels of that geo and bring up my gear. My mouth was dry and I drank from a trickle of peat water at the head of Strath Mhurain.

And then I was back on the slopes of Aird Mullaichean, walking in a daze, my mind facing again the mystery of that fire, conscious of a growing sense of uneasiness as I approached the rock outcrop that marked the entrance to that dark, subterranean fault. Had the crew of some trawler rowed into the geo and made a fire of the boat just for the hell of it? But that didn't explain the bones unless they'd killed a sheep and roasted it. And to burn the boat . . . On Laerg itself and all through the islands of the Hebrides boats were sacrosanct. No man would borrow so much as an oar without permission.

I picked up my torch and started back down the slabbed stairway. Darkness closed me in. The dank cold of it chilled the sweat on my body. I tried to tell myself it was only the strangeness of the place, my solitary stumbling in the black darkness and the cavernous sound of the sea that made me so uneasy. But who would come into that geo if he hadn't been told about it? Who would have known there was a boat there, firewood to burn? I was shivering then, and coming to the cave where the boat had been, I was suddenly reluctant, filled with a dreadful certainty. Twenty-two days. I'd had only a night at sea, a single cold night with little wind. But I knew what it was like now—knew that he couldn't possibly have survived . . . And then I was into the cave, my gaze, half-fascinated, half-appalled, following the beam of my torch, knowing what I was going to find.

Down on my knees, I reached out my hand to the bones, touched one, plucked it from the blackened heap with a feeling of sick revulsion as I recognised what it was. The end of the bone disintegrated into dust, leaving me with a knee joint in my hand. I poked around—a hip bone, femurs, pieces of the spinal column, the

397

knuckles of human fingers. It was all there, all except the head, and that I found tucked away under a slab of rock—a human skull untouched by the fire and with traces of hair still attached.

I put it back and sat for a moment, feeling numbed; but not shocked or even disgusted now that I knew. It had to be something like this. I was thinking how it must have been for him, his life soured by what had happened here, the prospect of discovery always hanging over him. And then automatically, almost without thinking, I stripped my anorak off and began to pile the grim relics of that wartime voyage on to it. There was more than the bones—buttons like rusted coins, the melted bronze of a unit badge, a wrist watch barely recognisable, all the durable bits and pieces that made up a soldier's personal belongings. And amongst it all an identity disc—the number and the name still visible: ROSS, I. A. Pres.

A pebble rattled in the darkness about me and I turned. But there was nothing, only the swell sloshing about in the great cavern of the geo, a faint, hollow sound coming to me from beyond the narrow defile of the fault. The last thing I did was to scatter the blackened stones about the cave, flinging them from me. Then, the pieces of bone bundled into my anorak, the last traces removed, I scrambled to my feet, and picking up my burden, started for the faulted exit that led to the geo.

I was halfway up the slope to it when the beam of my torch found him. He was standing by the exit, quite still, watching me. His face was grey, grey like the rock against which he leaned. His dark eyes gleamed in the torch beam. I stopped and we stood facing each other, neither saying a word. I remember looking to see if he were armed, thinking that if he'd killed Braddock ... But he'd no weapon of any kind; he was empty-handed, wearing an old raincoat and shivering uncontrollably. The sound of water on the geo was louder here, but even so I could hear his teeth chattering. 'Are you all right?' I said.

'Cold, that's all.' He took a stiff step forward, reaching down with his hand. 'Give me that, I'll do my own dirty work, thank you.' He took the bundled anorak from me.

'Who was it?' I asked. 'Braddock?' My voice came in a whisper, unnatural in that place.

'Give me the torch, will you.'

But I'd stepped back. 'Who was it?' I repeated.

'Man named Piper, if you must know.'

'Then it wasn't Braddock?'

'Braddock? No—why?' He laughed; or rather he made a noise that sounded like a laugh. 'Did you think I'd killed him? Is that it?' His voice was harsh, coming jerkily through the chattering of his teeth. 'Braddock died two days before we sighted Laerg.' And he added, 'You bloody fool, Donald. You should have

399

known me better than that.' And then, his voice still matter-of-fact: 'If you won't give me the torch, just shine it through here.'

I did as he asked and he went through the narrow defile in the rock, down the slope beyond into the geo, hugging the bundle to him. The falling tide had left my dinghy high and dry. The bows of his boat were grounded just astern of it. There were sails, mast and oars in it, two rusted fuel cans, some old lobster pots; but no clothing, not even oilskins. 'Got anything to drink with you?' he asked as he dumped the bundle.

I gave him my flask. His hands were shaking as he unscrewed the cap, and then he tipped his head back, sucking the liquor down. 'How long had you been there?' I asked.

'Not long.' He finished the whisky, screwed the cap back in place and handed me the empty flask. 'Thanks, I needed that.'

'Were you watching me all the time?'

'Yes. I was coming through the fault when I saw the light of your torch. Luckily it shone on your face, otherwise . . .' Again that laugh that had no vestige of humour in it. 'You reach a certain point . . . You don't care then.' He waded into the water, swung a leg over the side of the boat in a moment. 'Deep water . . . if I'd been able to do this at the time . . .' He swung the engine and it started at once, the soft beat of it pulsing against the walls. He pushed the gear lever into reverse. The engine revved and the bows grated and then he was off the beach and reversing slowly, back down the geo towards the grey light of the entrance. He backed right out and then disappeared, and I stood there in the half-darkness of the cavern's gloom, wondering whether he'd come back and if he did, what would happen then. Did he trust me? Or did he think I was like the rest of the world—against him? My own brother, and I wasn't sure; wasn't sure what he'd do, what was going on in that strange, confused mind of his—wasn't even sure whether he was sane or mad.

And all the time the drip, drip of moisture from the roof, the slop of water never still as the swell moved gently against the rock walls.

The beat of the engine again and then the boat's bows nosing into the gap below that hanging slab. It came in, black against the daylight, and him standing in the stern, a dark silhouette, his hand on the tiller. The bows grated astern of my dinghy and he clambered out, bringing the painter with him. 'Is the tide still falling?' he asked.

'For another two hours.'

He nodded, tying the rope to a rock. 'No tide table, no charts, nothing in the lockers, and bloody cold.' He straightened up, looking down at the rubber dinghy. 'How did you make out in that thing—all right?' And then he was moving towards me, his eyes fixed on my face. 'Why?' he demanded hoarsely. 'Why did you come here?'

'I knew you were headed for Laerg.' I had backed away from him.

'Did you know why?'

'No.'

'But you guessed, is that it?' He had stopped, standing motionless, his eyes still on me.

'How could I?' I was feeling uneasy now, a little scared, conscious of the strength of that thick-set body, the long arms. Standing like that, dark in silhouette, he reminded me of my grandfather—and the same crazy recklessness, the same ruthless determination. 'I just knew there was something, knew you had to come back.' And I added, 'Twenty-two days is a long time . . .'

'Yes, too long.' He seemed to relax then. He was looking about the cavern now and I could see his mind was back in the past. 'Thirteen days it took us. And then in the dawn I saw Tarsaval. God! I thought I'd never seen anything more beautiful.' He glanced about him, moving his head slowly from side to side, savouring the familiarity. 'This place—brings it back to me. We were five days . . . Yes, five, I think.'

'In here?'

He nodded, handing me back my anorak, empty now.

'How many of you?'

'Just the two of us—Leroux and myself. Alive. The other—he died during the night. We

402

were grounded, you see. On one of the rocks of Eileann nan Shoay, out there. Hadn't the strength to get her off. It was heavy, that raft. The tide did that, some time during the night, and when the dawn came we were right under the cliffs. That dawn—there was a little breeze from the nor'-east. Cold as ice, and the stars frozen like icicles fading to the dawn sky—pale blue and full of mares' tails. We paddled along the cliffs. Just got in here in time. The wind came out of the north. I'd never have stood that wind. We were frozen as it was, frozen stiff as boards, no heat in us—none at all. We hadn't fed for six days, a week maybe—I don't know. I'd lost count by then.' He turned his head. 'What made you come?' he asked again.

I shrugged. I didn't really know myself. 'You were in trouble . . .'

He laughed. But again there was no humour in that laugh. 'Been in trouble all my life, it seems. And now I'm too old,' he added, 'to start again. But I had to come back. I didn't want anybody to know—about that.' And he added, 'Not even you, Donald. I'd rather you hadn't known.'

I stared at him, wondering how much was remorse, how much pride and the fear of discovery. 'Did you have to do it?' I shouldn't have asked that, but it was out before I could stop myself, and he turned on me then in a blaze of fury.

'Have to? What would you have done? Died

like Leroux, I suppose? Poor little sod. He was a Catholic, I suppose if you're a Catholic . . .' He shook his head. 'Christ, man—the chance of life and the man dead. What did it matter? Lie down and die. I'm a fighter. Always have been. To die when there was a chance . . . that isn't right. Not right at all. If everybody lay down and died when things got tough—that isn't the way man conquered his world. I did what any man with guts would have done—any man not hidebound by convention; I had no scruples about it. Why the hell should I? And there was the boat—fuel for a fire ready to hand. I'll be honest. I couldn't have done it otherwise. But life, man—life beckoning . . . And that poor fellow Leroux. We argued about it all through the night, there in the cave with the wind whistling through that fault. God in heaven, it was cold—until I lit that fire.' He stopped then, shivering under that thin raincoat. 'Colder than last night. Colder than anything you can imagine. Cold as hell itself. Why do they always picture hell as flaming with heat? To me it's a cold place. Cold as this Godforsaken geo.' He moved, came a step nearer. 'Was the old man right? Is there a way out of here?'

'Yes,' I said. 'If you'd only tried . . .' I was thinking of the sheep that roamed the island wild. 'Didn't you try?'

'How could I? We only just had strength to crawl through to that cave. We were dead, man—both of us as near dead as makes no odds. You don't understand. When the ship went down . . . I wasn't going to have anything to do with the boats. I'd an escort. Did you know that? I was being brought back under escort. I saw those two damned policemen make bloody sure they got into a boat. They weren't worrying about me then. They were thinking of their own skins. I saw this Carley float hanging there, nobody doing anything about it. So I cut it adrift and jumped. Others joined me just before she sank. It was late afternoon and the sun setting, a great ball. And then she went, very suddenly, the boilers bursting in great bubbles. There were seven besides myself.' He paused then, and I didn't say anything. I didn't want to interrupt him. Nobody to confide in, nobody to share the horror of it with him; it had been bottled up inside him too long. But he was looking about the place again and I had a feeling that he had slipped away from me, his mind gone back to his memories. And then suddenly: 'You say the way out is still there—you've been up to the top, have you?'

'Yes.'

'Well, let's get out of here. Up into the fresh air.' He started to move up the beach towards the fault, and then he paused. 'What's it like up there? Fog, I suppose.'

'No, it's above the fog. The sun's shining.'

'The sun?' He was staring at me as though he

405

didn't believe me. 'The sun. Yes, I'd like to see the sun . . . for a little longer.' I can't describe the tone in which he said that, but it was sad, full of a strange sadness. And I had a feeling then—that he'd reached the end of the road. I had that feeling very strongly as I followed him up the slope and through the fault, as though he were a man condemned. 'Give me the torch a minute.' His hand was on it and I let him have it. For a moment he stood there, playing the beam of it on that recess, standing quite still and searching the spot with his eyes. 'Thanks,' he said. 'I couldn't bear to go, you see, with the thought that somebody would find that. It wouldn't have mattered—not so much—if I hadn't changed my identity. But taking Braddock's name . . . They'd think I'd killed the poor bastard. Whereas, in fact, I saved his life. Pulled him out of the water with his right arm ripped to pieces. Managed to fix a tourniquet. He was tough, that boy. Lasted longer than most of the others despite the blood he'd lost. Do you know, Donald—I hadn't thought of it. But when he was dying, that last night—he was in my arms, like a child, and I was trying to keep him warm. Though God knows there wasn't much warmth in me by then. The other two, they were lying frozen in a coma, and young Braddock, whispering to me—using up the last of his breath. You're about my build, Iain, he said. And his good arm fumbling at his pockets, he gave me his pay book, all his personal things and the identity disc from round his neck, and all the time whispering to me the story of his life, everything I'd need to know.' The beam of the torch was still fastened on the recess and after a moment he said, 'When a man does that— gives you a fresh start; and he'd got such guts, never complaining, not like some of the others, and none of them with so much as a scratch. Hell! You can't just pack it in. Not after that.' And then he turned to me suddenly. 'Here. Take the torch. You lead the way and let's go up into the light of day.' But instead of moving aside, he reached out and grabbed my shoulders. 'So long as you understand. Do you understand?' But then he released me and stepped back. 'Never mind. It doesn't matter. It's finished now.' And he gave me a gentle, almost affectionate push towards the cave's exit. 'We'll sit in the sun and listen to the birds. Forget the years that are gone. Just think of the old man and the way it was before he died. The island hasn't changed, has it? It still looks the way he described it to us?'

'Yes,' I said. 'It looks very beautiful.' And I climbed up through the continuation of the fault, up the slabbed stairway and out through the final cleft into the sunlight. The fog had thinned, so that it no longer looked like a sea below us, but more like the smoke of some great bush fire. It was in long streamers now, its tendrils lying against the lower slopes, fingering the rock outcrops, turning the whole world below us a dazzling white. Iain stood quite still for a moment, drinking it in, savouring the beauty of the scene just as I had done. But his eyes were questing all the time, searching the slopes of the hills and seaward where the rents in the fog were opening up to give a glimpse of the Atlantic heaving gently to the endless swell. The sunlight accentuated the greyness of his face, the lines cut deep by fatigue. He looked old beyond his years, the black hair greying and his shoulders stooped. As though conscious of my gaze he pulled himself erect. 'We'll walk,' he said gruffly. 'Some exercise—do us good.' And he started off towards the head of Strath Mhurain, not looking back to see if I were following him. He didn't talk and he kept just ahead of me as though he didn't want me to see the look on his face.

At the top of the Druim Ridge he paused, looking down into Shelter Bay where the fog was still thick. And when I joined him, he turned and started up the High Road, heading for the Lookout. He went fast, his head bent forward, and he didn't stop until he'd reached the top of Creag Dubh. Then he flung himself down on the grass, choosing the south-facing slope, so that when the fog cleared he'd be able to see down into Shelter Bay. 'Got a cigarette on you?' he asked.

I gave him one and he lit it, his hands steadier now. He smoked in silence for a while, drawing the smoke deep into his lungs, his head turned to feel the warmth of the sun, his eyes half-closed. 'Do you think they'll have guessed where I was going in that boat?' he asked suddenly.

'I don't know,' I said. 'Probably.'

He nodded. 'Well, if they have, they'll send a helicopter as soon as the fog clears. Or will they come in a ship?' I didn't answer and he said, 'It doesn't matter. From here you'll be able to watch them arrive.'

'And then?' I asked.

'Then . . .' He left the future hanging in the air. He was watching two sheep that had suddenly materialised on an outcrop below us. They were small and neatly balanced with shaggy fleeces and long, curved horns. 'It would be nice, wouldn't it,' he said, lying back with his eyes closed, 'if one could transform oneself— into a sheep, for instance, or better still a bird.' Startled by his voice, the sheep moved with incredible speed and agility, leaping sure-footed down the ledges of that outcrop and disappearing from view.

'You've nothing to worry about—now,' I said.

'No?' He raised himself on one elbow, staring at me. 'You think I should go back, do you? Tell them I'm not Braddock at all, but Sergeant Ross who deserted in North Africa. Christ! Go through all that.' He smiled, a sad, weary smile that didn't touch his eyes. 'Funny, isn't it—how the pattern repeats itself? Lieutenant Moore, Colonel Standing ... I wonder if that little bastard Moore is still alive. Ten to one he is and ready to swear he gave the only order he could. Probably believes it by now. No,' he said, 'I'm not going back to face that.'

He was silent then, lying there, smoking his cigarette—smoking it slowly, his face, his whole body relaxed now. I thought how strange the human mind is, blank one moment and now remembering every detail. The sun, shining down into the horseshoe curve of Shelter Bay, was eating up the fog. The whole world below us was a blinding glare. And high in the brilliant sky above an eagle rode, a towering speck turning in quiet circles. 'Well...' He shifted and sat up. 'I'll leave you now.' He looked around him, turning his head slowly, taking in the whole panorama of the heights. 'God! It's so beautiful.' He said it softly, to himself. Then, with a quick, decisive movement, he got to his feet. I started to rise, but he placed his hand on my shoulder, holding me there. 'No. You stay here. Stay here till they come, and then tell them ... tell them what you damn well like.' He dropped his cigarette and put his heel on it. 'You needn't worry about me any more.'

'Where are you going?' I asked.

But he didn't answer. He was staring down into the bay where the fog had thinned to white streamers with glimpses of the sea between. 'What's that? I thought I saw a ship down there.'

'I think it's a trawler,' I said.

'Are you sure it isn't . . .'

'No,' I said. 'It's a foreign trawler.' And I told him how I'd been down into the bay and heard the crew talking in a language I couldn't recognise.

He stood for a moment, staring down into the bay. The streamers of the fog were moving to a sea breeze and through a gap I caught a glimpse of the vessel lying at anchor with a boat alongside.

'Yes. A foreigner by the look of her.' Another rent and the view clearer. I could see men moving about her decks and a lot of radar gear on her upper works. And then his hand gripped my shoulder. 'Donald my Donald,' he said, and the way he said it took me back. 'Thanks for coming—for all your help. Something to take with me. I'd rather be Iain Ross, you know, and have a brother like you, than stay friendless as George Braddock.' And with a final pat he turned and left me, walking quickly down the Druim Ridge.

I watched him until he disappeared below the ridge, not moving from my seat because there wasn't any point. A little later he came into sight again crossing the top of Strath Mhurain, walking along the slopes of Aird Mullaichean until he reached the outcrop. He

411

paused for a moment, a small, distant figure standing motionless. And then he was gone and I sat there, seeing him still in my mind going down that subterranean fault, back into the geo and the waiting lobster boat. The bright sunlight and the warm scent of the grass, the distant clamour of the birds and that eagle still wheeling high in the vaulted blue; the whole world around me full of the breath of life, and I just sat there wishing I could have done something and knowing in my heart there was nothing I could have done.

I watched the fog clear and the trawler lift her boat into its davits. She got her anchor up then and steamed out of the bay. She was flying a red flag, and as it streamed to the wind of her passage, I thought I could make out the hammer and sickle on it. She rounded Sgeir Mhor, turned westward and disappeared behind the brown bulk of Keava. And later, perhaps an hour later—I had lost all track of time—a helicopter came in and landed on the flat greensward near the Factor's House. Men in khaki tumbled out, spread into a line and moved towards the camp. I got up then and started down to meet them, sad now and walking slowly, for I'd nothing to tell them—only that my brother was dead.

They found the lobster boat two days later. A trawler picked her up, empty and abandoned about eight miles north-east of Laerg. Nobody doubted what had happened. And in reporting it there was no reference to my brother. It was Major George Braddock who was dead, and I think it was the story I told them of what had really happened in North Africa that caused the various officers concerned, right up to the DRA, to be so frank in their answers to my questions. And now it is March again here on Laerg, the winter over and the birds back, my solitary vigil almost ended. Tomorrow the boat comes to take me back to Rodil.

I finished writing my brother's story almost a week ago. Every day since then I have been out painting, chiefly on Keava. And sitting up there all alone, the sun shining and spring in the air, the nesting season just begun—everything so like it was that last day when we were together on Creag Dubh—I have been wondering. A man like that, so full of a restless, boundless energy, and that trawler lying in the bay. Was he really too old to start his life again—in another country, amongst different people?

413

We hope you have enjoyed this Large Print book. Other Chivers Press or Thorndike Press Large Print books are available at your library or directly from the publishers.

For more information about current and forthcoming titles, please call or write, without obligation, to:

Chivers Press Limited
Windsor Bridge Road
Bath BA2 3AX
England
Tel. (01225) 335336

OR

Thorndike Press
P.O. Box 159
Thorndike, Maine 04986
USA
Tel. (800) 223-2336

All our Large Print titles are designed for easy reading, and all our books are made to last.